I0632995

THIS SERIES IS DEDICATED BY THE PUBLISHER TO

JOHN CALDER

AND TO THE MEMORY OF

MARION BOYARS

Mercury Books, an imprint of Michael Walmer, is set up to republish major works in translation which have been hard to procure in nice editions. The series design is an homage to the pioneering designs of the great John Sewell for Calder and Boyars.

GÖSTA BERLING'S SAGA

MERCURY BOOKS

1. Alphonse Daudet: KINGS IN EXILE
2. Selma Lagerlöf: GÖSTA BERLING'S SAGA

GÖSTA BERLING'S SAGA

by

SELMA LAGERLÖF

translated by
Lillie Tudeer and Velma Swanston Howard

Mercury Books

ADELAIDE
MICHAEL WALMER
2018

Gösta Berling's Saga first published 1891

Partial Tudeer translation first published 1898;
completed with added Howard chapters 1918

This Mercury Books edition published 2018

by

Michael Walmer
49 Second Street
Gawler South
South Australia 5118

ISBN 978-0-6480233-5-7 paperback

CONTENTS

PART I

	PAGE
The Pastor	3
The Beggar	15
The Landscape	33
Christmas Eve	39
The Christmas Dinner	57
Gösta Berling — Poet	73
The Cachucha*	91
The Ball at Ekeby	96
The Old Carriages	124
The Great Bear of Gurlita Cliff	144
The Auction at Björne	164
The Young Countess	200
Ghost Stories	234
Ebba Dohna's Story	252
Mamsell Marie*	279

PART II

Cousin Kristoffer*	297
The Paths of Life	305
Penance	324
The Iron from Ekeby	339
Lilliecrona's Home	356
The Dovre Witch	364
Midsummer	372
The Lady Musica	378
The Broby Parson	387

*Translated by Velma Swanston Howard

CONTENTS—*continued*

	PAGE
Squire Julius*	395
Plaster Saints	405
The Pilgrim of God	416
The Churchyard*	435
Old Songs	440
Death, the Deliverer*	455
The Drought	466
The Baby's Mother	483
Amor Vincit Omnia*	495
The Nygård Peasant Girl	503
Kevenhüller*	523
Broby Fair	537
The Forest Hut	549
Margarita Celsing	572

*Translated by Velma Swanston Howard

GÖSTA BERLING'S SAGA

PART I

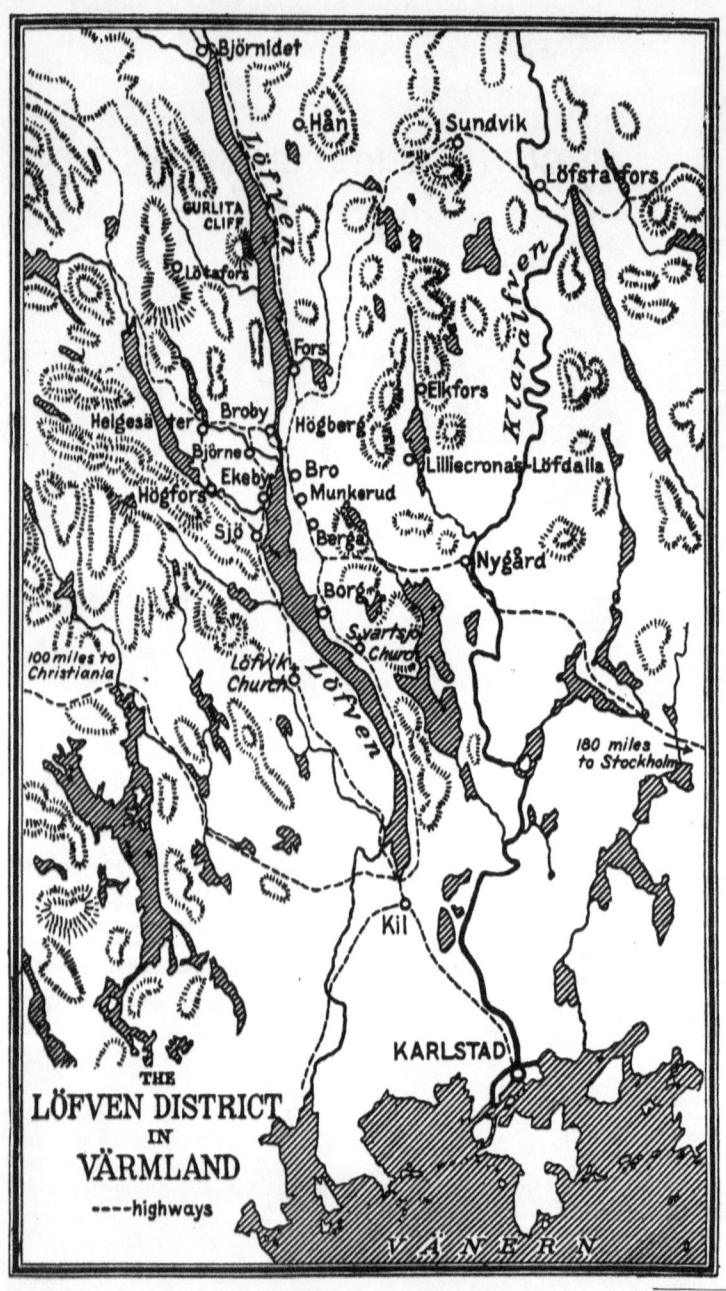

THE
LÖFVEN DISTRICT
IN
VÄRMLAND

----highways

The Pastor

THE pastor was mounting the pulpit steps. The bowed heads of the congregation rose—he was there, then, after all, and there would be service that Sunday, though for many Sundays there had been none.

How tall and slight and how strikingly beautiful he was! In helmet and coat of mail he might have stood as model for a statue of an ancient Athenian. He had the unfathomable eyes of a poet, but the lower part of his face was that of a conqueror, his whole being was instinct with genius and refinement and warm poetic feeling, and the congregation were awed to see him thus.

They had grown accustomed to see him staggering out of the tavern, with his boon companions, Colonel Beerencreutz and Kristian Bergh, "the strong captain."

He had been drinking so heavily that for several weeks he had been unable to perform the duties of his office, and the parish had been forced to lodge a complaint against him, first to the rector, and then to the Bishop and Council. The Bishop had come to investigate the matter and was sitting in the choir, wearing his gold cross of office upon his breast, and was surrounded by the clergy from Karlstad and from the immediate parishes.

There was no doubt that the preacher's conduct had exceeded all bounds. People were lenient in those days—between 1820 and 1830—in the matter of drink; but this man had utterly neglected his sacred duties for its sake, and he was now to be deprived of his office.

He stood in the pulpit as the last verse of the hymn was being sung.

A certainty grew upon him, as he stood there, that every one in the church was an enemy. The gentry in the gallery, the peasants filling the nave, the confirmation candidates in the choir, all were his enemies, and so were the organ-blower and the organist. The vestry-men's pew was full of enemies. They all hated and despised him, from the babies in arms to the stiff and rigid sexton who had fought at Leipzig. He longed to throw himself on his knees before them and beg for mercy. But a moment later, a silent storm of rage took possession of him. He remembered only too well what he had been but a short year ago, when he had stood in that pulpit for the first time. He gave no cause for reproach then. Now he stood there again and saw before him the man with the gold cross, who had come to condemn him.

While he read the introductory prayer, the blood surged to his face in waves of anger.

He could not deny the charge—he had been drinking. But who could blame him? Had they seen the parsonage where he lived? The pine forest stood dark and gloomy round his very windows; the moisture soaked through the black rafters and ran down the fungus-covered walls. Surely a man required the help of strong spirits to keep up his courage, when rain and driving snow rushed through the broken window-panes, when the ill-tilled soil hardly gave him enough to keep hunger from the door!

He thought he had been the very pastor for them; for they all drank. Why should he alone control himself? If a man buried his wife, he was dead drunk at the funeral; the man who christened his child gave a drinking bout after the christening; the people returning from church drank all the way home—a drunken pastor was the very man for them.

It was on his parochial rounds, when driving in his thin coat for miles over the frozen lakes, where the cold winds held high revel, or battling in his boat in storm and driving rain; when in whirling snowstorms he must leave his sledge, and lead his horse through mighty snowdrifts; when tramping through forest marshes—it was then he had learned to love strong drink.

The days dragged along in heavy gloom. Peasant and lord went their way with thoughts tied to earth till the evening brought freedom, when, loosened by wine, their spirits rose and cast aside their bonds. Inspiration came to them, their hearts glowed, and life grew beautiful—full of music and the scent of roses. To the young preacher, the tap-room of the tavern became transformed to a southern pleasure-garden; olives and grapes hung above him, marble columns gleamed through thick foliage, poets and philosophers strolled and conversed under the palm trees.

No!—the preacher in that pulpit knew that life without drink was unbearable in that isolated part of the world. All his hearers knew it too, yet they had come to condemn him.

They meant to tear away his priestly gown, because he had come a drunkard to the house of their God. Oh, the hypocrites, had they, did they really think they had, any other God than their drink?

He had finished the opening prayer, and now knelt to say "Our Father."

There was breathless silence in the church. Suddenly he clutched with both hands the band that held his gown in place; for it seemed to him that all the congregation, with the Bishop at their head, were creeping silently up the pulpit steps, intent on tearing it from his shoulders. He was on his knees and did not turn his head, but it seemed to him that he felt them pulling, and he saw them so distinctly —the Bishop and the dean, all the rectors and the vestry-men, pressing forward, and he pictured how they would all fall, one over the other, when the clasp gave way—even those who had not reached him but had been pulling at the coats of those before them.

He saw it so clearly, he could not help smiling, though the cold sweat broke out on his forehead. It was horrible.

He, to be an outcast on account of drink — a disgraced clergyman! Was there any one on earth more despicable?

He, to be a wayside beggar, to lie drunk in the ditches, go clad in rags, and consort with vagabonds!

The prayer was over, and he was about to read his sermon, when a thought struck him and checked the words on his lips. He remembered that this would be the last time he would stand in a pulpit and proclaim the glory of God.

The last time — that touched him. He forgot the Bishop and the drinking; he only felt that he must take the opportunity and bear witness to the glory of his God.

The nave of the church, with all his hearers, seemed to sink deep, deep down: the roof was raised, and he could see right into heaven. He stood alone, his soul soaring to the opening heavens, and his voice grew strong and joyous as he spoke of the glory of God.

He was inspired, and forgot his written text; while thoughts descended upon him like a flight of tame doves, and he felt that it was not he who spoke.

But he also knew that none could surpass him in splendor and majesty, as he stood there and bore witness to his God.

While the fire of inspiration burned, he spoke; but as it presently ebbed away, and the heavens closed, and the nave of the church rose again from the depths, he fell on his knees and wept, for he knew that life held for him no higher moment, and it was past.

After the morning service there was a vestry meeting, presided over by the Bishop, who inquired what cause of complaint the congregation had against their pastor.

No longer angry and defiant, as he had been before the sermon, the young man hung his head in shame. Oh, the wretched stories that would now be brought forward!

But no one spoke—there was silence round the big table in the vestry house.

He glanced round, first at the sexton—he was silent; then at the vestry-men, the richer peasants, the owners of the iron works—they were all silent. They sat with firmly closed lips and looked down at the table rather awkwardly.

"They are waiting for some one to speak first," he thought.

At last one of the vestry-men cleared his throat.

"I think I may say that we have a very exceptional pastor," he said.

"Your Lordship has heard how he can preach," put in the sexton.

The Bishop mentioned the unobservance of the church services.

"Our pastor may be ill occasionally, like any other man," replied the peasants.

He hinted at their previously expressed disapproval of his ways.

They defended him with one accord. He was so young, there was no danger but things would come right. Indeed, if he would only preach every Sunday as he had preached that morning, they would not exchange him for the Bishop himself.

There was no prosecution, there could be no judgment.

The pastor felt how his heart expanded, how lightly the blood flowed along his veins. Ah! he was no longer among enemies, he had won these people when he had least expected it, and he could retain his priestly calling.

When the meeting was over, the Bishop, all the clergy, and the chief parishioners went to dine at the parsonage.

The wife of a neighbor had undertaken to arrange matters, as the young preacher was unmarried. She had managed everything in the best possible manner, and for the first time he saw that the parsonage could be made habitable. The long dining-table had been carried out of doors, and stood under the pine trees, looking very inviting with its snowy cloth, its blue and white china, its glittering glass, and bright-colored serviettes. Two birch trees had been cut down and placed close to the house door as a decoration, juniper twigs were strewn over the hall floor, garlands hung from the ceiling, flowers decked every room, the smell of mould had been expelled, and the green window-panes shone cheerfully in the sunlight.

The young pastor was so radiantly happy, he felt sure he would never drink again.

All who sat at that dinner rejoiced; those who had forgiven past transgressions were happy, and the clergy were glad to have escaped a great scandal.

The good Bishop raised his glass, and told them that he had entered upon this visit with a heavy heart, for he had heard many evil reports. He had gone forth to meet Saul — but behold, Saul had been changed to Paul, who was to do greater work than any among them. And the reverend man spoke of the rich talents which were the portion of their young brother, and praised them highly, not with the intent of awakening his vanity, but as an encouragement to put forth all his strength and guard himself, as all they must do who have a more than usually heavy but precious burden to bear.

The young pastor drank no wine at that dinner, but he was intensely excited. The great and unexpected happiness affected him — the divine fire of inspiration had touched him, and he had won the love of his fellow-men; and when evening came, and all his guests had departed, the blood still coursed at fever heat through his veins. Late into the night, he sat in his room, letting the air stream in through the open window to cool that feverish excitement, that restless happiness which would not let him sleep.

Suddenly a voice broke the silence.

"Are you still awake, parson?"

And a man strode over the grass plot to the open window.

The pastor recognized Captain Kristian Bergh, one of his most staunch boon companions. An adventurer without house or home was this Captain Kristian—a giant in size and strength, as big as Gurlita Cliff, and as stupid as a mountain gnome.

"Of course I'm awake," he answered; "this is no night for sleeping."

And listen to what the Captain tells him! The giant, too, had his ideas upon the events of the day —he understood that the time had come when his friend might fear to continue in the old ways. He could never feel secure now—those clergymen from Karlstad, who had been here once, might come again; so he, Kristian Bergh, had laid his heavy hand to the good work, and had so arranged matters that they would never come again—neither they nor the Bishop. Hereafter, he and his friend might drink as much as they pleased at the parsonage.

Hear him, what a feat he has accomplished!

When the Bishop and his two companions had entered their carriage, and the door had been firmly closed upon them, he had climbed upon the driving seat, and had driven them a dozen miles on their homeward way in the clear summer night.

It was then they had learned that life sits insecurely even in the worthiest breasts. He had driven at a break-neck pace, as a punishment on them for not allowing an honest man to drink in peace.

He did not drive along the road, or guide the horses, but went over ditches, and half-cleared fields full of tree stumps. He tore down the hillsides and along the shores of lakes, where the water splashed over the wheels and the carriage half sank in the marshy ground, and over bare rocks, where the horses slid downward on stiffly braced feet. And meanwhile, behind the leather curtains, the Bishop and his companions were muttering prayers in terror for their lives — they had never known such danger before.

Imagine what was their appearance when they arrived at Rissäter post station, alive, but shaking like peas in a pod!

"What is the meaning of this, Captain Kristian?" asked the Bishop, as the Captain opened the door for him.

"The meaning is that the Bishop will think twice before making a second visitation to Gösta Berling," replied the Captain, having prepared the sentence beforehand.

"Greet Gösta Berling from me," answered the Bishop, "and say that neither I nor any other bishop will ever come to him again."

And this was the brave deed told at the open window on that summer night. Captain Kristian had only had time to return the horses to the post station and come on with the news.

"And now you can be at peace, good comrade," said he.

But ah! Kristian Bergh, the rectors sat with pale faces behind the leather curtains, but the face of this preacher is paler still. He even lifted his arm and aimed a fearful blow at the coarse, stupid face of the giant before him, but he checked himself, closed the window with a crash, and turned into the room, shaking his clenched fist above his head.

He, who with divine inspiration had proclaimed the majesty of God that morning, felt now that God had mocked him.

The Bishop could only think that Captain Bergh had been instructed; he must believe he had acted the hypocrite all day. He would be suspended and dismissed.

When morning came, the young pastor had left the parish. It was not worth while to remain and try to defend himself. God had mocked him. He would not help him. He knew he would be disgraced, God willed it so, and he might as well go at once.

This took place about 1820 in a distant parish in western Värmland.

It was the first misfortune that befell Gösta Berling; it was not the last.

Young horses who cannot bear the whip or spur find life hard. At every smart they start forward and rush to their destruction, and when the way is stony and difficult, they know no better expedient than to overturn the cart and gallop madly away.

The Beggar

ONE cold day in December a beggar was climbing the ascent to Bro. He was clad in the poorest rags, and his shoes were so worn that the cold snow wet his feet.

The Löfven is a long, narrow lake in Värmland, contracting at several points to a mere strait. It stretches northward to the Finn Forests and southward to Vänern. Several parishes lie along its shores, but the parish of Bro is the largest and most wealthy. It comprises a wide expanse of country, both on the eastern and western shores of the lake; but the larger estates, such as Ekeby and Björne, renowned for their riches and their natural beauty, lie on the western shore, and here also is the large village of Bro, with its parsonage and county court, its Major's house, and inn, and market-place.

The village is built on a steep slope. The beggar had passed the tavern at the foot of the hill, and was making his way to the parsonage, which stood on the crest.

Before him, on the road, a little girl was dragging a small hand-sledge laden with a sack of flour. The beggar overtook and spoke to her.

"What a little horse to drag such a heavy load!" he said.

The child turned and glanced at him. She was

small for her twelve years, and had sharp, inquiring eyes and a firmly closed mouth.

"Would to God the horse was smaller and the load bigger, so it would last longer," she answered.

"Are you taking home your own fodder, then?"

"Yes, I am. Young as I am, I must find my own living."

The beggar grasped the back of the sledge, intending to help it forward, but she turned instantly, saying,

"You need not think I shall give you anything for your trouble."

He laughed.

"You must surely be the daughter of the Broby parson," he exclaimed.

"That is just who I am. Many have a poorer father, none have a worse, though it is a shame his own child should say so."

"Is it true, then, that he is both a miser and wicked, this father of yours?"

"He is miserly, and he is wicked; but people say his daughter will be worse, if she lives."

"I should think they might be right. I should like to know where you got that sack of flour?"

"Well, it makes no difference if you know or not. I took the rye out of the granary this morning, and I've been to the mill with it."

"Won't he see it when you bring it home?"

"Well, you certainly never finished your apprenticeship. My father is away on parish duty, of course."

"There is some one driving behind us. I hear the snow creaking under the sledge runners. Think — if it should be he!"

The child listened and looked round, and then burst into a storm of tears.

"It is father," she sobbed. "He will kill me — he will kill me!"

"H'm, good advice is precious, and prompt advice is better than silver and gold," remarked the beggar.

"See," cried the child, "you can help me. Take the rope and draw the sledge, and father will think it is yours."

"What shall I do with it afterwards?" asked the man, as he threw the rope over his shoulders.

"Take it where you like at present, but when it gets dark, bring it to the parsonage. I'll be on the lookout for you. Mind you bring both sledge and flour; you understand?"

"I'll try."

"God have mercy on you if you don't," she shouted, as she sprang up the path to reach home before her father arrived.

The beggar turned the sledge, and with a heavy heart guided it back to the tavern.

He, poor wretch, had had his dream while wandering through the snow with half-frozen feet. He had dreamed of the great forest north of the lake, of the great primeval forest.

Here, in the parish of Bro, as he made his way from the Upper to the Lower Löfven, in this land of wealth and joy, where the estates lay side by side, and the great iron foundries adjoined one another, every path seemed too steep for him, every room too narrow, every bed too hard. A bitter longing for the quiet of the great forest had taken possession of him.

Here, he heard the thunder of the flails on every threshing floor, as if the grain were unfailing; here, loads of timber came in endless succession from the inexhaustible forests, and the heavy wagons of ore obliterated the deep ruts cut into the roads by the preceding carts; here, sledgefuls of guests drove from one estate to another, and it seemed to him as if Joy held the reins, and Youth and Beauty stood on the runners. Oh, how he longed, as he watched them, longed for the peace of the everlasting forest!

There the trees rise straight and column-like from the level, snow-covered ground. Wreaths of snow hang on the motionless branches; the wind is powerless, and can only sway gently the tops of the fir trees. He would go there, make his way into the very depth of the great forest, till his strength failed him, and he fell down under the great trees to die of hunger and cold.

He longed for the great murmuring grave which

awaited him beyond the Löfven, where the powers of death would at last gain the mastery over him, where hunger and cold and weariness and past drunkenness would at last destroy the body, which had been able to withstand so much.

He returned to the tavern, intending to remain there till the evening, and entered the tap-room, where he rested in heavy mood on the bench, still dreaming of the everlasting forest.

The landlady took pity on him, and gave him a glass of strong gin. She even gave him a second glass, as he begged so eagerly for it; but more than that she refused, and the beggar grew desperate. He must have some more of that strong, sweet drink, his heart must dance once more, his thoughts flame in the transport of intoxication! Oh, that sweet drink! Summer's sun and summer's song, summer's scent and beauty were surging in its white transparency. Once again, before he departed into night and darkness, he must drink of the summer's sun and joy.

So he bartered first the flour, then the sack, and lastly the sledge for drink. He had got sufficient now, and slept away the most of the afternoon in the tap-room.

When he awoke, he knew there was but one thing left for him to do. As his miserable body had so completely gained ascendency over his soul; as he had fallen so low that he could betray the trust of a child; as he was a living shame on earth, he must relieve the earth of the burden of so much wretchedness. He must free his soul and let it return to God.

As he lay half stupefied on the bench, he passed sentence upon himself. "Gösta Berling, disgraced clergyman, charged with stealing the sustenance of a hungry child, is sentenced to death. What death? —Death in the snowdrifts."

He clutched his cap and staggered out. He was not quite awake, nor was he sober, and he wept, thinking of his degraded soul which he was going to set at liberty. He did not go far, nor did he leave the highway. A deep drift lay close at hand; he cast himself into it and tried to sleep again.

None knew how long he lay there, but life still dwelt within him when, later in the evening, the parson's little daughter ran down the road with a light in her hand and found him lying there. She had expected him hours ago, and at last ran down to the village to find him. She recognized him at once, and tried to shake him, screaming loudly.

She *must* know what he had done with her sack of flour. He *must* revive, if only to tell her what had become of the sledge and meal-sack. Her father would kill her if the sledge were not forthcoming. She bit the hand of the sleeping man, scratched his face, and screamed as if crazy.

Just then some one drove by.

"Who the devil is screaming like that?" a harsh voice called.

"I want to know what this man has done with my meal-sack and my sledge," sobbed the child, continuing to beat with clenched fists on the beggar's breast.

"Is it a frozen man you are treating like that? Off with you, you wild cat!"

The new arrival was a big, rough woman. She got out of her sledge, and came to the drift; she lifted up the child by the back of her neck and flung her into the road, stooped, and slipping her arms under the unconscious man, carried him to her sledge and laid him gently down.

"Come with me to the tavern, wild cat," she called to the parson's daughter, "and we will see what you have to do with this affair."

An hour later the beggar was sitting on a chair near the door of the best room in the tavern, and before him stood the imperious woman who had saved his life.

As Gösta Berling now saw her, on her way home from inspecting the charcoal-burning in the forest, with sooty hands, a clay pipe in her mouth, dressed in a short jacket of unlined sheepskin over a striped woollen homespun skirt, with tarred boots on her feet and a sheathed knife thrust into the breast of her jacket,—as he saw her thus, with her grey hair brushed away from her beautiful face, he had heard

C

her described scores of times, and he knew at once he had fallen into the hands of the famous lady of the Manor, the Major's wife at Ekeby.

She was the most powerful woman in Värmland, the owner of seven foundries, accustomed to command and to be obeyed; and he was only a miserably weak man, waiting for death, destitute of everything, knowing full well that every path was too steep for him, every room too narrow, and he trembled as she looked at him.

She stood for some time gazing silently at the human wreck before her — at the red, swollen hands, the enfeebled body, and the splendid head, which even in its downfall was radiant in wild beauty.

"You are Gösta Berling, the mad parson?" she asked.

The beggar was silent.

"I am the Major's wife at Ekeby!"

A shudder ran through him. He clasped his hands tremblingly and lifted beseeching eyes. What would she do? Would she compel him to live? He trembled before her power. And he had so nearly gained the peace of the everlasting forest!

She opened the conversation by saying that the child had received her sledge and sack of flour, and that she had a refuge for him, as for so many other waifs and strays, in the cavaliers' wing at Ekeby Hall. She offered him a life of idleness and pleasure, but he answered that he must die.

Then she struck the table with her clenched fist, and gave him a piece of her mind.

"Oh, indeed, you want to die, do you? Well, I shouldn't have been so greatly surprised if I had found you to be really alive. But look at your half-starved body, your helpless limbs, and dim eyes! Do you mean to tell me there is anything left to kill? Do you suppose it is necessary to lie stiff and straight and to be nailed into a coffin to be dead? Don't you suppose that, standing here, I can see how dead you are, Gösta Berling? What have you but a skull in place of a head, and worms creeping out of your eyes? Don't you taste the earth in your mouth, and don't you hear your bones rattle when you move? You have drowned yourself in drink, Gösta Berling; you are already dead.

"Is it the shame of having once been a preacher that is driving you now to kill yourself? More honor would be gained if you would employ your talents and be of some use on God's green earth. Why didn't you come to me in your trouble, and I should have put things right for you? And now I suppose you expected to win some respect when you were laid out, and people spoke of you as a beautiful corpse?"

The beggar sat calm, almost smiling, while she thundered forth her anger. "No fear," he thought, joyfully; "the forest awaits me, she has no power to move me."

But suddenly the Major's wife was silent—and took two or three turns about the room. Then she drew up a chair to the fire, placed her feet on the hearth, and rested her elbows on her knees.

"Good God," she said, half laughing to herself, "what I said was so true, I didn't notice it myself. Don't you think, Gösta Berling, that most people in the world are dead or half dead? Do you think we are all alive? Ah, no!

"Look at me. I am the Lady of the Manor at Ekeby and the most powerful woman in Värmland. If I lift a finger, the county police must skip; if I lift two, the bishop does the same; and if I lift three, I can make the archbishop and council and all the judges and landed proprietors in Värmland dance a polka on Karlstad market-place. And yet I tell you, boy, I am nothing but a dressed-up corpse. God alone knows how little life there is in me!"

The beggar leaned forward in his chair and listened anxiously. The old lady rocked herself before the fire, and never glanced at him as she spoke.

"Don't you think," she continued, "that if I were a living soul, and saw you sitting there, miserable and sad, with thoughts of suicide in your mind, that I could dispel them in a breath? I should have tears and prayers to move you, and I should save you—but now—I am dead. God knows how little life there is in me!

"Have you never heard that once I was the beautiful Margarita Celsing? It was n't quite yesterday, but even yet I can weep my old eyes red when I think of her. Why is Margarita Celsing dead—and Margarita Samzelius living? Why should the Major's wife at Ekeby be alive, Gösta Berling?

"Do you know what Margarita Celsing was like? She was tall and slight and gentle, and knew no evil; she was a girl over whose grave the angels wept. She knew no evil, she knew no sorrow, and she was good to all. And she was beautiful, really beautiful.

"And there lived a splendid man in those days —his name was Altringer. God alone knows how he found his way up to the lonely foundry in the wilderness where Margarita lived with her parents. Margarita saw him—he was a splendid man—and he loved her.

"But he was poor; so they determined to wait for five years, as they do in the ballads.

"But when three years had passed, another man wanted her. He was ugly and wicked, but her parents believed him to be rich; and they forced Margarita, by fair means and foul, by blows and hard words, to take him as her husband. That day Margarita Celsing died. Since then, there only exists Major Samzelius' wife, and she is neither good nor gentle, she knows much evil, and thinks little of the good. I suppose you have heard what hap-

pened later. We lived at Sjö, here near the lake, the
Major and I; but he was not as rich as people had
said, and I had many hard days.

"And then Altringer came back, and he was a
wealthy man. He was Lord of Ekeby, the boun-
daries of which joined Sjö, and he was soon the
owner of seven foundries on the banks of the Löfven. He was clever and capable, a splendid man in
every way.

"He helped us in our poverty: we drove in his
carriage; he sent food to our kitchen and wine to
our cellar. He filled my life with pleasures and
amusements.

"The Major went to the wars, but little we
cared. I was guest at Ekeby one day, and he came
to Sjö the next. Oh, life in those days was one long
dance of pleasure along the shores of Löfven Lake!
But presently people began to talk about us. If
Margarita Celsing had lived, it would have hurt
her, but it was nothing to me. Yet I did n't understand the reason why I felt nothing,—that it was
because I was already dead.

"And tales of me were told to my father and
mother, as they worked among their mines in the
Älfdal forest. My mother lost no time in considering what she would do; she started off at once to
speak to me.

"One day, when the Major was away, and Altringer and some others were dining with me, she

drove up to the house. I saw her enter the room, but I could not feel her to be my mother, Gösta Berling. I greeted her as a stranger, and asked her to sit down and dine with us.

"She tried to address me as her daughter, but I told her she was mistaken, my parents were both dead, they had died on my wedding-day.

"And she entered into the comedy. She was seventy, and had driven a hundred and forty miles in three days, but she sat down to her dinner without further ceremony. She was a wonderfully strong woman.

"She remarked that it was unfortunate that I should have experienced such a loss on my wedding-day.

"'The greater misfortune was,' I replied, 'that my parents had not died a day earlier; then the wedding would never have come off.'

"'My lady is not happy in her marriage, then?'

"'Yes,' I answered, 'I'm happy now. I am happy in obeying the will of my dear parents.'

"She asked me if it was their will that I should bring shame upon myself and upon them in deceiving my husband. No honor was brought to them by my making myself the talk of the country-side.

"'They made their bed, and they must lie on it,' I replied. 'And, by the way, the strange lady might as well understand that I allowed no one to defame my father's daughter.'

"We ate our dinner, we two—but the men around us sat silent and dared hardly touch knife and fork.

"She remained a day with me, and then drove home again. But all the time I never felt her to be my mother. It seemed to me my mother was dead.

"When she was leaving, Gösta Berling, and I stood beside her on the steps, and the carriage had driven up, she said to me: 'I have been here a whole day, and you have not recognized me as your mother. I have travelled a long and lonely road to see you —a hundred and forty miles in three days—and I tremble for shame of you, as if I had been beaten. May you be disowned as I have been, cast out as I have been! May the roadside be your home, straw be your bed, and the lime-kiln your fireside! May shame and insult be your wage, and may others smite you as I smite you!'

"And she gave me a hard blow on my cheek.

"But I lifted her in my arms, carried her down, and placed her in the carriage.

"'Who are you,' I cried, 'to dare to curse me? Who are you to strike me? I will endure it from no one!'

"And I gave her back the blow again. The carriage drove away at that moment, and that was the first time, Gösta Berling, I felt that Margarita Celsing was dead. She had been good and guileless. Angels wept at her death. If she had lived, she would never have struck her mother."

The beggar sitting at the door listened, and her words drowned for a moment the tempting murmur of the everlasting forest. This imperious woman made herself his equal in sin, his sister in perdition, to give him the courage to take up his life again. He was to learn that sorrow and reproach rested on other hearts than his alone.

He rose and approached her.

"Won't you live your life, Gösta Berling?" she asked in a voice that broke into tears. "Why should you die? You may have been a good preacher, but the Gösta Berling you drowned in drink could not have been as blameless as the Margarita Celsing I killed in hatred."

Gösta kneeled before her. "Forgive me — I cannot," he answered.

"I am an old woman," she said, "hardened by troubles, and yet I sit here and give myself to the mercy of a beggar, whom I found in a snowdrift. It serves me right—at any rate, if you kill yourself, you can't tell anybody what a fool I've been."

"I am doomed. Don't make the fight too hard for me. I cannot live. My body has mastered my soul. I must set it free and let it return to God."

"Oh, indeed—you think it will go there?"

"Farewell—and thank you."

"Farewell, Gösta Berling."

The beggar rose and went with bowed head to the door. The woman made the way hard for him.

When he reached the door, he felt compelled to turn and glance back—and he met her look as she sat motionless by the fire and gazed at him.

He had never seen such a look on any face, and he stood and stared at her. She, who recently had been hot and angry and scornful, was transfigured; her eyes shone with sad and sympathizing love. There was something within him—within his own desponding heart, which broke at that look. He leaned his forehead against the door-post, stretched his arms over his head, and wept as if his heart were breaking.

Margarita Samzelius flung her pipe into the fire, and came to him with a movement as tender as a mother's.

"Hush—hush—my boy."

And she drew him down beside her on the bench near the door, so that he wept with his head pillowed on her knees.

"Are you still determined to die?"

He tried to rise, but she held him down by gentle force.

"I tell you, and it is for the last time, you can do as you like; but if you will live, I promise you to take the parson's daughter and make a good woman of her, so she will thank her God one day that you stole her flour."

He lifted his head and looked into her eyes.

"Do you mean it?"

"I promise, Gösta Berling."

Then he wrung his hands in despair. He saw before him the child's cunning eyes, her little drawn mouth and bony hands. She would receive protection and be cared for, and the marks of neglect would disappear from her body; the anger would be wiped out of her soul. The paths to the forest were closed to him.

"I will not kill myself while she is under your care," he said; "I knew you would compel me to live. I felt that you would be too strong for me."

"Gösta Berling," she answered, solemnly, "I have fought for you as for my own soul. I said to God: 'If there is anything of Margarita Celsing within me, let her come forth and save this man,' and He granted it. You felt her power, and could not go. And it was whispered to me that you would give up that terrible determination for the sake of that poor child. Oh, you wild birds, you fly daringly, but the Lord knows the net that will catch you!"

"He is a great and wonderful God," said Gösta Berling. "He has mocked me and rejected me, but He will not let me die. His will be done."

From that day, Gösta Berling became one of the cavaliers of Ekeby. Twice he attempted to make a living for himself. Once the Major's wife gave him a cottage and strip of land near Ekeby, and he tried to live the life of a workman. It answered for a time, but he grew weary of the loneliness and of the daily round of small duties, and returned to Ekeby. Later he became tutor at Borg to the young Count, Henrik Dohna. While there he fell in love with Ebba Dohna, the Count's sister, but she died just when he thought to win her, and after that he gave up all thought of being anything but a cavalier at Ekeby. It seemed to him that for an unfrocked clergyman all roads to amendment were closed.

The Landscape

NOW I must beg those of my readers who know this lake, this fertile plain, and those blue mountains, to skip a few pages. They can do this without compunction, for the story will be long enough without them. But you will understand that I must describe the country for those who do not know it, as it was the scene where Gösta Berling and the gay cavaliers of Ekeby spent their lives; and those who have seen it will understand too that the task surpasses the power of one who can only wield the pen.

I should have chosen to confine myself to saying that the name of the lake is the Löfven; that it is long and narrow, and that it stretches from the distant forests in the north of Värmland to the Vänern lowlands in the south; that a plain borders each side of the lake, and that a chain of undulating mountains surrounds the lake valley. But this is not sufficient, and I must try to picture in more graphic words the scene of my childhood's dreams, the home of my childhood's heroes.

The Löfven has its source far in the north, which is a glorious land for a lake, for the forests and hills gather water for it unceasingly, and streams and brooklets pour into it all the year round. It has fine white sand to recline upon; it has islands and promontories to admire and reflect; water-sprites and nixies make it their playground, and it soon grows strong and beautiful. Up in the north it is friendly and gay. You should see it on an early summer morning, when it lies wide awake under its veil of mist, to understand how happy it can seem.

It seems as if it would coquette with you at first, so gently, so gradually does it creep out of its light covering; and so enchantingly beautiful is it that you hardly recognize it, till suddenly it flings its veil aside and lies there naked and rosy, glittering in the sunshine.

But the Löfven is not content with a life of pleasure alone. It pushes its way through the sand-hills on the south; it contracts to a narrow strait, and seeks a new kingdom for itself. It soon finds one, and here again grows strong and mighty; it falls a bottomless depth, and adorns a cultivated landscape. But now its waters grow darker, its shores are less changeful, the winds are bleak, and the whole character of the lake is more severe; yet it remains ever proud and stately. Numbers of vessels and rafts pass over its surface, and it is late before it can go to its winter rest—not until Christmas. It is often in angry mood, and, turning white with sudden fury, wrecks the sailing boats, but it can also lie in dreamy quiet and reflect the sky.

But once again it longs to make its way into the world, though the hills are pressing close around it;

and it must contract again to a narrow strait, and creep between narrow sandy shores. Then it broadens out for the third time, but not with its former beauty and majesty. Its shores are lower and more monotonous, wilder winds blow, the lake goes early to its winter sleep. It is still beautiful, but it has lost the strength of its youth and manhood — it is a lake like any other. It throws out two arms to feel its way to the Vänern, and when it finds it, casts itself in aged weakness down the steep slope, and, after this last thundering exploit, sinks to rest.

A plain follows the course of the Löfven, but it has a hard fight to hold its own between the lake and the hills, from the cauldron-like valley, which is the lake's most northerly point, to the Vänern lowlands, where it finally gains the mastery, and spreads itself wide in indolent ease. The plain would have unquestionably preferred to follow the lake shores, but the hills give it no peace.

These hills are mighty granite walls, covered with forest, full of chasms, abounding in moss and lichen, difficult to penetrate into, and, in the days we are speaking of, the home of numberless wild beasts. There is many a tarn of inky black water and many a quagmire in those long, far-reaching ridges. Here and there you find a coal mine, or an opening in the forest where the timber has been felled; now and again a burned clearing, which shows that the hills allow of a little cultivation; but for the most part they lie in placid calm, content to let the lights and shadows play their everlasting game over their slopes.

And the plain, which is good and fertile and loves cultivation, wages constant war against the hills— in all friendliness, be it understood.

" It is sufficient," says the plain to the hills, "if you raise your walls around me; then I shall be amply protected."

But the hills cannot be persuaded. They send out long stretches of tableland to the lake; they make lovely points from which to get a view; and, in fact, it is so seldom that they will leave the shore that the plain hardly ever has a chance of rolling itself down to the soft sand of the lake shore. But it is useless to complain.

" Be thankful we are here," answer the hills. " Remember the time before Christmas, when day after day the icy mists roll over the Löfven. We are doing you a good turn by standing here."

The plain laments its want of room and that it has no view.

"You are stupid," reply the hills. "You should feel how it blows here near the water. At the least, it requires a granite back and a pine tree covering to bear it all. Besides which, you should be content with looking at us."

And that is what the plain does. You know what wonderful changes of light and shade and color pass over the hills. You have seen them in the midday light sinking to the horizon, pale blue and low, and at morning and evening rising in majestic height, as deep a blue as the zenith of heaven. Sometimes the light falls so sharply upon them, they look green or blue-black, and every fir tree, every path and chasm, shows clearly at a great distance.

Sometimes the hills draw aside and allow the plain to approach and look at the lake, but when it sees it in its anger, hissing and spitting like a wild cat, or sees it covered with cold mist (the water witches being busy with washing and brewing), it soon acknowledges that the hills were right, and returns willingly to its narrow prison.

For many, many generations the plain has been cultivated, and great things have been done there. Wherever a stream, in its rapid course, has flung itself over the sloping shores, mills and foundries have sprung up. On the light, open places, where the plain comes down to the lake, churches and parsonages have been built; and in the corners of the valleys, half way up the hillsides, on the stony ground where the corn will not grow, stand the peasants' huts and the officers' buildings and here and there a gentleman's mansion.

But it must be remembered that in 1820–30 the land was not nearly so cultivated nor so populated as it now is. Much was forest and lake and marsh which is now reclaimed.

D

The population was scanty, and the people made their living partly by carting and day work at the many foundries; while many left their homes to find work at a distance, for agriculture alone would not pay them. In those days they dressed in homespun, ate oat cakes, and were content with a daily wage of a krona. The poverty was great, but it was mitigated by an easy-going temperament and an inborn aptitude for handicrafts, which greatly developed when those people had to make their way among strangers.

And as these—the lake, the fertile plain, and the blue hills—make a most beautiful landscape, so these people, even to-day, are strong, courageous, and talented. Great progress has been made in their well-being and education.

May they greatly prosper, the dwellers near the lake and the blue hills! It is some of their stories I will now tell you.

Christmas Eve

SINTRAM was the name of the wicked proprietor of Fors; he, with the clumsy body of an ape, with long arms, bald head, and ugly grimacing face; he, whose whole delight it was to devise evil.

Sintram was the name of him who chose vagabonds and brawlers as workmen, and had only quarrelling and lying serving-girls about him, who maddened the dogs by thrusting pins into their noses, and lived happily amid hateful people and furious animals.

Sintram was the name of the man whose greatest pleasure was to masquerade as the Evil One in horns and tail and hoofs and hairy hide, and, suddenly appearing out of dusky corners, from behind the oven or the woodbox, frighten timid women and children.

Sintram was he who rejoiced to exchange old friendship for new enmity, and to poison the heart with lies.

Sintram was his name—and once he came to Ekeby.

. . . .

Drag the big wood sledge into the forge, pull it into the middle of the floor, and place the bottom of a tar barrel over it! That will serve as a table.

Bring up anything that will do to sit upon—
three-cornered bootmakers' stools and empty pack-
ing-cases. Bring out the torn old armchair without
a back, and the old racing sledge without runners,
and the ancient coach!

Drag out the old coach; it will do for the speaker's chair! Just look at it! one wheel is missing, and
the whole body of the carriage has disappeared, only
the driver's seat remains, the cushion is ragged and
mouldy, and the leather is red with age. The crazy
old thing is as high as a house. Prop it up, prop it
up, or it will go over!

Hurrah! it is Christmas Eve at Ekeby!

Behind the silken hangings of the double bed
sleep the Major and his wife, sleep and believe that
the cavaliers' wing is deep in slumber. The carters
and servant-girls may be asleep, overpowered by
porridge and strong Christmas ale, but not the gentlemen in the cavaliers' wing. How could any one
think it?

No bare-legged smiths turn the pieces of molten
iron, no sooty boys keep up the supply of coal; no
big hammer hangs like an arm with a clenched fist
from the ceiling—the anvil is bare, the furnace does
not open its red mouth to devour the coal, the
bellows do not creak. It is Christmas—the forge
slumbers.

Sleep, sleep! the cavaliers alone are awake. The
long pincers stand upright on the floor holding

candles in their claws. Out of the ten-gallon cauldron of brightest copper the flames flash blue into
the darkness of the roof. Beerencreutz's horn lantern hangs on the forge hammer. Yellow punch
gleams like sunlight in the punch-bowl. Here is a
table and benches, and the cavaliers intend spending Christmas Eve in the forge.

There is gaiety and carousal, music and song, but
the midnight festivity awakens no one. All noise
from the forge is drowned by the mighty thunder
of the waterfalls beyond it.

There is gaiety and carousal. Think if the Major's
wife were to see them! Well, she would probably
sit down and empty a glass with them. She is a sensible woman, a loud drinking song or a game of
Harlequin would not frighten her. She is the richest woman in Värmland, as gruff as a man, and as
proud as a queen. She loves song and the music of
violins. Cards and wine she likes, and a table surrounded with guests. She likes plenty in her pantry,
dancing and gaiety in her halls, and to have the
cavaliers' wing full of her pensioners.

Look at them sitting round their punch-bowl!
They are twelve — twelve men of might. There
is nothing effeminate about them, nor are they
dandies, but men whose renown will live long in
Värmland — brave and strong men.

They are not dried parchment nor closely tied-
up money-bags, but poor and reckless men, cava-

liers both day and night. They have not lived a life of ease as sleepy gentlemen on their own estates, but they are wayfarers, happy-go-lucky men, the heroes of a thousand adventures.

The cavaliers' wing has stood empty now for many years, and Ekeby is no longer the chosen refuge of homeless adventurers. Penniless noblemen and pensioned officers no longer traverse Värmland in their one-horse shays: but let the dead live again, let the joyous, careless, ever youthful men rise once again!

They could all play one musical instrument, some of them several. They were all as full of peculiarities and sayings and fancies and songs as an ant-hill is full of ants; but each had his special attribute, his highly prized cavalierly merit, which distinguished him from his companions. First of all I must mention Beerencreutz, the Colonel with the thick white moustache, the famous camphio-player and singer of Bellman's songs, and with him his friend and comrade in the wars, the silent Major Anders Fuchs, the great bear hunter. The third in the company would be little Ruster, the drum-major, who for years had been the Colonel's orderly, but his talent for brewing punch and for singing double-bass had raised him to the rank of cavalier. After him came the old ensign, Rutger von Örneclou, a lady killer, wearing a stock and wig and finely starched frill, and painted like a woman. He was one of the chief cavaliers, and so was Kristian Bergh, the strong captain, who was a doughty hero, but as easily deceived as the giant in the fairy tales. In the company of these two you often saw the little round Squire Julius. He was clever, amusing, and talented; artist, orator, and ballad singer, and a good story teller; and he was ever ready with a joke at the expense of the gouty little ensign or the stupid giant.

There was also the great German, Kevenhüller, the inventor of the self-propelling carriage and the flying machine, he whose name still echoes in those murmuring forests. He was a nobleman by birth and appearance, with a high twisted moustache, pointed beard, eagle nose, and small, squinting eyes set in a network of wrinkles. Here sat also the great warrior, Cousin Kristoffer, who never went beyond the walls of the cavaliers' wing, unless a bear hunt or a specially foolhardy adventure was "on the *tapis;*" and near him sat Uncle Eberhard, the philosopher, who had not come to Ekeby to spend his life in amusement, but that, exempt from the necessity of earning his bread, he might devote himself wholly to completing his great work on the Science of Sciences.

Lastly, I name the best of the troop, the gentle Lövenborg, the man too good for this world, and who understood little of its ways; and Lilliecrona, the great musician, who had a good home of his own, and always longed to be there, but who was forever chained to Ekeby, for his temperament required splendor and change to be able to endure life.

All these eleven men had left youth behind them, and some of them had passed middle age; but among them was one but thirty years old, in the full power of body and mind. This was Gösta Berling, the cavalier of cavaliers, who in himself was a greater orator, singer, musician, drinking champion, hunter, and gamester than all the others. He had every cavalierly virtue. What a man the Lady of the manor had made of him!

Look at him mounted on the speaker's chair! The darkness hangs from the ceiling behind him in heavy folds. His fair head shines out of it like the head of a young god — the youthful lightbearer who kindled chaos. He stands there, slight and beautiful, on fire with the love of adventure. But he speaks with great seriousness.

"Brother cavaliers, it draws toward midnight, our festivity is well on its way; it is time for us to drink the health of the thirteenth at table!"

"Dear Gösta," cried Squire Julius, "there is no thirteenth, there are only twelve of us."

"Every year one man dies at Ekeby," continued Gösta with increasing solemnity. "One of the guests of the cavaliers' wing dies — one of the joyous, careless, ever youthful men die. Well, what does it mat-

ter? Cavaliers may not grow old. If our shaking
hands could not lift a glass, our failing eyes not
distinguish the cards, what would life hold for us,
and what good are we in life? Of the thirteen who
celebrate Christmas Eve in the forge at Ekeby,
one must die: but every year brings a man to keep
up our number, a man experienced in all ways of
amusement. One who can handle both the violin
and the playing-cards must come and fill the empty
place. Old butterflies ought to die while the summer sun still shines. I drink to the health of the thirteenth!"

"But, Gösta, we are twelve," remonstrated the
cavaliers, leaving their glasses untouched.

Gösta Berling, whom they called the poet, though
he never wrote any poetry, continued with unruf-
fled calm:

"Brother cavaliers, have you forgotten who you
are? You are the men who hold joy by force in
Värmland! You lend life to the violin-bow, you
keep the dancing going, and songs and amusement
ring through the land. Your hearts have learned to
refrain from gold, your hands from money. If you
did not exist, dancing would die, summer would die,
and roses and song and card-playing, and in the
whole of this blessed land there would be nothing
but iron and foundry proprietors. Joy shall live just
as long as you do. For six years I have celebrated
Christmas Eve at Ekeby, and no one has yet had

the courage to drink to the thirteenth! Who is it that is afraid to die?"

"But, Gösta," they screamed, "when we are only twelve, how can we drink to the thirteenth?"

Despair was painted on Gösta's face.

"Are we only twelve?" he cried. "Why, must we then die out of the land? Shall we be but eleven next year, and ten the year after? Shall our names become a legend and our company be annihilated? I call upon him, the thirteenth, for I am here to drink his health. From the deep of the sea, from the bowels of the earth, from heaven or from hell, I call upon him who is to keep up the number of the cavaliers!"

And there was a rustling in the chimney, the door of the smelting-furnace was thrown open, and the thirteenth appeared. He came in hairy hide, with tail and hoofs and horns and pointed beard, and at sight of him the cavaliers sprang up with a shout.

But in unrestrained glee, Gösta screamed, "Behold the thirteenth, hurrah!"

And thus he appeared, man's ancient enemy, appeared to the foolhardy who were disturbing the peace of the Christmas Eve. The friend of the witches who have signed away their souls in blood on coal-black paper had come — he who had danced with the Countess of Tvarsnäs for seven days and could not be exorcised by seven priests.

A multitude of thoughts stormed through the

minds of the old adventurers at sight of him. They probably wondered on whose account he was out that night.

Some of them were inclined to hurry away in fear, but they soon learned that their horned friend had not come to fetch away any of them to his dark kingdom. The clinking sound of the punch glasses and the songs had tempted him in. He wished to enjoy the sight of men's happiness on that holy Christmas Eve, and to throw aside the burden of his rule for a time.

Oh, cavaliers, cavaliers! which of you remembers it is Christmas Eve? The angels are singing over the shepherds in the fields; children lie in their beds and fear to sleep too soundly that they may not miss the beautiful early morning service. It is soon time to light the Christmas candles in the church at Bro, and far away in the forest homestead the boys have been making a resinous torch, with which to light their sweethearts to church. In the windows of the houses the housewives have placed tiers of candles ready for lighting when the stream of church-goers begins to pass. The sexton starts the Christmas hymn in his sleep, and the old rector lies in bed and tries if he has still sufficient voice to chant "Glory to God in the highest, on earth peace, good will toward men."

Oh, cavaliers, it would have been better for you if you had been safe in your beds on this night of

peace instead of keeping company with the Prince
of Darkness!

But they cried him welcome as Gösta did. They
set a goblet full of wine in his hand, they gave him
the place of honor at the table, and seemed as glad
to see him as if his ugly, satyr-like face wore the
lovely features of their youth's beloved.

Beerencreutz invited him to a game of camphio;
Squire Julius sang him his best songs; Örneclou
talked to him of beautiful women, those charming
beings who sweeten existence. And he seemed to
enjoy himself, as with princely ease he leaned back
on the coach-seat of the old carriage, and lifted the
brimming goblet in his claw-beweaponed hand to
his smiling lips.

But Gösta Berling, of course, made him a speech.
"Your highness," he said, "we have expected you at
Ekeby for a long time, for you probably have some
difficulty in gaining access to any other paradise.
We live here without toiling, neither do we spin,
of which your highness is probably aware. Roast
sparrows here fly into our mouths, and the ale and
brandy flow in streams about us. This is a charming
place, you remark, my lord!

"We cavaliers have also expected you, because
our company has never really been complete. You
see the case is this—we are rather more than we
give ourselves out to be; we are the legendary troop
of twelve who go through Time. We were twelve

when we steered the world from the cloud-covered heights of Olympus, and twelve when we lived as birds in Ygdrasil's green crest. We follow wherever legend leads. Did we not sit twelve strong men round Arthur's Table, and were there not twelve paladins in the army of Charles the Great? One of us has been Thor, one Jupiter, as you can see to-day. The godlike splendor gleams sometimes through our rags; the lion's mane shows from under the donkey's hide. Time has used us badly, but when we are together, even the forge becomes Olympus, and the cavaliers' wing a Valhalla.

"But, your highness, we have not been complete in number. It is well known that in the fabled group of twelve there is always a Loki, a Prometheus. Him have we lacked! Your highness, I bid you welcome!"

"See, see," said the wicked one, "such grand phrases, such grand phrases! And I—I have no time to answer. Business, boys, business!—I must be off at once, or I would gladly serve you in any part you choose. Thanks for to-night's entertainment, old fellow, we'll meet again."

Then the cavaliers inquired where he was going, and he answered that the noble Fru Samzelius, the owner of Ekeby, was waiting to have her contract renewed. They were struck dumb with surprise.

She was a stern and capable woman, the Lady of

Ekeby. She could lift a sack of rye on her broad
shoulders. She accompanied the transport of ore
all the way from the mines at Bergslägen to Ekeby.
She could sleep like a carter on the floor of the
granary with a sack for her pillow. In the winter
she sometimes watched the charcoal burning; in
the summer she would follow a timber raft down
the Löfven. A capable woman was she. She swore
like a trooper, and reigned like a king over her
seven foundries and her neighbors' estates, reigned
over her own parish and the neighboring parishes—yea, over all the beautiful Värmland. But
to the homeless cavaliers she had been like a mother, and they had therefore closed their ears to the
whispers that told them she was in league with the
devil.

So, with great astonishment, they asked him what
contract she had made with him.

And their horned guest answered that he gave the
Major's wife her seven foundries on condition that
she sent him a man's soul every year.

Oh, what horror clutched at the hearts of the
cavaliers! They knew it, of course, but they had
never realized it. At Ekeby each year one of the
cavaliers died—one of the joyous, careless, ever
youthful men. Well, what did it matter? Cavaliers
may not grow old. If their shaking hands could not
lift a glass, or their failing eyes distinguish the cards,
what could life hold for them? What good were they

in life? Old butterflies ought to die while the sun shines.

But now, only now, they grasped the meaning of it all.

Alas, the woman! Had she given them so many good meals, had she allowed them to drink her strong brewed ale and her brandy, only that they might fall from the drinking-halls and gaming-tables at Ekeby down to the King of Darkness — one every year, one for every flying year?

Alas, the woman! the witch! Strong men had come to Ekeby, come thither to destruction. And she ruined them there. Their brains were like sponges, their lungs but dried ashes, their spirits were darkened when they sank back on their death-beds and were ready at last for the long journey — destitute of hope, or soul, or virtue.

Alas, the woman! Better men than they had died like that, and so, too, would they die.

But the paralysis of fear did not hold the cavaliers for long.

"You, Prince of Darkness," they shouted, "never again shall you make your bloody contract with that witch—she shall die. Kristian Bergh, the strong captain, has flung the heaviest hammer the forge contains over his shoulder, and he will bury it to the shaft in the hag's head. You will get no more souls from her.

"And as for yourself, we will lay you on the

anvil and loosen the great hammer. We will hold you with pincers under its blows, and teach you to go hunting for the souls of cavaliers."

He was a coward, was the dark gentleman, as is known of old, and the talk of the great hammer did not please him. He called Kristian Bergh back, and began bargaining with the cavaliers.

"Take the seven foundries, cavaliers, and give me the Major's wife."

"Do you think us as base as she is?" cried Squire Julius. "We will take Ekeby and all the other foundries, but you must manage the Major's wife yourself."

"What does Gösta say?" asked the gentle Löven-borg. "Gösta Berling must speak. We must have his opinion on such an important subject."

"This is madness!" cried Gösta. "Cavaliers, don't be made fools of by him! What have we against the Major's wife? Regarding our souls, it must be as fate ordains; but it won't be with my consent that we are ungrateful wretches, and act like rogues and villains. I have eaten at her table for many long years, and will not desert her now."

"Yes, go to the devil, if you feel inclined, Gösta. We would rather reign over Ekeby."

"But are you raving mad, or have you drunk yourselves out of your senses? Do you believe in all this? Do you believe that he over there is the Evil One? Don't you see that it is a cursed joke?"

"See, see!" cried the dark gentleman. "He has not noticed that he is in a fair way to be ready for me, and yet he has been at Ekeby for seven years. He has not noticed how far he has got."

"Oh, nonsense, man! Didn't I help you to hide yourself in the furnace over there?"

"As if that made any difference; as if I am not as good a devil as any other. Yes, yes, Gösta Berling, you are caught. You have become a fine specimen under Fru Samzelius' treatment!"

"She saved me; what am I without her?" said Gösta.

"Of course, of course, just as if she had no purpose in keeping you at Ekeby. You tempt many to fall. You have great talents. Once you tried to be independent; you let her give you a cottage, and you became a workman and earned your own bread, and every day she passed the cottage with a bevy of beautiful girls in her train. Marienne Sinclaire was with her once, and then you threw aside your apron and spade, Gösta Berling, and became a cavalier again."

"The road passed that way, you rascal."

"Yes, yes, of course, the road passed that way. Afterwards you went to Borg to be tutor to Henrik Dohna, and you very nearly became Countess Märta's son-in-law. Who was it contrived the young Ebba Dohna should hear you were only an outcast parson, and should say you nay? It was the

E

Major's wife, Gösta Berling — she wanted you back."

"What of it?" said Gösta. "Ebba Dohna died shortly after. I could not have won her in any case."

The dark gentleman came close up to him and whispered in his ear.

"Died — yea — certainly she died. She killed herself for your sake, but they never told you."

"You are no bad devil," said Gösta.

"It was the Major's wife who arranged it all, I tell you. She wanted you back in the cavaliers' wing."

Gösta burst into a loud laugh.

"You are no bad devil," he shouted wildly. "Why shouldn't we make a contract with you? You are able to give us the seven foundries, I suppose, if you feel inclined?"

"A good thing for you if you don't fight any longer against good fortune."

The cavaliers drew an easy breath. It had come to such a pass with them that they could do nothing without Gösta. If he had refused to join the affair, nothing would have come of it. And it was a great thing for the poverty-stricken cavaliers to be made masters of Ekeby.

"But notice," said Gösta, "we take the seven foundries to save our souls — not for the sake of being rich, prosperous people, who count their money and weigh their iron. We refuse to be dried-up parchment or tied-up money pouches; we are, and still remain, cavaliers."

"The very words of wisdom," mumbled the dark gentleman.

"So, if you give us the seven foundries for one year, we will take them; but remember this, if during that time we do anything which is uncavalier-like, anything sensible or useful or effeminate, you can take all the twelve of us, when the year is out, and give the foundries to whom you like."

The wicked one rubbed his hands with glee.

"But if we always behave like true cavaliers," continued Gösta, "you must never again make any contract about Ekeby, and you forfeit your wage for this year, both from us and from the Major's wife."

"That is hard," said the devil. "Oh, dear Gösta, I ought to get one soul, one poor little soul. I might as well have the Major's wife. Why do you spare her?"

"I don't buy and sell such goods," said Gösta. "But if you must have some one, you can take old Sintram at Fors; he is about ready for you, I can answer for it."

"See, see, that is worth mentioning," said the dark gentleman without blinking—"the cavaliers against Sintram. It will be a good year."

And so the contract was written with blood taken from Gösta Berling's little finger, on black paper supplied by the Evil One, with his own goose quill.

And when it was done, the cavaliers rejoiced. For a whole year everything that the world contained would be theirs, and afterwards there was always some way out of the scrape.

They pushed aside their chairs and formed a ring round the steaming kettle which stood in the middle of the floor. In their midst danced the Evil One, leaping high, till at last he threw himself down beside the kettle, tilted it over, and drank.

Then Beerencreutz threw himself down beside him, then Gösta, and after them all the other cavaliers, till they lay in a ring round the kettle, which was passed from mouth to mouth. At last a push sent it over, and the hot, sticky liquid streamed over them all.

When, swearing, they scrambled up, they found their dark friend had disappeared, but his golden promises still seemed to float like shining crowns over their heads.

The Christmas Dinner

FRU SAMZELIUS celebrated Christmas Day by giving a dinner-party at Ekeby. She took her place as hostess at a table spread for fifty guests, doing the honors with great splendor. The short fur jacket and striped skirt and clay pipe were cast aside. She rustled in silk, her bare arms were loaded with gold, and pearls gleamed on her white throat.

But where were the cavaliers? Where were the men who drank to the new owners of Ekeby out of the burnished kettle on the black floor of the forge?

In the corner near the fireplace the cavaliers were seated at a separate table; there was no room for them that day at the big central table. They were served later than the other guests, the wine flowed sparingly, none of the pretty women cast a glance in their direction, no one listened to Gösta's jokes.

The cavaliers were like tamed birds. They had had but an hour's sleep before they started to the early morning service at church, lighted on their way by torches and the stars. They saw the Christmas lights, they heard the Christmas hymns, and they became smiling children again. They forgot the Christmas Eve in the forge, as one forgets an evil dream.

The Lady of Ekeby was a powerful and great

dame. Who would dare lift his arm against her?
Whose tongue would dare to bear witness against
her? Certainly the cavaliers never could, who for so
many years had eaten her bread and slept beneath
her roof. She placed them where she chose; she
could exclude them from her festivity altogether
if she wished, and they were powerless. God bless
them! why, they could not exist away from Ekeby!

The guests at the big table were enjoying themselves. Marienne Sinclaire's beautiful eyes were
beaming, and you heard the low laugh of the gay
little Countess Dohna.

But the cavaliers were moody. Why were they
not with the other guests? What was the meaning
of this insulting arrangement of the table in the fireplace corner? As if they were not fit for the best
society?

The hostess sat between Count Dohna and the
rector of Bro, while the cavaliers hung their heads
like deserted children, and last night's thoughts
awoke within them. Gay nonsense and ridiculous
sayings were but shy guests at the smaller table, for
the anger and the promises of last night had entered
the hearts of the cavaliers.

Certainly Squire Julius managed to convince
Kristian Bergh that the roasted grouse which were
being handed round at the big table would not suffice for all the guests, but that did not cause much
amusement.

"I know they can't go round," he said. "I know how many there were. But the cook was not at a loss, Kristian Bergh; they have roasted crows for us at the little table."

But Colonel Beerencreutz's lips unbend only to a faint smile, and Gösta Berling had looked all day as if he were considering the advisability of murdering some one.

"Isn't anything good enough for cavaliers?" he said.

Captain Bergh was furious. Hadn't he cherished a lifelong hatred for crows, those abominable cawing things? He hated them so bitterly that he dressed himself in a woman's fluttering skirt and tied a kerchief over his head, and made himself a laughing-stock to every man, in the autumn, for the purpose of creeping within gunshot of them when they were feeding on the fresh grain in the corn-fields.

In spring he followed them to their dances on the bare meadows in mating time and shot them. He sought their nests in summer, and destroyed their half-hatched eggs and the screaming unfeathered young.

He now clutched the plate of grouse.

"Don't you think I recognize them?" he thundered to the servant. "Do you suppose I must hear them caw to know them? The devil — to offer Kristian Bergh a crow — the devil!"

And taking up the grouse one by one he flung them against the wall.

"The devil!" he shouted, "the devil! to offer crows to Kristian Bergh!"

Just as he was wont to throw the helpless nestlings against the cliffs he now threw the roasted grouse against the wall of the dining-hall.

Grease and gravy flew around him; the birds rebounded from the wall into the middle of the floor. And the cavaliers rejoiced. Then the angry voice of the Lady of Ekeby reached their ears.

"Turn him out!" she called to the servants.

But they dared not touch him. After all, he was Kristian Bergh, the strong captain.

"Turn him out!"

He heard the order, and, terrible in his anger, he turned to her as a bear turns from the fallen adversary to the new persecutor. He strode toward her table, his heavy tread shaking the floor, till he stood before her with only the end of the table between them.

"Turn him out!" thundered the Major's wife again.

But he was mad; his furrowed forehead and his great clenched fists filled all with awe. He was a giant in size and strength. Both guests and servants trembled and dared not touch him — no one dared touch him when such rage darkened his senses.

He stood before the Lady of Ekeby and defied her.

"I took the crows and threw them against the wall; dare you say I did wrong?"

"Out with you, Captain!"

"Sh — you woman! — to offer Kristian Bergh crows to eat! If I did the right thing, I would take you and your seven d——"

"A thousand devils! Kristian Bergh, don't you dare to swear! No one swears here but myself!"

"Do you think I fear you, you witch? Do you think I don't know how you got your seven foundries?"

"Silence, Captain."

"When Altringer died, he gave them to you, because he had been your lover."

"Will you be silent?"

"Because you had been such a faithful wife, Margarita Samzelius; and the Major took the gift, and let you manage the foundries, and pretended not to understand, and Satan backed the whole affair — but this is the end of it."

Margarita Samzelius sank into her chair, she was pale and trembling, and it was with a low, strange voice she reiterated, "Yes, this is the end of it, and it is your work, Kristian Bergh!"

At that tone Kristian Bergh shivered, his face changed, and anxious tears filled his eyes.

"I am drunk," he cried. "I don't know what I

am saying; I have said nothing. Have I not been
her dog and slave for forty years, her dog and slave
and nothing more! She is Margarita Celsing whom
I 've served all my life. I can say nothing ill of her.
What should I say of the beautiful Margarita Celsing? I am the dog that guards her door, and the
slave who bears her burdens. She may strike and
push me aside, but, you see, I bear it in silence. I
have loved her for forty years, how could I speak
evil of her?"

Ah, it was a wonderful sight to see him throw
himself down and pray forgiveness; and, as she sat
at the other side of the table, he crawled on his
knees till he reached her, and bent down to kiss the
hem of her skirt, and his tears wet the floor.

But not far from the Lady of Ekeby sat a strong
little man. He had curly hair, small, squinting eyes,
and a prominent under jaw, and he resembled a bear.
He was a man of few words. He was Major Samzelius.

He rose when he heard Kristian Bergh's last
words; so did his wife and all the fifty guests. The
women were trembling with fear of what was coming, the men stood helpless, and at the feet of
Margarita Samzelius lay Captain Kristian, kissing
the hem of her skirt and wetting the floor with his
tears.

The Major's broad hairy hands clenched slowly;
he lifted his arm to strike.

But the woman spoke first—in her voice lay a dull tone, which was unusual.

"You stole me," she cried. "You came like a robber and stole me. They forced me with blows and hard words to be your wife. I have only served you as you deserved."

The Major's broad fist was lifted; his wife fell back a step and then spoke again.

"The living eel squirms under the knife; a woman married by force takes a lover. Will you strike me now for what happened twenty years ago? Why did n't you strike then? Don't you remember he lived at Ekeby and we at Sjö? Don't you remember how he helped us in our poverty? We drove in his carriages, we drank his wine. Did we hide anything from you? Were not his servants your servants? Did not his gold weigh down your pockets? Did you not take the seven foundries? Then you were silent and took his gifts. It was then you should have struck, Berndt Samzelius, it was then!"

Her husband turned from her and gazed around at all those present, and he read in their faces that they thought her right—that they all thought he had taken Altringer's property and gifts as a price for his silence.

"I never knew it," he cried, and stamped on the floor.

"It is well, then, that you should know it now," she interrupted, with a mocking ring in her voice.

"I almost feared you might die without knowing it. For now that you know it, I can talk freely with you, who have been my lord and jailer. You may know it now, that, in spite of you, I was his from whom you stole me. You may know it now, all you who have slandered me."

It was the old love that shone in her eyes and rang in her voice. She had her husband before her, with his clenched fist; she read horror and contempt in the faces around her; she felt it to be the last hour of her power; but she could not help rejoicing when for the first time she spoke openly of what was the happiest remembrance of her life.

"He was a man — a splendid man. Who were you that you dared come between us? I never saw his like. He gave me happiness; and he gave me riches. Blessed be his memory!"

Then the Major dropped his arm without striking; he knew now how he would punish her.

"Out," he shouted, "out of my house!"

She stood motionless.

But the cavaliers gazed at each other with pale faces. It seemed as if all that the Evil One had prophesied was being fulfilled. This, then, was the result of the contract not having been renewed. If this was true, it must also be true that for more than twenty years she had been sending cavaliers to hell, and they also were destined for that journey. Oh, the wretch!

"Out with you!" screamed the Major. "Beg your bread by the wayside, you shall have no further joy of your riches, you shall have no dwelling in his houses! It is the end of the Lady of Ekeby, and the day you set your foot within my house I will kill you!"

"You turn me out of my own home?"

"You have no home — Ekeby is mine."

A feeling of helplessness came over her, and she fell back to the threshold; the Major following her closely.

"You, who have been the unhappiness of my life, are you to have the power to treat me so?" she wailed.

"Out — out!"

She leaned against the door-post, clasped her hands, and hid her eyes. She was thinking of her mother, and whispered to herself:

"May you be denied as I've been denied, may the roadside be your home, and the strawstack be your bed!" So it had come to pass — so it had come.

It was the good old rector from Bro and the Judge from Munkerud who came forward and tried to calm Major Samzelius. They said he would do wisest in letting all old stories die, let things be as they were, forget and forgive. But he shook aside the friendly hands from his shoulders. He was as terrible to cross as was Kristian Bergh.

"It is no old story," he cried. "I knew it not till to-day; I could not punish her unfaithfulness before."

At that his wife lifted her head and regained her old courage.

"You shall go before I do. Do you imagine I fear you?" she said, and came forward again.

The Major did not answer her, but he watched her every movement, ready to strike her down if he could not be quit of her in any other way.

"Help me, good gentlemen!" she cried; "help me to get this man bound and taken away till he regains the use of his senses. Remember who I am — and who he is. Think of it before I am obliged to yield to him. I manage all Ekeby, and he sits feeding his bears all day in their bear-hole. Help me, my good neighbors! There will be terrible misery here if I leave you. The peasant earns his livelihood by cutting my forests and carrying my ore. The colliers live by providing me with coal, and the lumbermen steer my rafts. I give the work which brings them riches. The ironsmiths and carpenters and day laborers all live by serving me. Do you think that man can hold my work in hand? I tell you that if you send me away, you bring down famine upon yourselves."

Again hands were raised in help, again an attempt was made to pacify the Major.

"No," he screamed, "out with her! Who dares

justify a faithless wife? I tell you, if she does not go voluntarily, I will lift her up and carry her to my wild bears."

Then, in her great distress, the Lady of Ekeby turned to the cavaliers.

"Will you allow me to be driven from my home, cavaliers? Have I let you freeze in winter? Have I refused you wine and ale? Did I require work from your hands because I gave you food and clothing? Have you not enjoyed yourselves at my side as trustfully as children? Have you not danced through my halls, and have not gaiety and laughter been your daily bread? Don't let this man who has been the great unhappiness of my life, don't let him drive me from my home, cavaliers! Don't send me to be a beggar by the wayside!"

During these words Gösta Berling made his way to a lovely dark-haired girl who was sitting at the big table.

"You were often at Borg five years ago, Anna," he said. "Tell me, was it the Major's wife who told Ebba that I was an unfrocked clergyman?"

"Help her, Gösta," the girl answered.

"You can understand, I suppose, that I wish to know first if she made a murderer of me?"

"Oh, Gösta, what terrible thoughts! Help her, Gösta."

"You won't answer me, I see—then Sintram told the truth."

And Gösta went back to the cavaliers, and would
not lift a finger to help Margarita Samzelius.

Oh! if she had not placed the cavaliers at a separate table in the chimney-corner, for the thoughts
of last night are astir in their hearts, and their faces
burn with anger hardly less than the Major's! Mer-
cilessly they stand aloof during her pleading. Everything they saw emphasized the facts they had learned
last night.

"One can see she did not get her contract renewed," muttered one of them. "Go to hell, you
witch!" screamed another. "We ought by right to
turn you out."

"You scoundrels!" shouted weak old Uncle Eberhard to the cavaliers; "don't you understand it
was Sintram?"

"Of course we know," answered Julius, "but what
of that? Can't it be true in spite of that? Does n't
he do the work of the Evil One? Don't they understand one another well?"

"You go, Eberhard, you go and help her — you
don't believe in hell," they cried, mockingly.

And Gösta Berling stood motionless, without
word or movement.

No — out of that screaming, threatening, muttering crowd of cavaliers she could get no help.

She turned again to the door, and lifted her
clasped hands to her eyes.

"May you be denied as I am denied!" she cried,

in her bitter sorrow. "May the wayside be your home, and the strawstack be your bed!" And she laid one hand on the door-handle, and lifted the other on high.

"Mark you — you who have beheld my down-fall — mark that your hour is coming soon. You shall be cast abroad, and your place shall be empty. How will you stand where I do not support you? You, Melchior Sinclaire, you have a heavy hand, and you let your wife feel it — take care! You, par-son of Broby, the punishment is coming! Madame Uggla, look to your home, poverty is at its doors! You beautiful women, Elizabeth Dohna, Marienne Sinclaire, Anna Stjärnhök, don't think I shall be the only one to fly from my home! Be on your guard, cavaliers, a storm is rising, and you will be swept away — your day is now past — yes, forever past! I do not mourn for myself, but for you, for the storm will go over your heads, and who can stand when I fall? Oh, my heart is heavy for the sake of the people! Who will give them work when I am gone?"

She opened the door, and then Kristian Bergh lifted his head and said, "How long must I lie here at your feet, Margarita Celsing? Will you not for-give me, that I may rise and fight for you?"

It was a hard struggle the Major's wife had with herself, for she knew that if she forgave him, he would fight her husband, and the man who had

F

loved her faithfully for forty years would probably be a murderer.

"Am I also to forgive?" she said. "Are you not the cause of all this trouble, Kristian Bergh? Go to the cavaliers and rejoice at your work!"

And so she left them. She went calmly, leaving terror behind her; she fell, but she was not without greatness in her fall. She did not stoop to weak repining, but even in her old age she rejoiced in the love of her youth. She did not stoop to wailing and tears when she left all behind her, and did not shrink from wandering through the land with a beggar's scrip and staff. She mourned over the poor and the happy, careless people on the banks of the Löfven, over the cavaliers, and all those whom she had protected and guarded. Deserted by every one, she had still strength to turn aside from her last friend, so as not to condemn him to being a murderer.

She was a powerful woman, great in strength of will and mighty in government. We shall hardly see another like her.

Next day Major Samzelius broke up his home at Ekeby, and moved to his own house at Sjö, which lies quite near the great foundry.

It had been plainly stated in Altringer's will, by which the Major had received the huge property of the seven foundries, that none of them were to be sold or given away, but after the death of the Major they were to pass to his wife and her heirs. As, therefore, he could not destroy the hated gift, he gave it into the hands of the cavaliers, thinking their bad management would do Ekeby and the other foundries the greatest harm.

And as no one in the land doubted that Sintram worked the will of his evil master, and as all his promises to the cavaliers had been so strangely fulfilled, they were all sure that the contract he had made with them would be carried out to the smallest detail, and they were determined to do nothing sensible or practical or uncavalier-like, and they were also quite convinced that the Major's wife was an abominable witch who had plotted their ruin.

Old Uncle Eberhard, the philosopher, made game of their belief, but who cared what such a man as Uncle Eberhard said — he was so obstinate himself in his beliefs that if he had stood in the midst of the fires of hell, and had seen all the devils grinning at him, he would still have said they were not there, because it was impossible that they should exist. Uncle Eberhard was a great philosopher.

Gösta Berling told no one what he thought. He certainly felt he had little cause to thank the Major's wife for making him an Ekeby cavalier, for it now seemed better to him to be dead than to know he had been the cause of Ebba Dohna's suicide. He lifted no hand in vengeance against the Major's wife, but neither would he help her. He could not. But the cavaliers had come to great power and splendor. Christmas was at hand with its fêtes and its pleasures; their hearts were full of joy, and, if any sorrow hung over Gösta Berling, he did not bear it in his face or on his lips.

Gösta Berling — Poet

IT was Christmas, and a ball was to be given at Borg. At that time — and it must be nearly sixty years ago — young Count Dohna lived at Borg. He was newly married, and his countess was both young and beautiful. Gay times were in store for the old estate.

Invitations had also come to Ekeby; but of all the cavaliers who were spending Christmas there, Gösta Berling, the poet, as they called him, was the only one who was inclined to accept.

Borg and Ekeby lie on opposite shores of the narrow Löfven Lake — Borg is in Svartsjö parish, Ekeby in Bro — and when the lake is frozen, it is only a dozen miles from one estate to the other.

The penniless Gösta Berling was fitted out by the old cavaliers for this festivity as if he were a king's son who upheld the honor of the kingdom. His coat with its shining gold buttons was new, his cambric frills were finely starched, his patent leather shoes shone. His overcoat was lined with the finest beaver, and a cap of sable fur covered his fair, curly head. They spread a bearskin with silver claws over his racing sledge, and he was to drive black Don Juan, the pride of the stable.

He whistled to Tankred, his white hound, and, snatching up the reins, drove away gaily, carrying with him an atmosphere of wealth and splendor.

It was early when he started. It was Sunday, and he heard the psalms being sung as he passed Bro Church. Afterwards he turned into the lonely forest road that led to Berga, Captain Uggla's home, where he intended to stop and dine.

Berga was not a rich man's house. Hunger knew the way to the Captain's thatch-covered dwelling, but he was received with jokes and laughter and entertainment, with song, as all other guests were, and he left as unwillingly as they did.

Old Mamsell Ulrika Dillner stood on the steps to welcome Gösta as he drove up. She was the housekeeper and managed the weaving-looms, and, as she curtsied to him, the false curls which hung round her brown old face danced with delight. She carried him off to the parlor, and poured forth the story of the changes and chances of the house and its inmates.

Trouble was at the door; hard times reigned at Berga. They had no horse-radish, even, to eat with their salt meat, and Ferdinand and the girls had yoked old Disa to a sledge and gone off to Munkerud to borrow some. The Captain was out shooting, and would probably bring home some tough old hare which required more butter in the cooking than it was worth. This was what he considered "provisioning the family"! But, anyway, it was bet-

ter than returning with a wretched fox—the worst
animal created, useless both living and dead.

And Fru Uggla? She had not left her room yet.
She was in bed reading a novel, as she did every
morning. An angel, such as she was, could not be
expected to do any work.

No, that must be done by those who are old and
grey like Mamsell Ulrika. Day and night she was
on her feet trying to keep things together. It was no
easy task; it was but the truth that they had had
no meat but bear hams all the winter. She certainly
expected no great wages—she had seen none as yet
—but they would not turn her out when she grew
too old to earn her bread. Even a housekeeper was
considered a human being here, and they would
certainly give old Ulrika a decent funeral when the
time came, if there was any money with which to
buy a coffin.

"For no one can say what may happen," she
said, drying her eyes, which always overflowed so
easily. "We are in debt to that wicked Sintram,
and he can sell us up any day. True, Ferdinand is
now engaged to Anna Stjärnhök, and she is rich,
but she will very soon tire of him. And then what
is to become of us and our three cows and nine
horses, our light-hearted girls who only think of
going from one ball to another, our fields where
nothing grows, our kind, good-natured Ferdinand
who never will be quite a man? What will become

of this whole blessed house, where everything except work thrives so contentedly?"

But the dinner-hour came, and the family assembled. Ferdinand, the quiet son of the house, and his
sisters arrived with the borrowed horse-radish. The
Captain, coming home from his shooting, had taken
a dip in the ice-covered river, and came in hearty
and strong, wrung Gösta's hand, and threw up the
windows to let in the fresh air. Fru Uggla appeared,
dressed in silk, with wide lace falling over the white
hands which Gösta was allowed to kiss.

They all welcomed him gladly, jokes passed
from one to the other, and they laughingly teased
him.

"Well, how are you all at Ekeby—how do you
like the promised land?"

"It flows with milk and honey," he answered.
"We empty the mountains of their iron, and fill our
cellars with wine. The fields bear gold with which
we gild life's misery, and we fell our forests to build
pavilions and skittle-alleys."

But Fru Uggla sighed and smiled, and one word
escaped her lips—"Poet."

"There are many sins on my conscience," answered Gösta, "but I've never written a line of
poetry."

"But still you are a poet, Gösta—you can't rid
yourself of that name. You have lived through more
poems than our poets have ever written."

And later, the Captain's wife spoke to him, mildly as a mother, about his wilfully wasted life. " May I live to see you become a man," she said; and Gösta felt the sweetness of being reproached by this gentle woman, who was his faithful friend, whose romantic heart was fired by the love of great deeds.

But when the merry meal was over, the cabbages and fritters, the horse-radish and Christmas ale enjoyed, and Gösta had made them laugh and cry with his tales of the Major and his wife and the Broby parson, sleigh-bells were heard in the yard, and a moment later Sintram entered the room.

He shone with satisfaction from the top of his bald head down to his long, flat feet. He swung his arms, and made such grimaces, it was evident he brought bad news.

" Have you heard," he cried, — " have you heard that the banns were called to-day at Svartsjö Church for Anna Stjärnhök and rich old Dahlberg? She must have forgotten that she was engaged to Ferdinand!"

No, they had not heard; they were all astonished and grieved. They already saw their home ravaged to pay the debt due to their cruel neighbor, their dearly loved horses sold, even the poor furniture which had come to them from their mother's old home. Their life of festivity and balls was over now —they must eat bear-meat again, and the young people must seek work among strangers.

Fru Uggla caressed Ferdinand, and let him feel the comfort of a never-failing love.

And the unconquerable Gösta Berling sat there among them with a thousand schemes surging in his brain.

"Listen," he cried; "this isn't the time for mourning. It is the parson's wife down at Svartsjö who has arranged it all. She has great influence over Anna since she has been living with her at the parsonage. It is she who has persuaded her to give up Ferdinand and take old Dahlberg; but they are not married yet, nor ever shall be. I am going to Borg; I will meet Anna there and talk to her. I will carry her away from the parsonage and old Dahlberg. I will bring her here to-night, and then he will not see much more of her."

So it was decided. Gösta drove alone to Borg, instead of taking one of the girls with him, but the best wishes of all followed him on his way. Sintram, rejoicing that old Dahlberg was to be outwitted, determined to remain where he was and see Gösta return with the faithless beauty. In a sudden outburst of kindness he even wrapped about Gösta his green travelling-rug — a present given him by Mamsell Ulrika.

But Fru Uggla came out on the steps with three small red bound books in her hand. "Take them," she said to Gösta, who was already seated in his sledge. "Take and keep them in case you fail. It is

Corinne, Madame de Staël's *Corinne*. I don't wish it to be sold at auction."

"I won't fail."

"Oh, Gösta, Gösta!" she said, and passed her hand over his uncovered head. "You strongest and weakest of men! For how long will you remember that the happiness of these poor people lies in your hands?"

Drawn by black Don Juan and followed by Tankred, Gösta again flew along the highway, the spirit of adventure flooding his soul. He felt himself a conqueror, borne forward by enthusiasm. The road took him past the parsonage at Svartsjö. He drove through the gate and asked if he might drive Anna Stjärnhök to the ball, and she consented. It was a lovely, self-willed girl who took her seat beside him. Who would not gladly ride behind Don Juan?

The young people were silent at first; then Anna opened the conversation — defiantly, as usual. "I suppose you heard what the pastor gave out in church to-day?"

"Did he say you were the loveliest girl between Löfven and Klarälfven?"

"How stupid you are! People knew that without his telling them. He published the banns for me and old Dahlberg."

"It is hardly likely I should have asked you to drive with me if I had known."

And Anna carelessly answered, "I daresay I could have done without you, Gösta Berling."

"But it is a great pity, Anna," Gösta said, thoughtfully, "that your parents are not living. Now you do what you like, and no one can depend on you."

"It is a greater pity you did not say so before; some one else could have driven me to the ball."

"The parson's wife must be of my opinion, that you require some one to take your father's place, or she would not have paired you off with an old creature like Dahlberg."

"The parson's wife had nothing to do with it."

"Dear me! was he really your own choice?"

"He is not marrying me for my money."

"No, of course not; it is only blue eyes and rosy cheeks that old men run after, and it becomes them finely."

"Gösta, are n't you ashamed of yourself?"

"Well, you must remember now that you have nothing further to do with young men. There will be an end now to your dancing and amusements. Your place will be on the sofa-corner, or perhaps you mean to play cribbage with your old man?"

They were silent after this, till they began the steep ascent to Borg Hall.

"Thanks for your trouble! It will be some time before I sleigh again with Gösta Berling," said Anna.

"Thanks for that promise! There are many, I

know, who have repented the day they ever went sleighing with you."

It was in no mild frame of mind that the defiant beauty entered the ball-room and glanced over the assembled guests. The first she saw was Dahlberg, small and bald, standing by the side of the tall, slight, fair-haired Gösta. She felt she could have turned them both out of the room.

Dahlberg came and invited her to dance — to be met with cutting astonishment.

"Are you going to dance? You don't usually do so!"

Her girl friends came forward to congratulate her.

"Don't pretend, girls; you know very well no one could fall in love with old Dahlberg. We are both rich, and it is therefore a suitable match."

The matrons pressed her hand and spoke of life's greatest happiness.

"Congratulate the pastor's wife," she said. "She is more delighted about it than I am."

There stood Gösta Berling, the gay cavalier, welcomed by all for his bright smile and his ready speech, which strewed gold-dust over life's grey way. It seemed to her that she had never really seen him before. He was no outcast, no homeless jester — he was a king among men, a born king.

Gösta and the other young men made a compact against her; she must be taught the wrong she did in giving herself, with lovely face and great wealth, to an old man. And they let her sit out ten dances.

She was furious.

At the eleventh dance a man of the most insignificant appearance, one with whom no one else cared to dance, approached her and invited her to waltz.

"As the bread is finished, the crusts must be brought on the table," she said.

Then they played forfeits. Fair-haired girls put their heads together and sentenced her to kiss the one she loved the best, waiting, with covert smiles, to see the proud beauty kiss old Dahlberg.

But she rose, stately in her anger, and said, "Shall I not rather box the ears of him I love the least?"

And the next moment Gösta's cheek burned from the stroke of her firm hand.

He flushed red, controlling himself, caught her hand, and holding it fast a moment, whispered, "Meet me in the red drawing-room downstairs in half an hour."

His blue eyes held her in magic fetters; she felt she must obey.

She met him there, proud and angry.

"What concern is it of yours, Gösta Berling, whom I marry?"

He could not speak kindly to her yet, nor did he think it good policy to mention Ferdinand at once.

"To sit out ten dances seems to me a light penance, but you want to break your promise without being censured? If a better man than I had passed sentence, it would have been severer."

"What have I done to you all that you cannot leave me in peace? It is because I have money that you persecute me so. I will throw it into the Löfven, and who likes can fish it up."

She hid her eyes in her hands and cried with vexation.

This touched him; he felt ashamed of his severity, and his voice grew caressing as he continued:

"Oh, child, forgive me, forgive poor Gösta Berling! You know very well that no one minds what I say or do! Who cares for such a wretch as I am? Who cares for my anger? You might as well cry over a gnat-bite! I was mad, but I wished to hinder our most beautiful and richest girl from marrying an old man. And now I have only hurt you."

He sat down on the sofa beside her, and put his arms round her, trying to support and raise her.

She did not draw back; she turned to him, and throwing her arms round his neck, wept, with her lovely head on his shoulder.

Ah, poet—strongest and weakest of men—it was not about your neck those arms should rest.

"If I had known this," she whispered, "I would never have consented to marry old Dahlberg. I have seen you for the first time to-day, and there is none like you."

Through white lips Gösta whispered, "Ferdinand."

She silenced him with a kiss.

"He is nothing — no one exists but you. I shall
be faithful to you alone."

"I am Gösta Berling," he answered, gloomily;
"you cannot marry me."

"It is you I love — you, the noblest of men. You
need do nothing, be nothing, you are born a king."

The poet's blood in him surged. She was so en-
chanting in her love, he clasped her in his arms.

"If you will be mine, Anna, you cannot stay at
the parsonage. Let me carry you away to-night to
Ekeby, and I will guard you there till we can be
married."

.   .   .   .

It was a wild drive through the night. Prompted
by the voice of their love they let Don Juan carry
them away. The creaking of the sledge runners
might have been the cries of their deceived friends,
what cared they? She clung to him, and he bent
down and whispered in her ear, "Can any bliss be
likened to stolen happiness?"

Who thought of the banns — they had love —
and of the anger of their friends? Gösta Berling
believed in fate. Fate had mastered them — no one
could fight against fate.

If the stars had been the wax candles lighted for

her wedding, if the sleigh-bells had been the church chimes calling the neighbors to witness her union with old Dahlberg, still she must have eloped with Gösta Berling, so powerful is fate.

They had passed the parsonage and Munkerud. They had about two miles before them to Berga, and then two again to Ekeby. The road followed the edge of the wood, and to the right of them lay dark mountains, to the left a long white valley.

Suddenly Tankred rushed after the sledge wildly. He seemed to lie at full stretch upon the ground, he passed over it so quickly, and shuddering with fear he leaped into the sledge and crouched at Anna's feet.

Don Juan started and broke into a gallop.

"Wolves," said Gösta.

They saw a long grey line following them near the fence. There were at least a dozen wolves.

Anna was not afraid. The day had been full of adventure, the night promised to be the same. That was life—to speed over the sparkling snow, defiant of men and beasts.

Gösta swore, bent forward, and brought the whip heavily over Don Juan.

"Are you afraid?" she asked.

"They are taking a short cut to that corner and will meet us where the road turns."

Don Juan was putting forth all his speed in the race with the wild beasts, and Tankred howled in

G

mingled fear and rage. They reached the turning at
the same time as the wolves, and Gösta drove off
the foremost with his whip.

"Ah, Don Juan, my boy, how easily you would
outstrip your pursuers if you had not to carry us
with you!"

They fastened the green travelling-rug behind
the sledge. The wolves were frightened, and kept
at a distance for a short time, but they soon conquered their fear, and one of them sprang with panting open jaws at the sledge, and Gösta flung Madame de Staël's *Corinne* down its throat.

Again they had a moment's respite while this
booty was devoured, but soon the wolves began to
tear at the rug, their quick breathing was heard behind. They knew there was no shelter to be hoped
for before they reached Berga, but worse than
death itself was the thought to Gösta of seeing the
people he had betrayed. He knew also that Don
Juan could not hold out much longer, and what
was to become of them?

Now they saw the Berga farmstead in the forest
clearing. Lights streamed from the windows. Gösta
knew too well for whose sake.

Just then the wolves fled, fearing the neighborhood of man, and Gösta drove past Berga; but he
did not get far, for, where the road turned into the
forest again, he saw a dark group fronting him —
the wolves awaited them.

"We must return to the parsonage, and say we went for a sleigh ride in the starlight. This won't do."

They turned, but the next moment the sledge was surrounded by the savage beasts. Grey bodies pressed near, white teeth gleamed, glaring eyes flashed; they howled with hunger and the thirst of blood. Their white teeth were ready to tear into soft human flesh. They sprang upon Don Juan, and hung to the harness. Anna sat and wondered if they would be eaten up entirely, or if people would find their torn limbs in the bloody trampled snow next morning.

"It is a case of life and death now," she said, bending down and grasping Tankred by his collar.

"Let him be, it would not help us. It isn't for his sake the wolves are abroad to-night."

And Gösta drove into the yard at Berga, the wolves following them to the very steps, so that he was obliged to beat them off with the whip.

"Anna," he said, as they reached the door, "it is not God's will. Keep a good countenance now, if you are the woman I think you."

The sleigh-bells had been heard indoors, and all the household came to meet them.

"He has brought her!" they cried, "he has brought her! Long live Gösta Berling!"

And they passed from one embrace to another. Many questions were not asked. It was late; their

perilous drive had unnerved them, and they needed
rest. It was sufficient for them all that Anna had
come. All was well, only *Corinne* and the green travelling-rug, Mamsell Ulrika's prized gift, had been
lost in the struggle.

.   .   .   .

The whole house lay in sleep when Gösta Berling
rose and crept downstairs. Unobserved by any one,
he took Don Juan out of the stable, yoked him to
his sledge, and was on the point of driving away
when Anna Stjärnhök came out of the house.

"I heard you go out," she said, "so I got up also.
I am ready to go with you."

He went up to her and took her hand.

"Don't you understand yet, Anna? It cannot
be. It is not God's will. I was here to-day to dinner
and heard their trouble about your faithlessness,
and I drove to Borg to bring you back to Ferdinand. But I never have been anything but a good-
for-nothing, and never will be anything else. I deceived him and took you for myself. My old friend
here believed me to be a true man, and I have deceived her. And another poor creature suffers cold
and hunger cheerfully to die among friends, and
I was ready to let Sintram turn her out. You were
so beautiful, and sin is so pleasant, and Gösta Berling is so easily tempted! Ah, what a wretch I am!
I know how they love their home, and I was about

to let it be ruined! I forgot all for your sake, you were so lovely. But now, Anna, since I have seen their joy I cannot keep you—no, I will not. Oh, my beloved! He above us plays with our wills. The time has come for us to bow under His chastening hand. Promise me that from this hour you will take your burden upon you. All in this house depend on you. Promise me that you will be their help and stay! If you love me, if you will lighten my heavy grief, promise me this! My dearest, is your heart so great that it can conquer itself and yet smile?"

And she received with ecstasy the call to sacrifice.

"I will do as you will—I will sacrifice myself cheerfully."

"And you will not hate my poor friends?"

She smiled sadly.

"As long as I love you, I shall love them."

"Now I know what a woman you are. Oh! it is hard to leave you."

"Farewell, Gösta; God be with you. My love shall not tempt you to sin."

She turned to go in; he followed her.

"Will you soon forget me, Anna?"

"Go now, Gösta, we are but human!"

He threw himself into the sledge, then she came again to him.

"Have you forgotten the wolves?"

"I am thinking of them, but they have done their

work. They have nothing further to do with me to-night."

Again he stretched out his arms to her, but Don Juan grew impatient and started. He let the reins hang, turning to look back, then leaned against the back of the sledge and wept like a man in despair.

"I had my happiness in my hand, and I have thrown it aside! I have cast it away myself! Why did I not keep it?"

Ah, Gösta Berling, thou strongest and weakest of men!

The Cachucha

WAR horse, war horse, old steed now tethered in the field, do you remember your youth? Do you remember the day of the battle, when you charged as if borne on wings, your mane flaring above you like flickering flames, your black chest glistening with frothy foam and splashes of blood? In harness of gold you bounded forward, the earth rumbling beneath you; and you trembled with joy, brave old steed. Ah, but you were splendid!

It is the hour of twilight in the cavaliers' wing. In the big room the cavaliers' chests stand against the wall, and their holiday clothes hang on hooks in a corner. The firelight from the hearth plays on the whitewashed walls and the checkered yellow curtains that hide the cubby-beds. The cavaliers' wing is no royal antechamber, no seraglio with cushioned divans and soft pillows.

Up there Lilliecrona's violin is heard. He, Lilliecrona, is playing the cachucha in the dusk of the evening; and he plays it over and over again.

Cut the strings! Break the bow! Why does he play that accursed dance? Why does he play it when Ensign Örneclou lies sick with the pains of gout, so severe that he cannot move in his bed! Snatch the fiddle from him and dash it against the wall, if he will not stop.

Master, is it for us you play the cachucha? Shall it be danced on the shaky floor of the cavaliers' wing, between narrow walls, blackened with smoke and grimy with dirt, under this low ceiling?

The cachucha, is it for us—for us cavaliers? Without howls the snowstorm. Would you teach the snowflakes to dance to the measure? Are you playing for the light-footed children of the storm?

Tremulous feminine forms, with hot blood throbbing in their veins, small sooty hands that have thrown aside the pot to take up the castanets, bare feet under tucked-up skirts, crouching gypsies with bagpipe and tambourine, Moorish arcades, marble-paved courts, moonlight and dark eyes—have you these, master? Else let the violin rest.

The cavaliers must dry their wet clothes by the fire. Shall they whirl about in top-boots, with spiked heels and soles an inch thick? All day they have plowed through knee-deep snow to reach the bear's lair. Think you they will dance in wet, reeking woollen clothes, with shaggy bruin for partner?

An evening sky glittering with stars, dark hair adorned with red roses, an atmosphere vibrant with blissful longing, untutored grace of movement, love rising from the earth, raining from the heavens, floating in the air—can you conjure these, master? Else, why make us yearn for such things?

Most cruel of men, would you sound the battle call to a tethered war horse! Rutger von Örneclou

is fettered to his bed with gout. Spare him the pain
of tender memories!

He, too, has worn the sombrero and the hair-net
of many colors; he, too, has worn the velvet jacket
and carried a stiletto in his girdle. Spare old Örneclou, master.

But Lilliecrona goes on playing the cachucha, and
Örneclou suffers like the lover who sees the swallow winging toward the distant abode of the beloved,
like the hart driven by the hounds past the cooling
spring.

For a moment Lilliecrona raises his chin from
the violin.

"Ensign, do you remember Rosalie von Berger?" he asks.

Örneclou swears a great oath.

"She was light as a candle-flame, and danced and
sparkled like the diamond at the tip of the fiddle-
bow. You must remember her at the theatre in Karlstad. We saw her when we were young, if you recall."

The ensign remembered. She was *petite* and be-
witching—all fire. Ah, *she* could dance the cachucha! And she taught all the young men in Karlstad to dance it and to play the castanets. At the
Governor's ball the ensign and Fröken von Berger
danced a *pas de deux* in Spanish costume. And he
had danced as one dances under fig-trees and mag-
nolias, like the Spaniard—the real Spaniard. No
one in all Värmland could dance the cachucha as

he danced it. What a cavalier was lost to Värmland when the gout stiffened his legs and great lumps formed on his joints! And what a gallant figure he had once been, so lithe, so handsome, so courtly! "Handsome Örneclou" he was called by the young girls, who were ready to start a deadly feud over a dance with him.

Lilliecrona again begins the cachucha, and Örneclou is carried back to other times. . . . Here he stands, there she — Rosalie von Berger! He is a Spanish lover, she a Spanish maiden. But a moment ago they were alone in the dressing-room. He was allowed to kiss her, but lightly, lest his blackened moustaches print a telltale mark on her cheek.

Now they dance! As one dances under fig-trees and plane-trees, so they dance. She draws away, he follows; he grows bold, she haughty; he is hurt, she solicitous. When at the end he falls on his knee and receives her in his outstretched arms, a sigh sweeps through the ball-room, a sigh of rapture. He was the Spaniard to the life. At just that stroke of the bow he had bent so, had put out his arms so, and poised his foot so, to glide forward on his toes. Such grace! What a model for a sculptor!

He does not know how it happened, but somehow he had got his foot over the edge of the bed and was standing up. Now he bends, raises his arms, snaps his fingers, and tries to glide across the floor

as in the days gone by, when he wore patent leather
shoes, so tight-fitting that the feet of his stockings
had to be cut away.

Bravo, Örneclou! *Bravo*, Lilliecrona, play life
into him!

But his foot fails him, he cannot rise on his toes.
He kicks out once or twice—more he cannot do—
and falls back on the bed.

Handsome Señor, you have grown old. Perhaps
the Señorita, too, is old?

It is only under the plane-trees of Granada that
the cachucha is danced by ever young *gitanas*—
ever young because, as with the roses, each year
brings new ones.

So now the time has come to cut the violin
strings. . . . No, no! play on, Lilliecrona, play the
cachucha, always the cachucha! Teach us that although our bodies have grown heavy and our joints
stiff, in our feelings we are ever the same—ever
Spaniards.

War horse, war horse, say that you love the trum-
pet-blast, which tempts you into a gallop, even
though you strain at your steel-linked tether till
your foot bleeds.

The Ball at Ekeby

OH, women of the olden days! To talk of you is to talk of Paradise; for you were perfect beauty, perfect light—ever youthful, ever charming, and as mild as the eyes of a mother when she gazes at her child. Soft as a little squirrel, you clung about man's neck, and your voice never shook with anger, your brow was never ruffled, your soft hand never grew harsh and hard. Like lovely saints, like bejewelled pictures, you stood in the temple of your homes. Incense and prayers were offered you, love worked its miracles by your power, and round your heads poetry cast its aureola.

Oh, women of the olden days! This is the story of how one of you gave her love to Gösta Berling.

Scarcely had Anna Stjärnhök's kisses died on his lips, scarcely had he forgotten the pressure of her arms around his neck, but sweeter lips and whiter arms were stretched toward him. He could do nothing but receive the loveliest of gifts, for the heart is incorrigible in its habit of loving. For every sorrow caused by love, it knows no other cure than a newer love, as those who have burned themselves with hot iron deaden the pain by burning themselves once more.

A fortnight after the ball at Borg a great festival was given at Ekeby.

It was a splendid fête, but ask not why or where-
fore it was given. For the only reason for which a
fête is worth giving — that eyes might shine, and
hearts and feet might dance, and joy might again
find a place among mankind; that hands might meet,
and lips might kiss.

But speak not of kisses!

And what a fête it was! Old men and women became young again and laughed and rejoiced when
they spoke of it. But then the cavaliers were sole
managers at Ekeby.

Fru Samzelius wandered through the country
with her beggar's scrip and staff, and the Major was
at Sjö. He could not be present at the ball, for smallpox had broken out at Sjö, and he was afraid of
carrying infection.

What a number of enjoyments were crowded
into those twelve hours, from the first popping of
the corks of the first bottles of wine at the dinner to
the last strain of the violins when midnight was long
passed! They sank back into eternity, those mirth-
crowned hours, frenzied with the fiery wine, the
choicest food, the loveliest music, the cleverest acting, and the most beautiful tableaux. They sank
back, giddy with the wild dancing. Where was there
so smooth a floor, such courtly cavaliers, such lovely
women?

Oh, women of the olden days! You knew well
how to brighten the feasts. Streams of fire, of genius,

and of youthful ardor touch all who approach you,
It was worth while to spend one's gold on the candles that lighted up your beauty, upon the wine
that awoke the gaiety in your hearts. It was worth
while to dance one's shoes to dust, and to wield the
violin bow till the arm dropped with weariness.

Oh, women of the olden days! You held the keys
of Paradise; the halls of Ekeby were thronged by
the loveliest of your train.

There was the young Countess Dohna, excit-
edly eager for dancing and all games, as was natural
for her twenty years; there were the lovely daughters of the Judge of Munkerud and the girls from
Berga; there was Anna Stjärnhök, a thousand times
more beautiful than before, in the quiet melancholy
which had come over her since the night she had
been chased by wolves; there were many who are
not forgotten yet, but who soon will be; and there,
too, was the beautiful Marienne Sinclaire.

Even she, the loveliest of the lovely, a queen
among people, the goddess-like, the fascinating
Marienne Sinclaire, deigned to come. She, the far-
famed beauty, who had shone at court and at many
a ducal castle, the queen of beauty, who received
the homage of the whole country — she, who ignited
the fires of love wherever she showed herself — she
had deigned to appear at the ball given by the cavaliers.

The honor of Värmland beamed afar in those

days, borne up by many a haughty name. There was much which its joyous children prided themselves upon. But ever when they talked of their many splendors, they spoke of Marienne Sinclaire.

The story of her conquests filled the land. They told you of many earls whose coronets might have graced her head, of the many millions which had been laid at her feet, of the brave swords and the poet's wreaths which had allured her.

And she possessed more than mere beauty. She was talented and learned. The best men of the time were happy to converse with her. She did not write, but many of her thoughts given to the souls of her friends have lived again in song.

To Värmland — to the bear-land — she came but seldom. Her time was spent in constant visits. Her father, the rich Melchior Sinclaire, lived with his wife at Björne, and allowed Marienne to travel about to her grand friends in the towns or to the great estates. He took pleasure in relating how much money she spent, and both the old people lived happily in the reflected glory of Marienne's splendor.

Her life was one of pleasure and adoration. The air about her was love. Love was her light and her life, and love her daily bread. She had been in love herself often — oh, so often! — but never had this love lasted for a sufficiently long time that out of it might be forged the chains that should bind for life.

"I am waiting for him—the grand conqueror," she used to say in speaking of love. "He has stormed no walls and surmounted no graves as yet. He has come tamely to me, having neither wildness in his eyes nor daring in his heart. I am waiting for the mighty one who will carry me out of myself. I want to feel the love so strong within me that I tremble before it. I only know the kind of love at which my intellect smiles."

She had the low voice and the refinement of a woman of high rank. They all bowed down to her in her country home, and felt their insignificance and ignorance of the ways of the fine world, but if she spoke, if she only smiled—all was well. She was a queen, and created a court and courtly manners wherever she went.

Her presence gave inspiration to the speeches and life to the wine. She gave speed to the violin bows, and the dancing went gayer than ever over the boards that she touched with her slender feet. She shone in the tableaux and in the acting.

Oh, no, it was not her fault—it was never her fault.

It was the balcony, the moonlight, the lace veil, and the cavalier dress that were to blame. The poor young people were innocent.

All that now follows, which led to so much unhappiness, was done with the best intention. Squire Julius, who could manage anything, had arranged a tableau chiefly that Marienne should be seen in great splendor.

Before a stage erected in the big salon at Ekeby sat a hundred guests, and watched a golden Spanish moon rise in a dark midnight sky. Then a Don Juan stole through the Seville street till he paused beneath a myrtle-covered balcony. He was disguised as a monk, but a white embroidered ruffle showed at his sleeve, and the gleaming point of a rapier protruded from his cloak.

He raised his voice and sang:

> "*I kiss no maiden dear,*
>   *Nor press my lips to a flagon's rim*
> *To taste the purling wine.*
>   *A cheek so clear*
>   *Set on fire by my glance,*
>   *Sweet eyes, seeking mine*
>   *As if by chance—*
> *Such worldly pleasures are not for me.*
>
> "*Come not in your beauty's might,*
>   *Señora, to the lattice here,*
> *I tremble at your sight.*
>   *I wear the cowl*
>   *And the rosary long,*
>   *To the Madonna still*
>   *Does my heart belong;*
> *In the water cruse I must drown my song.*"

When his voice died away, Marienne came out
upon the balcony dressed in black velvet and a lace
veil. She leaned over the rail and sang slowly and
ironically:

> "*Why do you stand, you holy man,*
>   *At midnight time, 'neath my lattice high,*
>   *Say, do you pray for my soul?*"

Then quickly, and with feeling:

> "*Nay, fly, — I pray;*
>   *They may find you here.*
>   *And your sword doth betray,*
>   *And the clank of your spur,*
>   *That the hooded monk is a fair cavalier.*"

At these words the monk threw aside his disguise,
and Gösta Berling stood under the balcony in a
Don's dress of silk and gold. He paid no heed to the
beauty's warning. On the contrary, he climbed one
of the balcony pillars, swung himself over the balustrade, and, as Squire Julius had arranged, fell at
the feet of the lovely Marienne.

She smiled graciously upon him and gave him
her hand to kiss, and as they gazed at each other,
lost in love, the curtain descended.

No one at Ekeby had ever seen anything lovelier than those two on that moonlit balcony. The
curtain had to be drawn up again and again. It was

like a thunder-cloud, out of which heaven's splendor gleamed, and every glance was followed by a deafening thunder of applause.

She was lovely, so wonderfully lovely, that Marienne. She had fair hair, and dark blue eyes under her dark eyebrows. The curve of her nose was incomparable in its audacity and refinement; her mouth and cheeks and chin were perfectly formed. Beside hers, all other faces looked coarse, and near her transparent complexion all others seemed dark and ugly. There was charm, too, in every glance, in every word, in every movement of the stately figure.

And before her knelt Gösta Berling, with a face as spiritual as a poet's and as daring as a conqueror's, with eyes that glittered with genius and humor, eyes that pleaded and insisted. He was strong and supple, fiery and fascinating.

While the curtain rose and fell, the young people stood motionless in the same attitude. Gösta's eyes held Marienne; they pleaded and insisted.

At last the applause died away, the curtain descended, and none saw them.

And then Marienne bent and kissed Gösta Berling. She did not know why she did it—she felt she must. He stretched his arms about her head and held her fast, and she kissed him again and again.

But it was the balcony and the moonlight. It was the veil and the cavalier dress, the song and

the applause, that were to blame; the poor young
people were not in fault. They had not intended it.
She had not refused the hands of earls and rejected
millions for love of Gösta Berling, neither had he
forgotten Anna Stjärnhök. No, they were not to
blame, they had not meant to do it.

It was the gentle Lövenborg, he with the tears in
his eyes and a smile on his lips, who acted as cur-
tain-puller that evening. Troubled by the memories of many sorrows, he paid little attention to
the things of this world, and had never learned
to manage them properly. Now, when he saw that
Gösta and Marienne had taken up a new position,
he thought it was part of the tableau, and he pulled
up the curtain.

They on the balcony noticed nothing till the
thunder of applause again deafened them.

Marienne started and tried to escape, but Gösta
held her firmly, whispering, "Stand still, they think
it part of the tableau."

He felt how her body trembled, and the glow of
her kisses died on her lips. They were obliged to
stand like this while the curtain again rose and fell,
and every time a hundred pairs of eyes saw them,
a hundred pairs of hands gave forth a storm of applause, for it was a lovely sight to see two so beautiful give a representation of love's happiness. No
one thought those kisses meant anything but a the-
atrical pretence; no one guessed that the Señora

shook with shame and the Don with anxiety. No one but believed it to be a part of the tableau.

At last Marienne and Gösta stood behind the scenes. She passed her hand over her forehead. "I don't understand myself," she said.

"For shame, Fröken Marienne," he said, with a grimace and a comic gesture of his arms, "to kiss Gösta Berling! for shame!"

She was obliged to laugh.

"One and all know Gösta Berling to be irresistible. My fault is no greater than that of others."

And they agreed to keep a good countenance, so that none should guess the truth.

"Can I be certain that the truth will never come out, Herr Gösta?" she asked, as they were about to join the other guests.

"You can, Fröken Marienne; the cavaliers will be silent, I can answer for them."

She dropped her eyes, and a peculiar smile curled her lips.

"And if the truth came out, what would people think of me, Herr Berling?"

"They would think nothing of it. They would know it meant nothing. They would think we were in our parts and continued to act."

Yet another question came creeping from the hidden eyes and the forced smile.

"But you, Herr Gösta? What do you think of it?"

"I think you are in love with me," he said, jest-
ingly.

"Don't believe anything of the kind," she smiled,
"or I shall be obliged to thrust this dagger into you
to prove that you are wrong."

"Women's kisses are dear," said Gösta. "Does
it cost a life to be kissed by Marienne Sinclaire?"

A glance flashed from her eyes, so sharp that he
felt it like a blow.

"I would rather see you dead, Gösta Berling—
dead—dead!"

These words awoke the old longing in the heart
of the poet.

"Ah," he said, "if your words were more than
words, if they were bullets out of a dark thicket,
if they were daggers or poison, and had the power
to destroy this wretched body and give my soul its
freedom!"

But she was again calm and smiling. "Childishness!" she said, and took his arm to rejoin the
guests.

They retained their costumes, and their triumph
was renewed when they showed themselves. All
praised them, no one suspected anything.

The ball began again, but Gösta shunned the
dancing-room. His heart was smarting from Marienne's glance as if it had touched it like sharp steel.
He understood too well the meaning of her words.
It was a shame to love him, a shame to be loved by

him — a shame greater than death. He would never dance again; he never wanted to see them again, those beautiful women. He knew it well — those lovely eyes, those rosy cheeks, burned not for him. Not for him was the fall of those light feet nor the chime of that low laughter. Yes, dance with him, flirt with him — that they would do, but none of them would seriously have chosen to give him her love.

The poet went away to the smoking-room, to the old gentlemen, and took his place at one of the card-tables. He happened to sit down near the master of Björne, who was playing "Knack," with an occasional turn at "Polish Bank," and had gathered a whole pile of sixpences and farthings before him. The stakes were already high, and Gösta drove them higher. The green bank notes came out, and the heaps of money increased before Melchior Sinclaire. But before Gösta, too, a pile of silver and paper gathered, and soon he was the only one who could hold out against the great land proprietor of Björne. Soon even Melchior Sinclaire's pile retreated over to Gösta.

"Gösta, my boy," said his opponent, laughing, when he had lost all he had in his purse and pocket-book, "what are we to do now? I am cleaned out, and I never play with borrowed money. I promised my mother I never would."

But he found a way — he gambled away his watch

and chain and his beaver cloak, and was on the point of staking his horse and sledge when Sintram interrupted him.

"Put up something to change the luck," was the advice of the wicked owner of Fors; "put up something to win."

"The devil knows where I am to find it!"

"Stake your heart's dearest treasure, brother Melchior — stake your daughter."

"You can do that without fear," said Gösta, laughing; "that stake I shall never take home."

The great Melchior Sinclaire could do nothing else than laugh also. He did not approve of Marienne's name being mentioned at the gaming-table, but the idea was so absurdly improbable he could not be angry. Stake and lose Marienne to Gösta? Yes, he could dare that.

"That is to say," he explained, "that if you can get her consent, I will set my blessing on the marriage on this card."

Gösta staked all his gains, and the game began. He won, and the proprietor of Björne gave up playing. He could not fight against Fortune, he saw.

Well, Gösta Berling, does not your heart beat at this? Don't you understand your fate? What was the meaning of Marienne's kisses and her anger? Don't you understand a woman's heart? And now this stake won too! Don't you see that fate wills what love wills? Up, Gösta Berling!

No, Gösta Berling is not in the mood for love-making to-night. He is angry over the hardness of hearts. Why should love only be healed by love? He knows too well the end of these pretty ditties. No one is constant to him; there is love for him, but no wife. It is no use trying.

The night goes on, midnight has passed. The ladies' cheeks begin to pale, their curls to straighten, their flounces to look creased. The matrons rise from the sofa-corners and remark that, as the fête has continued for twelve hours, it is time to go home.

And that would have been the end of the great ball, if Lilliecrona had not taken up his violin and played a last polka. The horses stood at the door, the old ladies were putting on their furs and quilted hoods, and the old gentlemen buttoned up their greatcoats and tied on their belts, but the young people could not tear themselves away from the dancing. They danced in their cloaks; they danced ring polka, swing polka, and every kind of polka; it was all one mad whirl. As soon as a man gave up his partner, another sprang forward and claimed her.

Even melancholy Gösta was drawn into the vortex. He meant to dance away his sadness and sense of degradation, he wanted to feel the wild joy of life in his veins again—he meant to be gay, he, as well as the others—and he danced so that the walls seemed to spin round, and his thoughts grew giddy.

Ah, who is the lady he has snatched from the crowd?

She is light and graceful, and he feels streams of fire flow between them. Oh, Marienne!

While Gösta danced with Marienne, Sintram was sitting already in his sledge in the courtyard, and near him stood Melchior Sinclaire.

The great land proprietor was impatient at having to wait for Marienne. He stamped on the snow with his big boots, and swung his arms, for it was bitterly cold.

"Perhaps, after all, you should not have gambled Marienne away to Gösta," said Sintram.

"Why not?"

Sintram put his reins in order and lifted his whip before he answered: "All that kissing did not belong to the tableau!"

Melchior Sinclaire raised his arm to strike, but Sintram was gone. He started his horse at racing speed, not daring to look back, for Melchior Sinclaire had a heavy hand and but short patience.

The master of Björne went back to the dancing-hall and saw Marienne and Gösta dancing together. The last polka was wildly, crazily danced. Some of the couples were pale, some blooming red, the dust hung like smoke over the room. The waxen lights burned low in the candlesticks, and amid all this ghost-like decay, Gösta and Marienne flew on and on, royal in their unwearied strength, with no blemish marring their beauty, happy in being able to indulge in the entrancing movement.

Melchior Sinclaire watched them for a time, then he went away and left Marienne to dance. He slammed the door after him, stamped down the steps, and without further ado seated himself in the sledge, where his wife already waited, and drove home.

When Marienne finished dancing and asked for her parents, they were gone.

When she was certain of this, she allowed no one to see her surprise. She dressed quietly, and went down into the courtyard, and the ladies in the dressing-room thought she had her own sledge waiting for her.

But in her thin, silk slippers, she was hurrying home without telling any one of her trouble. No one knew her in the darkness as she walked on the roadside; no one could think the tramp, who was driven deep into the snowdrifts by passing sledges, was beautiful Marienne Sinclaire.

When she could go securely along the middle of the road, she began to run. She ran as long as she could, then walked, then ran again. A miserable, aching fear drove her forward.

From Ekeby to Björne is about a mile and a half. Marienne was soon home, and yet she almost felt

she had come to the wrong place—for all the doors
were closed, and all the lights were out—she wondered if her parents had not yet arrived.

She went forward and knocked loudly at the hall
door. She clutched the latch and shook it till it re-
sounded all over the house. No one came to open,
but when she dropped the iron latch which she had
held, it tore away the frozen skin from her fingers.

Melchior Sinclaire had gone home to bar the door
against his only daughter.

He was intoxicated with much drinking, wild with
anger. He hated his daughter because she loved
Gösta Berling. Now he had locked the servants into
the kitchen and his wife into her bedroom, and he
swore a solemn oath to them that he would kill any
one who let Marienne in.

They knew he always kept his word. No one had
ever seen him so furious. No such sorrow had ever
touched him. If his daughter had come before him,
it is probable he would have killed her.

He had given her jewels and silken dresses; he
had let her learn all culture and wisdom. She had
been his pride, his honor. He had rejoiced over her
as if she wore a crown. She was his queen, his goddess, his adored, proud, beautiful Marienne! Had
he ever grudged her anything? Had he not always
felt himself to be too coarse to be her father? Ah,
Marienne!

Ought he not to hate her when she fell in love

with Gösta Berling and kissed him? Ought he not
to turn her out and bar his doors upon her, when
she had dishonored her grandeur by loving such a
man? If she stayed at Ekeby, or if she crept away to
some of the neighbors to get a lodging for the night,
if she slept in the snowdrift, it was all the same, she
was already trampled in the dirt, his lovely Marienne. Her glory was gone; the glory of his life was
gone too.

He lay in his bed and heard her knocking at the
door. What did it matter to him? Some one stood
there who was ready to marry an unfrocked parson—he had no home for such a woman. If he
had loved her less, if he had been less proud of
her, he might have let her in. He could not refuse
them his blessing—he had lost that in gambling to
Gösta; but to open his door to her—that he would
not do.

And the young girl still stood outside the door
of her home. Now she shook the latch in a fit of
fury; now she fell on her knees, and, clasping her
frozen hands together, begged forgiveness.

But no one heard her, no one answered, no one
opened.

Was it not awful? I am frightened in speaking of
it. She came from a ball where she had been queen;
she had been proud, rich, and happy, and in a moment she was cast down into bottomless misery.
Shut out of her home, given a prey to the snow;

not scorned, nor beaten, nor cursed, only shut out with cold, determined heartlessness.

Think of the frosty, starry night surrounding her, the great wide night with its desolate fields of snow, and the silent forests. All slept, all was sunk in painless sleep, there was only one living point in all that slumbering whiteness. All sorrow and fear and horror, which at other times seems spread over all the world, were concentrated in that one lonely point. O God! to suffer alone in the midst of that slumbering, icy world.

For the first time in her life, Marienne knew hardness and cruelty. Her mother would not leave her bed to let her in; old servants, who had taught her to walk, heard her, but would not move a muscle to save her; and why was she thus punished? Where was her refuge, if not here? If she had been guilty of murder, she would have come here believing they would forgive her. If she had fallen to the greatest depth of misery, and come here in rags, she would have approached the door confidently, expecting a loving welcome. That door was the entrance to her home, and behind it she could only expect to find love.

Had her father not tried her sufficiently; would he never open? Would'n't they open it soon?

"Father, father," she cried, "let me in. I am frozen and trembling. It is dreadful out here."

"Mother, mother, you have taken so many steps

to serve me, you have watched for me so many times, why do you sleep now? Mother, mother, awake this night also, and I will never cause you any more sorrow."

She called and then sank into breathless silence, to listen for an answer. No one heard her, no one answered.

She wrung her hands in agony, but no tears dimmed her eyes.

The long, dark house, with its closed doors and unlighted windows, lay mysterious, immovable in the night. What was to become of her without her home? She was dishonored, branded, as long as the heavens stand over the earth; and her own father had set the red iron on her shoulder.

"Father," she cried once more, "what will become of me? People will think the worst of me."

She wept in anguish, her body was rigid with cold.

Ah, that such trouble can envelop those who have stood so high. That it is so easy to be cast out into the deepest misery! Are we not then to fear life? Who of us sails securely? Round us surges sorrow like a foaming sea; see how its waves hungrily lick the sides of the vessel; see how they try to board her! Oh, there is no sure anchorage, no firm ground, no trusty ship, as far as the eye can reach, only an unknown heaven over the sea of trouble.

But silence! At last, at last! Light steps come through the entrance hall.

"Is it you, mother?" asked Marienne.

"Yes, my child."

"Can I come in now?"

"Your father won't let you in."

"I have walked in my thin shoes from Ekeby. I have stood here an hour and knocked and called. I am freezing to death. Why did you leave me?"

"My child, my child, why did you kiss Gösta Berling?"

"But tell my father that that does not mean that I love Gösta; it was in fun. Does he think I want to marry Gösta?"

"Go to the farm-bailiff's house, Marienne, and ask to remain there for the night. Your father is drunk, he won't hear reason. He locked me upstairs. I crept out when I thought he slept. He will kill me if I let you in."

"But, mother, shall I go to strangers when I have my own home? Are you as hard as my father? How can you allow him to shut me out? I will lie here in the snowdrifts, if you won't let me in."

Marienne's mother laid her hand on the latch, but at that moment heavy steps were heard on the staircase and a harsh voice called her.

Marienne listened — her mother hurried away; the harsh voice was scolding, and then . . . Marienne heard something awful — every sound in the silent house reached her ears. She heard the sound of a blow — of the stroke of a stick or a blow on the head, then a faint cry, then another blow; he was beating her mother—the fearful, tyrannous Melchior Sinclaire was beating his wife.

Marienne threw herself writhing in agony on the steps. She was crying now, and her tears froze on the threshold of her home.

Pity—mercy! Open, open, that she may give her own shoulders to the blows. Oh, that he could beat her mother! beat her, because she could not see her daughter lie in the snowdrifts, because she had tried to comfort her!

Great degradation swept over her that night. She had dreamed herself a queen, and now she lay outside the door of her home, hardly better than a whipped tramp. But she raised herself again in icy anger. Once again she raised her hand and struck the door and cried:

"Hear what I say—you—you—you who struck my mother. You shall yet weep. Melchior Sinclaire, you shall weep!"

And then Marienne turned and lay down in the snowdrift. She threw aside her fur mantle, and lay down in the black velvet dress which stood out so distinctly against the white snow. She lay and thought of her father coming out early for his morning walk, and finding her there. Her only wish was that he himself should find her.

.   .   .   .

Oh, Death, you pale friend, is it as true as it is com-

forting for me to know that I can never escape you?
Even to me, the most diligent of the workers among
men, you will come; loosen the worn shoes from my
feet, snatch the duster and the milk-can out of
my hand, and take my working clothes off my back.
With gentle force you will stretch me upon a lace-
embossed bed, you will wrap me in white linen, my
feet will not require any shoes, but my hands will be
covered with white gloves which no work will ever
soil. Crowned for the joy of rest, I shall sleep for a
thousand years. Oh, Saviour! The most diligent of
workers am I, and I dream with a shiver of delight of
the moment when I shall be taken to Thy kingdom.

Pale friend, my strength against yours is weakness, but I tell you that your fight was harder against
the women of the olden days. The strength of life
was greater in their slight bodies; no cold could cool
their fiery blood.

You laid Marienne on your bed, oh, Death, and
you sat by her side, as an old nurse watches by the
cradle of a child till it sleeps. You true old nurse,
who knows so well what is best for the children of
men, how it must anger you when its playmates
come, with laughter and shouts, and wake your
sleeping child! How angry you must have been
when the cavaliers lifted Marienne from her icy bed,
when a man's arms clasped her to his breast, and
when warm tears fell from his eyes on her face.

.   .   .   .

At Ekeby all the lights were out and the guests departed. The cavaliers stood alone in the cavaliers' wing round the last half-emptied punch-bowl.

Then Gösta tapped on the rim of the bowl, and made a speech in honor of you — women of the olden days. To talk of you was to talk of heaven, he said. You were perfect beauty, perfect light. Ever youthful, ever beautiful, and mild as the eyes of a mother when she gazed at her child. As soft as a little squirrel you hung about man's neck, and no one ever heard your voice shake with anger; your forehead never frowned, your soft hands never grew hard and rough. You were saints in the temple of your homes. Men lay at your feet, offering incense and prayer to you. By your power, love worked its miracles, and round your head poetry set its glittering aureola.

And the cavaliers sprang up, wild with wine and the intoxication of his words — their blood leaping with joy. Even old Uncle Eberhard and lazy Cousin Kristoffer did not draw back from the new project. Quickly they harnessed the horses to the big sledge and the racing sledges, and off they went through the cold night to pay homage to those to whom homage was due — to serenade those whose bright eyes and rosy cheeks had graced the halls of Ekeby.

Oh, it must have pleased you greatly, ladies, to

be awakened from the heaven of your dreams by
a serenade, sung by your most devoted admirers. It
must have pleased you much as it pleases a departing soul to awake to the music of Paradise.

But the cavaliers had not gone very far on their
way, for when they came to Björne, they found Marienne lying in the drift at the gate leading to the
house. They trembled with fear and with fury when
they saw her there. It was like finding a worshipped
saint lying plundered and desecrated outside the
church door; it was as if an unhung villain had
broken the neck and torn out the strings of a Stradi-
varius.

Gösta shook his clenched fist at the dark house.

"You children of hate," he screamed. "You hail-
stones and north wind—you destroyers of God's
pleasure garden!"

Beerencreutz lighted his horn lantern and threw
its beams upon the blue-white face. And the cavaliers saw her torn hands, and the tears which had
frozen in her eyelashes, and they sorrowed like
women, for she was not only a saint to them but
also a beautiful woman who had been a joy to their
old hearts.

Gösta Berling threw himself on his knees beside
her!

"Here she lies—my bride," he said. "She gave
me the bridal kiss some hours ago—and her father
promised me his blessing. She lies and waits for me

here in her snowy bed." And he lifted her in his strong arms.

"We will take her home to Ekeby," he cried. "She is mine now. I have found her in the snow-drift; no one can take her away from me. We will not wake them in that house. What has she to do inside the doors against which she had beaten her hands bloody?"

He was allowed to do as he wished. He laid Marienne in the first sledge and took his place beside her. Beerencreutz placed himself behind and took the reins.

"Take some snow and rub her, Gösta," he commanded.

The cold had but paralyzed her limbs—that was all. The excited heart still beat. She had not even lost consciousness; she knew the cavaliers had found her, but she could not move. So she lay stiff and motionless in the sledge, while Gösta sometimes rubbed her with snow, sometimes wept over her and kissed her, and she felt an unutterable longing to lift even one hand, so that she might return his caresses.

She remembered everything; lay there rigid and immovable and thought clearly as never before. Was she in love with Gösta Berling? Yes, she was! Was it only a caprice born of the night? No, it had been so for many years.

She compared herself with him and with the other

people in Värmland. They were all as unsophis-
ticated children. They followed every fancy that
drew them. They lived only a superficial life, and
had never analyzed the depths of their souls. But
she was different, as one does become by living
in the world; she could never give herself wholly
to anything. If she loved—yes, whatever it was
she did—it seemed as if one-half of herself stood
and looked on with a cold, scornful smile. She had
longed for a passion that should sweep her away in
unhesitating surrender. And now he had come, the
mighty victor. When she kissed Gösta Berling on
the balcony, she had forgotten herself for the first
time.

And now it came over her again, and her heart
beat so that she heard it. Would she never regain
the mastery over her limbs? She felt a mad delight
in being thrust out from her home. Now she would
be Gösta's without doubting. How foolish she had
been to force and bridle her love all these years.
Oh, it was glorious to give way to it, to feel her
blood rush madly along. But would she never, never
be freed from those chains of ice? She had been icy
hearted and yet fiery on the surface all her life; now
she was changed, she had a fiery soul in a body of
ice.

Then Gösta felt two arms slip round his neck in
a weak, almost powerless caress. He could only just
feel it, but Marienne meant to give expression to

all the repressed feeling within her by a passionate embrace.

When Beerencreutz saw this, he let the horse find its own path on the well-known road, while he gazed obstinately and continuously at the "Seven Sisters."

The Old Carriages

FRIENDS, if it should happen that you read this at night, as I write it, you must not draw a breath of relief and imagine that the good cavaliers were allowed to sleep undisturbed, after they arrived home with Marienne, and had arranged a comfortable bed for her in the best guest-chamber, opening out of the grand salon.

They went to bed, and they went to sleep; but theirs was not the good fortune to sleep in peace and quietness till midday, as it might have been ours, dear reader, if we had been up till four o'clock and our limbs ached wearily.

It must be remembered that during that time the Lady of Ekeby was wandering about the country with a beggar's scrip and staff, and that it never had been her way, when there was anything to be done, to wait for the convenience of tired wrong-doers. She was never less likely to do so than on that night, for she had determined to turn the cavaliers out of Ekeby.

The time was past and gone when she sat in splendor and might at Ekeby, and sowed joy over the earth as God sows the stars over the sky. And while she wandered homeless over the country, the honor and glory of the great estate lay in the hands of the cavaliers, to be guarded by them as the wind guards the ash-heap and the spring sunshine cherishes the snowdrifts.

Sometimes it happened that the cavaliers drove out six or eight together in their long sledge, tandem, with sleigh-bells and flowing reins, and if they met the Major's wife they did not hang their heads. The noisy party stretched out clenched fists at her; a sudden turn of the sledge obliged her to plunge deep into the snowdrifts, and Major Fuchs, the great bear hunter, always thought it necessary to spit three times as a safeguard against the evil omen of such a meeting.

They had no pity for her. She was to them a witch, as she went about the roadways, and if misfortune had overtaken her, they would have cared no more than he who on Easter Eve fires off his gun and hits a witch flying past on her broomstick.

It had become a matter of conscience with them, poor cavaliers, to persecute the Major's wife. People so often have been cruel and have persecuted one another pitilessly in trying to save their own souls.

When, late at night, the cavaliers turned from the drinking-table to the window, to see if the night was calm and starlit, they often saw a dark shadow glide over the courtyard, and they knew that the Lady of Ekeby had come to look again at her dear house, and then the cavaliers' wing shook with the scornful shouts of the old sinners, and mocking words were thrown at her from the open window.

In truth, pride and selfishness were ruining the hearts of the poor adventurers. Sintram had instilled hate into them, and they could not have been in greater danger if the Major's wife had remained at Ekeby. More die in the flight than on the field of battle.

She did not cherish any great anger against the men. Had the power been hers, she would have punished them as you whip unruly boys, and then received them into favor again. But she feared for the well-being of her beloved home, left in the hands of the cavaliers, to be guarded as the wolf guards the sheepfold and the storks guard the spring seed.

There are many who have suffered in the same way. She was not alone in seeing ruin descend over the beloved home, and feeling despair when the cherished homestead fell to pieces. Many have seen the home of their childhood return their gaze like a wounded animal. Many have felt themselves guilty when they have seen the old trees dying away in the grasp of the lichens and the garden walks covered with grass. They could have fallen upon their knees before the fields, which formerly were covered with rich harvests, and begged them not to blame them for their shameful condition. And they turn away from the poor old horses; some one braver must meet their eyes. And they do not dare stand at the yard gate and see the cows returning from pasture.

No place on earth is so wretched to enter upon as a ruined home.

Oh, I beg you—you who guard the fields and meadows and parks and the happy flower-gardens —guard them well! With love and work! It is not well that Nature should sorrow over mankind.

And when I think how this proud Ekeby suffered under the cavaliers' management, I could wish that Fru Samzelius had gained her desire and turned them out of Ekeby. It was not her wish to undertake the management herself again. She had only one intention—to free her home from those mad creatures, those robbers, those locusts, after whose passage no good seed could grow.

While she wandered over the country and lived on alms, her thoughts were constantly with her mother, and the feeling that no improvement of her lot was possible until her mother's curse was lifted gained firm hold in her mind.

No one had ever spoken of her death, so she was probably still alive at the forge in the Älfdal forests. Though ninety years old, she lived a life of unceasing toil, watching over her dairy in summer and the charcoal-burning in winter, constantly working and longing for the end of her life's mission.

And the Major's wife felt that her mother had been living all those years to be enabled at length to lift the curse from her shoulders. The mother could

not find it in her heart to die, who had called down
such trouble on her child.

And the Major's wife longed to go to her, so that
they both might secure peace. She would wander
through the dark forests, beside the shores of the
long river, till she reached the house of her youth.
She could have no rest till she had done that. There
were many who offered her a warm home and all
the gifts of faithful friendship in those days, but she
would not stay. Surly and angry, she went from one
estate to another, for she was oppressed by the curse.

She would go to her mother, but she must put her
house in order. She was not going to leave it in the
hands of such careless spendthrifts, drinkers, and
wasteful destroyers of God's good gifts.

Was she to go away and find her inheritance
dissipated on her return, her foundries standing
silent, her horses worn out, and her servants scattered abroad? Oh, no; once more she would rise in
strength, and turn out the cavaliers from Ekeby.

She understood very well how happy her husband
felt in seeing the estates being ruined. But she knew
him well enough to be sure that if she once could
drive away these locusts, he would be too indifferent
to find new ones. If the cavaliers were sent away,
her old bailiff would manage Ekeby on the old lines.

And thus her shadow had often been seen on
the dark roads about the foundries. She had crept
in and out of the crofters' huts, and had whispered

with the millers and the carters in the lower story of the water-mill, and had consulted with the blacksmiths in the dark forges.

They had all sworn to help her. The honor and glory of the old estate should not be left any longer in the hands of the careless cavaliers, to be guarded by them as the wind cherishes the ashes and the wolf the sheepfold.

And on the night when the gay gentlemen had danced and laughed and drunk, till, dead tired, they had thrown themselves on their beds, on that night they were to be turned out of Ekeby.

She let them enjoy themselves. She sat in the forge and waited for the conclusion of the ball. She had waited even longer, till the cavaliers returned from their expedition, waiting in silent expectation till it was told her that the last light had been extinguished in the cavaliers' wing and that the great house slept. Then she arose and went out. It was already five o'clock in the morning, but the dark starlit February night still hung over the earth.

The Major's wife commanded that all the people should assemble round the cavaliers' wing; she went herself to the chief entrance, knocked, and was admitted. The young daughter of the Broby parson, whom she had brought up to be a trusty servant, met her.

"My lady is heartily welcome," she said, and kissed her hand.

"Put out that light," commanded the Major's wife. "Do you think I cannot find my way here without a light?"

And she began a silent tour of inspection through the quiet house. She went from cellar to garret, and said good-by to it all. With stealthy footsteps they moved from room to room.

The Major's wife held communion with her memories; the servant neither sighed nor sobbed, but tear after tear fell unheeded from her eyes as she followed her mistress. The silver cupboard and the linen presses were opened, and the Lady of Ekeby passed her hand lovingly over the fine white damask cloths and the splendid silver tankards, and over the huge pile of feather bolsters in the maid's store-room. She must touch and handle everything, all the looms and spinning-wheels, and she probed the contents of the spice cupboard, and felt the lines of tallow candles which hung from a pole in the kitchen ceiling. "They are quite dry," she said; "they could be taken down and laid away."

She went down to the wine-cellar, tilted up the wine-casks gently, and ran her fingers over the rows of bottles. She was in the buttery and kitchen. She examined it all, and put out her hand in farewell to all in her house.

Lastly she entered the living-rooms. In the dining-room she placed her hand on the wide flaps of the big table.

"There are many who have eaten plentifully at this board," she said. And thus she went through all the rooms. She found the long wide sofas in their places, and she felt the cold surface of the marble tables borne up by the gilded griffins which supported the long mirrors with their trio of dancing goddesses.

"This is a rich house," she said. "He was a splendid man who gave me all this to rule over."

In the salon, where the dancing had lately been so gay, the stiff-backed chairs were ranged in order round the walls. There she went to the piano and gently struck a note. "Even in my time there was no lack of gaiety and laughter here," she said.

She also entered the best guest-chamber opening from the salon. It was quite dark in there, and in feeling her way she touched the face of her companion.

"Are you crying?" she asked, as she felt her fingers wet with tears.

The young girl burst into sobs.

"My lady," she cried, "my lady, they will ruin everything. Why do you leave us and let the cavaliers ruin your house?"

Then the Major's wife drew up the blind and pointed out into the yard.

"Have I ever taught you to weep and moan?" she cried. "Look out, the yard is full of men; tomorrow there won't be a cavalier left in Ekeby."

"And my lady is returning to us?" asked the girl.

"My time has not come yet," answered the Major's wife. "The roadway must still be my home and the strawstack my bed, but you shall guard Ekeby for me till I come."

And they went on. Neither of them knew that Marienne was sleeping in that room. But she was not asleep. She was wide awake, had heard and understood all. She had been lying on her bed, lost in a reverie of love.

"Thou Mighty One," she said, "who hast lifted me above myself! I lay in the deepest misery, and thou hast turned it to Paradise. My hands were wounded on the iron latch of the barred door, and my tears lay frozen on the threshold of my home. Hate froze my heart when I heard the blows my mother received, and I tried to sleep away my anger in the snowdrift, but Thou hast come to me. Oh, Love, thou child of fire, thou hast come to one who has been frozen to the heart. If I compare my misery with the blessedness I have from it, the misery is nothing. I am freed from all ties; I have no father, no mother, no home. Men will turn from me and believe ill of me. Well, it is thy will, oh, Love, for why should I stand higher than my beloved? Hand in hand we will go forth into the world. Gösta Berling's bride is a poor girl. He found me in the snowdrifts. So let us make our home together, not in wide

halls, but in a cotter's hut in the forest clearing. I
shall help him to watch the charcoal-stacks. I shall
help him to set traps for hares and partridges. I shall
cook his food and mend his clothes. Oh, my beloved
—shall I feel lonely and sad when I sit there watching for you? I shall—I shall, but not for the days
of riches. Only for thee, only for thee shall I long,
and hope for thy footsteps on the forest path, for,
thy glad song as thou comest home with thine axe
over thy shoulder. Oh, my beloved, my beloved, as
long as I live will I wait for thee!"

Thus lying and composing a hymn to the all-
conquering God of Love, she had not closed her
eyes when the Major's wife came in.

When they had left the room, Marienne rose and
dressed herself again. Once more she put on the
black velvet dress and the thin dancing-shoes. She
wrapped the bedcover round her as a shawl, and
hurried out once more in the awful night.

Quiet, starlit, and bitterly cold, the February
night still rested upon the earth. It seemed as though
it would never end, and the darkness and cold which
it spread abroad that night lasted long, long after
the sun rose again, long after the drifts which Marienne trampled through had melted into air.

Marienne hurried away for help. She could not
allow the men who had rescued her, had opened
their hearts and home to her, to be hunted out of
Ekeby. She would go to Sjö, to Major Samzelius.

K

She must hurry, it would take her an hour to get back.

When the Lady of Ekeby had said farewell to her home, she went down to the courtyard, and the strife round the cavaliers' wing began.

She placed the people round the tall, narrow building, the second story of which was famous as being the home of the cavaliers. In the biggest room there, with its plaster walls and the large chests painted red and the enormous folding-table where the cards were swimming about in the spilt wine, on the wide beds, hidden behind the yellow-striped curtains, slept the cavaliers.

And in the stables before their full mangers slept the cavaliers' horses, and dreamed of their youthful exploits. How happy in those restful days to dream of the wild feats of their youth! of their journeys to the horse-market, where they stood day and night under the open sky; of sharp canters from early service on Christmas morning; of trial races before exchanging owners, when drunken men, amid a rain of cutting blows, leaned far out of their vehicles, and swore fiercely in their ears. Happy so to dream, when they know they will never leave the full mangers and the warm stalls of Ekeby!

In the old coach-house, where the broken chaises and discarded sledges are placed, there is a wonderful assemblage of old vehicles. There are small hand-sledges and ice-hilling sledges painted in green and red and gold. There stands the first cariole seen in Värmland, brought there by Beerencreutz as spoil from the war of 1814. There are every conceivable kind of shay and chaise with swaying springs — post-chaises, extraordinary vehicles of torturing construction, with their seats resting on wooden springs. They are all there, all the murderous types of equipages which have been sung about in the times of road travelling. And there also stands the long sledge which holds all the twelve cavaliers, and poor, frozen, old Cousin Kristoffer's covered sledge, and Örneclou's family sledge with the moth-eaten bear-skin cover and the worn crest on the splashboard, and the racing sledges — innumerable racing sledges.

Many are the cavaliers who lived and died at Ekeby. Their names are forgotten, and they have no place any longer in people's hearts; but the Major's wife has gathered together all the old carriages in which they arrived at Ekeby, and preserved them in the old coach-house.

They also sleep and dream, and let the dust gather thickly over them. They never dream to leave Ekeby again — never again. So the leather bursts in the footbags, and the wheels fall to pieces, and the wood-work rots — the old carriages don't want to live any longer, they want to die.

But on that February night the Lady of Ekeby ordered the coach-house to be opened, and, by the light of torches and lanterns, she ordered the carriages belonging to the present set of Ekeby cavaliers to be brought out—Beerencreutz's old cariole and Örneclou's crested vehicle and the covered sledge which protected Cousin Kristoffer. She cared not whether the vehicle was intended for winter or summer use; she was only careful each should get his own.

And the old horses, which have been dreaming before their full mangers, they are also awakened.

Dreams shall for once come true.

Again you shall make trial of the steep hillside, and the mouldy hay in the shed of the village inn, and the cut of the drunken horse-seller's whip, and the mad racing over the slippery ice which you tremble to stand upon.

When the tiny grey Norwegian horses were harnessed to a tall, spindle-like chaise, and the big, bony, riding-horses to the low racing sledges, they were quite in keeping. The old animals snorted when the bits were forced into their toothless mouths, the old vehicles groaned and creaked. Brittle infirmity, which ought to rest in quiet till the end of the world, was brought out to the sight of all; stiff muscles, lame forefeet, spavin, and strangles were shown in the light of day.

The stablemen did manage at last to harness the horses to the old vehicles, and then asked their mistress in which vehicle Gösta Berling should be

placed, for, as you know, Gösta Berling was brought
to Ekeby in Fru Samzelius' own sledge.

"Harness Don Juan to our best racing sledge,"
she commanded, "and spread the bear-skin cover
with the silver claws over it." And when the groom
objected—"There is n't a horse in my stable I
would n't give to be freed from that man. Do you
understand?"

So the horses and carriages are ready, but the cavaliers are still asleep.

Now it is their turn to be brought out into the
wintry night, but it is a more daring exploit to take
them in their beds than to bring out the stiff old
horses and the rattling old carriages. They are daring, strong, fearful men, hardened by a hundred
adventures. They will resist to the death, and it will
be no easy task to take them in their beds, and bring
them down to the vehicles which are to convey
them away.

The Major's wife commanded that a stack of
straw standing near should be set on fire, so that
the light might shine into the cavaliers' room.

"The straw is mine—all Ekeby is mine," she said.

And when the strawstack was in flames, she cried,
"Wake them now." But the cavaliers slept on behind firmly closed doors. The crowd raised that
fearful, frightful cry, "Fire! Fire!"—but the cavaliers slept.

The heavy hammers of the master blacksmith

struck against the outer door in vain; a hard snow-
ball broke a window-pane and flew into the room,
striking the curtains of a bed—but the cavaliers
slept soundly.

They dream a lovely girl throws her handkerchief to them, they dream of the applause before the
curtain of the theatre, they dream of gay laughter
and the deafening noise of the midnight carouse.
It would require a cannon shot at their ear, a sea
of icy water, to awaken them.

They have sung and danced and played and
acted; they are heavy with wine, their strength is
gone; they sleep a sleep as deep as death.

That blessed sleep nearly saved them.

The people began to believe the silence hid some
menace. It might be that the cavaliers were away
seeking help. It might mean that they were standing on guard, with their fingers on the triggers
of their guns, behind the doors and the windows,
ready to shoot down the first man who entered.

The cavaliers were cunning and warlike men;
there must be some meaning in the strange silence.
Who could believe it of them that they would allow
themselves to be surprised like a bear in a hole.

The crowd shouted "Fire! Fire!" time after
time, without any result. Then, when they were all
trembling, the Major's wife took an axe, and broke
open the outer door.

Then, alone, she sprang upstairs, tore open the

door of the cavaliers' wing, and screamed again, "Fire! Fire!"

That voice echoed more clearly in the minds of the cavaliers than all the shouting of the crowd. Accustomed to obey its commands, twelve men sprang up out of their beds, saw the glare on the windows, snatched up their clothes, and sprang down the stairs into the yard.

But there, in the doorway, stood the master smith and two big carters, and great disgrace overtook the cavaliers. As one by one they came down, they were caught, thrown to the ground, their feet were tied, and they were borne away to the carriage which was destined for them.

Not one escaped — they were all caught. Beerencreutz, the fierce colonel, was tied and carried away as well as Kristian Bergh, the strong captain, and Uncle Eberhard, the philosopher.

Even the unconquerable, greatly feared Gösta Berling was overpowered. The Major's wife had succeeded; she was, after all, stronger than the cavaliers.

It was pitiful to see them as they sat bound on the vehicles. Hanging heads and fierce glances were to be seen — the courtyard echoed with oaths and wild bursts of impotent rage.

The Lady of Ekeby went from one to another.

"You are to swear," she said, "never to return to Ekeby."

"Begone, you witch!"

"You shall swear," she repeated, "or I will throw you, bound as you are, into the cavaliers' wing, and you shall die there to-night, for I will burn down the cavaliers' wing as sure as I live."

"You dare not."

"Dare not? Is n't Ekeby mine? Oh, you scoundrels! Don't you think I remember how you spat after me on the roadside? I should like to set fire to the building even now, and let you all burn. Did you lift a hand to help me when I was turned out of my home? No, swear now!"

And she looked furious, though perhaps she pretended to be more angry than she really was, and so many men with axes stood around her, the cavaliers were obliged to swear.

Then she ordered their clothes and boxes to be brought out and their hands to be untied, and the reins were placed between their fingers.

But time had passed, and Marienne had reached Sjö before this.

The Major was no late sleeper, he was up and dressed when she came. She met him in the yard; he had been to give his bears their breakfast.

He did not say much to her news, only went back to his bears, tied a nose-rope to each, led them out, and hurried away in the direction of Ekeby.

Marienne followed him at a distance. She was ready to fall, she was so tired, but she saw a bright flare of fire in the sky, and that nearly frightened her to death.

What a night that had been! A man had beaten his wife, and left his daughter to freeze to death outside his doors. Did a woman intend now to burn her enemies to death? Did the old Major intend to set his bears upon his own people?

She conquered her weakness, passed the Major, and ran wildly to Ekeby.

She was well ahead of him. She gained the courtyard and pushed her way among the crowd. When she gained the centre and stood face to face with the Major's wife, she cried as loudly as she could, "The Major! The Major is coming with his bears!"

There was great alarm among the people; all eyes turned to the Major's wife.

"You went for him," she said to Marienne.

"Fly," cried Marienne, still more eagerly. "Fly, for God's sake! I don't know what the Major will do, but he has the bears with him."

All stood with their eyes fastened upon the Major's wife.

"I thank you for your assistance, my children," she said, calmly, to the people. "All has been so arranged that you cannot be taken to task for this night's doings, nor will they harm you in any way. Go home now! I don't wish to see any of my people kill or be killed. Go now!"

The people stood motionless.

The Major's wife turned to Marienne.

"I know you love," she said; "you have acted in the madness of love. May the day never come when you are powerless to prevent the ruin of your home! May you ever be mistress of your own tongue and your own hand when anger fills your soul!"

"My children, follow me," she said, turning to the people. "May God guard Ekeby, I go to my mother. Oh, Marienne! when you have regained your senses, when Ekeby is destroyed, and all the country groans in famine, think then of your doings this night, and take pity on the people!"

And she left the courtyard, followed by all the crowd.

When the Major arrived he found not a living soul besides Marienne and a long row of horses harnessed to old vehicles — a long, wretched line of them, where the horses were not worse than the carriages, nor the carriages worse than their owners. They had all fared hardly in life.

Marienne went forward and unbound the cavaliers. She saw how they bit their lips and would not meet her eyes. They were ashamed as never before. They had never been so degraded in their lives.

"I was not better off when I lay on my knees on the steps at Björne a few hours ago," said Marienne.

And so, dear reader, I will not try to describe

the further events of that night—how the old carriages went back to the coach-house, and the old
horses to their stalls, and the cavaliers to the cavaliers' wing. The dawn began to spread itself over
the eastern hills, and the day came bringing quietness and calm. How much quieter are the bright,
sunny days than the dark nights, under whose shel-
tering wing the wild beasts hunt and the owls hoot!

Only this I must add: when the cavaliers came
upstairs again, and they found a few drops in the
punch-bowl still to pour into their glasses, a sudden enthusiasm swept over them.

"Skål, for the Major's wife!" they cried.

Oh, she was a mighty woman! What better could
they desire than to serve and adore her!

Was it not awful that the devil had such power
over her, and all she lived for was to send cavaliers'
souls to hell?

The Great Bear of Gurlita Cliff

IN the forest live evil beasts, whose jaws are armed with dreadful gleaming teeth or sharp beaks, whose feet have sharp claws that long to fasten upon a living throat, and whose eyes glimmer with the lust of murder.

There live the wolves, which come out at night, and give chase to the peasant's sledge, till the mother must take the child sitting on her knee and throw it out to save her own life and her husband's.

There lives the lynx, which the people call the "big cat," for it is dangerous to speak of it by its right name, in the forest at least. He who has talked of it during the daytime had better see to the doors and air-holes of his sheepfold at night, or it will find its way thither. It climbs up the wall, for its claws are as sharp as steel tacks, glides through the narrow opening, and throws itself upon the sheep. And it clings upon their necks, and drinks the blood out of the jugular vein, and kills and destroys till every sheep is dead. It does not stay its wild death-dance among the terrified animals while any of them show a sign of life.

And in the morning the peasant finds all his sheep dead with mangled throats, for the big cat leaves nothing living where it ravages.

In the forest, too, lives the great owl, which hoots

at twilight. If you anger him, then he swoops down upon you, and tears out your eyes, for he is not a real bird, but an evil spirit.

And there, too, lives the most terrible of all the forest beasts — the bear, which has the strength of twelve men, and, when once he has become blood-thirsty, can only be killed by a silver bullet.

Can anything give a beast a nimbus of greater terror than this, that he can only be killed by a sil-ver bullet? What are the secret, awful powers that dwell within him, and make him impervious to or-dinary lead! A child will lie awake many long hours, shuddering in fear of the wicked beast which the evil powers protect.

If you should meet him in the forest, tall as a moving mountain, you must not run away nor try to defend yourself; you must throw yourself down on the earth and pretend to be dead. Many little children have lain in fancy on the ground with a bear bending over them. He has turned them over with his paw, and they have felt his hot, panting breath on their faces, but they lay motionless till he went away to dig a hole to bury them in. Then they rose gently and crept away, first slowly, then in wildest flight. But think! Think if the bear had not found them to be really dead, but had given them a bite to make sure, or if he had been hungry and had eaten them at once, or if he had seen them when they crept away and had pursued them! Oh, God!

Terror is a witch who sits in the twilight of the
forests, and composes magic songs for the ears of
men, and fills their hearts with awful thoughts. Of
these are born Fear, which burdens life and veils
the beauty of the smiling landscape. Malicious is
Nature, and treacherous as a sleeping serpent, and
never to be trusted. There lies the Löfven Lake in
splendid beauty, but trust it not, it lies in wait for
its prey; every year it must receive its tribute of the
drowned. There lies the forest, enchantingly peaceful, but trust it not! The forest is full of wicked
beasts, possessed by the spirits of the witches and
the souls of murderous villains.

Trust not the brook with its sweet waters! It has
sickness and death for you, if you wade there after
sunset. Trust not the cuckoo, which calls so joyfully
in spring. In autumn it changes into a hawk with
cruel eyes and awful claws! Trust not the moss nor
the heather nor the ledge of rock: all Nature is
evil, possessed by invisible spirits which hate mankind. There is no place where you can set your foot
securely, and it is marvellous that feeble humanity
can withstand so much persecution.

A witch is Terror. Does she still sit in the darkness of the Värmland forests and sing her magic
songs? Does she still darken the beauty of the smiling landscape and crush the joy of life? Great has her
power been, I know well, for I too have had steel
put into my cradle and a piece of charcoal into my

bath; I know it well, for I have felt her iron grip upon my heart.

But you must not imagine I am going to tell you anything dreadful. It is only an old story about the great bear of Gurlita Cliff, and you are at liberty to believe it or not, as ought to be the case with all true stories of sport.

.   .   .   .

The great bear had his home on the fine mountain peak called Gurlita Cliff, which rose, precipitous and difficult of ascent, from the shore of the Upper Löfven.

The root of an overturned pine, about which the tufts of moss still hung, formed the roof and walls of his house. Pines and fir trees protected it, and snow covered it closely. He could lie there and sleep a calm, sweet sleep from one summer to another.

Was he then a poet, a gentle dreamer, this shaggy forest king, this cross-eyed robber? Did he wish to sleep away the bleak night of the cold winter and its colorless days, to be awakened by purling streams and the songs of birds? Did he lie there and dream of the reddening whortleberry banks, and of the ant-hills full of brown, spicy little insects, and of the white lambs that fed on the green slopes? Would he, happy creature, escape life's winter?

The drifting snow whirled, whistling, among the pine trees; the wolves and foxes were abroad, maddened by hunger. Why should the bear alone slumber? May he arise and feel how sharply the frost nips, and how heavy it is to walk in the deep snow!

He has bedded himself in so well, he is like the sleeping princess in the fairy tale. As she was awakened to life by love, so he will be awakened by the spring, by a sunbeam which finds its way between the branches and warms his nose, by some drops of water from the melting snowdrift which penetrates his fur coat. Woe to him who disturbs him before that time!

If only any one had inquired how the forest king wished to be awakened! If a shower of hail had not whisked suddenly between the branches and found its way into his skin like a horde of angry mosquitoes!

He heard sudden shouts and a great noise and shots. He flung the sleep from his limbs, and tore aside the branches to see what was the matter. There was work for the old fighting champion. It was not spring shouting and roaring outside his lair, nor could it be the wind, which sometimes threw the pine trees over and whirled the snow about, but it was the cavaliers — the cavaliers from Ekeby.

They were old acquaintances. He well remembered the night when Beerencreutz and Fuchs sat in ambush in a Nygård cowshed, where a visit was expected from him. They had just fallen asleep over their gin flasks, but woke up to find he was carrying away the cow he had killed out of the stall, and fell upon him with guns and knives. They recaptured the cow, and destroyed one of his eyes, but he managed to escape alive.

Yes, old acquaintances were they! The forest king remembered how they came upon him on another occasion, just as he and his royal consort and their children were lying down for their winter's sleep in their old castle on Gurlita Cliff. He had escaped, sweeping aside all that came in his path, and fleeing without heeding the bullets, but he was lamed for life by a shot in the thigh, and when he returned at night to his castle, he found the snow dyed red with the blood of his royal mate, and the royal children had been carried away to the dwellings of men, there to grow up as their servants and friends.

The ground trembled, and the snowdrift covering the bear-hole shook, as the great bear, the cavaliers' old enemy, broke out of his lair. Take care, Fuchs, old bear hunter; take care, Beerencreutz, colonel and camphio player; take care, Gösta Berling, hero of a thousand adventures!

Woe to all poets, all dreamers, all lovers! There stood Gösta Berling, his finger on the trigger of his gun, as the bear went straight toward him. Why did he not shoot? What was he thinking of?

Why did he not send a bullet into the broad chest. He was standing in the right place to do it, and the others had not the chance of a shot at the

L

right moment. Did he think he was on parade before the forest king?

Of course Gösta stood dreaming of beautiful Marienne, who was lying ill at Ekeby, having taken cold on the night when she lay in the snowdrift. He thought of her, who also was a sacrifice to the curse of hate that lies over the world, and he shuddered at himself at having gone forth to persecute and kill.

And there came the great bear straight to him, blind in one eye from the blow of a cavalier's knife, lame from a cavalier's bullet, angry and unkempt and lonely since they had killed his wife and carried off his children. And Gösta saw him as he was, a poor persecuted beast, whose life he did not care to take, for it was the only thing the poor creature possessed, when men had taken all else from him.

"He may kill me," thought Gösta, "but I won't shoot."

And while the bear rushed toward him, he stood as quietly as if on parade, and when the forest king came right in front of him, he shouldered his gun and took a step aside.

Then the bear pursued his way, knowing full well there was no time to lose. He plunged into the forest, forced a way through drifts as high as a man, rolled down the steep slopes, and fled irreclaimably, while all the cavaliers who had stood with their guns at full cock, waiting for Gösta's shot, now discharged them after him.

But in vain. The ring was broken and the bear was gone. Fuchs scolded, Beerencreutz swore, but Gösta only laughed. How could they expect a man as happy as he was to kill any of God's children?

The great bear of Gurlita Cliff escaped with his life from the fray, but he had been thoroughly awakened from his winter sleep, as the peasants soon had cause to know. There was no bear who could tear open the low, cellar-like roofs of their sheep-folds so easily; none could so cunningly avoid a carefully arranged ambush.

The people on the Upper Löfven were soon in despair what to do about it. They sent again and again to the cavaliers, begging them to come and shoot him.

And day after day and night after night, during all the month of February, the cavaliers made their way to the Upper Löfven in search of the bear, but he always escaped them. Had he learned cunning from the fox and sharpness from the wolves? While they were guarding one farmyard, he was laying the neighboring yard waste; while they searched for him in the forest, he was giving chase to a peasant driving over the ice. He had become the most audacious of marauders; he crept into the garret and emptied the goodwife's honey-pot, and killed the horse standing harnessed to her husband's sledge.

But by and by people began to understand what kind of a bear he was, and the reason why Gösta Berling had not shot at him. Dreadful as it was to think of, this was no ordinary bear! No one need think of killing him unless he carried a silver bullet in his gun. A bullet of mingled silver and bell metal, cast on a Thursday night at new moon in a church tower, without the priest or sexton or any living mortal knowing about it, would certainly bring him down, but such a bullet was not easy to procure.

.   .   .   .

There was one man at Ekeby, more than the others, who was mortified at this state of things. It was, of course, Anders Fuchs, the bear hunter. He lost both appetite and sleep in his anger at not being able to kill the big bear of Gurlita Cliff, till at last he also began to understand that the bear could only be felled by a silver bullet.

Major Anders Fuchs was not a handsome man. He had a clumsy, heavy body and a broad, red face with hanging pouches under his cheeks and a many-doubled chin. His small black moustache stood as stiff as a brush above his full lips, and his black hair was close and thick, and rose straight up on his head. Besides this, he was a man of few words and a great eater. He was not a man whom women met with sunny smiles or open arms, and he did not waste any tender glances on them either.

No one thought he would ever see a woman to whom he would give preference, and anything in connection with love or sentiment was utterly foreign to his nature.

So when he went about longing for moonlight, you must not imagine he wished to make the good lady, Luna, a confidant in any tender love trouble; he was only thinking of the silver bullet which must be moulded by the light of the new moon.

On a Thursday evening, when the moon was only two fingers' width and hung over the horizon for a couple of hours after sunset, Major Fuchs betook himself from Ekeby without telling any one where he was going. He had a fire-steel and a bullet form in his game-bag and his gun on his back, and he went toward Bro Church to see what Fortune had in store for an honest man.

The church lay on the eastern shore of the narrow strait between the Upper and the Lower Löfven, and Major Fuchs was obliged to cross Sund Bridge to reach it. He marched down thither in deep thought without looking up at the Bro Hills, where the houses were sharply outlined against the clear evening sky, or toward Gurlita Cliff raising its round head in the evening glow. He stared only at the ground, and wondered how he was to get hold of the church key without any one discovering the theft.

When he reached the bridge, he heard some one

screaming so wildly that he was obliged to raise his head.

A little German, Faber by name, was organist at Bro at that time. He was a slender man, wanting in both dignity and weight; and the sexton was Jans Larsson, a doughty peasant, but poor, for the Broby parson had cheated him out of his patrimony, five hundred dalers. The sexton wanted to marry the organist's sister, the little, refined Fröken Faber, but the organist would not hear of it, and thus the two were enemies. That evening the sexton had met the organist on the bridge and straightway fallen upon him. He caught him by the chest, lifted him over the parapet of the bridge, and told him he would drop him into the strait if he would not promise him the hand of the little lady. Still the German would not consent; he kicked and screamed and still persisted in his " No," though he saw beneath him the stream of black, open water rushing between its white banks.

"No, no!" he screamed, "no, no!"

And it is very possible that the sexton, in his fury, would have allowed his captive to drop down into the cold, black water, if Major Fuchs had not come upon the bridge just then. He was startled, placed Faber on his feet again, and disappeared as rapidly as possible.

Little Faber fell upon the Major's neck and thanked him for saving his life, but Major Fuchs thrust him aside and said it was nothing to be thankful for. The Major had no love for the Germans since he lay quartered in Putbus on the Rügen during the Pomeranian war. He had never been so near starving to death as during that time.

Then little Faber was for running to Justice Schärling and charging the sexton with attempting to murder him, but the Major soon convinced him that it was not worth while to do so; for in that country it cost nothing at all to kill a German, not a penny, and to prove the truth of his words, he offered to throw him into the strait himself.

Then Faber calmed himself, and invited the Major to go home with him and eat some sausages and drink warm German beer.

The Major accepted, for he thought the organist was sure to have a church key, and they went up the hill on which Bro Church stood, with its rectory and the sexton's and organist's dwellings around it.

"Please excuse things," said little Faber, when he and the Major entered the room. "We are not in very good order to-day, we have been so busy, my sister and I. We have killed a cock."

"You don't say so!" exclaimed the Major.

Directly afterwards little Fröken Faber came into the room carrying great earthenware jugs full of beer. Now every one knows that the Major did not look upon women with the kindest of glances, but he was obliged to look graciously on the little lady

who was so neat in her pretty cap and laces. The
fair hair was brushed so smoothly on her forehead,
and the homespun dress was so neat and so beautifully clean, her little hands were so busy and eager,
and her little face so rosy and round, that he found
himself thinking that if he had seen that bit of
womankind twenty-five years ago, he would certainly have felt forced to pay court to her.

But though she was so rosy and helpful and so
neat, her eyes were quite red with crying. It was just
that which gave him such tender thoughts regarding her.

While the men ate and drank, she passed in and
out of the room. Once she came to her brother,
curtsied, and asked, "Will my brother say how the
cows are to be placed in the shed?"

"Place twelve on the left and eleven on the right;
they will not be crowded then," replied little Faber.

"It is extraordinary how many cows you have,
Faber!" exclaimed the Major.

But the truth of the matter was that the organist
had only two cows, but he called one Twelve and the
other Eleven, so that it should sound grand when
he talked of them.

The Major learned that the cowhouse was being
rebuilt, so that the cows were out of doors during
the day, and were placed at night in the woodshed.

And going in and out of the room, the little
Fröken came to her brother again, curtsied, and

said, "The carpenter was asking how high the cow-house was to be built.'"

"Measure by the cows," replied the organist. "Measure by the cows."

Major Fuchs thought that a very good answer.

And without further ado the Major found himself asking the organist why his sister's eyes were so red, and he learned that she was crying because her brother would not allow her to marry the sexton, who was a poor man and encumbered with debt.

That made the Major sink still deeper in thought. He emptied one jugful after another and ate one sausage after another without noticing what he was doing. Little Faber shuddered at such an appetite and such thirst, but the more the Major drank and ate, the clearer grew his mind, and the more determined he became to do something for the little Fröken.

He was Major Fuchs, the bear hunter, the man who ate up in one evening a piece of brawn which the Judge's wife at Munkerud had intended to last all through the Christmas holidays, and he was pleased and in gentle mood at the thought of what splendid sausage he was eating. Yes, he would certainly see to it that Fröken Faber's eyes need weep no more.

Meanwhile he kept his eye on the big key with the curved handle hanging near the door, and no sooner had little Faber, who had been obliged to keep the Major company at the beer-jugs, laid his head on the table and was snoring, than the Major clutched the key, put on his cap, and hurried away.

A few minutes later he was feeling his way up the steeple stairs, lighted by his tiny horn lantern, and reached at last the bell tower, where the bells opened their wide throats above him. Once there, he scraped some bell metal off one of them with a file, and he was just on the point of taking the bullet form and a small pan out of his game-bag when he discovered that he was without the most important thing of all—he had brought no silver with him. If there was to be any power in that bullet, it must be cast in that belfry. Now all was complete : it was Thursday night and there was a new moon, and no one knew of his being there, and yet he could not cast his bullet. There in the silence of the night he sent up such a mighty oath, it fairly rang in the bells above him.

Just then he heard a slight noise in the church below, and thought he heard steps on the stairs. Yes, so it was, heavy steps were ascending the stairs.

Major Fuchs, standing there swearing so that the bells trembled, became a trifle thoughtful at this turn of affairs. He wondered who it could be coming to help him cast his bullet. The footsteps approached nearer and nearer. He who climbed the stairs was certainly bound for the belfry.

The Major crept in among the beams and rafters, and put out his lantern. He was not frightened exactly, but everything depended on his doing his work unseen. And no sooner was he concealed, than the new-comer's head rose to the level of the floor.

The Major recognized him—it was the miserly Broby parson. He, nearly crazy with covetousness, was in the habit of hiding his treasure in the most extraordinary places. Now he came to the belfry with a packet of notes which he wished to conceal there. He did not know that any one saw him; he lifted a board in the floor, placed the money under it, and departed again.

The Major was not backward, he lifted the same board. What heaps of money—rolls and rolls of notes, and among them, leather pouches full of silver! The Major took just as much silver as he needed for his bullet, and did not disturb the rest.

When he descended from the belfry, the silver bullet was in his gun. He marched away wondering what more fortune had in store for him that night. There is something extraordinary about Thursday nights, as everybody knows. He took a turn in the direction of the organist's house. Think, if that wretch of a bear knew that Faber's cows stood in a miserable shed, hardly better than being under the open sky!

Well, was that not something big and black he saw making its way over the field toward the cowshed? It must be the bear.

He laid his gun to his cheek and was quite prepared to fire, when he suddenly changed his mind.

Fröken Faber's red eyes appeared before him in the darkness. He thought he would like to help her and the sexton, but, of course, it was a great sacrifice for him to give up the chance of killing the great bear of Gurlita Cliff. He said afterwards that nothing in his life had been so hard to do as that, but as the little Fröken was so particularly nice and sweet, he did it.

He went to the sexton's house, woke him, dragged him out half-naked, and told him that he must shoot the bear which was creeping round Faber's woodshed.

"If you shoot that bear, he will certainly give you his sister," he said, "for you will at once become an honored man. That is no ordinary bear, and the best man in the country would think it an honor to kill him."

And he placed his own gun in his hand, loaded with the bullet made of silver and bell metal, cast in a belfry on a Thursday night at new moon, and he could not help trembling with envy that another than he was to shoot the great forest king, the old bear of Gurlita Cliff.

The sexton aimed—aimed, God help us, as if he meant to shoot the Great Bear or Charles' Wain, which, high in heaven, circles round the Polar Star, and not a bear walking on the earth—and the gun went off with a report which was heard even on Gurlita Cliff.

But whatever he aimed at, the bear fell. That is always the case when you shoot with a silver bullet. You hit the bear in the heart even if you aim at Charles' Wain.

The people rushed out at once from all the cottages near, wondering what had happened, for never did a shot sound louder or awake so many sleeping echoes as that did, and the sexton was greatly praised, for the bear was a real trouble to all the country-side.

Little Faber also came out, but Major Fuchs was cruelly deceived. There stood the sexton, highly honored by his neighbors, and he had saved Faber's own cows, yet the little organist was neither touched nor thankful. He did not open his arms to the sexton as to a brother-in-law and a hero.

The Major wrinkled his brows and stamped his foot in anger at such narrow-mindedness. He wanted to explain to the avaricious, mean little man what a feat had been done, but he began to stammer so, he could not get a word out. And he grew more and more angry at the thought of having uselessly sacrificed the great honor of killing the bear.

Oh! it was simply impossible for him to conceive how the man who had accomplished such a feat was not accounted worthy of winning the proudest bride.

The sexton and some young men were going to flay the bear. They went to the grindstones to sharpen their knives, and the other people went home and to bed, and Major Fuchs was left alone with the dead bear.

Then he went off to the church again, turned the key once more in the keyhole, climbed once more the narrow, crooked stairs, woke the sleeping pigeons, and entered the belfry.

Afterwards, when the bear was flayed under the Major's supervision, they found a parcel of notes worth five hundred dalers in his jaws. It was impossible to account for their presence there, but after all, it was no ordinary bear, and as the sexton had killed it, the money was clearly his.

When this became known, little Faber, too, began to understand what a glorious deed the sexton had done, and he declared he would be proud to own him as a brother-in-law.

On Friday evening Major Fuchs returned to Ekeby, after having graced an assembly at the sexton's held in honor of the dead bear, and another at the organist's in honor of the new engagement. He walked along with a heavy heart; he felt no delight over his vanquished enemy, and took no pleasure in the splendid bear-skin which the sexton had presented to him.

Perhaps some might imagine that he mourned because little Fröken Faber belonged to another?

Oh, no! that caused him no grief. But what went to his heart was that the old one-eyed forest king was now dead, and he had not been the man to kill him with a silver bullet.

He went up to the cavaliers' wing, where the cavaliers sat round the fire, and without a word he threw the bear-skin down before them. You must not think he related his adventures there and then; it was long, long years before he could be persuaded to tell the true facts of the case. Neither did he make known the Broby parson's hiding-place, and the parson probably never missed the money.

The cavaliers examined the skin.

"It is a beautiful skin," said Beerencreutz; "I wonder why he rose from his winter sleep, or perhaps you shot him in his lair?"

"He was shot in Bro."

"Well, he was not as big as the Gurlita bear, but he must have been a splendid beast," said Gösta.

"If he had been one-eyed," said Kevenhüller, "I should believe you had shot the old man himself, he is so big; but there is no wound or scar near his eyes, so it can't be he."

Fuchs swore first over his stupidity, but afterwards his face lighted up till he looked quite handsome. So the great bear had not fallen to another man's shot!

"Lord God, how good Thou art!" he said, and clasped his hands.

The Auction at Björne

WE young people must often wonder at the stories told us by our elders. "Did you dance every night as long as your beautiful youth lasted?" "Was life for you one long adventure?" we asked them. "Were all girls lovely and amiable in those days, and did Gösta Berling elope with one of them after every ball?"

Then the old people shook their heads and told of the whirling of the spinning-wheels and the boom of the looms, of cooking, of the thunder and crash in the track of the axe through the forests; but before long they harked back again to the old stories. Sledges drove up to the hall door and raced through the dark woods with their load of gay young people, the dancing grew wild, and the violin strings snapped. The wild wave of adventure rushed tumultuously along the shores of Lake Löfven, and its noise was heard afar. The forests swerved and fell, all the powers of destruction were loose, flames flared, the rapids swept away their prey, and wild beasts prowled hungrily round the homesteads. Under the hoofs of the eight-footed horses all quiet happiness was trampled in the dust. And wherever the wild hunt passed, men's hearts flamed up tempestuously, and the women fled from their homes in pale dismay. And we sat wondering, silent, frightened, and yet blissfully happy. "What people they were," we thought to ourselves; "we shall never see their like!"

"Did people in those days never *think* of what they were doing?" we asked.

"Certainly, they did," our elders answered.

"But not as we think," we persisted. Then our elders did not understand what we meant.

For we were thinking of the wonderful spirit of self-analysis which had already taken possession of our minds; we were thinking of him with the icy eyes and the long, knotted fingers — he, who sits in the darkest corner of our souls, and plucks our being to pieces as old women pluck scraps of wool and silk. Piece by piece, the long, hard fingers have dissected us till our whole being lies there like a heap of rags — till all our best feelings, our innermost thoughts, all we have said and done is examined, ransacked, disintegrated, and the icy eyes have watched, and the toothless mouth has sneered and whispered, "See, it is but rags, nothing but rags."

One of the people of those old days had opened her soul to that spirit. He sat there watching at the font of all impulse, sneering both at the good and the evil, understanding all, judging nothing, examining, searching, and plucking to pieces and paralyzing all emotions of the heart and all strength of thought by smiling scornfully at everything.

Marienne Sinclaire bore the spirit of self-analy-

M

sis within her. She felt his eyes follow every step, every word of hers. Her life had become a play, at which she was the only spectator. She was no longer a human being—she was neither wearied, nor did she rejoice, nor could she love. She played the part of the beautiful Marienne Sinclaire, and the spirit of self-analysis sat with staring eyes and busy fingers and watched her acting. She felt herself divided into two, and half of her being—pale, unfeeling, and scornful—watched the other half's transactions; and the spirit which thus plucked her asunder had never a word of kindness or sympathy for her.

But where had he been, the pale watcher beside the springs of impulse, on the night she had learned to feel life's fulness? Where was he, when she, the wise Marienne, kissed Gösta Berling before the eyes of two hundred people, and when she threw herself into the snowdrift to die in despair? The icy eyes were blinded, and the sneer was paralyzed, for passion had swept through her soul. The wild wave of adventure had thundered in her ears. She had been a whole being during that one awful night.

Oh, god of self-scorn, when Marienne lifted at last her frozen arms to Gösta's neck, then, like old Beerencreutz, thou wert compelled to turn thy eyes from earth and look at the stars! That night thou hadst no power. Thou wast dead while she sang her love hymns, dead when she hurried to Sjö for the Major, dead when she saw the flames redden-

ing the sky over the treetops. See, they have come,
the strong storm birds, the demon birds of passion.
With wings of fire and claws of steel, they have
swooped down upon thee, and flung thee out into
the unknown. Thou hast been dead and destroyed.
But they, the proud and mighty, they whose path
is unknown and who cannot be followed — they
have swept onward, and out of the depths of the
unknown the spirit of self-observation has arisen
again, and again taken possession of Marienne's
soul.

She lay ill at Ekeby all through February. She
had taken smallpox at Sjö, when she went to find
the Major, and the awful sickness had her completely at its mercy, for she had been frightfully
chilled and wearied during that night. Death had
been very near her, but toward the end of the
month she grew better. She was still weak, and was
greatly disfigured. She would never again be called
beautiful Marienne. This misfortune, which was
to bring sorrow over all Värmland as if one of its
best treasures had been lost, was known, as yet,
only to Marienne and her sick nurse. Even the
cavaliers were not aware of it. The room in which
the smallpox reigned was closed to all. But where
is the spirit of self-analysis stronger than in the
long hours of convalescence? There it sits and stares
and stares with its icy eyes, and plucks and plucks
to pieces our being with its knotted fingers. And if

you look closely, you see behind him another pale being who stares and sneers and paralyzes, and behind him still another and another, all sneering at one another and the whole world. While Marienne lay there and stared at herself with those icy eyes, all feeling died within her. She lay there and played the part of being ill and being unhappy; she played at being in love and being revengeful. She was all this, and yet it was but acting a part. Everything became unreal under the gaze of those eyes watching her, which, again, were watched by another pair, and another, and another in an endless perspective. All life's powers were asleep; she had had strength for burning hate and overwhelming love for one night only. She did not even know if she loved Gösta Berling. She longed to see him to prove if he could carry her out of herself.

While the illness raged she had only one clear thought. She took care that the nature of the fever should remain unknown. She would not see her parents: she had no wish for reconciliation with her father. She knew he would repent if he heard how ill she was. So she commanded that her parents, and others too, in fact, were to be told that her eyes, which were always weak when she visited her native place, compelled her, for a time, to remain in a darkened room. She forbade her nurse to say how ill she was and forbade the cavaliers sending for a doctor from Karlstad. She certainly had the smallpox, but it was a mild case—the medicine-chest at Ekeby contained all that was necessary to save her life. She never thought of dying: she only waited to be well enough to go with Gösta to the pastor and arrange for the banns to be published. But now the fever had left her. She was cool and prudent again. It seemed to her as if she alone was wise in this world of fools. She neither loved nor hated; she understood her father, she understood them all. He that understands does not hate. She had been told that Melchior Sinclaire was going to have an auction at Björne and make away with all his possessions so that she would have nothing to inherit from him. They said he intended making the wreck as complete as possible. He would sell the furniture and household goods first, then the horses and cattle and farm implements, and lastly, the estate itself; and he intended putting the money in a bag and sinking it in the Löfven. Her inheritance would be ruin, dissipation, and dismay. Marienne smiled approvingly when she heard this. Such was his character; he was sure to act like that.

It seemed extraordinary to her that she should have poured forth that poem of love. She, too, had dreamed of the miner's hut—she, as well as others. It was wonderful to her that she had ever had a dream. She sighed for nature—she was weary of constantly acting a part. She had never had a strong feeling. She hardly mourned her lost beauty, but she

shuddered at the thought of pity from strangers.
Oh, a second of self-forgetfulness, a gesture, a word,
an act which was not premeditated!

One day, when the room had been disinfected, and
she lay dressed upon the sofa, she sent for Gösta
Berling. They told her that he had gone to the auction at Björne.

. . . .

At Björne there was, in truth, a great auction going
on. It was an old and wealthy estate, and people
had come from great distances to take part in the
sale.

Melchior Sinclaire had gathered all the household belongings into the great salon. There were
thousands of things there, thrown in heaps which
reached from the floor to the ceiling.

He had gone about the house like a destroying
angel on Judgment Day, and gathered together all
he intended to sell. The kitchen utensils, the black
cauldrons, wooden chairs, tin pots, and copper pans
were left in peace, for they did not remind him of
Marienne, but there was little else that escaped his
wrath.

He broke into Marienne's room, carrying away
everything. Her doll cupboard stood there and her
bookcase, the little chair he had ordered to be carved
for her, her clothes and ornaments, her sofa and
bed — they must all go.

And he went from room to room. He snatched up anything he took a fancy to, and carried great burdens down to the auction room. He panted under the weight of sofas and marble tables, but he persisted in his work. And he threw it all down in the greatest confusion. He had torn the cupboards open and brought out the family silver. Away with it! Marienne had used it. He gathered up armfuls of snow-white damask and smooth linen towels with wide open-work hems — honest, homemade stuff, the fruit of years of toil — and tumbled it all in a heap. Away with it! Marienne was not worthy to inherit it. He stormed through the rooms with piles of porcelain, caring little if he broke dozens of plates, and he carried off the teacups on which the family crest was painted. Away with them! Let who will use them. He brought downstairs mountains of bed-clothes from the garrets — pillows and bolsters so soft, you could sink in them as in a wave. Away with them! Marienne had slept in them.

He cast furious glances at the well-known furniture. There wasn't a chair or a sofa that she had not used, nor a picture that she hadn't looked.at, nor a chandelier that hadn't lighted her, nor a mirror that hadn't reflected her beauty. Gloomily he shook his fist at that world of memories. He could have rushed at them with lifted club and broken them in pieces.

Yet it seemed to him an even greater revenge to

make an auction of it all. Away to strangers with
it! Away to be soiled in the cotters' huts, to be
destroyed in the charge of the stranger! Didn't he
know them well? Those old pieces of furniture,
fallen from high estate, to be seen in the peasants'
huts, fallen as his daughter had fallen! Away with
them all to the four corners of heaven, so that no
eye could find them, no hand could gather them
together again!

When the auction opened, he had filled half the
salon with an incredible jumble of household goods.

Across the room he had placed a long counter.
Behind this stood the auctioneer and cried the goods,
and the clerk sat there making notes, and Melchior
Sinclaire had a cask of gin standing beside him.
At the other end of the room, in the hall, and out
in the yard, stood the buyers. There was a great
crowd of people and much shouting and laughter.
The sale was brisk, and one thing was cried after
another, while by the side of his cask, with all his
possessions in indescribable confusion behind him,
sat Melchior Sinclaire, half drunk and half crazy.
The hair stood stiffly erect above his red face, his
eyes rolled bloodshot and furious. He shouted and
laughed as if he were in the best of tempers, and he
called up every purchaser and gave him a glass of
his gin.

Among those who saw him thus was Gösta Berling, who had come in with the crowd, but avoided

being seen by Melchior Sinclaire. He became
thoughtful at the sight, and his heart contracted as
with a foreboding of misfortune.

He wondered where Marienne's mother could
be while all this was going on, and he went, much
against his will, but driven by fate, to seek her.

He went through many rooms before he found
her. The great land proprietor had but short patience and little liking for women's tears and wailing. He had grown tired of seeing her tears flow at
the fate overtaking all her treasures. He was furious to see that she could mourn over linen and
bedclothes when his beautiful daughter was lost
to them, and with clenched fists he had driven her
before him through all the house, into the kitchen,
and even into the pantry.

She could go no further, and he had been satisfied at seeing her there, crouching under the step-
ladder awaiting a blow, perhaps a death-blow. He
let her remain there, but he locked the door and
put the key into his pocket. She might remain there
while the auction lasted. She would not starve, and
his ears were spared her wailing.

There she sat still, a prisoner in her own pantry, when Gösta walked down the corridor to the
kitchen, and he saw her face at a high little window which opened in the wall. She had climbed
up the step-ladder and was gazing out of her
prison.

"What is Aunt Gustafva doing up there?" he asked.

"He has locked me in," she whispered.

"What! Melchior Sinclaire?"

"Yes, I thought he would kill me. But, Gösta— get the key of the salon door and go into the kitchen and open the pantry door with it so that I can get out. That key fits."

Gösta obeyed, and a few minutes later the little woman was in the kitchen, which was quite deserted.

"Aunt should have told one of the servant-girls to open the door with that key," said Gösta.

"Do you think I would teach them that trick? I should never have anything left in peace in the pantry after that. And besides, I began to put the upper shelves there into order. They needed it. I can't understand how I allowed so much rubbish to collect there."

"Aunt has so much to look after," said Gösta.

"It's too true. If I am not seeing to everything, neither the spinning nor weaving goes right. And if . . . " She paused and wiped a tear from her eyes. "God help me, what nonsense I'm talking!" she said. "I won't have much to look after now. He is selling all we have."

"Yes, it is a miserable business," said Gösta.

"You remember the big glass in the drawing-room, Gösta? It was so beautiful because the glass

was all in one piece and without a scratch, and
there wasn't a spot on the gilding. I got it from my
mother, and now he wants to sell it."

"He is mad."

"You may well say so. It can't be anything else.
He won't stop till he has beggared us, and we must
tread the road like the Major's wife."

"It will not go so far as that."

"Yes, Gösta. When the Major's wife left Ekeby,
she foretold misfortune for us, and it has come.
She wouldn't have allowed it—she would never
have allowed him to sell Björne. And think of it—
his own porcelain—the real china cups from his
own home are to be sold! She would never have
allowed it."

"But what is the matter with him?" asked Gösta.

"Oh, it is all because Marienne has not returned.
He has gone about waiting and waiting. He has
walked up and down the lane for days waiting for
her. He will go mad with longing, but I daren't
say anything."

"Marienne thinks he is angry with her."

"Oh, no, she doesn't think that; she knows him,
but she is proud and will not take the first step.
They are proud and hard, both of them, and they
are in no trouble. It is I who must stand between
them."

"Aunt knows that Marienne is going to marry
me?"

"Oh, Gösta, she never will do that. She says it only to madden him. She is too spoiled to marry a poor man, and too proud, too. Go back now and tell her that if she does not come home soon, all her inheritance will be wasted. He will destroy it all without getting anything for it."

Gösta was really angry with her. There she sat on the big kitchen table, and had no heart for anything but her looking-glass and her porcelain.

"You ought to be ashamed, Aunt Gustafva," he exclaimed. "You turn your daughter out into the snowdrifts, and then you think it simply wickedness of her not to return home. And you think no better of her than that she would desert one she cares for because she will be disinherited?"

"Dear Gösta, don't be angry — you also. I hardly know what I'm saying. I tried to open the door for Marienne, but he dragged me away. They always say that I don't understand things. I don't grudge you Marienne, Gösta, if you can make her happy. It isn't so easy to make a woman happy, Gösta."

Gösta looked at her. How could he have lifted an angry voice against her? She looked so frightened, so hunted to death; but she was kind hearted.

"Aunt has not inquired how Marienne is," he said, softly.

She burst into tears.

"Don't be angry if I ask," she cried. "I have

longed to ask you all the time. Think of it—I know nothing about her except that she is alive. I have heard nothing from her all this time, not even when I sent her some clothes, and I thought neither of you meant to tell me anything."

Gösta could not withstand the pity of it. He was wild and giddy. God sometimes sent His wolves after him to compel his obedience, but the tears of that old-mother and her wailing were worse to bear than the howling of the wolves. He told her the truth.

"Marienne has been ill all the time," he said. "She has had smallpox. She was to sit up to-day on the sofa. I have not seen her since that first night."

With a bound Fru Gustafva was on the floor. She left Gösta standing there and rushed at once to her husband. The people in the auction room saw her come and whisper something eagerly in his ear. They saw his face redden, while his hand resting on the tap of the cask twisted it till the gin flowed over the floor. It seemed to all that she brought important news which would stop the sale. The auctioneer's voice ceased, the clerks stopped writing, there were no further bids.

Melchior Sinclaire awoke from his thoughts. "Well," he screamed, "aren't you to go on?" And the auction was in full swing again.

Gösta still sat in the kitchen when Fru Gustafva came back weeping to him. "It was no use," she said; "I thought he would stop when he heard Marienne had been ill, but he lets them continue. He would like to stop, but he is ashamed now."

Gösta shrugged his shoulders and bade her farewell.

In the hall he met Sintram.

"A devilish funny affair," exclaimed Sintram, rubbing his hands. "You are a master-hand at getting up such things, Gösta."

"It will be funnier still in a little while," whispered Gösta. "The Broby parson is here with a sledgeful of money. They say he wants to buy all Björne and pay the money down, and I should just like to see Melchior Sinclaire then, Uncle Sintram."

Sintram dropped his head between his shoulders and laughed to himself a long time. Then he made off to the auction room and straight to Melchior Sinclaire.

"If you want a glass, Sintram, you have got to make a bid first."

Sintram went up close to him. "You have good luck as usual, Melchior," he said. "A great man has come to Björne with a sledgeful of money. He is ready to buy Björne with all its goods and chattels. He has arranged with a number of people to do the bidding for him. I suppose he doesn't want to show himself at once."

"You may as well say who it is, and I will give you a smack for your trouble."

Sintram took the smack and retreated two steps before he answered, " It is the Broby parson, Brother Melchior."

Melchior Sinclaire had many better friends than the Broby parson. There was a feud of many years' standing between them. There were stories of the great land proprietor having lain in ambush on dark nights on the road where the parson must pass, and having given many a good honest thrashing to that toady and grinder of the poor.

And though Sintram had retreated a few steps, he did not quite escape the great man's anger. He got a wineglass between his eyes and the whole cask on his feet, but this was followed by a scene which gladdened his heart for many a day.

"Does the Broby parson want my estate?" screamed Sinclaire. "Are you standing there and bidding for the Broby parson? You ought to be ashamed; you ought to know better!" He caught up a candlestick and an inkstand and flung them at the crowd. It was his heart's bitterness finding expression. Roaring like a wild beast, he shook his fist at the bystanders, and flung whatever he could lay his hands on at them. The brandy bottles and glasses flew across the room; he was beside himself with rage. "The auction is over," he shouted. " Out with you! Never while I live shall the Broby parson possess Björne. Out with you all; I'll teach you to buy in for the Broby parson!" He attacked the auctioneer and the clerks; in trying to escape, they overturned the counter, and the furious squire was in the midst of the crowd. A stampede ensued —more than a hundred men rushed toward the door fleeing from one. And he stood still shouting, "Out with you!" He sent curses after them, and now and then he swung over his head a chair, which he had used as a weapon. He followed them into the hall, but no further. When the last stranger left the doorstep, he returned to the salon and bolted the door after him. Then he gathered together a mattress and a pair of cushions, and lay down and went to sleep amid all the wild disorder, and did not wake till next day.

When Gösta got home he was told that Marienne wished to speak to him. It was just what he wanted. He had wondered how he might see her. When he entered the dimly lighted room in which she lay, he was obliged to pause a moment at the door, for he could not distinguish her.

"Stay where you are, Gösta," said Marienne to him. "It is perhaps dangerous to come near me."

But Gösta had come, taking the stairs in two strides, trembling with eager longing. What cared he now for infection? He longed for the bliss of again seeing her. She was so beautiful, his beloved. No one had such soft hair, such a clear, open brow; all her face was a play of lovely curves. He thought of her eyebrows, sharply and clearly pencilled like

the stamens of a lily, of the daring curve of the
nose, and the soft wave of the lips, and the long
oval of her cheek, and the refined cut of her chin.
And he thought of the clear complexion, of the be-
witching expression made by the black eyebrows
under the fair hair, and of the blue eyes in their
white setting, and of the gleam of light which hid
in the corners of them. She was so lovely, his beloved. He thought of the warm heart hiding under
her haughty mien. She had strength for love and
self-sacrifice under that fine skin and those proud
words. It was bliss to see her again. He had made
two steps of the stairs, did she think he would stand
now at the door? He sprang through the room and
knelt at her sofa. He meant to see her, kiss her,
and bid her farewell. He loved her, and would probably never cease to love her, but his heart was accustomed to suffering. Oh, where was he to find her,
the rose without support or root which he might
gather and call his own? He could not even keep
her he had found deserted and half dead in the
snowdrift. When would his love raise its song, a
song so high and pure that no discord would rend
it? When could his happiness build on a ground
which no other soul longed for? He thought of his
farewell to her.

"There is great trouble in your home to-day,"
he would say. "My heart ached at the sight of it.
You must go home and bring your father to his

senses. Your mother lives in constant fear of her life. You must go home again, my dearest."

He had those renunciating words on his lips, but they remained unuttered. He fell on his knees by the pillow, and he took her head between his hands and kissed it, and after that he found no words. His heart was beating so violently, it threatened to burst its bonds. The smallpox had gone over the lovely face. Its complexion was coarsened. Never again would the red blood show in the fair cheeks, nor the blue veins line the temples. The eyes lay heavy under swollen lids, the eyebrows were gone, and the white of the eyes was tinged with yellow. All was ruined. The daring curves were lost in heaviness. There were many who mourned Marienne Sinclaire's beauty, now lost. All over Värmland the people grieved over her lost fairness, her shining eyes and beautiful hair. Beauty is prized there as nowhere else, and the people sorrowed as if they had lost one of the brightest jewels in their crown, as if the sunniness of life had received a flaw.

But the first man who saw her after she had lost her beauty did not grieve.

Unutterable feelings filled his soul. The longer he gazed at her, the happier he grew. His love increased like a river in spring-time, it swelled from his heart in waves of fire, it filled all his being, it rose to his eyes in tears, sighed on his lips, shook in his hands and in all his being.

Oh, to love her, protect and cherish her! To be her slave, her guardian!

Love is strong when it has gone through the fire of pain. He could not talk to Marienne of separation and self-sacrifice now. He could not leave her. He was indebted to her for his life. He would have committed crimes for her sake.

He could not speak one sensible word, only wept and kissed her, till the old nurse came to say it was time he should go.

When he was gone, Marienne lay and thought of his being so moved. "It is good to be loved like that," she thought.

Yes, it was good to be loved, but how was it with herself? What did she feel? Oh, nothing, less than nothing.

Was her love dead, or what had become of it? Where had the child of her heart hidden itself? Did it live, had it crept into the darkest corner of her heart and lay there freezing under the gaze of those icy eyes, frightened by that pale, sneering laugh, half smothered under those hard, knotted fingers?

"Oh, my love," she sighed, "my heart's child! Do you live, or are you dead, as dead as my beauty?"

.   .   .   .

Next day the great squire, Melchior Sinclaire, went early to his wife.

"See that everything is put in order again here,
Gustafva," he said; "I am going to bring Marienne home."

"Yes, dear Melchior, I will put it all in order
again," she answered.

And everything was clear between them.

An hour later he was on his way to Ekeby.
There were not many nobler-looking or kindlier
old gentlemen than the great squire, as he sat in
his sledge in his best fur coat and belt. His hair
was smoothly combed, but his face was pale, and his
eyes appeared to have sunk in their sockets.

And there seemed no end to the glory which
streamed from heaven that February morning. The
snow glittered like a girl's eyes when the first notes
of a waltz are being played. The birches stretched
their fine network of red-brown branches over the
sky, and some of them had fingers of small, sparkling icicles. There was a glory and holiday glitter
about the day. The horses pranced, lifting high their
forefeet, and the coachman cracked his whip in
pure joy. After a short drive, the sledge drew up
before the great entrance to Ekeby.

A servant came out.

"Where are your masters?" asked the squire.

"They are hunting the great bear on Gurlita
Cliff."

"All of them?"

"All of them, sir. He that has not gone for the

sake of the bear has certainly gone for the sake of the provision basket."

Melchior Sinclaire laughed till it echoed in the empty yard. He gave the servant a daler for his sharp answer.

"Go and tell my daughter that I have come to fetch her. She won't freeze, for I have the sledge cover and a wolf-skin rug to wrap her in."

"Will not the squire please to enter?"

"Thanks. I am well enough here."

The man disappeared, and Melchior began his waiting. He was in such splendid mood that day, nothing could anger him. He expected to wait some time for Marienne, probably she was not up yet. He must amuse himself by looking about him.

A long icicle hung from the point of the roof, and the sun gave himself much trouble in melting it. It began from the top, melted a drop, and wanted it to run down the icicle and fall to earth, but before it reached halfway, it froze up afresh, and the sunshine made another effort and another, but always failed. At last there came a free-lance of a little sunbeam, which took possession of the tip of the icicle—a tiny little sunbeam, which shone and glittered with eagerness, till at last it gained its point, and a drop fell with a splash to the ground.

The great land proprietor watched it and laughed. "That wasn't at all so stupid of you," he said to the sunbeam.

The courtyard was quiet and deserted. Not a sound was heard from the big house, but the squire was not impatient. He knew that womenkind need a long time to get ready.

He looked at the dovecot. There was a wire over the opening. The birds were shut in for the winter so that the hawks might not get them. Every now and then a dove came and stuck its white head through the bars.

"She is waiting for spring," said Sinclaire, "but she must have patience yet."

The pigeon came so regularly to the bars that he took out his watch and timed her. She put out her head precisely every third minute.

"No, my little friend," he said; "do you think that spring can be ready in three minutes? You must learn to wait."

And he had to wait himself, but he was in no hurry.

The horses scraped the snow impatiently with their feet at first, but they soon became drowsy standing blinking in the sunshine. They leaned their heads together and went to sleep.

The coachman sat stiffly on his seat, with his reins and whip in his hand, facing the sun, and slept—slept so soundly that he snored.

But Melchior Sinclaire was not asleep. He never felt less like it. He had seldom spent such pleasant hours as while waiting there for Marienne. She had been ill. She could not come before, but she would come now. Of course she would, and all would be well again. She would understand now that he was not angry with her. He had come for her himself with two horses and a sledge.

Near the opening of the beehive a great titmouse was engaged upon a perfectly fiendish trick. He must have his dinner, of course, and he tapped, therefore, at the opening with his sharp little beak. Inside the hive the bees hung in a big, dark cluster. Everything within was in the strictest order. The workers dealt out the rations, and the cup-bearers ran from mouth to mouth with the nectar and ambrosia. With a constant creeping movement those hanging in the middle of the swarm changed places with those on the outside, so that warmth and comfort might be equally divided.

They hear the titmouse tapping, and the whole hive becomes a buzz of curiosity. Is it a friend or an enemy? Is there danger to the community? The queen has a bad conscience, she cannot wait in peace and quietness. Can it be the ghosts of murdered drones that are tapping out there? "Go and see what it is," she orders Sister Doorkeeper, and she goes. With a "Long live the Queen!" she rushes out and—ha!—the titmouse has got her! With outstretched neck and wings, trembling with eager-ness, he catches, kills, and eats her, and no one carries the tale of her fate to her companions. But the titmouse continues to tap and the queen to send forth her doorkeepers, and they all disappear. No one returns to tell her who is tapping. Ugh! it is awful to be alone in the dark hive—the spirit of revenge is there. Oh, to be without ears! If one only felt no curiosity, if one could only wait in patience!

Melchior Sinclaire laughed till tears filled his eyes at the silly womenkind in the beehive and the sharp, greeny-yellow little rascal outside.

There is no great difficulty in waiting when you are sure of your object, and when there is so much to engage your thoughts.

There comes the big yard dog. He steps along on the tips of his toes, keeps his eyes on the ground, and wags his tail gently, as if he were on the most indifferent errand. Suddenly he begins digging in the snow. The old rascal has certainly buried stolen goods there; but just as he lifts his head to see if he can enjoy in peace, he is surprised to see two magpies sitting right before him.

"You thief!" cry the magpies, looking like conscience itself, "we are police constables; give up your booty."

"Silence! you rabble, I am the yard bailiff."

"Just the man," they sneer.

The dog springs at them, and they fly up with lazy wing. He rushes on, jumping and barking; but while he hunts one, the other has returned to

the meat. She pulls and tears at it, but cannot lift
it. The dog snatches it away, places it between his
forepaws, and begins his dinner. The magpies seat
themselves before him, and continue their dispar-
aging remarks. He glances savagely at them, and
when it gets quite too bad, he springs up and chases
them away.

The sun began to sink behind the western hills.
Melchior Sinclaire looked at his watch; it was three
o'clock, and mother had had dinner ready at twelve.

Just then the servant came out and said Marienne wished to speak to him.

He placed the wolf-skin rug over his arm and
marched up the stairs in the best of humors.

When Marienne heard his heavy step on the
stairs, she did not know whether she would accompany him home or not. She only knew she must put
an end to the waiting. She had hoped the cavaliers
would come home, but they did not. She must then
take matters in hand herself, she could not bear it
any longer. She had imagined he would go his way
in anger after waiting five minutes, or that he would
break the door in, or set fire to the house.

But there he sat, calm and smiling, and waited.
She felt neither love nor hate toward him; but an
inner voice seemed to warn her against giving herself into his power again, and besides, she wished to
keep her word to Gösta.

If he had fallen asleep, if he had spoken or been

restless or shown a sign of doubt, if he had even
ordered the sledge to stand in the shade — but he
was all patience and certainty — sure, so infectiously
sure, that she would come if he only waited.

Her head ached, every nerve quivered. She could
get no peace while he sat there. It seemed as if his
will were dragging her, bound hand and foot, downstairs.

Then she decided to speak to him.

Before he came she made the nurse pull up the
blinds, and she lay so that her face was distinctly
seen. By this she meant to put him to the proof;
but Melchior Sinclaire was a wonderful man that
day.

When he saw her, he made no gesture, no cry of
surprise. It seemed as if he saw no difference in her.
She knew how he had prized her beauty; but he
showed no grief now, and kept control over all his
being so as not to cause her any farther sorrow.
This touched her, and she began to understand how
it was that her mother still loved him. He showed
no sign of hesitation. He came with no reproaches
or excuses.

"I will wrap you in the wolf-skin, Marienne. It
isn't cold, it has been lying on my knee all the
time."

In any case he went forward to the fire and
warmed it. Afterwards he helped her to rise, wrapped
the fur about her, drew a shawl over her head, pulled

it under her arms, and tied it at the back. She let him do it. She had no will. It was good to be commanded, it was restful to have no will. Best of all for one so tortured by self-analysis, for one who owned neither a thought nor a feeling that was her own!

Melchior Sinclaire lifted her up, carried her down to the sledge, threw back the cover, placed her beside him, and drove away from Ekeby.

She shut her eyes and sighed, half in satisfaction, half in sadness. She was leaving life, real life, behind her, but after all, it was a matter of indifference to her, who could not really live, but only play a part.

.   .   .   .

A few days later her mother arranged that she should see Gösta. She sent for him while her husband had gone for a long walk up to the timber stacks, and took him to Marienne.

Gösta entered the room, but he neither greeted nor spoke to her. He remained standing at the door, looking at the floor like an awkward boy.

"But, Gösta!" exclaimed Marienne. She was sitting in her armchair and looked at him half amused.

"Yes, that is my name."

"Come here, come nearer to me, Gösta."

He came forward quietly, but did not lift his eyes.

"Come nearer, kneel here!"

"Good God! what is the use of all this?" he exclaimed, but obeyed.

"Gösta, I wanted to tell you I thought it best to come home."

"We will hope that they do not turn Fröken Marienne into the snowdrifts again."

"Oh, Gösta, don't you love me any more? Do you think me so ugly?"

He drew her head down and kissed her, but he was just as cold as before.

She was really amused. If he chose to be jealous of her parents, what did it matter? It would pass. It amused her now to win him back. She hardly knew why she wanted him, but she did. She remembered that he had freed her from herself once at least; he was probably the only one who could do it again. And she began to speak eagerly to him. She said it had not been her intention to desert him, but they must, for the sake of appearances, break this engagement for a time. He had seen himself that her father was on the verge of madness, and her mother lived in constant fear of her life. He must understand that she had been obliged to return home.

Then his anger found words. She need not pretend. He would no longer be her plaything. She had jilted him as soon as she found she might return home, and he could not love her any more. On the day when he came home from the bear hunt and found her gone without a word of farewell, his blood had stood still in his veins, and he had nearly died of sorrow. He could not love her after the pain she had caused him. And she had never really loved him. She was a coquette who wanted some one to kiss and caress her here at home too — that was all.

Did he think, then, she usually let young men kiss and caress her?

Oh, yes, why not? Women were not so holy as they looked. They were made up of selfishness and coquetry. No, if she knew what he had felt when he came home from the woods and found her gone! He felt as if he had waded in ice water. He would never get over that pain. It would follow him all his life, and he would never be the same again.

She tried to explain to him how it all happened; she reminded him that she had been true through it all.

Yes, but it was all the same, for he did n't love her any longer. He had seen through her, she was selfish. She never had loved him, she had left him without a word.

He constantly returned to this, and she almost enjoyed the scene, for she could not be angry. She understood his anger so well, she did not even fear any real break between them. But at last she grew anxious. Had such a change really taken place that he cared no more for her?

"Gösta," she said, "was I selfish when I went to Sjö for the Major? I remembered very well that the smallpox was there. Neither is it pleasant to be out in thin shoes in the cold snow."

"Love lives by love, and not by service and good works," he replied.

"You want us to be strangers in the future?"

"Yes."

"Gösta Berling is very changeable."

"They say so."

He was apathetic, impossible to awaken, and really she felt herself even colder. Self-analysis sat and sneered at her attempt to play at being in love.

"Gösta," she pleaded at last, "I have never wilfully wronged you, even if it has seemed like it. I beg you, forgive me!"

"I cannot forgive you."

She knew that if she had had any whole feeling about her she could have won him, and she tried to act a passionate love. The icy eyes mocked her, but she tried in any case. She did not want to lose him.

"Don't go, Gösta, don't leave me in anger. Think how ugly I have become now. No one will love me again."

"I don't love you either," he answered. "You must get accustomed to having your heart trampled upon, as others do."

"Gösta, I have never been able to love any one

but you. Forgive me, and don't leave me. You are the only one who can save me from myself."

He pushed her aside.

"You are not speaking the truth," he said, with icy calm. "I don't know what you want of me, but I see you are lying. Why would you keep me? You are so rich, there will always be lovers for you."

So he left her. And as soon as he closed the door, longing and pain made entrance in all their majesty into Marienne's heart. It was Love, her heart's one child, who came forth from the corner where the icy eyes had hidden him. He, the longed-for one, came now when it was too late. All-powerful, he took possession, and longing and pain bore up his kingly mantle.

When Marienne could with certainty say to herself that Gösta Berling had deserted her, she experienced a purely physical pain, so dreadful that she nearly lost consciousness. She pressed her hands against her heart, and sat for hours in the same position, fighting her tearless grief. And she suffered —she, herself, not a stranger nor an outsider. She, herself, suffered it all. Why had her father come and separated them? Her love had not been dead. It was only that in the weakness subsequent to her illness she could not feel its power.

Oh, God, oh, God, to lose him! Oh, God, to have awakened too late! He was the only man who had conquered her heart. She could bear all from him.

Angry words and harshness from him only bowed
her down in humble love. If he struck her, she would
creep to his hand like a dog and kiss it. She did not
know what to do to find alleviation for this dumb
pain.

She caught up a pen and some paper and began
to write. She wrote of her love and her longing, and
she begged not for his love but for mercy. It was
a kind of verse that she wrote. When she finished,
she thought that perhaps if he saw it he might believe in her love. Why should she not send it to
him? She would send it next day, and she quite
believed that it would bring him back to her.

Next day she went about in mental strife with
herself. What she had written seemed so weak, so
feeble. It had neither rhyme nor metre: it was only
prose. He might laugh at such poetry, and her pride
awoke, too. If he did not love her, it was a great
degradation to beg for his love. Now and again pru-
dence whispered that she ought to be thankful to
have escaped the connection with Gösta Berling and
all the wretched circumstances it would bring in its
train. But the aching of her heart was so great that
her feelings, after all, must have their way.

Three days later she put the verses in an envelope
and wrote Gösta Berling's name upon it. Still they
were not sent. Before she found a suitable messenger, she heard such tales of Gösta Berling that she
felt it was too late to win him back. But it became

the sorrow of her life that she had not sent the verses in time to win him. All her pain circled round that point. "If I had not waited so long; if I had not let so many days go by." Those written words would have given her happiness or at least life's reality. She was certain they would have brought him back.

Sorrow did for her the same service love would have done. It moulded her into a whole individuality with a strength of devotion for good or evil. Strong feelings streamed through her soul, never again frozen by the spirit of self-analysis. And so, in spite of her lost beauty, she was greatly loved. Yet they say she never forgot Gösta Berling. She mourned him as one mourns over a wasted life.

And her poor verses, which were much read at one time, have long since been forgotten. Yet they are very touching, as I look at them, written on yellowed paper in faded ink, in a close, elegant handwriting. There is the longing of a whole life bound up in those poor words, and I copy them with a mysterious sense of awe, as if some secret strength lay in them.

I beg you to read and think them over. Who knows what power they might have had if they had been sent? They are passionate enough to bear witness to true feeling. Perhaps they would have brought him back to her. They are tender and wistful in their awkward formlessness. No one would

o

wish them different. No one would wish them bound
in the chains of rhyme and metre, and yet it is sad
to remember that it was perhaps this imperfection
which prevented her sending them in time.

I beg you to read them and to love them. It was
a human heart in great need that inspired them.

> " *Child, you have loved, but ne'er again*
> *Shall you taste of the pleasure of love.*
> *The storms of passion have shaken your soul;*
> *Be thankful you'll now be at rest.*
> *Ne'ermore shall you soar to the heights of love;*
> *Be thankful you now are at rest!*
> *Ne'er again shall you sink to the depths of pain—*
> *Ne'er again.*

> " *Child, you have loved, but ne'er again*
> *Will your soul ever burst into flame.*
> *You were filled, like a field of sun-dried grass,*
> *For a moment with burning fire.*
> *Before the clouds of smoke and the burning coal,*
> *Heaven's birds fled forth with frightened screams.*
> *Let them turn again! for never again—*
> *You'll ne'er burn again.*

> " *Child, he is gone—*
> *And with him all love and the pleasures of love—*
> *He whom you had loved, as if he had taught*
> *Your pinions flight in the heavens above,*

He whom you loved, as if he had given you
The only safe spot in an overwhelmed world.
He is gone—he who alone understood how to open
    The door of your heart.

"I would entreat you for one thing, oh, my beloved! —
Lay not on me the burden of hate!
The weakest of all weak things is it not a human heart?
How should it then endure the awful thought
That it is a torment to others?
Oh, my beloved, if you would kill me,
Seek not daggers or poison or rope;

"Let me but know that you would have me turn
From earth's green fields, from the kingdom of life,
And I will sink into my grave.
You gave me the life of life, you gave me love,
But you take your love again. Oh, I know it well,
But turn it not to hate!
Oh, remember — I would still live —
Yet I would die beneath the burden of hate."

The Young Countess

THE young Countess slept till ten o'clock every morning, and liked to have fresh bread every day on the breakfast table. The young Countess did tambour work and read poetry; she understood nothing of cooking or weaving. The young Countess was decidedly spoiled. But she was joyous and let her happiness shine upon everything and everybody. The long sleep in the morning and the fresh bread were easily forgiven her, for she was a spendthrift in doing good to the poor and was friendly to every one.

Her father was a Swedish nobleman, who had spent all his life in Italy, kept prisoner there by the beauty of the country and by one of its beautiful daughters. When Count Henrik Dohna had travelled in Italy, he had been received in their home, he had learned to know the daughters, had married one of them and brought her back to Sweden.

She, who had always known Sweden and had been brought up to love all that was Swedish, was very happy in the "Bear Country." She whirled along so gaily in the long dance of pleasure that circled round the Löfven shore, you might imagine she had always lived there. She understood little of what it meant to be a countess. There was no stateliness, no stiffness, no patronizing air about that gay young creature.

The old gentlemen were perhaps the most fond of her. After they had seen her at a ball, you could be quite certain that every one of them — the Judge at Munkerud and the Rector of Bro, Melchior Sinclaire and the Captain at Berga — they all confided to their wives in the strictest confidence that if they had met her thirty or forty years ago—!

"Yes, but she certainly had not been born then," cried the old ladies. And the next time they met they teased the young Countess about stealing the hearts of the old gentlemen from them.

The old ladies watched her with a certain amount of anxiety. They remembered so well Countess Märta. She, too, had been joyous and good and beloved when she first came to Borg. And she was now nothing but a vain coquette, and could think of nothing but amusement. "If she only had a husband who would make her do some work," said the old ladies. "If she would only set up a loom"—for to weave is a comfort for all sorrow, it absorbs all other interests, and has been the saving of many a woman.

The young Countess wished very earnestly to be a good housewife. She knew of nothing better than to be a happy wife in a happy home, and often during one of the big assemblies she came and sat down among the old ladies.

"Henrik wishes so much that I should become

a clever manager," she used to say, "as his mother
is. Do teach me how you set up a loom!"

And the old ladies sighed a two-fold sigh — the
first over Count Henrik, who could imagine his
mother to be a good housewife; and the second over
the difficulty of initiating any one so young and
ignorant into such a complicated thing. You had
only to mention skeins and heddles, mounting single and double threading, and it all spun round in
her head.

No one who saw the young Countess could
help wondering why she married that stupid Count
Henrik.

He who is stupid is to be pitied, whoever he is,
but he is most to be pitied if he lives in Värmland.
There were already many stories abroad about his
stupidity, and he was only a few years over twenty.
The way he entertained Anna Stjärnhök during a
sleighing party is a specimen.

"You are very beautiful, Anna," he said.

"Nonsense, Henrik!"

"You are the most beautiful girl in all Värmland."

"Certainly I'm not."

"You are, in any case, the loveliest at this sleighing party."

"Oh, no, Henrik, I'm not."

"Well, you are certainly the best looking in this
sledge. You can't deny that?"

No, she could not deny that.

For Count Henrik was not handsome. He was as ugly as he was stupid. They said of him that the head on his shoulders had been an inheritance in the family for a few hundred years, therefore the brain was so worn out in the present possessor. "It is clear he has no head of his own," they said; "he has borrowed his father's. He dare not bend it, he is afraid it might drop off. He is already quite yellow and wrinkled; his head has evidently been in use both in his father's and grandfather's time, otherwise the hair would not be so thin and his lips so bloodless and his chin so sharp."

He was constantly surrounded by a crowd of jokers who tempted him into saying stupid things, and then they collected them, spread them abroad, and helped them out.

It was a mercy he noticed nothing. He was dignified and pompous in all he did, he never dreamed others were different; respectability had taken bodily shape in him — he moved languidly, he walked stiffly, he never turned his head without his whole body following it.

One day, some years ago, he had been at Munkerud, at the Judge's. He had ridden there in tall hat, yellow riding-trousers, and shining boots, sitting stiffly and proudly in his saddle. His arrival passed off very well, but when he rode away it happened that one of the overhanging branches in the birch alley knocked his hat off. He descended, put his hat on, and rode away once more under the same branch. Again the hat was knocked off. This was repeated four times.

The Judge came out at last, and said, "Suppose you try riding to the side of the branch next time!"

And he passed it successfully the fifth time.

And yet, in spite of his ancient head, the young Countess was fond of him. Of course, when she saw him in Rome, she did not know he was surrounded by such a martyr-like halo of stupidity. There had been something of a youthful glamour over him then, and they had been married in such very romantic circumstances. You should have heard her relate how Count Henrik eloped with her. Monks and cardinals had been furious that she should desert her mother's religion and become a Protestant. All the populace were in an uproar, her father's palace was besieged, and Henrik was pursued by bandits. Her mother and sister prayed her to give up the marriage, but her father was wild to think the Italian rabble should dare to try and hinder him from giving his daughter to whomever he chose. He commanded Count Henrik to elope with her, and as it was impossible for them to be married at home without it being discovered, she had crept with Henrik along back streets and all kinds of dark passages to the Swedish Consulate, and when she had abjured her Catholic faith and become a Protestant,

they were instantly married and came north in a
swiftly travelling coach. "There was no time for any
banns, you see, it was quite impossible," the young
Countess used to say; "and, of course, it wasn't as
nice being married at the Consulate as in one of
the beautiful churches, but Henrik couldn't possibly get me in any other way. They are all so hasty
there—both papa and mamma and the cardinals
and monks, all of them. We were obliged to keep
it secret, and if the people had seen us leave home,
they would certainly have killed us both—just to
save my soul. Henrik's was, of course, lost already."

But the young Countess was fond of her husband
even when they arrived at Borg and lived a quieter
life. She loved the splendor of the old name he
bore and the fame of his adventurous forefathers.
She liked to see how her presence softened him, and
to hear his voice take another tone when she talked
to him. And besides he was fond of her and spoiled
her, and, after all, she was married to him. The young
Countess could not imagine a married woman not
caring for her husband.

In a certain way he answered her ideal of man-
liness. He was just and loved the truth. He had
never broken his promised word. She considered
him a true nobleman.

.   .   .   .

On the 18th of March, the high sheriff, Schärling,

celebrated his birthday, and there were many who drove up Broby Hill that day. From east and west, known and unknown, the invited and uninvited guests came on that occasion to the official residence. All were welcome. There was meat and drink for all, and in the dancing-hall there was room enough for the dancers from seven parishes.

The young Countess was there too, as she was everywhere where you could expect dancing and amusement. But she was not gay when she arrived, it almost seemed as though she had a presentiment that it was now her turn to be involved in the wild wave of adventure.

She sat and watched the setting sun while driving to the assembly. It sank from a cloudless sky, and left no golden-edged cloudlets after it. Pale grey twilight pierced by gusts of chilly wind covered all the country.

She saw the strife of day and night, and how everything living seemed to fear it. Horses hurried forward the last load to gain their stables as quickly as possible. The wood-cutters hurried home from the forest, the dairymaids from the farmyard. Wild beasts howled in the forest clearing. Day, the beloved of mankind, was conquered.

Colors faded, the light disappeared. Cold and ugliness was all she saw. All she hoped, all she loved, all she had ever done seemed wrapped in the twilight's grey coverlet. It was an hour of weariness, depression, and helplessness for her, as it was for all nature.

She remembered that her heart, which now in its joy lifted all life into a shimmer of purple and gold, might lose its strength to raise her world.

"Oh, helplessness, my own heart's helplessness!" she said to herself. "Crushing goddess of the twilight, one day you will conquer my soul, and I shall see life ugly and hard, as perhaps it is, and my hair will whiten then, and my back will bend, and my mind will grow dull."

At that moment the sledge swung into the courtyard, and, as she looked up, her eyes fell upon a barred window in a side wing of the house and on a grim face looking out of it.

The face was that of the Major's wife at Ekeby, and the young Countess knew that all her pleasure was spoiled for that evening.

It is possible to be joyous when you don't know sorrow and only hear it mentioned as a guest in another country. It is more difficult to keep the heart gay when you stand face to face with dark, cruel trouble.

The Countess knew that the high sheriff had arrested the Major's wife, and that she was to be tried for what had taken place at Ekeby on the night of the ball there; but she had never dreamed that she would be kept in the official residence, so near them that they could see her room, so near

that she could hear the dance music and the sound
of their voices. And the thought of the Major's
wife took all the Countess's pleasure away.

Of course she danced both waltz and quadrille,
minuet and anglaise, but between the dances she
crept to the window and looked across the courtyard to the side wing. There was a light in the
room there, and she could see Margarita Samzelius
pacing backward and forward. She seemed never to
rest, but to walk to and fro unceasingly.

The Countess found no pleasure in dancing, she
was thinking all the time of the Major's wife pacing
restlessly up and down her prison like a caged beast.
She wondered how the others could dance; there
were many there who must be quite as touched at
the knowledge of their old friend being so near
them as she was, but none of them showed a trace
of it. The Värmlanders are a reserved people.

After each glance through the window, her feet
grew heavier and the laugh caught in her throat.
Schärling's wife saw her at last, as she brushed the
vapor from the window-pane and tried to look out,
and came and whispered to her, "Such a misfortune! Oh, dear, it is such a misfortune!"

"I feel it nearly impossible to dance to-night,"
whispered the Countess.

"It is against my wish we have a ball at all while
she is imprisoned here," answered Fru Schärling.
"She has been in Karlstad since she was arrested.

She is to be tried very soon, and they brought her
here to-day. We could not put her into the wretched
jail at the courthouse, so she was given the weav-
ing-room in the side wing. She would have been
in my drawing-room, Countess, if all these people
had n't come to-day. You know her so slightly, but
she has been like a mother and queen to us all.
What will she think of us dancing here while she
is in such trouble? It is a mercy that only a few
know she is here."

"She ought never to have been arrested," said
the Countess, sternly.

"That is true, but there was no other way, unless
worse were to happen. There is no one who would
deny her right to setting her own strawstacks on
fire and turning the cavaliers out of Ekeby, but
the Major is hunting the country for her. God alone
knows what he might have done if she had n't been
arrested! Schärling has had much unpleasantness
for arresting her. Even in Karlstad they were angry
that he had not looked through his fingers at the
doings at Ekeby, but he did what he thought was
best."

"But will she be condemned now?" asked the
Countess.

"Oh, no, Countess, she won't. The Lady of Ekeby
will never be found guilty, but I am afraid it will
all be too much for her. She will go mad. You can
imagine such a proud woman cannot bear being

treated like a criminal. I think it would have been wisest to have let her alone; she would have escaped him in her own way."

"Let her out," said the Countess.

"That can be done by others rather than the sheriff and his wife," whispered Fru Schärling. "We must guard her—especially to-night, when so many of her friends are here. Two men keep watch at her door, and it is barred so that no one can get at her. But if some one got her away, both Schärling and I should be so glad."

"Could I see her?" asked the young Countess.

Fru Schärling caught her hand eagerly and led her out. They threw shawls over their shoulders, and then crossed the courtyard.

"It is very possible she won't speak to us," said the sheriff's wife; "but she will see, at least, that we have not forgotten her."

They entered the first room in the wing, where the two men sat at the barred doors, and they were allowed entrance into the further room. It was a large chamber full of looms and other work instruments. It was commonly used as a weaving-shed, but it had a barred window and a strong lock on the door, and could, in case of necessity, be used as a jail.

The Major's wife continued her tramp up and down without paying any attention to them.

She was on a long journey. She remembered nothing but that she was on her way to her mother, who was waiting for her in the Älfdal forests. She had no time to rest; she must cross the hundred and forty miles that separated them; she must go on, and quickly, for her mother was over ninety years old, and she would be dead soon. She had measured out the floor into ells, and then counted up the ells into fathoms, and the fathoms into half-miles and miles.

The way seems long and weary to her, and yet she dare not rest. She wades through deep snow-drifts; she hears the murmur of the everlasting forests as she walks onward. She takes her mid-day and evening meal, and rests in the huts of the Finns and the charcoal-burner's shanty. Sometimes, where there is no human habitation for many, many miles, she is obliged to gather branches and make a bed for herself at the root of an overturned pine.

And at last she reaches her destination—the long miles are all behind her, the forest opens out, and a red house stands in a snow-covered yard. The Klar-älfven rushes along in a series of small rapids, and by the well-remembered thunder of its waters she realizes she is at home.

And her mother, who sees her coming like a beggar as she desired, comes to meet her.

When the Major's wife reached this point, she always looked up, glanced about her, saw the barred door, and remembered where she was.

Then she wondered if she was not going mad, and sat down to rest and think. But after a time she was again on the march, counting the ells and fathoms into miles, taking a short rest at the huts along the way, and sleeping neither day nor night till she had gone over the hundred and forty miles again.

During the time of her imprisonment she had hardly ever slept, and the two women who had come to see her gazed at her anxiously. The young Countess ever afterwards remembered her as she looked then. She often dreamed of her, and woke with tears in her eyes and a cry on her lips.

The old lady was so broken down; her hair was so thin, and loose ends streamed from the thin plait. Her face looked weak and hollow, her clothes were disordered and ragged, but she had still enough of the old imperiousness of the powerful Lady Bountiful about her so that she did not only inspire pity, but also respect.

But the young Countess chiefly remembered her eyes—sunken, retrospective, the light of reason in them not yet destroyed, but ready to die out—with a fierce gleam in their depths, so that you feared she might attack you with biting teeth and with clawing hands.

They had stood watching her for some time, when the Major's wife paused before the young Countess and looked at her severely. The Countess took a step backward, and clutched Fru Schärling's arm.

The old woman's face suddenly awoke to life and gained expression, and her eyes looked out upon the world with understanding. "Oh, no! oh, no!" she said, and smiled; "it isn't as bad as all that, my young lady."

She directed them to sit down, and seated herself with the air of stateliness belonging to the old days—to the great assemblies at Ekeby and the state balls at the Governor's residence at Karlstad. They forgot the rags and the prison, and saw again the proudest and richest woman in Värmland.

"My dear Countess," she asked, "what could have induced you to leave the dancing and visit a lonely old woman like me? You must be very good."

Countess Elizabeth could not answer. Her voice shook too much, and Fru Schärling answered for her that she could not dance while thinking of the Major's wife.

"Dear Fru Schärling," she said, "has it gone so far with me that I spoil the young people's pleasure? You must not cry for my sake, my dear little Countess," she continued. "I'm a wicked old woman who deserve my fate. You don't think it right to strike your mother?"

"No, but—"

The Major's wife interrupted her, smoothing the fair curly hair over her forehead. "Child, child," she said, "how could you marry that stupid Henrik Dohna?"

P

"But I love him!"

"I see how it is, I see how it is—a good child
and nothing more, crying with those that weep, and
laughing with those that rejoice, and obliged to say
'Yes' to the first man who says 'I love you.' Yes,
yes. Now go in and dance, my dear Countess, dance
and be gay. There is no ill in you."

"But I want to do something for you!"

"Child," she answered, with dignity, "there lived
an old woman at Ekeby, who held the winds of
heaven in her hand. Now she is imprisoned and the
winds are free. Is it wonderful that a great storm
rages through the land?

"I am old, and I've seen it before. I know it, I
know that God's fearful storm is upon us. Sometimes it sweeps over the great nations, sometimes
over small forgotten communities. God's storm forgets no one: it overwhelms the great and the small.
It is wonderful to see its approach.

"Oh, blessed storm of the Lord, blow over the
earth! Voices in the air, voices in the water, sound
and terrify! Make God's storm thunder, and make
it fearful. May its stormy gusts sweep over the earth,
beating against shaking walls, breaking the rusty
locks and the houses that are falling to ruin.

"Terror shall spread over the country. The little
birds' nests shall fall from their hold in the pine
trees, and the hawk's nest shall fall from the fir-top
with a great noise, and even into the owl's nest on

the mountain ledge shall the wind hiss with its dragon tongues.

"We thought all was well here among us, but it was not. God's storm was needed. I understand, and I do not complain. I only wish to go at once to my mother."

She seemed to sink together suddenly.

"Go now, young woman," she commanded. "I have no more time; I must go at once. Go now, and beware of those who ride on the storm clouds!"

And she returned to her restless walk. Her features lost their firmness, her eyes grew vacant. The Countess and Fru Schärling left her.

As soon as they were again among the dancers, the Countess went straight to Gösta Berling.

"I bring you a greeting from the Major's wife, Herr Berling," she said. "She expects you to help her out of prison."

"Then she must continue to expect it, Countess."

"Oh, help her, Herr Berling!"

Gösta gazed sternly before him. "No," he replied; "why should I help her? What have I to thank her for? All she has done for me has been my ruin."

"But, Herr Berling—"

"If she had not existed," he said passionately, "I should now be sleeping in the everlasting forest. Must I feel it necessary to risk my life for her, because she made me an Ekeby cavalier? Do you

think, Countess, there is any renown to be gained
in that capacity?"

She turned from him without answering, she was
so angry, and went to her place, thinking bitterly
of the cavaliers. They are all there to-night with
their horns and violins, and they intend to let the
bows fly over the strings till they wear out, and
without giving a thought to the fact that the gay
music must penetrate to the prisoner's miserable
room. They have come there to dance till their
shoes go to dust, and they never think that their
old benefactress can see their shadows swing by on
the dimmed window-panes.

Oh, how ugly and grey the world had become!
What a shadow trouble and harshness were casting
over her soul!

A little later, Gösta Berling came and asked her
to dance.

She refused shortly.

"The young Countess will not dance with me?"
he asked, flushing hotly.

"Neither with you nor any of the Ekeby cavaliers," she answered.

"We are then not considered worthy of the
honor?"

"It is no honor, Herr Berling; but I find no pleasure in dancing with those who have forgotten all
the precepts of gratitude."

Gösta had already swung round on his heel.

The scene had been witnessed by many, and every one thought the Countess right. The ingratitude and heartlessness of the cavaliers had awakened universal disapproval.

But in those days Gösta Berling was more dangerous to cross than a wild beast of the forest. Ever since he came home from bear-hunting and found Marienne had left Ekeby, his heart was like an open sore. He had an aching desire to injure some one—any one—to spread sorrow and misery around him.

"If she desires it, she shall have it," he said to himself; "but she must not spare her own skin. The Countess likes elopements, she shall have more than she likes of them." He had nothing against an adventure. For eight days he had sorrowed for a woman's sake. It was enough. He called up Beerencreutz, the Colonel, and Kristian Bergh, the Strong Captain, and trusty Cousin Kristoffer, who never hesitated at a mad adventure, and held counsel with them how best to revenge the damaged honor of the cavaliers.

.   .   .   .

Soon after this the ball came to an end. A long line of sledges drove up to the door. The gentlemen·put on their fur coats, the ladies sought their wraps in the deepest confusion of the dressing-room.

The young Countess hastened to leave that hateful ball, and was ready first. She stood in the middle of the room, smiling at the excitement round her, when the door was thrown open and Gösta Berling crossed the threshold.

No man had the right to enter that room. The old ladies had their heads uncovered after putting away their splendid caps, and the younger ladies had tucked up their skirts so that their frills might not get crushed on the homeward drive.

But without paying attention to arresting cries, Gösta Berling strode forward to the Countess, lifted her in his arms, and rushed out of the room into the hall and out upon the doorsteps with her.

The cries of the astonished women did not stop him, and when they reached the hall door, they saw him throw himself into a sledge with the Countess still in his arms.

They heard the driver crack his whip and saw the horse spring forward. They recognized the driver —it was Beerencreutz, the horse was Don Juan —and with fear in their hearts for the fate of the Countess, they called to their husbands.

The men lost no time in questions, but dashed to the sledges, and with the Count at their head, they started after the runaways.

Meanwhile Gösta Berling sat in the sledge, holding the young Countess securely. He had forgotten all his sorrows, and, wild with the maddening spirit of adventure, he sang a song of love and roses.

He held her pressed closely to him, but she made

no attempt to escape. Her face lay, white and stony, on his breast.

What shall a man do when a pale, helpless face lies so near him, when he sees the fair hair swept aside, which usually shadows the shining brow, and the eyelids lie heavily over the gleam of smiling grey eyes? What shall a man do when red lips whiten under the gaze of his eyes?

Why, kiss them, of course—kiss the pale lips, the closed eyes, and white brows.

But at that the young Countess awoke. She threw herself aside. She was like a steel wand, and he was obliged to exert all his strength to prevent her from throwing herself out, till he forced her at last, conquered and trembling, into a corner of the sledge.

"See," he said, quite calmly to Beerencreutz, "the Countess is the third that Don Juan and I have carried away this winter; but the other two hung round my neck with kisses, and she will neither be kissed by me nor dance with me. Can you understand these women, Beerencreutz?"

When Gösta had left the courtyard, while the women were screaming and the men cursing, when the sleigh-bells rang, and the whips cracked, and all was shouting and confusion, the men who were guarding the Major's wife grew frightened.

"What is the matter?" they thought. "Why do they shout so?"

Suddenly the door was thrown open, and a voice cried to them, "She is gone. He has carried her off!"

Out they flew, running like madmen, without finding out if it was the Major's wife or some one else who had been carried away. They had good luck too, and managed to climb into a passing sledge, and it was a long time before they learned whom they were trying to overtake.

But Bergh and Cousin Kristoffer marched calmly to the door of the improvised jail, broke the lock, and opened it for the Major's wife.

"The Lady of Ekeby is free," they said.

She came out. They stood as straight as ninepins on each side of the door, but did not meet her eyes.

"Your horse and sledge await you downstairs."

She went down, seated herself, and drove away. No one followed her, and no one knew whither she went.

Down Broby Hill, toward the ice-bound Löfven, Don Juan rushed. The proud racer flew over the snow; the frosty air whistled in the faces of the drivers; the sleigh-bells rang out; the moon and stars glittered, and the snow lay blue and white, shining with its own splendor.

Gösta felt his poetic fancy awakened. "Beeren-creutz," he cried, "this is life. As Don Juan carries away the young women, so Time carries away the individual. You are Necessity steering the course. I am Desire which tames the will, and so she is carried helpless, ever deeper and deeper downward."

"Don't talk nonsense," growled Beerencreutz; "they are after us,"—and a whistling cut of the whip urged Don Juan to still greater speed.

"There are the wolves, here is the booty," cried Gösta. "Don Juan, my boy, imagine yourself a young elk. Break your way through the ensnaring bushes, wade through the marsh. Leap from the crest of the hill range into the clear lake, swim over with proudly lifted head, and vanish, vanish into the dense darkness of the firwood. Run, Don Juan, run like a young elk!"

Joy filled his wild heart at the speed. The shouts of his pursuers were songs of exultation. Joy filled his wild heart when he felt the Countess shake with fear, and heard her teeth chattering.

Suddenly he loosened the iron grasp in which he had held her. He stood upright in the sledge, and swung his cap.

"I am Gösta Berling," he shouted, "the lord of ten thousand kisses and thirteen thousand love-letters. Hurrah for Gösta Berling! Catch him who can!"

And the next moment he was whispering to the Countess, "Is n't the speed fine? Is n't our drive royal? Beyond Löfven lies Vänern, beyond Vänern lies the sea—endless stretches of clear, blue-black ice, and beyond it all a shining world. Rolling thunder in the freezing ice, shrill shouts behind us, shooting stars in the heavens, and ringing sleighbells before us! Forward—forever forward! Now, do you wish to make trial of such a journey, Countess?"

He had freed her, and she pushed him aside violently.

The next moment found him on his knees at her feet.

"I am a wretch, a miserable wretch. You should not have angered me. You stood there so proud and pure, and never dreamed that a cavalier's fist could reach you. You are loved by heaven and earth; you should not increase the burden of those whom heaven and earth despise."

He snatched her hands, and pressed them to his face.

"If you but knew," he pleaded, "what it meant to know yourself an outcast! You don't care what you do—you never care."

Just then he noticed that her hands were uncovered. He drew a pair of large fur gloves out of his pockets, and put them on for her.

And with that he became quite calm. He seated himself in the sledge as far as possible from the Countess.

"It is n't worth while being frightened, Countess," he said. "Don't you see where we are driving to? You can surely understand that we never intended to do you any harm!"

She had been nearly out of her senses with fear, and only noticed now that they had crossed the river, and Don Juan was drawing them up the steep hill to Borg.

They pulled up before the steps, and allowed the Countess to alight at her own door; but as soon as she was surrounded by protecting servants, she regained her courage and presence of mind.

"Take charge of the horse," she commanded the coachman. "These gentlemen who have driven me home will surely come in for a few moments. The Count will be here directly."

"As the Countess desires," replied Gösta, and stepped immediately out of the sledge, and Beerencreutz, too, threw the reins aside without a moment's hesitation. But the young Countess preceded them, and showed them, with hardly concealed exultation, into the salon.

She had probably expected they would hesitate to accept her proposal to await her husband's return. Of course, they could not know what a stern and just man he was. They did not seem to fear the judgment he would mete out to them for having so violently laid hold of her and compelled her to take that drive. She wished to hear him forbid them ever to set foot in her house again.

She wanted to see him call in the servants and

point out the cavaliers as men who were never again to be admitted within the doors of Borg. She wished to hear him express his scorn, not only for the way they had treated her, but also for their ingratitude toward the Major's wife, their benefactress.

Yes, he, who to her was all tenderness and consideration, would rise in just wrath against her captors. Love would lend fire to his words. He who protected and cared for her as for a being of another world, he would never allow rough men to descend upon her like hawks upon a sparrow. The little woman glowed from head to foot with the desire for revenge. Her husband would help her in her helplessness and drive away all the dark shadows.

But Beerencreutz, the Colonel, with the thick white moustache, strode unconcernedly into the dining-room and walked up to the fire, which was always burning there when the Countess was expected home from a ball.

Gösta remained in the darkness near the door, and silently watched the Countess while the servants relieved her of her outer garments. As he sat looking at her, he rejoiced as he had not done for many years. It was so clear to him — as certain as if it had been revealed to him — that within her dwelt the most beautiful soul. It lay bound and sleeping yet, but it would awaken. He rejoiced greatly at having discovered all the purity and the goodness and the innocence that lay hidden within her. He

could almost have laughed at her standing there
looking so angry, with burning cheeks and frowning eyebrows.

"You don't know how good and sweet you are,"
he thought. That side of her character which inclined toward the world of the senses would never
do her real self justice. But from that hour, Gösta
Berling was compelled to be her servant, as one
serves all that is beautiful and godly. Yes, it was no
good regretting that he had treated her so roughly.
If she had not been so frightened, if she had not
pushed him aside so wildly, if he had not felt that
all her being was shuddering at his coarseness, he
would never have known, never have guessed, what
a noble and sensitive spirit dwelt within her.

He never had believed it before. She had only
cared for dancing and amusement, and she had found
it possible to marry that stupid Count Henrik.

Yes, now he would be her slave till death —
"dog and slave," as Captain Kristian used to say,
"and nothing more."

Gösta Berling sat near the door with folded hands,
and held a kind of adoration service. Since the day
he had felt the fire of inspiration touch him, he
had never experienced such blessedness in his soul.
Though Count Henrik came into the room with
a crowd of men, all swearing and lamenting over
the cavaliers' many pranks, it did not distract him.
He let Beerencreutz meet the storm, and he, the

man of many adventures, stood calmly at the fireplace with his foot on the bars and his elbow on his
knee, and gazed at the storming crowd.

"What is the meaning of this?" the little Count
screamed.

"It means," Beerencreutz replied, "that as long
as there remains womankind on earth, there will
always be fools to dance to their piping!"

The young Count grew very red in the face.

"I ask what this means!" he repeated.

"I also ask," mocked Beerencreutz, "I ask what
it means when Henrik Dohna's Countess refuses
to dance with Gösta Berling!"

The Count turned questioningly to his wife.

"I could not, Henrik," she cried; "I could not
dance with him or any of them. I thought of the
Major's wife whom they were allowing to die in
prison."

The little Count straightened his stiff body and
stretched out his old-fashioned head.

"We cavaliers," continued Beerencreutz, "allow
no one to insult us. She that will not dance with us
must drive with us. The Countess has received no
harm, and that can be the end of the matter."

"No," said the Count, "that can't end the matter. I am answerable for my wife's doings. I desire
to know why Gösta Berling did not apply to me
when my wife insulted him."

Beerencreutz smiled.

"I desire to know," repeated the Count.

"One does not ask leave of the fox to take his skin," said Beerencreutz.

The Count laid his hand on his narrow chest.

"I have the reputation of being a just man," he cried. "I judge my servants, why cannot I judge my wife? You cavaliers have no right to judge her. The punishment you meted out to her, I put aside. It has never taken place, gentlemen, it has never taken place."

Count Henrik shrieked out the words in the highest falsetto. Beerencreutz sent a rapid glance over the company. There was not one of them — Sintram and Daniel Bendix and Dahlberg, and whoever they all were who had followed them in — who was not grinning at the way he was outwitting the stupid young Count.

The Countess did not understand at first. What was it that had never taken place? Her fear, the hard grip of the cavaliers' hands upon her, the wild songs, the wild words and kisses, were they all to be brushed aside? Was there nothing in this evening's events that was not influenced by the grey goddess of twilight?

"But, Henrik—"

"Silence!" he said, straightening himself to pass sentence upon her! "Woe to you, a woman, who have wished to be a judge over men. Woe to you, my wife, who have dared to insult a man whose hand

I press in friendship! What affair is it of yours that the cavaliers put the Major's wife in prison? Have they not the right? You can never know how a man is angered to the depths of his soul when he hears of a woman's infidelity. Are you also going to tread the downward path, that you take her part?"

"But, Henrik—"

She cried out like a child, and stretched out her arms as if to ward off the cruel words. Probably she had never heard such anger directed against herself. She was so helpless among all those hard men; and now her only defender turned against her. Her heart would never again have strength to illumine the world.

"But, Henrik, it is you who should defend me!"

Gösta Berling was attentive now, when it was too late. He did n't in the least know what to do. He wished her well, but he dared not thrust himself between husband and wife.

"Where is Gösta Berling?" asked the Count.

"Here," replied Gösta, and he made a well-meant attempt to laugh the matter aside; "the Count was probably on the point of making a speech, and I fell asleep. What do you say to our going home now and leaving you to get to bed?"

"Gösta Berling, as my wife refused to dance with you, I command her to beg your pardon and to kiss your hand."

"My dear Count Henrik," said Gösta, smilingly,

"my hand is n't suitable for any young lady to kiss. Yesterday it was red from the blood of an elk; tonight it was black with soot after a fight with a coalheaver. The Count has passed a noble and high-minded sentence—that is sufficient. Come, Beerencreutz."

The Count placed himself in his way.

"Stay," he said, "my wife must obey. I desire her to know what it is to act on her own responsibility."

Gösta looked helpless. The Countess was quite pale, but she did not move.

"Go!" said the Count.

"Henrik—I can't."

"You can," he answered, sternly; "you can, but I know what you want. You want to force me to fight the man, because you are capricious and don't like him. Well, if you won't give him satisfaction, I must. You women are always delighted when men are killed for your sake. You are in fault, but you will not make amends for it. I must therefore do it. I am obliged to fight a duel, my Countess, and in a few hours I shall be a bloody corpse."

She gave him a long look, and she saw him as he was, stupid, cowardly, inflated with pride and vanity, the most pitiable of men.

"Calm yourself," she said, and she was now cold as ice; "I will do it."

But now Gösta Berling seemed out of his mind.

"Countess, you shall not, never, never! You are

Q

only a child, a weak, innocent child, and *you* — to
kiss my hand! You have such a white and pure
soul. I will never again come near you, never again!
I bring death and desolation and destruction over
all the good and innocent. You shall not touch me!
I shrink from you as fire from water, you shall not
touch me!"

He put his hands behind his back.

"It is nothing to me now, Herr Berling. It is
nothing at all now. I beg your pardon, and I beg
you to let me kiss your hand!"

Gösta still kept his hands behind his back. He
considered the situation and moved nearer the door.

"If you will not receive the satisfaction my wife of-
fers you, I must fight you, Gösta Berling, and I must
also deal to her another and severer punishment."

The Countess shrugged her shoulders. "He is
crazy with fear," she whispered; "let me do as he
commands. What does it matter if I am humiliated?
It is what you wished from the first."

"Did I wish it? Do you believe I wished *that?*
Well, if I have no hands to kiss, you must then
believe I never meant it," he cried.

He sprang to the fire and plunged his hands in.
The flames wrapped round them, the skin crinkled,
the nails cracked, but Beerencreutz caught him by
the back of the neck at the same moment and flung
him out upon the floor. He stumbled against a chair
and remained sitting. He was almost ashamed now

of doing such a thing. Would she think he had done it for effect? To do it before a roomful of people must seem as if it were done for effect. There hadn't been the least danger in it.

Before he could think of rising, the Countess was on her knees beside him. She caught hold of the reddened, sooted hands, and looked at them.

"I will kiss them — kiss them," she cried, "as soon as they are not too tender and painful." And the tears poured from her eyes as she saw the blisters rising under the burned skin.

Thus he became to her the realization of an unknown nobility. That such things could still happen in the world! That it had been done for her sake! What a man he was, able to do all, as mighty in good as in evil, a man of great achievements, a man of strong words and brilliant deeds! A hero, a hero! Created different, of different clay from other men! The slave of a caprice, of the desire of a moment, wild and fearful, but the possessor of a furious strength, fearing nothing.

She had been so oppressed all the evening, and had seen only sorrow and cruelty and cowardliness about her. Now all was forgotten. The Countess was again happy in living. The goddess of twilight had been conquered, and light and color again clothed the world.

.   .   .   .

On the same night the cavaliers were shouting and

swearing in the cavaliers' wing at Gösta Berling. The old gentlemen wished to go to sleep, but it was impossible. He gave them no peace. It was in vain they put out the lights and drew their bed-curtains; he continued talking.

He told them first what an angel the young Countess was, and how much he worshipped her. He would serve and adore her. He was happy in the knowledge that every one had forsaken him. He would now devote his life to her service. She scorned him, naturally, but he would be content to lie at her feet like a dog.

Had they ever noticed Low Island in the Löfven? Had they seen it from the south, where the rugged cliff raised itself abruptly from the water? Had they seen it from the north, where it sank into the lake in gentle slope, and where the narrow sandbanks, covered with tall, beautiful pines, wound out into the shallow water and formed lovely little lakes? There, on the precipitous height where the remains of an old castle were still standing, he would build a palace for the young Countess—a marble palace. Wide stairs would be hewn in the rock leading down to the lake, where gaily flagged boats would land. There would be shining halls and high towers with gilded pinnacles. It would be a suitable home for the young Countess. That old wooden hovel at Borg Point was not worthy she should set her foot in it.

When he had gone on like this for some time, a snore now and then penetrated the yellow-striped curtains, but most of the cavaliers swore and railed over him and his mad ideas.

"Fellow-men," he continued, solemnly, " I see God's world covered with men's handiwork or remains of their handiwork. The pyramids weigh down the earth, the Tower of Babel pierces the sky, beautiful temples and grey castles have been raised from the dust. But of all that has been built by hands, what has not fallen to ruin or will fall? Oh, fellow-men, throw aside the bricklayer's trowel and mortar-board! Spread your apron over your head and lie down and build fair dream castles! What has the spirit to do with temples of clay and stone? Learn to build everlasting castles of dreams and visions!"

And thereupon he went off laughing to bed.

When soon afterwards the Countess heard that the Major's wife had been set at liberty by the cavaliers, she gave a dinner party in their honor, and her long friendship with Gösta Berling dated from that time.

Ghost Stories

OH, children of a later day! I have nothing new to tell you; nothing but what is old and almost forgotten. Tales from the nursery, where the children sit on low stools round the white-haired story-teller, tales from the workmen's kitchen, where the farm laborers and crofters gather about the pine-wood fire. From the leather sheaths hanging round their necks they draw their knives and butter themselves thick slices of soft bread, as they sit about and chat, while the steam rises in clouds from their wet clothing. And I have tales from the sitting-room, where old gentlemen sit in their rocking-chairs and, inspired by a glass of steaming toddy, talk of the days that are past and gone.

And listening to these stories, a child, standing at the window on a wintry night, would see, instead of the clouds, cavaliers sweep over the sky in their light shays; to her the stars were waxen lights shining from the old mansion on Borg Point, and the spinning-wheel which hummed in the next room was turned by old Ulrika Dillner, for the child's head was full of these men and women of the olden days, and she lived and dreamed among them.

And if you send her, whose whole soul is filled with those old stories, through the dark garret to the pantry beyond, to fetch flax or some crackers, what a rush of little feet, what a hurried dash is made down the stairs, over the entry, and into the kitchen! For in the dark upstairs, she has remembered the stories told of the wicked Sintram, the owner of the iron works at Fors, he who was in league with the devil.

The bones of Sintram are at rest long years ago in Svartsjö churchyard, but no one believes his soul is with God, as is written on his tombstone.

As long as he lived, he was one of those men to whose house on long, rainy Sunday afternoons there came a heavy calash drawn by four black horses. A darkly clad, elegant gentleman descended and went in to help the master of the house while away with cards and dice the dreary monotony of the hours which were his despair. Those card parties were kept up till after midnight, and when the stranger drove away at dawn, he always left behind him some gift which carried misfortune with it.

Yes, as long as Sintram lived, he was one of those whose coming was heralded by unseen powers. One of those whose shade went before them, their carriages rolled into your courtyard, whips cracked, their voices were heard on the steps, the hall door opened and shut, the dogs were roused at the loud noise they made, and yet there was no one, nothing to be seen, it was only the apparition which always preceded them.

Ugh, those fearful people whom the wicked spir-

its seek! What was that big black hound seen at
Fors in Sintram's time? It had awful gleaming
teeth and a long tongue, dripping with blood, hanging out of its panting mouth! Once when the farm
men were in the kitchen having dinner, it came and
scratched at the kitchen door. All the servant girls
screamed with fright, but one of the biggest and
strongest of the men caught up a burning log from
the hearth, opened the door, and thrust it down the
dog's throat.

It had rushed away, howling horribly, flames and
smoke pouring out of its mouth; sparks whirled
about it, and its footsteps on the road shone like
fire.

And was it not awful, too, that although Sintram
drove away upon his journeys with his black horses,
horses never brought him home again. When he
returned at night, black bulls drew his carriage.
People living by the roadside saw their long black
horns outlined against the sky, heard their bellow-
ing, and were terrified at the shower of sparks struck
out by their hoofs and the carriage wheels on the
dry gravel.

Yes, there was ample cause for the scurrying of
small feet over the wide floors of the garret. Imagine if something dreadful, if he whose name it was
best not to mention were to come out of the dark
corner! You could not feel sure he would not do it.
It was not only to the wicked he showed himself.

Had not Ulrika Dillner seen him? Yes, both she and Anna Stjärnhök could tell you about it.

. . . .

Friends, children of men! You who dance and you who laugh, I pray you that you dance carefully and laugh kindly, for much sorrow may come to pass if your thin-soled, silken shoe treads upon a tender human heart instead of the hard floor planks, and your gay, silver-ringing laugh may drive a soul to despair.

It must have been that the young people had trampled too hard upon old Ulrika Dillner; their laughter must have sounded too overbearing in her ears, for suddenly there came over her a great and irresistible longing for the title and dignity belonging to a married woman. She said "Yes" to Sintram's long courtship, married him, and took her place at Fors as his wife, leaving her old friends at Berga, the old work she was accustomed to, and the old struggle for daily bread.

It was a hastily arranged wedding; Sintram proposed at Christmas, and they were married in February. Anna Stjärnhök was to spend the winter with the Ugglas and more than filled Ulrika's place, thus leaving her free to go forth and win for herself the title of Fru.

Her conscience had nothing to reproach her with, yet she regretted the step she had taken. It was

anything but a comfortable home she had come to;
the big empty rooms were full of a mysterious terror. As soon as it grew dark, she began to be afraid
and to shudder. She almost died of homesick-
ness. The long Sunday afternoons were the worst—
there seemed no end to them, nor to the train of
painful thoughts which passed slowly through her
mind.

And so it happened, one Sunday in March, when
Sintram had not returned home after church, she
went upstairs into the salon and sat down at her
harpsichord. It was her only comfort. The old harpsichord, with a piper and shepherdess painted on
its white cover, was her own property, inherited
from her parents' home. She could tell it all her
grief, and it would understand.

But isn't it both pitiful and ridiculous? Can you
guess what she played? A polka—when she was in
such great distress!

Oh, she knew nothing else. Before her fingers
stiffened round the dusting switch and the carver,
she had learned this one polka, and her fingers
remembered it still. She knew no funeral march
nor passionate sonata—not even a mournful folk-
song—nothing but that polka.

And she played it whenever she had anything
to confide to the old clavier; when she could have
wept, and when she wished to laugh. She played it at
her own wedding, when she came to her new home,

and she played it now. The old strings understood her well enough—she was wretched—wretched.

A passer-by, hearing the sound of the polka, might have thought that Sintram was giving a ball to his neighbors and friends—it was such an extraordinarily cheery and lively air. In the old days it rang gaiety in and hunger out of Berga, and all were ready to dance when it sounded. Rheumatic muscles burst their bonds, and its gay strains had tempted eighty-year-old cavaliers to try the polka. All the world would have danced to that polka, but old Ulrika wept.

She had surly, ill-tempered servants and savage animals around her; she longed for kind and smiling faces, and the polka must express her great longing.

People found it difficult to remember that she was Fru Sintram. They still called her Mamsell Dillner, and the polka expressed her sorrow over the vanity which had tempted her to run after the dignity accorded to a married woman.

She played as if she meant to break the strings of the harpsichord; there was so much she must drown in its tones—the cries of the ill-used peasantry, the curses of the crofters, the taunting laughter of defiant servants, and, worst of all, the shame —the shame of being a bad man's wife.

To that same tune Gösta Berling had led out young Countess Dohna to the dance, Marienne Sinclaire and her many admirers had danced to it, and

even the Lady of Ekeby had kept time to it in the
days when handsome Altringer lived. She saw them,
couple after couple, united by youth and beauty,
as they whirled before her, and a stream of gaiety
passed from her to them and back to her. It was
her polka which made their cheeks burn and their
eyes shine like that. She was far from it all now, but
the polka still rang out; there were so many happy
memories to drown!

She played, too, to deaden her fear. Her heart
grew faint with fright when she saw the black
hound, or heard the servants whisper about the
black bulls—and she played the polka, over and
over again, to deaden that fear.

Presently she noticed that her husband had returned. She heard him come into the room and sit
down in the rocking-chair. She recognized his way
of rocking and the noise made by the rockers scrap-
ing against the deal floor so well that she did not
turn toward him.

And still, as she played, the rocking continued
till it drowned all the sounds of her polka.

Poor old Ulrika, so wearied, so helpless and
lonely, alone in the enemies' country, without a
friend to complain to, with no better companion
than an old harpsichord which answered her grief
with a polka!

It was like a laugh at a funeral or a drinking
song in church. And while the chair still rocked

behind her, it suddenly seemed to her that her harpsichord was laughing at her, and she stopped abruptly in the middle of a bar. She got up and glanced behind her. A moment later she was lying unconscious on the floor. It was not her husband sitting there—but another—he whose name it is best for children not to mention, who would frighten them to death if they met him in the dark garret.

.   .   .   .

Ah, if your soul has been satiated with such stories as these, is it possible to free yourself from their power? To-night the wind is howling outside, and a fecus palm and a rosebush are beating their stiff leaves against the balcony pillars—the sky hangs darkly over the far-reaching hills, and I, sitting here, with my lamp lighted and my curtains drawn aside, I, already growing old and therefore bound to be sensible, still feel the same creepiness upon my spine as when I heard the story; I am compelled to raise my eyes from my work and glance round repeatedly to see that no one has stolen into the room and is hiding in that corner; I must glance into the balcony to be sure that no black head raises itself over the railing. This fear, fostered by the old ghost stories, never leaves me, and, when the nights are dark and I am alone, it grows so overwhelming that I must cast aside my pen, creep into bed, and draw the blankets over my head.

It was the great secret wonder of my childhood
that Ulrika Dillner lived through that afternoon.
I could not have done it.

It was fortunate that Anna Stjärnhök drove up
to the house about that time! She found Ulrika
lying on the floor in the salon and brought her back
to consciousness. I should not have been so easy to
bring back to life. I should have been dead.

I hope, dear friends, that you will never see the
tears of the aged, and that you may never stand
helpless when a grey head leans against your breast
to find support, and old hands are clasped upon
yours in silent prayer. May you never see the aged
sink in sorrow which you cannot lighten. For what is
the grief of youth? It has still strength and hope, but
how terrible it is to see the old weep — what despair
you feel when they, who have been the support of
your young life, sink down in helpless misery.

Anna Stjärnhök sat and listened to old Ulrika,
and she saw no way of helping her. The old woman
cried and trembled, her eyes were wild — she ram-
bled on and talked incoherently, almost as if she
no longer remembered where she was. The thousand wrinkles which covered her face were twice as
deep as usual, the false curls which hung round her
face were uncurled and disordered by her tears, and
the long, thin figure shook with sobs.

At last Anna felt she must put a stop to it. She
had decided what she would do. She would take

Ulrika back to Berga. Although she was undoubt-
edly Sintram's wife, she could not remain at Fors.
She would go mad if she remained with him. Anna
decided to take her away.

How frightened and yet how delighted Ulrika
was with this decision!

But oh, no, she certainly would not dare to leave
her husband and her home. He might, perhaps,
send the black dog after her.

But Anna conquered, partly by deception, partly
by threats; and in half an hour she had her in the
sledge beside her. Anna drove herself, and old Disa
was in the shafts; the roads were bad, for it was late
in March, but it did Ulrika good to be sitting again
in the well-known sledge, behind the horse which
had served Berga as faithfully and as long as she
herself had done.

Being of a cheerful temperament and a dauntless
mind, this old household drudge stopped crying
by the time they passed Arvidstorp; at Högberg
she was already laughing, while at Munkerud she
was telling Anna her experiences in her youth with
the Countess at Svaneholm.

They turned into the lonely deserted district beyond Munkeby. The road climbed every height it
could possibly reach, it crept to the top in lengthy
curves, leaped down in steep descent, and then
rushed as rapidly as possible over the level valley
to climb the nearest height again.

They were just about to drive down the hill at Vestratorp when old Ulrika paused suddenly in her talk and caught Anna by the arm. She was staring at a big black dog on the roadside.

"Look!" she cried.

The dog turned and set off into the woods. Anna did not see him very clearly.

"Drive!" cried Ulrika; "drive as quickly as you can. Sintram will hear directly that I am gone."

Anna tried to laugh her out of her fancy, but it was impossible.

"We shall hear his sleigh-bells directly, you'll see. We shall hear them before we reach the top of the next hill."

And while old Disa took a breath on the top of Elofsbacke they heard sleigh-bells below them.

Old Ulrika grew quite wild with fear. She trembled, sobbed, and wailed as she had done in the salon at Fors. Anna tried to whip up old Disa, but the horse only turned its head and gave her a look of the profoundest astonishment. Did she imagine old Disa did not know the right time to trot and when to walk? Was she going to teach her to pull the sledge, teach *her*, who knew every stone, every bridge and gate, and every hillock on the road for the last twenty years?

And the sleigh-bells sounded nearer.

"It is he—it is he—I know his bells," wailed Ulrika.

The sound still approached. Sometimes it seemed so loud that Anna turned her head, expecting to see the head of Sintram's horse just behind their sledge—sometimes it died away. Now they heard it on the right, now on the left of the road, but they saw no one. It seemed as though the sleigh-bells followed them.

And just as such bells rang in melodies, sang, talked, and answered when you returned at night from a ball, so they sang and talked and answered now. The whole forest echoed with their tune.

Anna Stjärnhök began to wish something would appear—to see Sintram and his red horse. That dreadful bell-ringing began to unnerve her.

She was not afraid, she had never been afraid, but those sleigh-bells distracted and tortured her.

"Those sleigh-bells torment me," she said at last, and immediately the words were caught up by the bells. "Torment me," they rang; "torment, torment, torment me," they sang in every possible tone.

It was not long since she had driven over this same road hunted by wolves. In the darkness she had seen white teeth glance in gaping mouths, she had expected her body to be torn to pieces by the savage brutes, but she had not been afraid. She had never lived through a more glorious night. Strong and beautiful the horse had been that carried her, strong and beautiful, too, was the man who had shared the joy of adventure with her.

R

Oh, this old horse and this helpless, trembling comrade! She felt herself so helpless, too, she could have wept. It was impossible to escape from that dreadful, irritating ringing.

She drew up and got out of the sledge. There must be an end to it; why should she flee, as if she were afraid of the wicked, contemptible wretch?

At last she saw a horse's head appear out of the gathering twilight, then a whole horse, a sledge, and in the sledge sat—Sintram.

She noticed, however, that it did not appear as if it had come along the road, this sledge with horse and master, but seemed as if it had been created under her eyes, and appeared just as it was finished.

Anna threw the reins to Ulrika and went to meet Sintram.

He pulled up his horse.

"See, see," he cried, "what exceptional luck I have! Dear Fröken Stjärnhök, may I hand over my companion into your sledge? He is going to Berga this evening, and I am in a hurry to be at home."

"Where is your companion?" asked Anna.

Sintram threw open the sledge cover, and showed Anna a man sleeping at the bottom of the sledge. "He is a little tipsy," he said, "but it won't matter. He is sure to sleep soundly. Any way he is an acquaintance of yours, Fröken Stjärnhök—it is Gösta Berling."

Anna started.

"Yes, I may say," continued Sintram, "that she who gives up her beloved sells him to the devil. That was the way I got into his claws. One thinks one is going to do so much good; sacrifice is a good thing, but love, that is evil."

"What do you mean? What are you talking about?" Anna asked, shaken with feeling.

"I mean that you shouldn't have let Gösta Berling give you up, Fröken Anna!"

"It was God's will—"

"Yes, yes, of course, to sacrifice one's self is right, to love is wrong. The good Lord does not like to see people happy. He sends wolves after them; but what if it wasn't God's doing, Fröken Anna? Suppose it was I who called my nice grey lambs from Dovrefjäll to chase that young man and woman? Suppose I sent them because I feared to lose one of my elect? Suppose it wasn't God who did it?"

"You must not tempt me to doubt on that point, Herr Sintram," said Anna, in a weak voice, "or I am lost."

"See here," said he, leaning over the sleeping man, "look at his little finger. That tiny cut never heals. The blood was drawn from there when he signed the contract. He is mine. There is a peculiar power in blood. He is mine—it is only love that can free him . . . but if I keep him, he will be a fine fellow."

Anna Stjärnhök fought against the enchantment

which seemed to be enveloping her. It was stupidity, rank stupidity, no one could sign away his soul to the devil; but she had no control over her thoughts, the twilight hung so heavily over her, the forest round about was so dark and quiet. She could not escape the hour's mysterious dread creeping over her.

"Perhaps you think," continued Sintram, "there is n't much to be destroyed in him? But there is. Has he ever ground down the peasants or deceived his poor friends or played falsely? Has he been the lover of married women?"

"I shall believe you are the devil himself, Herr Sintram!"

"Let us exchange, Fröken Anna—you take Gösta Berling, take him and marry him. Take him and give your friends at Berga money. I give him up to you—and, you know, he is mine. Remember it was n't God who sent the wolves after you that night, and let us exchange!"

"And what will you take in his place?"

Sintram grinned.

"I, what will I have? Oh, I shall be satisfied with little. I only ask for that old woman in your sledge, Fröken Anna."

"Satan—tempter," Anna cried, "leave me! Am I to fail an old friend who depends upon me? Am I to leave her to you, that you may drive her to madness?"

"See, see, be calm, Fröken Anna! Think it over! There is a fine young man and there an old worn-out woman. One of them I must have. Which shall it be?"

Anna Stjärnhök laughed despairingly.

"Do you think we can stand here and exchange souls as one exchanges horses at Broby market-place?"

"Yes, just so — but if you wish, Fröken Anna, we will arrange it in another way. We must remember the Stjärnhök honor."

And he suddenly began to call and shout to his wife, who was sitting alone some distance ahead in the other sledge, and to Anna's unspeakable horror, she obeyed him at once, stepped out of the sledge, and came trembling toward them.

"See, see," said Sintram, "what an obedient wife! Fröken Stjärnhök has nothing to do with it if she comes when her husband calls. Now I will lift Gösta out of my sledge and leave him here on the road. Leave him forever, Fröken Anna, — and who likes may take him up."

He bent down to take the sleeping figure, but Anna, bending down and looking directly into his eyes, hissed out like a tortured animal —

"In God's name, go home at once! Don't you know who is sitting in the rocking-chair and waiting for you? Dare you let that gentleman wait?"

It was to Anna almost the most terrible of that

day's dreadful occurrences to see the effect of those words. Sintram clutched at his reins, turned, and drove homeward, lashing the horse to wildness with his shouts and blows. Down the steep hillside they flew at a dangerous pace, while a line of sparks flashed under the sledge runners and the horse's hoofs on the rough March roads.

Anna Stjärnhök and old Ulrika stood alone on the road, but they had no word to say to each other. Ulrika trembled at the sight of Anna's wild eyes, and Anna had nothing to say to the poor creature for whose sake she had sacrificed her lover.

She longed to scream, to throw herself on the ground and strew the snow and sand upon her head.

She had known the beauty of sacrifice before, now she felt its bitterness. To sacrifice her love was nothing in comparison to offering up the soul of her lover!

They reached Berga in silence, but when they arrived and the sitting-room door opened, Anna Stjärnhök fainted for the first and last time in her life. There in the room sat Gösta Berling and Sintram, chatting in all good fellowship, the toddy glasses on the table. They must have been there quite an hour.

Anna Stjärnhök fainted, but old Ulrika stood calm. She had noted that all didn't seem quite right with their pursuer on the road.

Afterwards it was arranged between Captain

Uggla and Sintram that Ulrika should remain at Berga. He took it all very good-naturedly; he certainly did not wish her to go mad, he said.

.   .   .   .

Oh, children of a later day!

I cannot demand that any one should believe these old stories. They may be nothing but lies and fancies, but the fear which rolls over the human heart, till it wails like the floor planks under Sintram's rocking-chair, the doubt which rings in your ears, as the sleigh-bells rang in Anna Stjärnhök's in the lonely forest, are they only lies and fancies?

Oh, if they only were!

Ebba Dohna's Story

BEWARE of the beautiful promontory on the east shore of the Löfven, of the proud promontory round which the bays curve in gentle waves, where Borg Hall stands. The Löfven is never so beautiful as seen from its crest. No one knows how lovely is this lake of my dreams, if from Borg promontory he has not watched the morning mists glide away from its gleaming surface, and from the window of the little blue cabinet where so many memories live seen it reflect a rosy sunset.

But I still say—beware of going thither.

For you may be tempted to remain in the sorrow-laden halls of the old estate; you will perhaps become the owner of this beautiful spot, and if you are young, rich, and happy, you may make your home here with a young bride, as many another has done.

No; better never to have seen the beautiful promontory, for happiness cannot dwell in Borg. Know that, however rich, however happy you may be, those old-fashioned floors will soon drink *your* tears; those walls, which have echoed so many sounds of sorrow, will also echo *your* sighs.

There lies an untoward fate over that beautiful estate It seems as though sorrow were buried there, but could find no rest in its grave, and rose again to terrify the living. If I were master at Borg, I would search the stony ground of the pine wood, and under the cellar floor of the mansion, and in the fertile earth of the surrounding fields, till I found the worm-eaten corpse of the witch, and I would give her a grave in consecrated ground at Svartsjö churchyard. And at her funeral there should be no lack of bell-ringers; the bells should peal loud and long over her; and I would give rich gifts to the priest and the sexton, that they might wed her to everlasting rest with redoubled vigor.

Or if this were ineffective, I would let fire encircle the bulging wooden walls some stormy night and let it destroy it all, so that no one could ever again be tempted to live in that unhappy house. And afterwards no one should enter upon that fated place, only the black daws from the church tower might found a colony in the tall chimney stack which raised itself black and awful over the charred ground.

Yet I should certainly be frightened to see the flames leap over the roof, to see thick smoke, reddened by the flare of the flames and flaked with sparks, pour forth from the old mansion. I should fancy I heard the wail of homeless memories in the roar and crackling of the flames, and saw homeless ghosts float in their blue points. I should remember how sorrow and unhappiness beautifies, and I should weep, feeling that a temple of the old gods had been doomed to destruction.

But silence, you who croak of misfortune! Wait till night, if you would hoot in concert with the forest owl. Borg still gleamed on the height of the promontory, protected by its park of mighty pire trees, and the snow-covered fields below glittered in the blinding sunlight of a March morning, and the glad laugh of the gay little Countess Elizabeth was heard within its walls.

On Sundays she used to go to Svartsjö church, which lay near Borg, and gather together some friends to dinner. The Judge from Munkerud and his family and the Ugglas from Berga, the curate and his wife and wicked Sintram usually came, and if Gösta Berling had come to Svartsjö over the ice of the Löfven, she invited him too. Why should she not invite Gösta Berling?

She probably did not know gossips already whispered that Gösta went to the east shore so often for the purpose of meeting the Countess. Perhaps he also went to sup and gamble with Sintram; but no one thought much of that, they all knew his body was like iron, but it was quite another thing with his heart. No one believed that he could see a pair of bright eyes and fair hair curling round a white forehead without falling in love.

The young Countess was very kind to him; but there was nothing exceptional in that, for she was kind to all. She seated ragged urchins on her knee; and when driving, if she passed any poor old wretch on the wayside, she made the coachman pull up and took the wanderer into her sledge.

Gösta sat in the little blue cabinet, where you have the lovely view northward over the lake, and read poetry to her. There was no harm in it. He did not forget what she was. A Countess! and he was a homeless wanderer and adventurer; and it did him good to associate with some one who stood high and holy over him. He might as well think of falling in love with the Queen of Sheba, who decorated the front of the gallery in Svartsjö church, as with the Countess Dohna.

He only desired to serve her as a page serves his mistress — to be allowed to fasten on her skates, hold her wool skeins, or steer her coasting sledge. There could be no question of love between them, but he was the kind of man to find pleasure in a romantic, harmless sentiment.

The young Count was silent and serious, and Gösta was gaiety itself. He was just the companion the Countess desired. No one seeing her dreamed of her cherishing an unlawful passion. She cared only for dancing — dancing and gaiety. She would like the world to be quite level, without any stones or hills or lakes, so that you could dance over it all. She would like to dance all the way from her cradle to her grave in her narrow, thin-soled silken shoes.

But gossip is not very merciful toward young women.

When these guests dined at Borg, the gentlemen usually went after dinner into the Count's room to smoke and take a nap; the old ladies sank into the armchairs in the salon and leaned their worthy heads against the high-cushioned backs; but the Countess and Anna Stjärnhök went away into the blue cabinet and exchanged endless confidences.

And on the Sunday following the one on which Anna had taken old Ulrika Dillner back to Berga, they were sitting there again.

No one on earth was more wretched than Anna. All her gaiety was gone, as was the happy audacity with which she met every one and everything that threatened to touch her.

All that had taken place that day had sunk, in her consciousness, into the twilight from which it had emanated. She had not a single clear impression.

Yes, one—which poisoned her soul.

"If it was not God," she kept whispering to herself,—"if it was not God, who sent the wolves?"

She demanded a sign, a miracle. She searched the heavens and the earth, but she saw no hand stretched from the skies to point out her way. No cloud of smoke and fire went before her.

As she sat opposite the Countess in the little blue cabinet, her eyes fell upon a small bouquet of blue anemones which the Countess held in her white hand. Like lightning it flashed across her that she knew where they had grown, that she knew who had plucked them.

There was no necessity to ask. Where in all the country did blue anemones grow in April but in the birchwood on the shore slope near Ekeby?

She gazed and gazed at the small blue stars — those happy flowers who win all hearts; those little prophets who, beautiful themselves, are glorified in the glamour of all that they foretell, of all the beautiful to come. And as she looked at them, anger began to shake her soul — anger which rumbled like thunder and streamed like lightning. "By what right," she thought, "does the Countess wear that bunch of anemones plucked on the shore road from Ekeby?"

They were all tempters — Sintram, the Countess, every one tried to tempt Gösta to evil ways; but she would defend him, she would defend him against them all. If it cost her her heart's blood, she would do it.

She felt she must see those flowers torn from the Countess's hand and cast aside, trampled, destroyed, before she left the little blue cabinet.

She felt this, and began a strife against the little blue stars. In the salon the old ladies leaned their heads against the backs of their armchairs, and suspected nothing; the old gentlemen puffed their pipes in peace and quietness in the Count's room — all was calm, only in the little blue cabinet raged

a fierce strife. Ah, they do well who can hold their
hands from the sword, who can bear in patience, can
quiet their hearts and let God guide their path! The
uneasy heart is forever going astray; evil ever makes
the evil worse.

But Anna Stjärnhök thought she had at last seen
a sign.

"Anna," said the Countess, "tell me a story."

"What about?"

"Oh," said the Countess, caressing the bouquet
with her white fingers, "don't you know something
about love, something about loving?"

"No, I know nothing about loving."

"How you talk! Isn't there a place here called
Ekeby, a place full of cavaliers?"

"Yes," said Anna, "there is a place here called
Ekeby, and there are men who suck out the marrow
of the country, who make us incapable of earnest
work, who ruin the youth growing up around them,
and lead our geniuses astray. Do you want to hear
love stories about *them?*"

"Yes, I do—I like the cavaliers."

Then Anna spoke—spoke in short, curt sentences like an old hymn book, for she was nearly
stifled by stormy feeling. Hidden passion trembled
in every word, and the Countess, both frightened
and interested, listened to her.

"What is the love and the faith of a cavalier?
A sweetheart to-day, another to-morrow, one in the

east, one in the west. Nothing is too high for him,
nothing too low; one day a count's daughter, the
next a beggar girl. Nothing in the world is so roomy
as his heart. But wretched, wretched is she who loves
a cavalier! She must search for him while he lies
drunk on the wayside. She must silently watch him
laying waste the home of her children at the gam-
bling-table. She must endure seeing him hanging
about strange women. Oh, Elizabeth, if a cavalier
begs a decent woman for a dance, she ought to refuse him; if he gives her flowers, she ought to throw
them away and trample on them; if she loves him,
she ought to die rather than marry him. Among the
cavaliers was one who was a disgraced clergyman. . . .
He was dismissed from his calling because he drank.
He was drunk in church: he drank the sacramental
wine. Have you heard of him?"

"No."

"After he was suspended, he ranged the country
as a beggar. He drank like a madman. He would
even steal to get gin."

"What is his name?"

"He is no longer at Ekeby. The Major's wife
took him in hand, gave him clothes, and persuaded
your mother-in-law, Countess Märta, to make him
tutor to your husband, young Count Henrik."

"A discharged clergyman?"

"Oh, he was a young and strong man, and
learned. There was nothing the matter with him as

long as he did not drink. And Countess Märta was
not very particular. It amused her to tease the rector
and curate. Still she ordered that no one was to
speak of his past life to her children, for her son
would have lost all respect for him, and her daughter could not have endured him, for she was a saint.

"So he came here to Borg. He always remained
near the door, sat on the extreme edge of his chair,
was silent at table, and disappeared into the park as
soon as visitors arrived.

"But there, in the lonely paths, he used to meet
Ebba Dohna. She was not of those who loved the
noisy fêtes that stormed through the halls of Borg
since Countess Märta had become a widow. She was
not of those who sent daring glances out into the
world. She was so shy and gentle. Even when she
was seventeen, she was but a tender child, but
she was very beautiful, with her brown eyes and the
fair flush on her cheeks. Her thin, slim figure bent
slightly forward. Her narrow little hand slipped into
yours with a shy pressure. Her little mouth was the
most silent of mouths, and the most serious. And
her voice — her sweet, low voice, which pronounced
the words so slowly and distinctly — never rang with
any healthy youthfulness or warmth, but its tired
tones sounded like a wearied musician's closing
chords.

"She was not like other girls. Her feet trod the
earth so lightly, so silently, as if she were but a

frightened visitant here; and her glances sank so as not to be disturbed in the view of glorious inner visions. Her soul had turned from earth while she was but a child.

"When a child, her grandmother used to tell her stories, and one evening they sat before the fire together, but the stories were finished. *Carsus and Moderus*, and *Lunkentus*, and *The Beautiful Melusina* had all lived before her. Like the flames, they had flashed through a brilliant life, but now the heroes were all slain and the beautiful princess had turned to ashes, till the next blaze in the fireplace should waken them to life again. But the child's hand still rested on her grandmother's dress, and she softly stroked the silk — that funny silk which squeaked like a little bird when you touched it. And that movement was her prayer, for she was one of those children who never pray in words.

"Then the old lady began to tell her gently of a little child who was born in the land of Judea — a little child who was born to be a great king. The angels had filled the world with songs of praise when he had been born. The kings of the East had sought him, guided by the star of heaven, and had presented him with gold and incense, and old men and women prophesied his glory. And the child grew to greater wisdom and beauty than other children. When only twelve years old, his wisdom was greater than that of the high priest and the scribes.

s

"And the old lady told her of the most beautiful thing the world had ever seen—of the life of that child while he remained on the earth among the wicked people who would not acknowledge him as their king. She told her how the child became a man, while wonderful miracles ever surrounded him.

"All on earth served and loved him, all but men. The fish allowed themselves to be caught in his net, bread filled his baskets, water turned to wine when he wished it. But men gave him no golden crown, no glittering throne. There were no courtiers to bow before him. They allowed him to go away and live as a beggar.

"Yet he was so good to them—he healed their sick, gave sight to the blind, and raised the dead.

"'But,' said the old lady, 'men would not receive him as their lord. They sent their soldiers against him and took him prisoner. They mocked him, dressing him in a silken mantle and a crown and sceptre, and made him bear his heavy cross to the place of execution.

"'Oh, my child! the good king loved the hills. At night he used to ascend thither and hold converse with the dwellers of the heavens, and he liked to sit on the side of a mountain in the daytime and talk to the listening multitude. But now they led him up the mountain to crucify him. They drove nails through his hands and feet, and hung the good king upon a cross as if he had been a robber and a murderer.

"'And the people mocked him. Only his mother and his friends wept that he should die before he became king.

"'Oh, how the dead world sorrowed at his death!

"'The sun lost its light, and the mountains shook; the veil of the temple was rent, and the graves opened to allow the dead to rise and show their sorrow.'

"The child lay with her head on the grandmother's knee, and sobbed as if her heart would break.

"'Don't cry, dear; the good king rose again and went to his father in heaven.'

"'Grandmother,' she sobbed, 'did he never receive his kingdom here?'

"'He sits at the right hand of God.'

"But that did not comfort her. She wept as hopelessly and as unrestrainedly as only a child can weep.

"'Why were they so cruel to him? Why were they allowed to be so cruel to him?'

"The old lady was almost frightened at such overwhelming sorrow.

"'Say, grandmother, that you did not tell the story rightly! Say that it ended differently, that they were not so cruel to the good king, and that he received his kingdom here on earth!'

"She flung her arms around her grandmother, tears still streaming from her eyes.

"'Child, child,' her grandmother said to comfort her, 'there are people who believe he will return. The world will then be in his power, and he will rule it. It will be a beautiful kingdom and last for a thousand years. And the evil beasts shall become good, and the children shall play in the adder's nest, and the bear and the ox shall feed together. Nothing will harm or destroy, the spears shall be turned into scythes, and swords shall be forged into ploughshares. And all shall be joy and gladness, for the good shall inherit the earth.'

"Then the child's face brightened beneath her tears.

"'Will the good king have a throne, grandmother?'

"'A throne of gold.'

"'And servants and courtiers and a golden crown?'

"'Yes.'

"'Will he come soon, grandmother?'

"'No one knows when he will come.'

"'May I then sit on a cushion at his feet?'

"'Yes, certainly you may.'

"'Grandmother, I am so happy,' she cried.

"Evening after evening, for many winters, those two sat by the fire and talked about the good king and his kingdom. The child dreamed of it both day and night, and she never wearied of aggrandizing it in fancy with all the beautiful she could imagine.

"It is often the case with the silent children about us that they cherish a dream which they dare not talk about. There are wonderful thoughts inside many a head of soft hair; the brown eyes see many wonderful visions behind their drooping eyelids; many a fair maid has her bridegroom in heaven; many a rosy cheek would anoint the feet of the good king with precious ointment, and dry them with her hair.

"Ebba Dohna dared not tell any one about it, but since that evening she had lived for the Lord's Millennium alone, and to await his coming.

"When the evening sun lighted up the portals of the west, she wondered if he would not appear there, shining in quiet splendor, followed by millions of angels, and pass by her, allowing her to touch the hem of his mantle.

"She often thought, too, of the pious women who had loved him as devotedly as she did, and hung veils over their heads, and never raised their eyes from earth, but imprisoned themselves in the quiet of grey cloisters and the darkness of small cells so as to see uninterruptedly the glorious visions that rise from the darkness of the soul.

"Thus she had grown up, and such was her character, when she and the new tutor began to meet in the lonely park. I will speak no more ill of him than I must. I try to believe that he loved that child who chose him as her companion in her lonely walks.

I believe his soul again took wing as he walked by
the side of that silent girl, who had never confided
in any one before. I think he felt himself like a child
again too, good and virtuous.

"But if he loved her, why did he not remember
that he could give her no worse gift than his love?
He, one of the outcasts of the world, what was
he doing, what was he thinking of, as he walked by
the side of the Count's daughter? What did he, the
discharged pastor, feel when she confided her reli-
gious dreams to him? What was he, who had been
a drunkard and brawler, and would be one again
as soon as the opportunity offered — what was he
doing by the side of her who dreamed of a bridegroom in heaven? Why did he not flee, flee far from
her? Would it not have been better for him to wander stealing and begging through the country than
that he should walk there in the silent pine wood
and be good and virtuous and devout again, when
his past life could not be lived over again, and it
was unavoidable that Ebba Dohna should learn to
love him?

"You are not to think he looked a miserable
drunkard with ashy cheeks and red eyes. He was
ever a stately man, beautiful and strong in body and
soul. He bore himself like a king, and had an iron
constitution which was not impaired by the wildest
life."

"Is he still alive?" asked the Countess.

"Oh, no, he must be dead now. It is all so long ago."

There was something within Anna Stjärnhök that trembled at what she was doing. She began to think she would never tell the Countess who the man was, that she would let her believe him dead.

"At that time he was still young," she continued her story; "the joy of life awoke again within him. He had the gift of speech and a fiery, inflammable heart. There came an evening when he spoke to her of love. She did not answer him, but told him of what her grandmother had described to her in the winter evenings and of the land of her dreams. Afterwards she made him promise, made him swear, that he would be one of God's preachers, one of those who would prepare the way for him, that his coming might be hastened.

"What could he do? He was a discharged clergyman, and no path was so impossible for him as the one she had wished him to tread. But he dared not tell her the truth: he had not the heart to distress the sweet child he loved. He promised all she asked.

"Not many words between them were required after that. It was clear that she would one day be his wife. It was not a love of kisses and caresses. He hardly dared approach her closely; she was as sensitive as a fragile flower; but her brown eyes were raised from the ground sometimes in search of his. On moonlight nights, when they sat upon the veranda, she used to creep close to him, and he kissed her hair without her noticing it.

"But, you understand, his sin lay in his forget-fulness of both past and future. That he was poor and had no position in life, he might easily forget; but he ought to have remembered that the day would surely come when love would rise against love in her mind, earth against heaven, and when she must choose between him and the glorious Lord of her dreams. And she was not one of those who could survive such a strife.

"So passed the summer, the autumn, and winter. When spring came, and the ice in the Löfven broke up, Ebba Dohna lay sick. The springs were melt-ing in the valleys, the brooks were swelling, the ice on the lakes was insecure, roads were impassable both for sledges and wheeled vehicles. Countess Dohna wanted a doctor from Karlstad — there was no one nearer — but she commanded in vain. Nei-ther threats nor prayers could induce any of the ser-vants to go for him. She begged the coachman on her knees, but he refused. She had cramp and hys-terics, she was so alarmed over her daughter. She was as uncontrolled in sorrow as in joy was Count-ess Märta.

"Ebba Dohna had inflammation of the lungs, and her life was in danger, but there was no doctor to be had.

"Then the tutor rode to Karlstad. To cross the

country when the roads were in such a state was
to venture his life, but he did it. He crossed the
lakes on swaying ice, and climbed neck-breaking
heaps of it, where it was stacked; he was obliged
sometimes to cut steps for his horse in the high
blocks, sometimes he dragged it out of the deep
mire of the road. They said the doctor refused to
accompany him, but that he forced him to do so at
the point of his pistol.

"When he came back, the Countess was ready
to cast herself at his feet. 'Take everything,' she
cried, 'take what you will — my daughter, my land,
or my money!'

"'Your daughter,' said the tutor."

Anna Stjärnhök suddenly became silent.

"Well, and afterwards — and afterwards?" asked
the Countess.

"That is enough," answered Anna, for she was
one of those miserable people who are always in
fear and doubt. She had been in doubt all the week.
She did not know what she wanted. That which
seemed right to her one moment seemed wrong the
next. Now she wished she had never begun this
story.

"I begin to believe you are mocking me, Anna.
Don't you understand I *must* hear the end?"

"There isn't much more to say. The hour of
strife had come to Ebba Dohna, love rose against
love, earth against heaven. . . .

"Countess Märta told her daughter of the wonderful journey the young man had made for her sake, and that as a reward she had given him her hand.

"Ebba Dohna was so far convalescent that she lay dressed upon the sofa. She was tired and pale and even more silent than usual. When she heard these words, she lifted her reproachful, mournful brown eyes to her mother and said, 'Mamma, have you given me to a discharged clergyman, to one who has forfeited his right to be God's servant, to a man who has been a beggar and a thief?'

"'But, child, who has told you this? I thought you knew nothing about it!'

"'I heard it—I heard your visitors talking about it the day I fell ill.'

"'But remember, Ebba, he saved your life.'

"'I remember that he has deceived me. He should have told me who he was.'

"'He says you love him.'

"'I have done so. I cannot love him who has deceived me.'

"'In what way has he deceived you?'

"'You would not understand, mamma.'

"She did not care to talk to her mother about the Millennium of her dreams which her lover was to help her to realize.

"'Ebba,' said her mother, 'if you love him, you must not think of what he has been, but marry him.

The husband of Countess Dohna will be sufficiently rich and sufficiently powerful for his youthful sins to be forgiven him.'

"'I am not thinking of his youthful sins, mamma. It is because he has deceived me and can never be what I wished him to be that I will not marry him.'

"'Ebba, remember I have given my word.'

"The girl became deadly pale.

"'Mamma, I tell you, if you make me marry him, you part me from God.'

"'I am determined to make you happy,' said her mother, 'and I am sure you will be happy with this man. You have already made a saint of him. I have determined to put aside the usual requirements of our station, and to forget that he is poor and despised, to give you the opportunity of raising him. I feel I am doing what is right. You know how I despise all old conventionalities.'

"But she said this because she could not endure any one to contradict her. Perhaps, too, she meant it when she said it. Countess Märta was not easy to understand.

"Ebba lay quietly on her sofa for a long time after her mother left her. She fought her fight. Earth rose against heaven, love against love; but the love of her childhood won the battle. As she lay there on that very sofa, she saw the west flush into a glorious sunset. She felt it was a greeting from the good king, and as she was not strong enough to

be true to him if she lived, she determined to die.
She could do nothing else when her mother wished
her to be the wife of one who could not be a servant of the king. She went to the window, opened
it, and let the cold, damp evening again envelop her
poor, feeble little body.

"It was easy for her to bring about her death.
It was certain she would have a relapse, and she did.

"No one but I knew that she had sought her
death. I found her at the window. I heard her rav-
ings in her fever. She liked me to remain by her
side during her last days.

"It was I who saw her die, who saw her, one
evening, stretch out her arms to the glowing west,
and die, smiling, as if she had seen some one step
out from the sunset radiance to meet her. I also was
to carry her last greeting to the man she had loved.
I was to ask him to forgive her that she could not
be his wife. The good king would not allow it.

"But I have not dared to tell the man he was
her murderer. I have not dared to lay the burden of
such sorrow upon him. And yet, he that lied and
won her love was he not her murderer? Was he not,
Elizabeth?"

Countess Dohna had long since ceased caressing
the blue anemones. Now she stood up, and the
bouquet fell to the ground.

"Anna, you are still mocking me. You say the

story is old, and that the man is dead long ago.
But I know it is hardly five years since Ebba Dohna
died, and you say you were a witness to it all. You
are not old. Tell me who the man is."

Anna Stjärnhök began to laugh.

"You wanted a love story, and you have had
one which has cost you both tears and distress."

"Do you mean that it is not true?"

"It is nothing but lies and fancy, my dear."

"You are malicious, Anna."

"Perhaps—I am not too happy. I can tell you
—but the old ladies have wakened, and the gentlemen are entering the drawing-room—let us join
them."

She was arrested on the threshold by Gösta Berling, who had come in search of the young ladies.

"You must have patience with me," he said,
laughingly; "I am only going to annoy you for ten
minutes, but you must hear some poetry."

He told them that he had dreamed that night
more vividly than usual—dreamed that he wrote
poetry. And he—the so-called "poet," though he
had borne the name innocently hitherto—had got
up in the middle of the night and, half asleep,
half awake, had begun to write. And he had found
quite a long poem on his writing-table in the morning. He never could have believed it of himself.
The ladies must hear it, and he read:

" *Now rose the moon, and with it came the day's most lovely hour,*
And from the clear, pale, lofty dome, she poured her shimmer
down
On the veranda wreathed in lovely flowers;
While at our feet the lily spread
Its scent, its chalice tipped with gold;
And on the hard, broad stairway there
We grouped together, young and old,
Silent at first, and let our feelings sing
Our hearts' old songs in that most lovely hour.

" *From the mignonette bed a lovely scent was all around diffused,*
And from the dark and gloomy tangle of the undergrowth
The shadows crept over the dewy plot.
Our spirits, freed, now flew on high
To regions which they scarce could reach,
To the pale blue shining dome on high,
Whose brightness scarce revealed a star.
Ah! who could flee a throbbing of the heart
When shadows sport and mignonette perfumes the air.

" *A Provence rose shed silently its last, pale, fading leaves,*
And yet no sportive breeze had claimed the sacrifice.
So, thought we, would we give our life,
Vanish in air like a dying tone,
Like autumn's yellow leaves, without a sigh.
Oh! ye strain at the length of our years, disturb
Thus Nature's peace — to grasp a vision.
Death is Life's wage, so may we pass in peace
As a Provence rose sheds silently its last pale leaves.

"On quivering wing a lonely bat flew swift and noiseless by.
  Passed and repassed, and was ever seen where'er the moonlight
    And in the downcast hearts it raised   [fell;
    The question never answered yet—
    Deep as sorrow—old as pain—
  'Oh, whither go ye, what paths shall ye tread
  When the verdant paths of the earth ye leave?
Can ye point the spirit's path to another?'—No,
'Twere easier to guide the bat which fluttereth by just now.

"On my shoulder, then, my darling leaned her head, her soft,
      sweet hair,
  And softly she did whisper to him whom she thus loved—
    'Ne'er dream my soul will flee from thee
    To distant spheres when I am dead;
    My homeless spirit will find its way
    To thee, oh, love! and dwell in thee.'
  What pain! My heart was nigh to break.
Would she then die? Was this night then her last?
Was this my parting kiss upon my darling's face?

"Now many years have passed since then—I sit again and oft
  In that old favorite place of mine, when nights are dark and
      still;
  But I shrink from the moon—she knows how oft
    On the veranda I have kissed my love.
    Her shimmering light she used to blend
    With the tears I shed on my darling's hair.
  Oh, the woe of memory! It is my curse.
My soul is the home of hers! What doom can he await
Who has bound to his a soul so pure and fair!"

"Gösta," said Anna, in a would-be laughing tone, though fear clutched at her throat, "they say that you have lived through more poems than have ever been written by those who do nothing else all their lives; but I advise you to keep to your own style of poem. Those verses are clearly a night production."

"You are cutting, Anna."

"To come and read to us about death and misery! Aren't you ashamed?"

But Gösta was not paying further attention to her, his eyes were fixed on the young Countess. She sat quite motionless, immovable as a statue. He thought she was going to faint.

But with much trouble a word passed her lips.

"Go!" she said.

"Who is to go? Is it I?"

"The parson must go," she ejaculated.

"Elizabeth, do be silent!"

"The drunken parson must leave my house!"

"Anna, Anna," cried Gösta, "what does she mean?"

"Go away, Gösta; it is best you should go."

"Why should I go? What is the meaning of this?"

"Anna," said the Countess, "tell him—tell him . . ."

"No, Countess, you must tell him yourself."

The Countess Elizabeth bit her teeth together and mastered her feeling.

"Herr Berling," she said, approaching him, "you have a wonderful faculty for making people forget who you are. I have not heard till to-day. I have just been told the story of Ebba Dohna's death, and that it was the knowledge that the man she loved was unworthy of her love which caused her death. Your poem has shown me that you are the man. I cannot understand how a man with a past such as yours dares to show himself in the society of a decent woman. I cannot understand it, Herr Berling. Is my meaning sufficiently clear?"

"It is, Countess. I will only say one word in defence. I was convinced—I have been convinced all the time that you knew all about me. I have never tried to hide anything, but there is no pleasure in shouting out one's bitterest griefs from the housetops—least of all to do it one's self."

And he left them.

At the same moment Countess Dohna set her foot upon the little bouquet of blue anemones.

"You have done what I desired," said Anna Stjärnhök to her in a hard voice; "but this is the end of our friendship. You need not think I will forgive you for having been cruel to him. You have dismissed him, scorned and hurt him, and I—I would follow him to prison, to the pillory if need be. I will guard and defend him. You have done what I desired, but I shall never forgive you."

"But, Anna, Anna!"

T

"If I told you that story, do you think I did it with a glad heart? Have I not been tearing my heart out bit by bit while sitting here?"

"Then, why did you do it?"

"Why? Because—because I did not wish him to be the lover of a married woman. . . ."

Mamselle Marie

O HARK, hark! There is a buzzing over my head. It must be a bumblebee that comes flying. And what a fragrance! As true as I live, it is boy's-love and sweet lavender and hawthorne and lilac and white narcissus. How delightful to have all this steal in upon you on a grey autumn evening in the midst of the town. I have only to think of that precious little corner of the earth, and immediately I hear the hum of tiny wings and the air about me is filled with sweet perfumes. In a twinkling I am transported into a little square rose-garden, full of flowers, protected by a privet-hedge. In the corners are lilac bowers with wooden seats, and between the flower beds, which are formed in the shape of hearts and stars, wind narrow paths, strewn with white sea-sand. On three sides of this rose-garden are woods. Semi-wild rowan and hagberry trees stand nearest it, their scents blending with the perfume of the lilacs. Beyond are some clusters of silver-stemmed birches, which lead to the spruce forest—the real forest, dark and silent; bearded and prickly. And on the fourth side stands a little grey cottage.

The rose-garden of which I am thinking was owned some sixty years ago by an old Fru Moreus of Svartsjö, who earned her living making quilts for the peasants and cooking the food for their feasts.

Dear friends, of the many good things that I wish for you, above all I would name a rose-garden and a quilting-frame — a great, wobbly, old-fashioned quilting-frame, with worn screw-taps and chipped rollers, at which five or six persons can work at the same time and hold a stitching contest, where all hands vie with each other to produce neat stitches on the under-side; where one munches roasted apples, and chatters, and "journeys to Greenland to hide the ring," and laughs till the squirrels out in the wood tumble headlong to the ground from fright. A quilting-frame for winter and for summer a rose-garden. Not a garden on which one must lay out more money than the pleasure is worth, but a rose-garden such as they had in the old days, the kind you tend with your own hands; with little brier trees crowning the brow of the small hillocks and wreaths of forget-me-nots encircling the foot, and where the big floppy poppy, which sows itself, springs up everywhere on the grassy borders, and even in the sand-path; also there should be a sun-browned moss sofa, overgrown with columbine and crown imperials.

Old Fru Moreus, who had three lively and industrious daughters, was in her day the proud possessor of many things. She owned a little cottage near the roadside, had a nest-egg tucked away at the bottom of an old chest, had stiff silk shawls and straight-backed armchairs, and besides, she had learned to do any number of things that are useful to know for one who must earn her own bread. But the quilting-frame, which brought her work the year round, and the rose-garden, which gave her joy the whole summer long, were to her the best of all.

In Fru Moreus's cottage was a lodger, a little weazened spinster about forty years of age, who occupied a gable-room in the attic. Mamselle Marie, as she was called, held views of her own about many things, as is apt to be the case with those who sit much alone and let their thoughts dwell on what their eyes have seen.

Now Mamselle Marie believed that love was the root of all the evil in this mundane world. Every night before going to sleep, she would fold her hands and say her evening prayers. When she had said "Our Father" and "Lord bless us," she always prayed God to preserve her from love.

"It could only end in misery," she would say, "for I am old and homely and poor. May I be spared from falling in love!"

Day after day she sat in her attic chamber, knitting curtains and table-covers in shell-stitch, which she sold to the gentry and the peasants. She was knitting together a little cottage of her own. A cot on the hillside opposite Svartsjö Church was what she wanted—a cottage on high ground from which one could have a fine open view, that was her dream. But of love she would have none.

When on a summer evening she heard the sound of violin music from the crossroads, where the fiddler sat on a stile, and the young folks danced till the dust whirled about them, she would go a long way around through the wood to escape hearing and seeing.

The day after Christmas, when the peasant brides came to be dressed by Fru Moreus and her daughters, while they were being adorned with wreaths of myrtle and high satin crowns broidered with glass beads, with gorgeous silk sashes and breast bouquets of hand-made roses and skirts garlanded with taffeta flowers, she kept to her room so as not to see them decked out in Love's honor.

And when on winter evenings the Moreus girls sat at the quilting-frame in the cosy living-room, where a fire crackled on the hearth and the glass-apples swung and sweated before the blaze; when handsome Gösta Berling and the good Ferdinand, dropping in for a visit, would pull the thread out of the needles and fool the girls into making crooked stitches, the walls fairly ringing with the merry chatter and the love-making, as hands met hands under the quilting-frame — then, vexed, she would hurriedly gather up her knitting and quit the room. For she hated lovers and the ways of Love.

But Love's misdeeds she knew, and of these she

could tell! She wondered that Amor still dared show himself on this earth, that he was not frightened away by the wails of the forsaken, by the curses of those whom he had turned into criminals, by the lamentations of others whom he had cast into hateful bondage, and she marvelled that his wings could bear him so lightly, that he did not fall into the abyss of oblivion, weighed down by shame and remorse.

To be sure, she, like others, had once been young, but she had never been in love with Love. Never had she let herself be tempted to dance or to take or give a caress. Her mother's guitar hung in the attic, dusty and unstrung, but Mamselle Marie had never thrummed inane love-ditties on it. Her mother's potted rose-tree stood in the window; she watered it, that was all, for she was not fond of flowers, those children of love. Its leaves sagged with dust, spiders spun webs between the stems, and the buds never opened.

In Fru Moreus's rose-garden, where butterflies fluttered and birds sang, where fragrant blossoms wafted their love messages to circling bees—where everything spoke of the detestable Amor—she seldom set foot.

Then there came a time when the Svartsjö folk had an organ put into their church. A young organ-builder arrived in the parish, and he too became a lodger at Fru Moreus's cottage.

It was he who built in the organ which has such
extraordinary tones, whose thundering bass sometimes bursts forth in the middle of a peaceful an-
them — how or why, none can say — and sets all the
children howling in church at Christmas matins.

That the young organ-builder was a master of
his craft may well be doubted, but he was a bonny
fellow with sunshine in his eyes. He had a pleasant
word for every one, — for rich and poor, old and
young.

When he came home from his work in the evening, he would hold Fru Moreus's skein, dig side
by side with the young girls in the rose-garden,
declaim *Axel* and sing *Frithiof*, and he picked up
Mamselle Marie's ball of thread as often as she let
it drop, and even set her clock going.

He never came away from a ball without having
danced with every woman there, from the oldest
matron to the youngest slip of a•girl, and when
some adversity befell him, he would sit down beside
the first woman he chanced to meet and make her
his confidant. He was the manner of man women
create in their dreams. It cannot be said that he
spoke to any one of love, but he had not been many
weeks at Fru Moreus's before all the girls were in
love with him. As for poor Mamselle Marie, she
had prayed her prayers in vain.

That was a time of sorrow and a time of joy.
Tears rained on the quilting-frame, blotting out the

chalk lines. Evenings, a pale dreamer often sat in
the lilac bower, and up in Mamselle Marie's little
room the newly strung guitar twanged to old love
songs, which Marie had learned from her mother.

The young organ-builder meanwhile went about,
happy and care-free, lavishing his smiles and atten-
tions upon these languishing women, who quarrelled over him while he was away at his work.
Then, at last, came the day when he must depart.

The conveyance was at the door, the luggage had
been tied on behind, and the young man said farewell. He kissed Fru Moreus on the hand, gathered
the weeping girls in his arms, and kissed them on
the cheek. He wept himself at having to leave there,
for he had passed a pleasant summer in the little
grey cottage. At the very last he looked around for
Mamselle Marie.

She came down the old attic stairs in her best
array, the guitar strung round her neck on a broad,
green silk ribbon, a bouquet of "moon-roses" in her
hand; for that summer her mother's rose-tree had
bloomed. She stood before the young man, struck
her guitar, and sang:

> "Thou 'rt going far from us. Ah, come back again!
> 'T is friendship's voice that entreats thee.
> Be happy, forget not a true, loving heart,
> Which in Värmeland's valleys awaits thee."

Whereupon she put the nosegay in his buttonhole

and kissed him square on the mouth; then she vanished up the attic stairs like an apparition.

Amor had taken revenge on her and made her
a spectacle for all men. But she never again com-
plained of him, never again put away the guitar, and
never, never forgot to care for her mother's rose-
tree.

"Better unhappiness with Love than happiness
without him," she thought.

.   .   .   .

Time passed. The Major's wife had been driven out
of Ekeby, and the cavaliers had come into power.
Thus it happened, as related, that Gösta Berling,
one Sunday evening, read a poem to the Countess at
Borg, after which he was ordered out of the house
and told never to enter it again.

'T is said that when Gösta shut the hall door after
him, he saw several sledges drive up to Borg, and
cast a furtive glance at the little lady seated in the
first sledge. Dark as that hour had been for him,
it became darker still at sight of her. He hastened
away, lest he be recognized. Forebodings of disaster
filled his mind. Had the conversation inside called
up this woman? One misfortune always brings another.

Servants came hurrying out, carriage aprons were
unbuttoned, and pelts thrown to one side. Who had
come? Who was the little lady that stood up in

the sledge? Ah, it was actually she herself, Märta Dohna, the celebrated Countess!

She was the gayest and maddest of women. A pleasure-loving world had placed her on a throne and crowned her its queen. Play and Laughter were her subjects, and in the lottery of life she had drawn music, dancing, and adventure.

Though now close on to fifty, she was one of the wise, who do not count the years. "He who cannot lift his foot to dance," she said, "nor open his mouth to laughter, he is old; he feels the atrocious burden of years, but not I."

King Pleasure did not reign undisturbed in the days of her youth, but change and uncertainty only increased the delight of his charming presence. His Majesty of the butterfly wings had tea one day in the rooms of the ladies-in-waiting at the palace in Stockholm, and danced the next in Paris. He visited Napoleon's camps, sailed the blue Mediterranean with Nelson's fleet, attended a congress in Vienna, and risked going to Brussels on the eve of a famous battle to attend a ball.

And where King Pleasure was, there too was Märta Dohna, his chosen queen. Dancing, playing, jesting, Countess Märta flitted the whole world round. What had she not seen, what lived! She had danced thrones down, played *écarté* for principalities, caused devastating wars with her banter. Merriment and folly had been her life, and would be always. Her feet were not too old for dancing, nor her heart for love. When did she ever weary of masquerades and comedies, of droll tales and plaintive ballads?

When Pleasure betimes was homeless in the great world converted into a battlefield, she would take refuge for a longer or shorter period at the Count's old manor on the shores of Lake Löfven, as in the time of the Holy Alliance, when the princes and their courts had become too dull for her ladyship. It was during one of these visits that she had thought it well to make Gösta Berling her son's tutor. She always enjoyed her stay at Borg. Never had Pleasure a more ideal kingdom, with gay, beautiful women and adventure-loving men. There was no lack of feasts and balls, of boating-parties on moonlit lakes, nor sleighing-parties through dark forests, nor thrilling heart-experiences.

But after her daughter's death the Countess had ceased coming. She had not visited Borg in five years. Now she came to see how her daughter-in-law bore the life among the pines, the bears, and the snows. She deemed it her duty to find out whether the tiresome Henrik had quite bored her to death, with his stupidities, and she meant to play the gentle angel of domesticity. Sunshine and happiness were packed in her forty leather portmanteaux, Mirth was her handmaiden, Play her companion, Banter her charioteer.

As she tripped up the steps, she was met with open arms. Her old rooms had been put in order. Her companion, her maid, her footman, her forty leather portmanteaux and her thirty hat-boxes, her dressing-rolls, her shawls, and her furs were by degrees brought into the house. There was bustle and excitement from cellar to attic, a slamming of doors and a running on the stairs. It was quite evident that Countess Märta had arrived!

.   .   .   .

It was a beautiful spring evening, though only April, and the ice in the lake had not yet broken up. Mamselle Marie had opened her window and was sitting in her room, picking her guitar and singing. She was so absorbed in her music and her memories that she did not notice that a carriage had drawn up at the door of the cottage. In the carriage sat Countess Märta, who was highly amused at the sight of Mamselle Marie seated at the window, hugging her guitar and, with eyes turned heavenward, singing old, long-forgotten love-ditties.

Presently the Countess got out of her carriage and went into the cottage, where the girls sat as usual at the quilting-frame. She was never haughty: the winds of the Revolution had swept over her and blown fresh air into her lungs.

It was not her fault that she was a Countess, she used to say; but at all events she would live the life that was most pleasing to her. She had just as good a time at peasant weddings as at court balls, and when there was no one else at hand, she entertained her maids. She brought joy wherever she appeared, with her pretty little face and her exuberant spirits.

The Countess ordered quilts of Fru Moreus and complimented her daughters; she looked about the rose-garden and told of her adventures on the journey, for she was always having adventures, and she finally climbed the attic stairs, which were dreadfully steep and narrow, and sought out Mamselle Marie in her gable-room. The Countess's dark eyes beamed on the lonely little woman, and her mellow voice caressed her ear.

She gave her an order for curtains, and declared she could not live at Borg without having knitted curtains at all her windows, and for every table she must have one of Mamselle's covers.

Taking up the guitar, she sang to her of love and happiness and told her stories, and the little Mamselle was quite carried away into the gay, festive world. And the Countess's laugh was so musical it set all the little half-frozen birds out in the rose-garden warbling, and her face, which was hardly pretty now, for her complexion had been ruined by cosmetics and there was a sensual expression about her mouth, looked so beautiful to Mamselle Marie, that she wondered how the little looking-glass could let it vanish once it had been mirrored on its shining surface.

At parting, she kissed Mamselle and asked her to come to Borg. Poor Mamselle Marie's heart was as empty as the swallow's nest at Christmas. Though free, she sighed for chains like a slave freed in' old age.

Again there came for her a time of joy and a time of sorrow; but it did not last long—only one short week.

Every day the Countess sent for her and entertained her with anecdotes of her suitors, and Mamselle Marie laughed as she had never laughed before. They became the best of friends, and the Countess soon knew all about the young organ-builder and about the parting.

At twilight she would have Mamselle sit in the window-seat in the little blue cabinet, hang the guitar-ribbon round her neck, and make her sing love songs. The Countess sat where she could see the old spinster's shrunken figure and ugly little head silhouetted against the red evening sky, and she likened the poor Mamselle to a languishing maid of the castle. Her songs were all of tender shepherds and cruel shepherdesses, and her voice was the thinnest voice imaginable; so one can easily understand that the Countess had her little laugh at the ludicrousness of it all.

There was a party at Borg, as was natural when

the Count's mother had come home. It was not a grand affair, only the parish folk being invited; but every one had a jolly time, as usual.

The dining-hall was on the lower floor, and after supper the guests did not go upstairs again, but ensconced themselves in the adjoining room, which was Countess Märta's living-room. The Countess picked up Mamselle Marie's guitar, and began to sing for the company.

She was a merry-maker, this Countess, and a clever mimic. Now she had taken it into her head to mimic Mamselle Marie. Turning her eyes heavenward she proceeded to sing in a thin, squeaky voice.

"No no, no no, Countess!" pleaded Mamselle Marie.

But Märta Dohna was having sport, and the guests could hardly help laughing, though no doubt they felt sorry for poor Mamselle Marie.

The Countess took from a pot-pourri jar a handful of dried rose-leaves and, with tragic gestures, went up to Mamselle Marie, and sang with mock emotion:

> *"Thou 'rt going far from us. Ah, come back again!*
> *'Tis friendship's voice that entreats thee.*
> *Be happy, forget not a true, loving heart,*
> *Which in Värmeland's valleys awaits thee."*

Then she strewed the rose-leaves over her head. Everybody laughed except Mamselle Marie, who went white with fury. She looked as though she could have torn out the Countess's eyes.

"You're a bad woman, Märta Dohna," she said. "No honest woman should associate with you."

Countess Märta was angry too.

"Out with you, Mamselle!" she cried. "I have had enough of your silliness."

"I shall go," answered Mamselle Marie, "but first I must be paid for my covers and my curtains, which you've put up here."

"The old rags!" exclaimed the Countess. "Do you want to be paid for such rubbish? Take them away! I never wish to see them again. Take them away with you at once!"

Whereupon the Countess tore down the curtains and threw them, with the table-covers, at Mamselle Marie.

The next day young Countess Elizabeth begged her mother-in-law to make her peace with poor Mamselle; but she would not, for she was weary of her.

The young Countess then bought of Mamselle Marie the whole set of curtains and put them up at all the windows in the upper story, and Mamselle felt herself fully redressed.

Countess Märta chaffed her daughter-in-law a

U

good deal about her fondness for knitted curtains.
She could also mask her anger — keep it smoulder-
ing for years. A very clever person was this Countess Märta Dohna.

GÖSTA BERLING'S SAGA

PART II

Cousin Kristoffer

IN the cavaliers' wing there was an old bird of prey that always sat in the chimney-corner and kept an eye on the fire. He was grey and unkempt. His small head, with its big beak and lustreless eyes, drooped mournfully on the long, thin neck that stuck out above a shaggy collar. For this bird of prey wore a coat of fur summer and winter.

Formerly he belonged to the flock which, in the train of the great Emperor, had swept over all Europe; but what name and title he bore none ventured to guess. In Värmland they merely knew that he had taken part in the tumultuous struggle, had distinguished himself mightily, and was finally compelled to flee from an ungrateful fatherland, taking refuge with the Swedish Crown Prince, who advised him to disappear in distant Värmland. The times were such that he whose name had made nations tremble was glad that here none knew him by that once dreaded name. Having given his word of honor not to leave Värmland nor to reveal his identity, he had been sent by the Crown Prince to Ekeby Hall, with a letter of introduction to the Major. Thus it happened that the doors of the cavaliers' wing opened to him.

At first people wondered who the distinguished stranger could be that lived under an assumed name;

but in the course of time they came to regard him
as one of Värmland's cavaliers. Every one called
him Cousin Kristoffer, without knowing how he had
acquired the name.

It is not well, however, for a bird of prey to live in
a cage. One can understand that he has been accustomed to something quite different from hopping
from perch to perch and eating out of a keeper's
hand. His blood has been fired by the excitement
of battle and braving danger. Drowsy peace sick-
ens him.

True, the other cavaliers were not tame birds
either, though none fretted at captivity as did Cousin Kristoffer. A bear hunt was the only thing that
could enliven his drooping spirits, a bear hunt or
a woman — one particular woman.

He had come to life some ten years before, when
he first met Countess Märta, who was even then a
widow — a woman as uncertain as war, as inciting
as danger, a brilliant, audacious creature; her he
loved.

And there he sat growing old and grey, unable
to ask her to be his wife. It was five years since he
had seen her, and he was withering and pining like
a caged eagle. Each year found him more shrunken
and hopeless — drawing farther into his pelt and
nearer to the fire.

.   .   .   .

Thus he sat, buried in his pelt and shivering, on the day the Easter shots are fired at evening and the Easter witch is burned. The other cavaliers had gone out, but he was huddled, as usual, in the chimney-corner.

Oh, Cousin Kristoffer, Cousin Kristoffer, don't you know that she is come, the smiling and alluring Spring?

Nature has awakened from her winter sleep, and in the blue sky winged genii tumble about in wild glee. As thick as the blossoms on the brier-bush, their shining faces peer through the clouds.

Mother Earth has come to life again. Happy as a child, she leaps from her bath in the spring floods and her shower of spring rains. Rock and soil glisten. "Back to the rhythm of Life!" chant the tiniest atoms. "We shall rush like wings through ether; we shall shimmer on the blushing cheeks of maidens."

The blithesome spirits of Spring take possession of our bodies, and dart like eels through the blood, setting the heart in motion. There is the same murmur everywhere, in the heart and in the flower; to all living things the winged spirits attach themselves and ring out, as with a thousand tocsins: "Life and joy, life and joy! The smiling Spring is come!"

But Cousin Kristoffer sits still and does not understand. With head bowed on his stiffened fingers, he dreams of a rain of bullets and the glories of the battlefield.

One can but pity the lonely old refugee in the cavaliers' wing without a country or a people; he who never hears the sound of his mother tongue, he who will some day have a nameless grave in the Bro churchyard.

Oh, Cousin Kristoffer, you have been sitting dreaming long enough! Up and drink the sparkling wine of life! Know that a letter has come to the Major this very day, a royal letter bearing the seal of Sweden. Though addressed to the Major, it concerns you, old eagle. It would be a delight to watch you when you read that letter, to see your head lift and your eye regain its wonted brightness, as the cage door opens and you see the wide heavens spread for your longing wings.

.   .   .   .

Cousin Kristoffer burrowed deep down to the bottom of his chest and brought forth his long-put-away gold-laced uniform, and donned it; then he pressed his plumed hat on his head, mounted his fine white saddle-horse, and rode away from Ekeby.

Straightening in the saddle, he set off at a gallop, his fur-lined dolman fluttering, and his hat-plume waving in the breeze.

The man had grown young like the earth itself; he, too, had awakened from a long winter's sleep. The gold on his uniform had not lost its lustre, and the bold warrior-face under the cocked hat wore a proud look.

Wonderful indeed was the ride! Springs gushed from the ground, and crocuses popped up their heads wherever he passed. Twittering birds circled round the freed captive, and all nature rejoiced with him.

He was a conquering hero. Spring went before him on a floating cloud; he could scarcely contain himself for joy. Round about Cousin Kristoffer rode a staff of old comrades-at-arms. There was Happiness, standing on tiptoe in the saddle; there was Honor mounted on a splendid charger, and Love on a fiery Arabian steed. The inquisitive thrush called to him:

"Cousin Kristoffer, Cousin Kristoffer, whither are you riding, whither are you riding?"

"To Borg for to woo, to Borg for to woo," Cousin Kristoffer answered.

"Ride not to Borg, ride not to Borg!" screamed the thrush. "A man unmarried has no sorrow."

But he would not heed the warning. Up the hills and down the hills he rode, until at last he was there. He sprang from the saddle, and was instantly conducted into the presence of his lady.

Countess Märta was most gracious. Cousin Kristoffer felt sure that she would not refuse to bear his distinguished name and be the queen of his castle. He put off the moment of rapture when he

should show her the royal letter, and found pleasure in the waiting.

She chatted and regaled him with innumerable
anecdotes. He laughed at her quips, and was altogether entranced. They happened to be sitting in
one of the rooms where Mamselle Marie's knitted
curtains were hung, and the Countess told him their
story. She made it as funny as she could, of course,
and ridiculed the old Mamselle.

"You see," she laughed—"you see how bad I
am. These curtains now hang here that I may be
reminded of my sin every hour of the day. Was
ever such penance put upon any one! Oh, those
abominable shell-stitch curtains!"

The great warrior looked at her with flaming
eyes.

"I too am old and poor," he said, "and I have
sat for ten years in a chimney-corner yearning for
the one *I* love. Does your ladyship laugh at that
also?"

"Ah, that is another matter!" exclaimed the
Countess.

"God has deprived me of both fatherland and
happiness, forcing me to eat the bread of strangers," Cousin Kristoffer continued gravely, "and I
have learned to respect poverty."

"You too!" cried the Countess, throwing up her
hands. "Dear me, how virtuous every one is these
days!"

"Let me say to you, Countess, that if God some day should give me back my lost wealth and power, I shall put them to better use than sharing them with a worldly creature, a heartless, painted monkey that mocks at the unfortunate."

"In that you would do right, Cousin Kristoffer."

Turning on his heel, Cousin Kristoffer walked out of the house and went back to Ekeby. But the happy genii did not accompany him now, the thrush did not call to him, and he no longer saw the smiling Spring.

He arrived just as the Easter shots were about to be fired and the Easter witch was to be burned.

The Easter witch is a big straw doll with a rag face, on which eyes, nose, and mouth are sketched with charcoal. Dressed in witches' garb, with the long-handled oven-rake and broom placed beside her, and the horn with oil hung round her neck, she was all ready for her ride to hell.

Major Fuchs loaded his shotgun and emptied it into the air. Whereupon a heap of dried branches was lighted, the witch was cast on the pyre, and was soon burning lustily. The cavaliers, in accordance with a time-honored custom, did what they could to destroy the power of evil.

Cousin Kristoffer, with sombre mien, stood looking on. Suddenly he drew from his cuff the royal letter and threw it on the fire. God alone knew what was in his thought. Perhaps he imagined it was the

Countess herself burning there. Or, he may have felt that, inasmuch as the woman he had idolized was, after all, but straw and rags, nothing else mattered.

He returned to the cavaliers' wing, rekindled the fire, put away his uniform, and once again settled down in his chimney-corner. With each passing day he grew more listless, more grey and shaggy, dying by degrees, as do eagles in captivity.

Though no longer a captive, he did not care to make use of his freedom. All the world was open to him; the battlefield, honor, life awaited him; but he had not the strength to spread his wings for flight.

The Paths of Life

DREARY are the paths which men must tread on earth, through desert and marsh and over the hills. Why must so much sorrow go uncomforted, till it loses its way in the desert, or sinks into the marsh, or stumbles from the hills? Where are the fairy princesses in whose footsteps roses spring? Where are they who should strew flowers over the dreary way?

Now, the poet Gösta Berling has determined to get married. He is only seeking a bride poor enough, lowly enough, and sufficiently an outcast to be a fit mate for a crazy parson. Noble and beautiful women have loved him, but they are not to compete for his hand. The outcast will choose among the outcasts. Whom will he choose, whom will he seek out?

Sometimes there came to Ekeby a poor girl selling brooms, from a desolate village up among the hills. There, where poverty and misery ever reigned, many of the people were not in the full possession of their faculties, and the broom girl was one of them. But she was beautiful. Her thick black hair was bound in such heavy plaits her head could hardly carry them; her cheeks were delicately rounded, her nose was straight and not too large, her eyes were blue. She had a melancholy, Madonna-like type of beauty, as one sometimes finds it even now among the girls on the shores of the long Löfven.

Such is the bride Gösta Berling has chosen. A half-crazy beggar girl will be a fit wife for a disgraced parson. Nothing could be more suitable. It is only necessary he should go to Karlstad for the rings, and afterwards they will have another gay day on the Löfven shores. Let them laugh once more at Gösta Berling, when he is betrothed to the broom girl, and when he marries her! Let them laugh! Has he ever conceived a more amusing escapade?

Dreary are the paths men tread on earth, over desert and marsh and mountain. Must the outcast go the way of the outcasts? The way of anger and trouble and unhappiness? What does it matter if he stumbles and falls! Is there any one to restrain him? Is there any one who would stretch out to him a supporting hand, or offer him a pleasant drink? Where are the fairy princesses who should strew roses over the dreary paths?

No, no, the sweet young Countess at Borg must not interfere with Gösta Berling's plans! She must think of her reputation, she must think of her husband's anger and her mother-in-law's spite, she must not try to restrain him. During the long service in Svartsjö church she may clasp her hands and bow her head and pray for him. During sleepless nights she may weep and fear for him, but she has no

flowers to strew in his, the outcast's path, no drop
of water to give to the thirsty, no light clasp of the
hand which might draw him back from the edge of
the precipice.

Gösta Berling did not trouble to lavish silks and
jewels upon his chosen bride, he let her go from
house to house selling brooms, as she had been accustomed to do; but when he had gathered together
all the men and women of rank in the whole country side to a great festival at Ekeby, he intended to
proclaim his betrothal. He would call her in from
the kitchen just as she was after her long tramp, with
the dust and the dirt of the road on her clothes, perhaps in rags, perhaps uncombed, with wild eyes
and a stream of wild words on her lips. And he would
ask the guests if he had not chosen a fitting bride,
if the crazy parson should not feel proud of such a
beautiful girl, of that wild, Madonna-like face and
those blue, dreamy eyes.

It had been his desire that no one should know
anything about this beforehand, but the secret got
abroad, and among those who heard of it was young
Countess Dohna. But what could she do to hinder him? The betrothal day had arrived, and it was
already twilight. The Countess stood at the window of the little blue cabinet, and gazed toward
the north. She almost thought she could see Ekeby,
though tears and mist intervened. She fancied she
saw the big three-storied house with its lighted win-

dows and the champagne being poured out into
the glasses, and could hear the healths being drunk
and Gösta Berling proclaiming his betrothal with
the broom girl. If she were near, or could lay her
hand gently on his arm, and even give him a kindly
glance, would he turn from the angry path of the
outcasts? If a word from her had driven him to
such folly, would a word from her check him?

She shuddered at the thought of the sin he had
committed against that poor unfortunate child. She
shuddered at the sin committed against that poor
creature, who would now be tempted to love him,
perhaps, for a day's amusement. And yet she shuddered most at the sin he was committing against
himself, chaining a heavy burden to his life, which
would forever weigh down the strength of his spirit.
And the fault was chiefly hers. She had turned him
with hard words into the outcast's path. She, whose
duty it was to bless and to mitigate pain, why had
she twined another thorn into the sinner's crown
of thorns?

Well, she knew what to do. She would order the
black horses to be harnessed to the sledge, she would
hurry over the Löfven to Ekeby, and, standing
before Gösta Berling, she would tell him she did
not scorn him, that she did not know what she said
when she turned him away from her house. . . . No,
she would do nothing of the kind, she would be
ashamed, and would not dare to utter a word. She

was a married woman, and must be careful. There would be so much gossip if she were to do anything like that. But if she did not do it, what would happen to him? She must go.

Then she remembered such a drive was impossible. No horse could cross the ice of the Löfven again that season. It was melting and already detached from the shores. It lay free, broken, and fearful to look at. The water gurgled over and through it; in some places it had collected in black pools, in others the ice was shining white. But it was chiefly grey, dirty from the melting snow, and the roads wound like long black ribbons over its surface. How could she think of venturing upon such a journey? Old Countess Märta, her mother-in-law, would never allow her. She must sit beside her all the evening and listen to her stories about the court, which were the old lady's delight. Still, night came at last, her husband was away from home—she was free. . . .

She could not drive, she dared not call a servant to go with her, but her fear drove her out—she could not help herself.

Dreary are the paths men tread on earth, over desert and marsh and mountain. But that night's path over the melting snow, to what can I compare it? Was it not the very path the fairies themselves have to tread, an insecure, swaying, slippery path, the path of those who would heal the hurt, of those

who would right the wrong, the path of the light-
footed and the quick-eyed, and of the living, courageous heart?

Midnight had passed before the Countess reached
Ekeby shore. She had fallen often, and had sprung
over wide clefts; she had run swiftly over places
where the water filled at once the traces of her footsteps; she had stumbled, she had crept carefully
over dangerous places. It had been a dreary way,
and she wept as she went onward. She was wet and
tired, and out there on the ice, the darkness, loneliness, and desolation had frightened her. At last,
before she reached the shore, she was obliged to
wade through water a foot deep, and when she
reached it she had no heart for anything but to sit
down upon a stone and cry from weariness and helplessness.

Dreary are the paths that the children of men
tread, and sometimes the fairies fall beside their
flower baskets, just when they have reached the
way which they should strew with roses.

But this young and delicately nurtured little lady
was a loving heroine. She had never trod any such
path in her own bright fatherland. She might well
sit by the shores of that fearful lake, wet, tired,
unhappy as she was, and think of the flower-edged
paths of her southern home. Oh, but it was no longer
a question of north and south to her! She was fairly
in the stream of life. She was not weeping for her

home. She wept because she was so tired that she could not reach the path she wished to strew with roses. She wept because she thought she had come too late. Then she saw a number of people running quickly along the shore. They passed without seeing her, but she caught their words.

"If the dam goes, the forge goes," one cried. "And the mill and the workshops and the blacksmiths' houses," cried another.

Then the Countess gained new courage, rose, and followed the men.

. . . .

The forge and the mill at Ekeby lay upon a narrow promontory, round which the Björksjö River rushed. It thundered upon the point, white from the mighty fall above, and to protect the buildings on shore from the rush of the waters a gigantic breakwater had been built. This breakwater had grown old, and the cavaliers were masters at Ekeby; in their days dancing went over the hills, but no one took time to see what frost and time and tide were doing to the old stone breakwater.

Then came the spring flood, and the dam began to give way. The waterfall at Ekeby is a mighty granite stairway, down which pour the waves of the Björksjö River. They are giddy with the speed, and tumble over and strike one another. They rise in fury and dash spray over one another—stumble

over a stone or a piece of timber and then up again,
to fall again and again and again — foaming, hissing, roaring.

Now these wild, excited waves, maddened with
the spring air, crazed with their new found liberty,
were rushing to storm the old breakwater! Hissing
and tearing at it, they hurled themselves high against
it and then fell back as if they had hurt their white
crests. They made a splendid storming party. They
used huge pieces of ice as shields, they built the floating beams into a battering-ram, they bent, broke,
and beat against the poor breakwater till suddenly
it seemed as if some one shouted to them, "Take
care, take care!" Then they all rushed backwards,
and after them came a big stone, loosened from the
dam, and fell with a thundering splash into the
stream. This seemed to surprise them, they paused,
they rejoiced, they held a consultation, then on
again. They were at it again with icy shields and
thick battering-rams, mischievous, cruel, and wild,
mad with the lust of destruction. "If only the breakwater were away," cried the waves, "if only the
breakwater gives way, it will then be the turn of the
forge and the mill. To-day is the day of freedom —
away with men and their work! They have soiled us
with coal, they have dusted us with flour, they throw
the yoke of labor upon us as upon oxen, they
have driven us round the water-wheel and dammed
us up, cramped us in the mill wickets, compelled

us to turn the heavy wheels, to carry the clumsy beams. But we shall have freedom now. The day of freedom has come. Hear it, you waves of the Björksjö —hear it, brothers and sisters, in marsh and fen, in mountain, stream, and forest brook! Come, come, rush down the Björksjö River—come with new strength, thundering, hissing, ready to break through the restraint of centuries, come! The bulwark of tyranny shall fall. Death to Ekeby!" And they came; wave after wave rushed over the fall to dash its head against the dam, to lend its help to the great work. Giddy with spring's new freedom, they came with united force and loosened stone after stone, piece after piece of the falling breakwater.

But why do men let the wild waves rage without resisting their onslaught? Is Ekeby dead?

People there were, a helpless, bewildered, confused crowd. The night was dark; they could not distinguish one another nor see their way. The falls thundered loud; the sound of breaking ice and grinding timbers was overpowering; they could not hear themselves speak. The wild whirl that inspires the roaring waves filled their heads—their hearts, too; they had no thought nor any reason left.

The foundry bell pealed. Let them that have ears to hear, hear. We here at Ekeby Foundry are nearly lost. The river is upon us. The dam is failing, the foundry is in danger and the mill and our own poor houses—loved in spite of their lowliness.

The waves must have thought the bells were calling to their friends, for no more people made their appearance. But far in the forest and marshes a sudden hurry awakens. "Send helpers, send helpers!" rings the bell. "We are free at last, after centuries of slavery; come, come!" The roaring waves and the ringing bell sing a death song over Ekeby's honor and glory.

And meanwhile word is sent again and again to the cavaliers. Are they in the humor to think of foundry or mill? A hundred guests are assembled in Ekeby's halls. The broom girl waits in the kitchen; the exciting moment has come. The champagne is purling in the wine-glasses; Julius is rising to make a speech. All the old adventurers at Ekeby are rejoicing at the numbness of astonishment which will soon descend upon the assembled guests.

Out on the ice of Löfven Countess Dohna is treading a dangerous path to be able to whisper a few words of warning to Gösta Berling. At the fall the waves are storming against Ekeby's honor and might; but in its spacious halls there reigns joy and eager excitement; the waxen candles shine, and wine flows; no one gives a thought to what is taking place in the darkness of the stormy spring night.

The moment arrived. Gösta rose and went out to bring in the bride. He was obliged to cross the hall, and the great doors stood open; he paused, looked out into the black night, and he heard — he

heard. He heard the bell pealing and the roar of the
waters. He heard the thunder of the breaking ice,
the noise of the grinding timbers, the wild waves
roaring a scornful, jubilant song of freedom. And he
dashed out into the night, forgetting all else. They
might stand round the table with lifted glasses and
wait till doomsday; he cared no more for them. The
bride might wait, Squire Julius's speech die on his
lips. No rings would be exchanged that night—the
paralyzing astonishment would not descend upon
the brilliant assembly.

Now, woe to you, you wild waves! You must fight
in earnest now for your freedom, for Gösta Berling
has come upon the scene, the people have found a
leader, courage awakens in the frightened hearts,
the defenders climb the breakwater: now begins a
mighty battle.

Hear him shout to the people; he takes command and sets them all to work.

"We must have light, light, first of all; the mill-
er's horn lantern is of no use here. See those strawstacks; take them up to the crest of the hill and set
fire to them. That is work for the women and children. But quick, make a huge blazing pile of straw
and keep it afire! It will light our work, and call help
from far and near. And do not let it die out; bring
more straw; let clear flame flare to heaven!

"Here, men, is work for you. Here are beams
and planks, bind a dam together which we can sink

before the failing wall. Quick, quick, to work, make
it strong and steady! Find stones and sandbags to
sink it with. Quick, swing your axes, let your hammers thunder, the gimlets bite into the wood, and
the saws grate in the dry planks!

"And where are the boys? Here, you good-for-
nothings! Find poles and boat-hooks, and come out
into the midst of the tumult. Out upon the breakwater with you, boys, into the midst of the waves
that whirl and seethe and cover us with foam. Ward
off, weaken, turn aside those blows under which the
old dam is falling. Turn aside the timbers and hold
fast the loosening stones with your hands; hang on
to them, grip them with claws of iron. Fight, boys,
you wild rascals! Out upon the wall with you, and
we will fight for every handful of earth!"

Gösta took his place at the end of the breakwater and stood there deluged in spray. The ground
swayed beneath him, and the waves thundered and
roared, but his wild heart rejoiced at the danger and
the strife and dismay. He laughed and had gay nonsense for the boys on the wall beside him; he felt he
had never spent a more enjoyable night.

The work of defence went rapidly forward; the
flames flared, the carpenters' axes crashed, and the
dam still stood.

The other cavaliers and their hundred guests also
came down to the waterfall. People came from far
and near, and all helped either at keeping the fire

alight or working at the improvised dam, at filling the sandbags, or out on the trembling, quaking breakwater.

Ah! the carpenters have finished the new dam; it must be sunk before the shaking breakwater. Hold ready the sandbags and stones and boat-hooks, so that it may not be torn away, and that victory shall remain with man and the vanquished waves return to their slavery.

Then, at the critical moment, it happened that Gösta caught sight of a woman sitting on a stone near the river bank. The light from the bonfire illuminated her figure where she sat staring at the waves. He could not see her very distinctly through the mist and spray, but his eyes were drawn irresistibly toward her. He gazed at her again and again; he felt that woman had a special mission to him.

Among all the hundreds who were out at work on the river bank, she alone sat idle, and his glance turned to her, till at last he saw her and no one else. She sat so near the stream that the waves dashed against her feet, and their spray flew over her. She must have been dripping wet. She was darkly clad, and had a dark shawl over her head, and sat in a crouching position, supporting her chin on her hands, and stared fixedly at him out on the breakwater. He felt those staring eyes, drawing him and calling him, though he could not distinguish the features, and at last he thought of nothing but the woman sitting at the edge of the waves.

"It is the mermaid from the Löfven who has risen in the river here to tempt me to destruction," he thought. "She sits there and calls and calls to me; I must go and drive her away."

The white-crested waves seemed to be her vassals; she excited and drove them in their attacks on him.

"I really must drive her away," he repeated. And he caught up a boat-hook, sprang on shore, and hurried in her direction.

He left his place at the end of the breakwater to drive that apparition away. In that moment of excitement it seemed as if the powers of the deep were fighting with him, and he felt obliged to drive away that dark figure sitting on the stone by the river bank.

Oh, Gösta, why was your place vacant at the critical moment? They were bringing the improvised dam; a long row of men stood on the breakwater; they had ropes and stones and sandbags in readiness to weigh it down and hold it in place; they were ready, waited, and listened. Where was the leader? Where was the voice of command?

No, Gösta Berling had followed the mermaid; his voice was silent, and no one heard his command.

So the work was continued without him — the waves swept aside, the heavy timbers plunged down, and after them the sandbags and stones. But how can the work be done without a leader? There is no order, no care taken. The waves rushed forward again and again; they flung themselves with renewed fury against the new hindrance; they rolled the sandbags aside, tore the ropes, loosened the stones, and succeeded — succeeded. Scornful, jubilant, they raised the whole raft on their strong shoulders, pulled and dragged at it, and had it at last completely in their power. Away with the miserable piece of defence; into the Löfven with it! And so on again at the failing, helpless old breakwater.

But Gösta Berling was intent upon driving the sea-nymph away. She saw him approach, swinging the boat-hook, and grew frightened. It almost seemed as if she intended to throw herself into the water, but she bethought herself, and sprang toward the land.

"You witch!" cried Gösta, swinging the boat-hook over her. She turned hurriedly into the yellow bushes on the bank, became entangled in the thick branches, and stood motionless.

Then Gösta threw the boat-hook aside, and laid his hand on her shoulder.

"You are out late to-night, Countess Elizabeth?"

"Leave me alone, Herr Berling; let me go home."

He obeyed instantly, and turned away from her.

But as she was not only a fine lady, but a kind
little woman who could not endure the thought
that she had been the cause of any one's trouble —
as she was one of the fairies who always had enough
roses in her basket to strew upon the very dreariest
of paths — she repented directly and followed him,
catching hold of his hand.

"I came," she said, stammering, "I came to —
Oh, Herr Berling, you have not done it, say you
have not done it! I was so afraid when you ran
toward me, but I wanted to see you so much. I
wanted to say that you must forget what I said that
day, and come to see us as usual."

"How did you get here?"

She laughed nervously. "I knew, of course, I
should come too late, but I did not wish any one to
know I was going, and besides, you know, there is
no possibility of driving over the ice."

"And you have walked over the ice?"

"Yes, certainly; but please, Herr Berling, let me
know the truth. Are you already betrothed? You
know that I hope you are not. It is so wrong, you
see, and it seems as if I were to blame for it all. I
am a stranger, and do not know the customs of the
country. It has been so lonely at Borg since you
came no more."

To Gösta Berling, standing there among the wet
bushes on the swampy ground, it seemed as if some
one had thrown a shower of roses over him — as

if he waded in them over his knees, they gleamed before his eyes in the darkness, he greedily drank in their perfume.

"And you have done this?" he repeated.

He must answer her and put an end to her anxiety, though he felt such great delight in it. Oh, how warm and how fair everything seemed, when he thought of the road she had crossed, of how wet and cold and anxious she was, how tearful her voice sounded!

"No," he said; "I am not betrothed."

Then she caught his hand again and caressed it. "I am so glad, so glad," she cried, and her heart, which before had been frozen with fear, shook with sobs.

There were flowers enough now in the poet's path, and all darkness, anger, and hate melted out of his heart.

"How good you are—how very good you are," he exclaimed.

Before them the waves were storming against the honor and glory of Ekeby. The people had no leader; no one inspired their hearts with hope and courage, and the breakwater fell. The waves plunged over it, and then dashed exultantly against the promontory where the mill and foundry stood. No one fought them now; no one thought of anything but of saving their own lives and their property.

It was quite a matter of course to those young

people that Gösta should accompany the Countess home; he could not leave her in the dark nor let her cross the dangerous ice alone again. They never once remembered that he was needed at the foundry, for they were so happy at being friends again.

It is easy to believe they loved one another, but who can be sure of it? Only disjointed and stray accounts of the brilliant events of their lives have reached me, and I know nothing — less than nothing, of what passed in their innermost hearts.

What can I tell you of the motives which inspired their actions? I only know that a young and beautiful woman risked her life, her honor, her reputation, and her health, that night, to bring a miserable wretch back into the right path. I only know that Gösta Berling let the honor and glory of beloved Ekeby fall that night to accompany her, who, for his sake, had overcome the fear of death and shame and punishment.

I have often followed them in my thoughts over the ice on that dreadful night, which for them had such a happy ending. I do not think there was any secret love in their hearts which they repressed and tried to crush down, as they clambered over the ice, chatting happily of all that had taken place during the time they had been separated.

He was again her page, her slave who lay at her feet, and she was again his lady.

They were gay and happy, and neither of them

said a word that might betoken love. Laughingly
they splashed their way through the shore water;
they laughed when they found their way and laughed
when they lost it, when they stumbled, when they
fell, and when they scrambled up again; they laughed
at everything. Life was again to them an amusing
game, and they had been naughty children who had
quarrelled. Oh, how perfect it was to make it up and
begin over again.

Reports came and went, and in time the story of
the perilous crossing made by the Countess reached
Anna Stjärnhök.

"Ah!" she said, "I see that God has more than
one string to His bow. I will hush my heart to rest
and remain where I am needed. God will make a
man of Gösta Berling without my help."

Penance

DEAR friends, if it should happen that you meet a poor creature on your path, a poor little being who lets his hat hang on his back and carries his shoes in his hand, refusing protection against the heat of the sun and the stones in his way—a waif who willingly calls down ruin upon his own head—pass him by in silent dismay! It is the penitent—the penitent on his way to the Holy Places.

The penitent must wear the coarse gown and live on bread and water, even if he be a king. He must walk and never drive; he must beg and never own. He must sleep on thorns, and he must wear out the hard pavement of the Holy Places with his constant kneeling. He must swing the knotted scourge over his own back. No pleasure can he take except in suffering—no happiness except in sorrow.

Young Countess Elizabeth once wore the coarse gown and trod the thorny path. Her heart accused her of sin. It longed for pain as the weary long for a refreshing bath, and she brought awful ruin upon herself when she stepped down joyfully into a cloud of suffering.

Her husband, the young Count with the head of an old man on his shoulders, came home on the morning after the night when the Ekeby Mill was destroyed by the spring flood. He had hardly arrived home when his mother, Countess Märta, sent for him and told him a wonderful tale.

"Your wife was out last night, Henrik. She was away a long time, and she was accompanied by a man. I heard him saying good-night to her. I know, too, who it was. I heard her go, and I heard her return, though it was not her intention that I should. She is deceiving you, Henrik,—she is deceiving you—the hypocrlte! She has never loved you, my poor boy. Her father simply wanted her to make a good marriage, and she took you because you were rich."

She was so plausible that Count Henrik became furious. He would have a divorce—he would send his wife back to her father.

"No, my friend," said Countess Märta; "in that case she would go to the bad altogether. She is spoiled and badly brought up; let me take her in hand and bring her back to the path of duty."

And the Count called in his wife and told her that she was to yield utter obedience to his mother's wishes.

What a scene was that! Surely none more pitiful had ever taken place in that old house, wedded as it was to sorrow. The young wife heard many hard words from her husband. He stretched his arms to heaven and charged it with letting his name be dragged through the mire by a shameless woman.

He shook his clenched fist before her face, asking her if she knew of a punishment severe enough for a crime such as hers.

She was not at all afraid of him, for she was sure she had done right. She replied that she had a cold in the head, and that was quite punishment enough.

"Elizabeth," said Countess Märta, "this is not a thing to joke about."

"We," the young woman answered, "have never agreed about the right time for joking or seriousness."

"But you ought to be able to understand, Elizabeth, that no honest woman leaves her home in the middle of the night to wander about with a well-known adventurer."

Then Elizabeth Dohna saw that her mother-in-law had determined to ruin her. She understood she must fight with every faculty, or that woman would draw down a fearful misfortune upon her.

"Henrik," she cried, "don't let your mother stand between us! Let me tell you how it all happened. You are just—don't judge me unheard. Let me tell you how it all happened, and you will see that I have only done what you taught me."

The Count nodded a dumb assent, and Elizabeth told him how she had driven Gösta Berling into bad ways. She told him all that had taken place in the little blue cabinet, and how her conscience had forced her to try and save the man to whom she had

been so unjust. " I had no right to judge him," she
said; "and my husband has himself taught me that
no sacrifice is too great when we wish to atone for an
injustice. Isn't it true, Henrik?"

Count Henrik turned to his mother.

" What does my mother say?" he asked. He was
stiff with dignity now, and his high, narrow forehead
lay in majestic folds.

"I," answered his mother, "I say Anna Stjärnhök was a clever girl, and knew very well what she
was doing when she told Elizabeth that old story."

" My mother deigns to misunderstand me," continued her son. "I ask what my mother thinks of
this story. Has the Countess Märta tried to talk
over her daughter, my sister, to marry a disgraced
clergyman?"

Countess Märta was silent a moment.Ah,that stupid, stupid Henrik! He was off again on the wrong
tack. Her dog was after the hunter now and allowing the hare to escape. But if Countess Märta had
no answer then, it was not long before she had. "My
dear friend," she said, with a shrug of her shoulders, "there is a reason for letting these old stories
of that unfortunate man rest—the same reason
which compels me to beg you to avoid all public
scandal. It is in fact highly probable that he perished last night."

She spoke in a mild, pitying tone, but there was
not a word of truth in what she said.

"Elizabeth has slept so late this morning, and has not heard that men have been sent all round the lake to seek Herr Berling. He has not returned to Ekeby, and they fear he has been drowned. The ice on the lake broke up this morning. Look! the storm has split it up into a thousand pieces."

Countess Elizabeth looked out—the lake was almost clear.

Then she bewailed herself. She had thought to escape God's justice; she had lied and dissembled, and had covered herself with the white mantle of innocence.

In wildest despair she threw herself down before her husband, and her confession poured over her lips.

"Judge me and cast me out! I have loved him—never doubt that I have loved him! I tear my hair for the sorrow of it. I do not care for anything now he is dead. I don't care to defend myself. You may know all the truth. I have taken the love of my heart from my husband and given it to a stranger. Oh, wicked woman that I am! I am one of those who have been tempted by forbidden love."

Youthful, despairing—lying there at the feet of your judges, tell them all!

Welcome martyrdom, welcome disgrace! How you will bring the lightning of heaven over your fair young head!

Tell your husband how terrified you were when love, powerful and irresistible, came over you—

how you shuddered over the worthlessness of your
heart. You would rather have met the churchyard
ghost than the demons in your own soul.

Tell them that, denied the face of God, you felt
yourself unworthy to tread the earth. You have
striven with tears and prayers. "O God, save me!
O Son of God, who cast out the devils, save me!"
you have cried.

Tell them how you thought it best to hide your
sin. No one should know your wretchedness. You
thought to please God in doing this. You thought
you were doing God's errand when you wished to
save the man you loved. He knew nothing of your
love. He should not be lost for your sake. Did you
know what was right or what was wrong? God alone
knew it, and He has judged you. He has thrown
down the idol of your heart. He has led you into
the great, the healing path of the penitent!

Tell them that you knew that salvation did not
lie in hiding it. Demons love the darkness. May
the hands of your judges grasp the scourge! The
punishment will fall like healing balm on the sore
of your sin. Your heart longs for suffering.

Tell them all this, while you kneel on the floor
and wring your hands in tempestuous grief, crying
out in wild tones of despair, and welcoming with
a shrill laugh the thought of punishment and disgrace, till your husband takes hold of you and drags
you up from the floor.

"Behave yourself like a Countess Dohna, or I must beg my mother to chastise you as a child."

"Do with me what you will."

Then the Count pronounced sentence:

"As my mother has prayed for you, you may remain in my house, but in the future she commands, and you obey."

See the path of the penitent! The young Countess has become one of the servants. How long, oh, how long?

How long will a proud heart be subdued? How long will impatient lips be silent and a hasty hand held back? The misery of abasement is sweet. While the back aches with the heavy work, the heart is quiet. To those who sleep a few short hours on a hard bed of straw sleep comes unbidden.

The older woman might be changed into an evil spirit to torture the younger one sufficiently. She thanks her; the evil is not yet dead within her. Hunt the sleepy head up every morning at four o'clock. Give the inexperienced worker an endless day's work at the heavy looms. It is right; the penitent might not have strength to swing the scourge with sufficient force.

When the great spring wash was at hand, Countess Märta made the young Countess stand at the tubs in the wash-house. She went herself to inspect her work. "The water is too cold in your tub," she said, and took boiling water out of the cauldron and poured it over her bare arms. The day was cold, when the washerwomen went down to the lake to rinse the clothes. Stormy winds and squalls rushed by and covered them with mingled snow and rain. Their skirts were dripping wet and heavy as lead. It was hard work to wield the beating staff, and the blood started from under the delicate finger-nails. But Countess Elizabeth did not complain. Blessed be the goodness of God! Where has the penitent his happiness but in suffering? And the knotted scourge falls as softly as rose leaves on the penitent's back.

The young Countess soon heard that Gösta Berling lived. The older woman had only trapped her into a confession. Well, what did it matter? See God's path! See God's guidance! He has driven the sinner thus into the path of atonement.

One thing she grieved about. What will become of her mother-in-law, whose heart God, for her sake, has hardened? Oh, He will judge her kindly! She must be hard to help the sinner to win God's love again.

She did not know how often a soul, having proved all the good things of the world, turns to find pleasure in cruelty. When flattery and caresses, the madness of dancing and excitement of gambling have satiated the impatient darkened soul, it dives down to its depths and finds cruelty there. In the torture of men and animals there is still to be found a font

of joy for deadened feelings. Countess Märta was
not conscious of doing evil. She believed herself
to be punishing a frivolous wife, so she lay awake
sometimes in the night contriving new tortures.
Woe to her! What sacrilege she committed! She was
turning work, the great healer, into a torment and
a curse.

One evening she went over all the house and
ordered the young Countess to light her way. Elizabeth carried the candle without a candlestick.

"The candle is burnt out," she said presently.

"When the candle is finished, the candlestick
burns," Countess Märta replied, and she went on,
till the flame died out in the blistered hands.

But that was childishness. There is a suffering
of the soul that outweighs all the pains of the body.
Countess Märta invited her guests, and made the
lady of the house serve them at table herself. That
was the penitent's great festival day. Strangers would
see her in her disgrace. They would see she was no
longer worthy to sit at her husband's table. Oh, with
what scorn their cold eyes would rest upon her!

But it was worse than that—a thousand times
worse. Not a glance met hers. All sat silent and depressed around the table, men and women equally
cast down.

But she gathered up all this as burning coals
to heap upon her head. Was her sin then so awful?
Was it a sin to be near her?

Then came the temptation. Anna Stjärnhök, who had been her friend, and the Judge from Munkerud, her neighbor at table, caught hold of her, when she approached them, snatched the dish of meat out of her hands, drew up a chair, and refused to let her go.

"Sit down, child, sit down!" said the Judge; "you have done no harm." And all the other guests declared with one accord that, if she would not remain at table, they would all leave at once. They were no hangman's servants; they were not in Märta Dohna's pay. They were not so easily deceived as the sheepheaded Count.

"Oh, my friends, my dear friends, don't be so kind to me! You compel me to confess my sin. There is some one I have loved too much."

"Child, you do not know what sin is! You do not know how innocent you are! Gösta Berling did not even know you cared for him. Take your place in your own house; you have done no wrong."

They encouraged her for a time, and were themselves as gay as children. Laughter and jokes circled round the table.

These hasty, easily moved people, they were so kind-hearted, but still they were sent by the tempter. They tried to convince her she was a martyr, and openly showed their scorn for Countess Märta, as if she were a witch. But they did not understand. They did not know how the soul longs for purity, and how the penitent is forced to expose himself to the burning heat of the sun and the roughness of his path.

Sometimes Countess Märta compelled her to sit all day at her embroidery frame, while she told her endless stories about Gösta Berling, the preacher and adventurer. If her memory did not suffice, she invented, with the one object that his name should sound for days in Elizabeth's ears. This she feared most. During such days she felt that the penance would never end. Her love refused to die. She thought she would die herself before that—her strength was failing her. She was often very ill.

"But where does your hero tarry?" asked Countess Märta, scornfully. "I have expected him day after day at the head of the cavaliers. Why does he not storm Borg, set you upon the throne, and throw me and your husband, bound, into the tower? Are you forgotten already?"

She almost wished to defend him, and say that she had forbidden him to help her. But no, it is best to be silent—to be silent and to suffer.

Day by day, she was being worn away by the fire of over-excitement. She was in a constant fever, and was so tired she could hardly hold herself upright. She longed only to die. The strong currents of her life were conquered; love and joy dared not stir within her, and she no longer feared suffering. It seemed as if her husband no longer remembered that she existed. He imprisoned himself in his room nearly all day, studying undecipherable manuscripts and essays printed in an old-fashioned blurred print.

He read letters of nobility on parchment, to which the Swedish seals hung large and round, formed in red wax and guarded in a carved wooden case. He examined armorial bearings of lilies on a white field and blue griffins; he understood that kind of thing and translated it easily —and re-read again and again old funeral ovations and the dates of the births and deaths of the noble Counts of Dohna, where their exploits are compared to the heroes of Israel and the gods of Hellas. You see these old things had always given him pleasure. But he did not trouble himself to think any further about his young wife.

Countess Märta had said that which had killed all his love: "She took you for your money." No one can bear to think of that; it kills all love, and he was now quite indifferent to what became of the young woman. If his mother could bring her back to the path of duty, so much the better. Count Dohna cherished a great admiration for his mother.

This miserable state of things lasted a month. Still it was not such a stormy and tumultuous time as it sounds when the separate events are gathered together within the bounds of a few written pages. Countess Elizabeth seems to have been always calm to outward appearance. It was but once, when she heard of Gösta Berling's death, that she lost her self-control; but so great was her sorrow that she could not retain her love for her husband, that she would probably have allowed Countess Märta to torture her to death, if one evening the old house-keeper had not spoken to her.

"The Countess should tell the Count. What a child you are! Good God! perhaps you do not know yourself what you have to expect; but I see, of course, what is the matter." But it was just this that she could not speak about to her husband, while he cherished such hard suspicions about her.

That night she dressed herself quietly and left the house. She was clad in the usual peasant girl's dress, and had a small bundle in her hands. She intended to leave her home and never to return.

It was not to escape the torment and the suffering, but she believed now that God had given her a sign, and that she had permission to go that she might husband her strength and health.

She did not turn to the west over the lake, for there lived the man she loved so much. Neither did she go north, for there dwelt many of her friends; nor south, for far, far in the south lay her father's home, and she did not wish to approach a step nearer it. But she went east, for there she had neither home nor loved friends; she knew no one, and there was neither help nor comfort there. She did not go with a light heart, for she did not feel forgiven of God; but still she was happy that in the future she would bear the burden of her sin among strangers. Their indifferent glances would rest upon her as soothingly as steel against a swollen limb. She would walk on till she found a poor crofter's hut in a forest clearing, where no one would recognize her.

"You see what has come upon me, and my parents have turned me out," she would say. "Let me have food and a roof over my head here till I can work for my bread; I am not without money." So she walked on through the clear June night, for May had gone in hard suffering. Oh, the month of May, the beautiful time when the birches blend their pale green with the dark masses of the pine forests, and the south wind returns from afar laden with balmy warmth!

Ungrateful must I seem, more than others, I who have received your gifts, you lovely month! Not a word have I said in praise of your beauty!

Oh, May, you dear bright May! have you ever seen a child sit on its mother's knee listening to fairy tales? As long as it hears about cruel giants and the bitter suffering of beautiful princesses, it keeps its head up and its eyes open; but if its mother begins to talk of happiness and sunshine, the little one shuts its eyes and falls asleep quietly with its head against its mother's breast. And I, dear May,

am just such a child! Let others listen to tales of
flowers and sunshine, but as for me I choose the
dark nights, full of visions and adventures, the hard
fates, and the sorrowful passion of agonized hearts.

The Iron from Ekeby

IT was spring, and the iron from all the Värmland foundries must be sent to Göteborg.

But there was no iron to send from Ekeby. They
had occasionally been short of water in the autumn,
and the cavaliers had managed Ekeby all the spring.
During their occupation, strong bitter ale foamed
down the granite steps of the Björksjö waterfall,
and the long Löfven might have been filled with
brandy instead of water. While they reigned, no iron
entered the forges, but the smiths stood in their
shirt-sleeves and wooden shoes before the furnaces
and turned enormous steaks over on long spits,
while the smithy boys held larded capons in long'
pincers over the glowing coals. In those days dancing went over the foundry hills. The men slept on
the turning-lathes and played cards on the anvils.
In those days no iron was forged.

Then spring came, and the iron from Ekeby began
to be expected at the merchant's office in Göteborg.
They turned over the contract made with the Major and his wife, which spoke of many hundred
tons that might be expected.

But what did the cavaliers care about the contract? They made merry, and there was joy and
music and banqueting in the land. All they attended
to was that dancing went over the foundry hills.

Iron came from Stömme—iron came from Sölje.
The iron from Kynsberg wound its way through
the wilderness down to Vänern. It came from Udde-
holm and from Munkfors and from all the many
ironworks; but where was the iron from Ekeby?

Was not Ekeby by far the greatest of Värmland's
foundries? Did no one guard the honor of the old
estate? As ashes before the wind it lay in the hands
of careless cavaliers. They led the dance over the
hills, and their foolish hearts took thought of little
else.

But the rapids and the rivers, the cutters and the
lighters, the harbors and the sluices wondered and
asked, "Is n't the iron coming from Ekeby?" And
there was whispering and questioning from forest
to lake, from hill to dale, "Is n't the iron coming
from Ekeby? Is there never any more iron coming
from Ekeby?"

And deep in the forest the charcoal-stack laughed,
and the big hammer-heads in the dark foundry
seemed to sneer; the coal mines opened their wide
mouths and roared with laughter, and the office-
desk in the merchant's office in which the contract
lay twisted itself in contortions of glee. "Have you
heard of anything so funny? They have no iron at
Ekeby—the best of Värmland's foundries has no
iron."

Up, you careless, homeless cavaliers! Will you
let such shame overtake Ekeby? As you love this,

the most beautiful spot on God's green earth, as it is the aim of your longing heart when on far journeys, as you cannot name it among strangers without tears filling your eyes — up, cavaliers, and save the glory of Ekeby! Well, but if the hammers of Ekeby had rested, the six lesser foundries must have been at work? There must be more than enough iron, of course.

So Gösta Berling went to talk to the managers of the six foundries.

Now, it must be remembered that he did not think it worth while to go to Högfors on the Björksjö River just above Ekeby. That lay so near that it was as good as under the control of the cavaliers. But he drove thirty miles or so north, till he came to Lötafors. It was beautifully situated; there was no doubt about that. The upper Löfven spread out before it, and behind it stood Gurlita Cliff with its steep ascending crest and its air of wilderness and romance suited to an old mountain. But as for the foundry, it certainly wasn't all it ought to be; the fly-wheel was broken and had been so the whole year. But why had it not been mended?

"The carpenter, my dear friend — the carpenter, who is the only man in the whole province who could put it right, has been engaged at another place. We could not forge a single ton of iron."

"Well, why did you not send for him?"

"Send for him? As if we had not sent for him

z

every day! But he could not come; he has been building skittle-alleys and summer-houses at Ekeby."

Then Gösta Berling suddenly perceived what he
had to expect from this journey.

He went further north to Björnidet. It also had
a beautiful and practical site, befitting a castle. The
chief building commanded a crescent-shaped valley, which was surrounded on three sides by mighty
hills, and on the fourth by the Löfven, which here
has its source. And Gösta knew well that there was
no better place for moonlight promenades and love-
making than that long walk beside the shore, past
the waterfall, down to the foundry, which was built
between huge arches blasted out of the rock itself.
But iron, was there any iron? No, of course not!
They had no coal, and they were unable to get the
money from Ekeby to pay the coal-breakers and
carters. Work on the place had been standing still
all winter.

Then Gösta turned southward again. He went
to Hån on the east side of the Löfven, and to
Löfstafors, far in the deep forest, but matters were
no better there. There was no iron anywhere, and
it seemed this was the fault of the cavaliers.

So Gösta returned to Ekeby, and the cavaliers
gloomily considered the fifty tons or so which lay
in the stores, and their heads were heavy with grief,
for they heard all nature sneering at Ekeby, and
it seemed to them that the ground trembled with

sobs, and the trees threatened them with angry
gestures, and all the grass and every herb sorrowed
over the lost glory of Ekeby.

.   .   .   .

But why so many words and so much astonishment? "Here comes the iron from Ekeby!" There
it was, loaded on barges on the Klarälf shore, ready
to sail down the river, ready to be weighed on the
iron weights at Karlstad, ready to be taken by a
Vänern sloop to Göteborg. So Ekeby's honor was
saved after all.

But how was it possible? At Ekeby there were
no more than fifty tons of iron, and at the other
foundries none at all. How was it possible, then,
that the heavily loaded barges were to carry such
an immense amount of iron to the weights at Karlstad? Well, you must ask the cavaliers that question. They were all on board the heavy ugly vessels, for they intended to take the iron themselves
from Ekeby to Göteborg. None of the usual barge-
men, not a single ordinary mortal, was to accompany them. The cavaliers took possession with
provision baskets and wine bottles, with their violins and guns and fishing-rods and playing-cards.
They intended to do everything for their beloved
iron, and they would not desert it before it was
unloaded on the quay at Göteborg. They were determined to load and unload, to manage the sails

and the rudder themselves. They were just the right men for such an undertaking. Was there a sand-bank in the Klarälfven or a reef in Vänern which they were not familiar with? Did not the tiller and tackle lie as lightly in their hands as a violin-bow or a bridle? If they loved anything in the world, it was the iron on those barges. They were as careful of it as of the finest glass, and they spread a tar-paulin over it. Not a scrap of it lay exposed. Those were the heavy grey bars which were to uphold Ekeby's honor. Strangers should not cast their in-different glances upon it. Oh, Ekeby, thou land of our delight, may thy glory shine!

Not one of the cavaliers had remained at home. Uncle Eberhard had deserted his writing-desk, and Cousin Kristoffer had left his chimney-corner. Even the gentle Lövenborg was here. Not one of them remained behind when it was a question of Ekeby's honor. But for Lövenborg there was no pleasure in seeing the Klarälfven. He had not seen it for thirty-seven years, nor entered a boat all that time. He hated the shining surface of the lakes and the grey rivers, for he was always reminded of dreary things when he saw the water; but to-day he, too, was unable to remain at home—even he must accompany the barges to help in rescuing the honor of Ekeby.

Thirty-seven years ago Lövenborg saw his be-trothed drowned in the Klarälfven, and since then his poor head had often been strange; and now, as he stood and looked at the river, his old brain got more and more confused. The grey river which flowed by, with its many glittering wavelets, was a huge serpent with silver scales lying in wait for its prey. The high, yellow sandhills with their sedge-covered crests, through which the river had cut its path, were the walls of a pitfall, at the bottom of which the serpent lay; and the broad road which made an opening in its walls and waded down through deep sand to the ferry where the barges were moored was the very door to the dreadful death-hole. And the little old man stood and stared before him with his small blue eyes. His long, white hair flew in the wind, and his cheeks, which usually bloomed a gentle pink, were now quite white with fear. He was as sure as if he had been told that some one would come along that road and throw herself into the mouth of that waiting serpent.

The cavaliers were just about to cast loose, and had already grasped the long poles to push the barges out to midstream, when Lövenborg cried, "Stop, I say; stop for God's sake!"

They quite understood that his head was beginning to be confused on feeling the barge swing under his feet, but, unconsciously, they arrested their lifted poles, and he who had felt that the river lay in wait and that some one would surely come and throw herself into it, pointed with a warning gesture up the road as if he saw some one coming along it. Every one knows that life is lavish of such meetings as that which now followed. He who can still feel astonished may perhaps find it wonderful that the cavaliers should be on board their barges at Klarälfven Ferry on the very morning after the Countess Elizabeth had left her home and started on her tramp eastward. But it would certainly have been even more extraordinary if she had found no help in her need. It happened now that she, having walked all night, came along the road to the ferry just as the cavaliers were ready to push off, and they remained standing watching her while she spoke to the ferryman, and he untied his boat. She was dressed like a peasant girl, and they had no idea who she was. But they still stood and looked at her, because there was something familiar about her appearance. And while she was there talking to the ferryman, a cloud of dust rose on the road, and out of the dust-cloud appeared a big, yellow calash. She knew at once it was from Borg, that they were in search of her, and that she would be caught. She could not hope to escape in the ferry- man's boat, and the only hiding-place she saw was on the cavaliers' barges. She rushed toward them without seeing who was on board; and it was as well she did not see, for she would probably have chosen to throw herself under the horses' feet rather than have taken flight thither.

When she came on board, she only cried, "Hide me, hide me!" Then she tripped and fell down upon the cargo. But the cavaliers begged her to be calm and pushed from land at once, the barge swinging out into midstream and drifting down toward Karlstad just as the calash drove up to the ferry.

Count Henrik and his mother were in the carriage, and the Count sprang out to ask the ferryman if he had seen Countess Elizabeth, but as he was rather embarrassed at being obliged to make inquiries after a runaway wife, he only said, "There is something missing."

"Really?" said the ferryman.

"There is something missing; I ask you if you have seen anything?"

"What is it you wish to know?"

"Well, that does not matter, but there is something missing. I ask you if you have ferried anybody over this morning."

In this way he learned nothing, and Countess Märta was obliged to talk to the man herself. She found out in a minute that the girl they were in search of was on board one of those barges which were steadily gliding away.

"Who are the people on board those barges?" she asked.

"Oh, they are the cavaliers, as we call them."

"Oh!" said the Countess; "in that case your

wife is in good hands, Henrik. We may as well return home at once."

.   .   .   .

No such joy, however, prevailed on the barges as Countess Märta imagined. As long as the yellow calash was visible, the frightened young woman had crouched down upon the cargo without moving or saying a word. She only stared at the shore.

It is probable that it was only when she saw the yellow calash disappear in the distance that she recognized the cavaliers. Again she sprang up, and it seemed as if she wished to make another attempt to escape, but she was checked by the nearest bystander, and she sank down with a low wail. And the cavaliers dared not speak to her nor ask her questions; she looked as if she were on the verge of madness. The heads of these cavaliers were truly being weighed down with responsibility. This iron was in itself a heavy burden for inexperienced shoulders; and besides this, they were now to watch and guard a young high-born lady who had run away from her husband.

When they had met her during the winter festivities, more than one of them had remembered a little sister whom he had loved in the old days. When he had played and struggled with her he had been obliged to handle her gently, and when he talked to her he had learned to be careful and say no bad words. If a strange boy had played roughly with her or had sung ugly songs, he had fought him with the greatest fury and nearly pommelled the life out of him, for his little sister should never hear anything wicked, nor suffer any pain, nor ever meet with evil or hatred.

Countess Elizabeth had been a gay little sister to all of them. When she placed her small hand in their broad, hard fists, it seemed just as if she had said, "See how frail I am, but you are my big brother — you shall guard me against others and against yourself." And they were courtly knights as long as they saw her. Now they looked on her with fear and hardly knew her. She was wasted and thin—her neck had lost its roundness, her face looked transparent. She must have struck her head against something during her night tramp, for a drop of blood fell now and again from a little cut near her temple, and the curly hair that hung over her forehead was clotted with blood. Her skirt was dirty after the long walk over the dew-damp roads, and her shoes were the worse for wear. The cavaliers had a dreadful feeling that this was a stranger. The Countess Elizabeth they knew had n't such wild, glowing eyes. Their poor little sister had been hunted to the verge of madness. It seemed as if a soul descended from the other world was fighting with the real soul for the possession of that tortured body.

But there was no need that they should alarm themselves as to what they should do with her. The old thought awoke within her. This was temptation again — God was trying her again. Again she was among friends. Would she leave the penitent's path?

She rose up and cried that she must go.

They tried to calm her. They told her she might feel safe with them; they would guard her against her would-be captors.

She only begged to be allowed to step down into the little boat following the barge and row to land to continue her flight alone.

But they would not let her go. What would become of her? It was best she should remain with them. They were only poor old men, but they would certainly find some way of helping her.

Then she wrung her hands and prayed them to let her go, but they were obliged to refuse her prayer. They saw how weak and wretched she was, and they thought she might very probably die on the roadside.

Gösta Berling stood at a little distance and gazed down into the water. Perhaps she would rather not see him. He did not know, but his thoughts smiled and danced in any case.

"No one knows where she is," he thought. "Now we can carry her back with us to Ekeby. We can keep her hidden there, we cavaliers, and we will be very

good to her. She shall be our queen, our empress;
but none will know she is there, we will guard her so
well. Perhaps she would be happy among us, cherished like a daughter by all the old men. She might
make men of us; we might even come to drink
almond milk and talk French. And when our year
is over, what then? With time comes help."

He had never dared ask himself if he loved her.
He could not hope to possess her without sin, and
he would never draw anything low or mean over
her. He knew that. But to have her hidden at Ekeby,
and to be kind to her when others had been cruel,
and to let her enjoy everything that life gave—ah,
what a dream, what a blessed dream!

Then he awoke from his dream, for the young
Countess was in wild despair, and her voice had the
piercing tone of desperation. She had thrown herself upon her knees to the cavaliers, praying to be
allowed to leave the barge.

"God has not forgiven me yet," she cried; "let
me go!"

Gösta saw that none of the others had the strength
to obey her, and he realized that he must do it.
He, loving her, must do it.

He experienced a difficulty in walking, as if every
limb in his body strove against the power of his
will, but he dragged himself to her and said he
would row her to land.

She rose instantly. He lifted her into the boat

and rowed toward the eastern shore. He pulled to a little landing-place and helped her out of the boat.

"What will now become of you, Countess?" he asked.

She lifted her finger solemnly and pointed to heaven.

"When you are in trouble, Countess——"

He could not speak, his voice failed him, but she understood, and answered, "I will send for you when I need you."

"I would have guarded you from all harm," he said.

She gave him her hand in farewell, and he could say nothing more. Her hand lay cold and nerveless in his. Elizabeth was unconscious of anything but those inner voices which compelled her to go away among strangers. She hardly knew that it was the man she loved whom she was leaving now.

So he let her go and rowed back to the cavaliers. When he reached the barge he trembled with fatigue and seemed to be worn out and powerless. He felt as though he had done the hardest day's work of his life.

He held his courage up a few days longer, till the honor of Ekeby was saved. He carried the iron to the weights at Kanikenäset; after that his strength and courage of life deserted him for a long time. The cavaliers noticed no change in him as long as they were on board.

He strained every nerve to keep the gaiety and laughter going, for it was by gaiety and laughter that the honor of Ekeby was to be saved. How was the game to be theirs, if they played it with troubled faces and discouraged hearts?

If it is true what report said, that the cavaliers had more sand than iron in their barges—if it is true that they carried the same bars backward and forward to the scales at Kanikenäset, till the many hundred tons were weighed out—if it is true that this could be done because the manager there and his people were feasted so well from the provisions and wine-baskets brought from Ekeby—you can easily imagine, then, that the time went gaily on the iron barges.

Who can tell? But if this was the case, it is certain that Gösta Berling had no time to suffer. He knew little now of the joy of adventure, and as soon as he dared he sank down in despair.

"Oh, Ekeby, my land of delight!" he then cried, "let thy honor shine clear!"

As soon as the cavaliers received the quittance from the manager of the weigh-scales they loaded their iron into a Vänern sloop. It was usual that the shipowners undertook the delivery of goods down to Göteborg, and the Värmland proprietors had no further trouble about their iron after they had received the quittance that the delivery was correct. But the cavaliers refused to do their work by halves, and they intended to accompany the iron all the way to Göteborg.

Mischance met them on the way thither. A storm broke out in the night; the sloop became unmanageable, drifted upon a reef, and sank with all its precious burden, violins and gambling cards and wine bottles—all went to the bottom. But if you looked at the matter sensibly, what did it matter that the iron was lost? The honor of Ekeby was saved. The iron had passed the scales at Kanikenäset. And if the Major was obliged to sit down and inform the merchants in the big city in a curt letter that he would not receive their money, as they had not received his iron, it also mattered very little: Ekeby was so rich, and its honor was saved.

But if the harbors and sluices, if the coal mines and the coal stacks and cutters and barges began to whisper wonderful things? If a gentle sighing went over the forests that the whole journey was a fraud, if all Värmland declared that there never was more than a miserable fifty tons of iron on the barges, and that the shipwreck was carefully arranged? It would be a daring exploit done, a truly cavalier-like joke. And by such exploits, the honor of the old estate was not risked.

But it was so long ago; it is possible that the cavaliers brought iron from another foundry, or that they found it in some forgotten warehouse. The truth of the affair will never come to light. The master of the scales will at least never admit that any deception was possible, and he ought to know.

When the cavaliers came home, they heard some news. Count Dohna's marriage was to be dissolved. The Count had sent his lawyer away to Italy to find proofs of the illegality of the marriage. The man returned later in the summer with satisfactory evidence. Of what this consisted, I don't know for certain. People said that the marriage in Italy had not been performed by the right priest. I know no more than that it is true in any case that the marriage between Count Dohna and Elizabeth von Thurn was pronounced by the Justice in Borg to be no marriage at all.

The young woman knew nothing of all this, for she was living among peasants in a distant part of the country, if she was alive at all.

Lilliecrona's Home

AMONGST the cavaliers was one whom I mentioned as being a great musician. He was a tall, large-limbed man with a big head and a mane of black hair. He was certainly not much over forty at that time, but he had an ugly, roughly chiselled face and a quiet manner, which made many people think him older than he was. He was a good fellow, but of a very melancholy temperament.

One afternoon he took his violin under his arm and left Ekeby. He bade no one farewell, yet it was not his intention to return. The life there disgusted him, since he had seen Countess Elizabeth's misery. He therefore marched away, walking all day and all night, without resting, till at early sunrise he came to a little farmstead, called Löfdala, which was his property.

It was so early no one was awake yet. Lilliecrona sat down upon the green bench outside the main building, and looked at his surroundings. Good God, it would be difficult to find a lovelier place. The grass-plot before the house lay on a gentle slope, and was covered with fine, pale green grass. The sheep were allowed to nibble it, and the children rushed over it in their play, but it was ever smooth and green. The scythe never touched it; but once a week, at least, the mistress of the house

had all the stray branches and bits of straw and dry
leaves swept away. He looked at the walk before
the house, and drew his feet under him suddenly.
The children had raked the sand into a fine pat-
tern the evening before, and his huge feet had made
dreadful havoc of their work. How wonderfully
things grew here! The six mountain-ash trees which
guarded the grass-plot were as tall as beeches, and
spread wide like oaks. Such trees were rare, and
they were very beautiful. Their thick stems were
covered with green lichen, and the big clusters of
white flowers stood out in relief against the dark
foliage. It reminded him of the evening sky with
its cluster of stars. It was impossible not to be
struck by the way in which the vegetation flourished there. There stood an old willow, so thick
that two men could not clasp hands round it. It
was decayed and hollow now, and the lightning had
destroyed its crown, but it refused to die. Every
spring brought a fringe of fresh green from the old
main stem to prove that it was still alive. That
bird-cherry near the east gable had grown large
enough to shade the whole house. The turf roof
was covered with its fallen blossoms, for the cherry
trees had just finished flowering. And the birches
standing in clumps on the fields certainly had their
Paradise here. They developed as many different
styles of growth as if they were determined to imi-
tate every other species. One resembled a lime,

AA

growing in a thickly leaved arch; another stood straight and narrow like a poplar, and a third hung its branches like a weeping willow. Not one resembled its neighbors, and they were all beautiful.

Then Lilliecrona rose and walked round the house. There lay its flower-gardens, so wonderfully lovely that he paused and caught his breath. The apple trees were in blossom. Yes, he had known that before. He had noticed them on all the other estates; it was only that they never bloomed anywhere else as in this garden, where he had seen them blossom ever since he was a child. He walked with folded hands and careful steps up and down the walks. They were white, and the trees were white — one or two with a tint of pink. He had never seen anything so lovely. He knew every tree as one knows one's brothers and sisters and playfellows.

The flowers of the winter cress were rose-colored, and the crab apple trees were nearly red. But the old ungrafted apple tree was the loveliest; no one could eat its small, sour fruit, but it was lavish with its flowers, and looked like a big snowdrift in the brightness of the early morning.

For remember, too, it was early morning. The dew made all the leaves glitter, and all the dust was washed away. Over the forest-covered mountains, which sheltered the house and garden, the first sunbeams were pouring. It seemed as if they had set the pine-tops on fire. The faintest mist — the finest beauty mist — hung over the young clover fields, over the rye and wheat and the oats which had just come up, and the shadows lay as sharply defined as on a moonlight night.

He stood and considered the large spice-beds between the garden walks. He knew that both the mistress and her girls had had their work here. They had dug and raked and manured and pulled up the weeds and worked the earth till it became fine and light. After they had made the bed even and the edges sharp, they had taken ropes and measuring poles and marked out lines and squares. Afterwards they had stamped up and down between the squares with little steps, and had then sowed and set their plants, till all the lines and squares were filled. The children had helped too, and had been perfectly happy in doing so, though it had been hard work for them to bend and stretch their arms over the wide beds. And their help had been wonderfully useful, as any one could understand.

All the plants were just coming up now.

God bless them! How bravely they stood there, both the peas and the beans with their two thick little leaves, and how evenly and nicely the turnips and carrots had come up! The curly little parsley leaves were the funniest; they had lifted a scrap of the mould over them, and were playing at hide-and-seek with life as yet. And there stood a little bed where the lines were not very straight, and where

the small squares might have been samplers of all
that could be set or sown.

It belonged to the children.

And Lilliecrona suddenly lifted his violin to his
chin and commenced to play. The birds were beginning to sing in the big clump of bushes that sheltered
the garden from the north wind. It was impossible
for any mortal gifted with a voice to be silent—the
morning was so fair. The violin-bow played by itself. Lilliecrona walked up and down the paths and
played. "No," he thought, " there can be no lovelier place than my home." What was Ekeby in comparison? His home was thatched with turf and was
but one story high. It lay in the forest clearing, with
the mountains above and the long dale before it.
There was nothing wonderful about it—there was
no lake, no waterfall, no shores nor park, but it was
very beautiful for all that. It was beautiful, because
it was a good and peaceful home. Life was easy
to live there. Things that, in other places, would
have brought forth bitterness and anger were here
smoothed away so mildly. Thus it should be in a
true home.

The lady of the house lay sleeping in a room
which overlooked the garden. She awoke suddenly
and listened. She did not move—but lay and smiled
to herself. The music approached, until it seemed
as if the musician stood under her window. It was
not the first time he had stood there. He, her hus-

band, sometimes came like that—when they had been unusually wild over there at Ekeby.

He stood there confessing and begging forgiveness. He described the evil powers which tempted him from all he loved best—from her and the children. But he did love them.

While he played, she got up and dressed, hardly knowing what she did, she was so absorbed in the music.

"It was not the luxury of good living which tempted me away," he played on, "nor the love of other women, nor honor, but the rich variety of life —its beauty, its bitterness and richness, which I long to feel around me. But now I have had enough of it—now I am tired and satisfied. I will leave my home no more! Forgive me, and have sympathy with me!"

Then she drew aside the curtain and opened the window, and he could see her beautiful, kind face.

She was good and wise. Her face brought a blessing like the sun's on all she looked upon. She managed and guided everything. Wherever she was, things grew and flourished; she carried happiness about with her.

He swung himself up to the window-sill, and was as happy as a young lover. Afterwards he carried her down in his arms to the garden and under the apple trees, and showed her how lovely it all was, and pointed out the vegetable beds and the children's gardens and the funny little parsley leaves.

There was great joy and excitement when the children awoke—father had come home. They laid hands on him at once. He must see everything new —the birds' nests in the willow, the little fish which were swimming by thousands in the shallows of the pond.

Then father, mother, and children took a long walk over the fields. He must see how thick the rye was, and how the clover grew, and how the potato plants were pushing out their crumpled leaves. He must see the cows as they came home from pasture, and visit all the new arrivals in the cow-house and sheepfold, seek for eggs, and give sugar to the horses. The children hung about him all day. No lessons, no work—nothing but to stroll about with father.

In the evening he played polkas for them, and he had been such a good comrade and playfellow all day that they fell asleep with a prayer on their lips that their father might always remain with them!

He remained eight whole days, and was pleased as a boy all the time. He was in love with everything at home, with his wife and children, and never thought of Ekeby.

But there came a morning when he was absent again. He could not stand it any longer, there was too much happiness at Löfdala for him. Ekeby was a thousand times worse, but Ekeby was in the midst of the whirl of events. Oh! how much there was there to dream and play about. How could he live away from the cavaliers' exploits and the long Löfven lake, when the wave of wild adventure rushed along its shores?

Everything went on so smoothly on his own little estate. Everything grew and flourished under the mild sway of its mistress. Every one went about quite happy. Everything which might have brought differences and hate in other places passed there without pain or dismay. Everything was just as it should be. And if the master of the house longed to live as a cavalier at Ekeby, what did it matter? Is there any use in bewailing that the sun sinks every evening in the west and leaves the world in darkness? Who is invincible without submissiveness? Who can conquer without patience?

The Dovre Witch

THE Dovre witch was abroad on the shores of the Löfven. She was small and hunchbacked and wore a leather coat and belt studded with silver. How did she come from her wolf-hole to the world of men? And what did she seek in our green valleys? She came a-begging, for, although she was so rich, she was miserly and loved gifts. She had hidden thick, white layers of silver in the clefts of the rocks and far among the mountains. Her great herds of black, yellow-horned cows fed on dewy meadows, yet she wore birch-bark shoes and a leather coat, the rough seams of which showed through the accumulated dirt of centuries. Her pipe was filled with moss, and she begged from the very poorest. Shame upon her, who was never grateful, and seemed never to have received enough.

She was very, very old. When did the beautiful glamour of youth rest over that broad face with its brown skin shining with fat, over the flat nose and the small eyes which gleamed through the dirt like bright coals among the ashes? When did she, as a girl, sit on a saeter knoll, and answer the shepherd boy's love song with a note on her cow-horn? She had lived for several centuries. The oldest did not remember the time when she did not wander begging through the country. When their fathers were young, she was an old-woman—and she is still alive to-day. For I, who write this, have seen her.

She was a mighty woman, she, the daughter of the ancient Finnish sorcerers, who bowed down to no man. Her broad feet left no timid marks upon the dust of the highway. She brought the hail and pointed the lightning. She could drive the herds astray and send the wolves into the sheepfolds. There was little good she could do, but much evil, and it was best to be on good terms with her. If she asked for your only lamb and a whole pound of wool, it was best you gave it to her, or the cows might suffer, or your child might die, or the miserly housewife might herself go out of her mind.

She was never a welcome guest, but it was wisest to meet her with a smiling face. Who can tell on whose account it was that she was wandering through the valley? She did not come simply to fill her beggar's basket. Evil omens followed her. The army-worm crept forth, owls and foxes screamed in the twilight, red and black caterpillars, spitting forth venom, crept forth from the forest to the very threshold of your door.

She was proud—mighty wisdom elevates the mind. Costly runes were inscribed on her staff, and she would not sell it for all the gold in the dale. She could sing magic songs and brew magic drinks, was wise in herbs, could ride the storm, and was learned in all witchcraft. If I could only interpret the wonderful thoughts of her aged heart! Coming from the darkness of the forests and from the mighty hills, what did she think of the people in the valleys? Believing in Thor, the great giant-killer, and the great Finnish gods, the Christians were, in her eyes, like tame house-dogs before a grey wolf. Untamed as the snow-storm, strong as the rapids, she could never love the sons of the country side.

Yet she often came from the mountains to view their dwarfish ways. Men shuddered when they saw her, but the strong daughter of the wilderness went securely among them, guarded by fear. The daring exploits of her forefathers were not forgotten, nor her own. As a cat trusts to its claws, so she trusted in her god-inspired magic. No king was so secure on his throne as she was in the domain of terror in which she reigned.

So the Dovre witch wandered through many villages, and she came at last to Borg, and did not hesitate to approach Count Dohna's mansion. She seldom took the kitchen-way, and now she marched straight up the wide steps of the terrace. She planted her broad birch-bark shoes on the flower-bordered walks as securely as if she trod her mountain paths.

It happened that Countess Märta had just stepped out upon the terrace to view the fine beauty of the June morning. At the end of the walk two servant girls paused on their way to the larder. They had come from the bath hut where meat was being smoked, and they carried freshly smoked hams on a pole between them.

"Will the Countess deign to come and smell them?" asked one of the girls. "Is the meat sufficiently smoked?"

Countess Märta, who was mistress at Borg Hall at that time, bent over the balustrade to look at the meat; but at the same moment the old witch laid her hand upon one of the hams.

Look at the shining, brown rind and the thick layer of fat, and smell the fresh scent of juniper on the newly smoked hams! Oh, food for the lost gods!

The witch wanted all this, and laid her hand upon it.

The daughter of the mountain was not accustomed to beg and pray for what she wanted! Was it not by her clemency that flowers bloomed and men flourished? Frost and devastating storms and floods were in her power—therefore it did not become her to beg and pray. She laid her hands upon what she wished, and it was hers. But Countess Märta knew nothing of the old woman's power.

"Go away, you beggar," she said.

"Give me the ham," replied the Dovre witch, the leader of the wolfpacks.

"She is mad!" cried the Countess, and she ordered the servant girls to go on with their load.

The eyes of the aged dame flamed with anger and desire.

"Give me the brown ham," she repeated, "or you will fare badly."

"I would rather give it to the magpies than to such a one as you."

The old woman shook with a storm of fury. She stretched the rune stick above her head and swung it round wildly, her lips muttered strange words, her hair rose on her head, her eyes blazed, and her face was contorted.

"You shall the magpies eat — they shall eat you," she screamed at last. And she turned away, mumbling curses and swinging her staff. She turned homeward; she went no farther south on that occasion, for the daughter of the mountain had executed the errand on which she had come from the hills.

Countess Märta stood still on the terrace and laughed at the ungovernable rage of the old beggar; but the laugh died suddenly on her lips, for there they came. She could not believe her eyes. She thought she must be dreaming. But there they were, the magpies that were to eat her.

They flew toward her from park and garden, scores of magpies, with their claws extended and their beaks outstretched. They came with noise and laughter and black and white wings gleaming before her eyes, and behind them she saw all the magpies of the neighborhood swarming, and all the sky was filled with their black and white bodies. Their polished, metallic feathers shone in the sharp

morning sunshine; their throat feathers were ruffled as if they were fighting hawks. They flew in
narrowing circles round Countess Märta, swooping
down with claws and beaks at her face and hands,
and she was forced to turn and rush into the hall
and shut the door behind her. She leaned against
it, panting with fright, while the laughing magpies
circled outside. And thus was she shut away from
the beauty and greenness of summer and from all
the joy of life. The future held for her only closed
rooms and drawn curtains, despair and fear and
bewilderment bordering on madness.

This story may sound crazy, but it must be true.
Hundreds will recognize it and bear witness that
such is the old tradition. The birds settled down
on the balustrade and on the roof; they sat there as
if waiting to throw themselves upon Countess Märta
as soon as she showed herself. They took up their
quarters in the park, and there they remained. It was
impossible to drive them from the place, and it was
only worse if you tried to shoot them. For every
one that fell came ten new arrivals. Sometimes great
numbers of them flew away to feed, but they always
left faithful sentinels on guard. And if Countess
Märta showed herself, if she looked out of the window, or even drew aside a curtain for a moment,
or attempted to go out upon the steps, they surrounded her instantly. The whole swarm flew headlong toward the house with the thunder of beating

wings, and the Countess fled into her innermost room.

She lived in her bedroom, opening out of the red drawing-room. I have often heard that room described as it was during that fatal time when Borg was besieged by the magpies. Heavy curtains over the doors and windows, thick carpets on the floors, and creeping, whispering servants.

Pale despair abode in the heart of the Countess. Her hair turned grey and her skin wrinkled; she became an old woman in the course of a month. She could not harden her heart in doubt of the fateful sorcery. She sprang up from her dreams at night with loud cries that the magpies were eating her. She wept long days over the hard fate that she could not avoid. Fearing people, afraid that the flock of birds would follow in the wake of every one entering the house, she usually sat with her hands over her face, rocking herself in her armchair, miserable and enervated, in the close air of the room, now and then starting up with a cry or a wail.

No one could have had a more bitter life. No one could help pitying her!

I have not had much to tell you about her, and what I have said has not been kind. My conscience almost smites me. She was kind-hearted and joyous when she was young, and many amusing stories about her have gladdened my heart, though this has not been the place to tell you about them.

But it is the truth, though poor Countess Märta did not know it, that the soul is ever hungering. It cannot live on vanity and frivolity alone. If it gets no other nourishment, it tears to pieces, like a wild animal, first others, lastly itself.

This is the meaning of the saga.

Midsummer

IT was as hot a midsummer as it is to-day when I am writing. The loveliest season of the year had come.

This was the time when Sintram, the wicked owner of Fors foundry, grew frightened and anxious. He was furious over the conquest light had won over the hours of darkness. He fretted over the leafy verdure of the trees and the many-colored carpet spread over the earth.

Everything was clothed in beauty. The road, grey and dusty as it was, had its border of flowers, blue and yellow midsummer flowers, shevril and birdsfoot trefoil. And when the splendor of the midsummer day lay over the hills, and the trembling air carried the ringing of Bro church bells up to Fors, when the sweet quiet of the hallowed day reigned over all the land, Sintram rose in wrath.

It seemed to him that God and men had dared to forget that he existed, and he determined that he, too, would go to church. All who rejoiced at the summer weather should see him, Sintram, the man who loved darkness without a dawn, death without resurrection, winter without spring!

He put on his wolfskin coat and his thick fur driving-gloves. He ordered the red horse to be harnessed to a racing sledge and the sleigh-bells to be fastened on, and, clad as if there were thirty degrees of frost, he drove to church. He thought the sparks flying beneath the runners were due to the severe cold, the foam on the horse's back he imagined to be rime frost. He felt no warmth; he diffused cold as the sun diffuses heat.

He drove over the wild plain north of the Bro church, the road leading him through large well-to-do villages and fields where the larks were singing. I have never heard larks sing as they do over those fields, and I have often wondered if he was able to deaden his hearing against the voices of those many hundred songsters.

There was much by the wayside that must have angered him if he had given it a glance. He would have seen two birches standing at the door of every cottage, and, on looking through the windows, he could have seen the walls and ceilings of the rooms covered with garlands of flowers and green branches. The meanest little beggar girl carried a bunch of lilacs in her hand, and every peasant girl had a bouquet of flowers wrapped carefully in her handkerchief.

In the cottage yards the maypoles still stood with their fallen flowers and withered garlands. The grass around them was trampled, for there had been dancing there during Midsummer night.

Down on the lake the timber-rafts covered the surface of the Löfven. Their little sails were hoisted in honor of the day, though there was no wind to fill them, and every mast was crowned for the mid-summer fête.

Along the many roads leading to Bro, the church folk were gathering, the women looking very stately in their light, hand-woven summer dresses finished in readiness for that day. All were dressed for the midsummer fête.

They could not cease rejoicing over the peace of the day and the rest from their every-day work, at the summer's warmth and the promising harvest, and the strawberries that grew red by the roadside. They remarked upon the stillness of the air, the cloudless sky, and the singing of the sky-larks, and said, "It is evident this is the Lord's Day."

Then Sintram drove by, swearing and swinging his whip over his toiling horse. The sand scraped horribly under the sledge runners, and the shrill tinkle of his sleigh-bells drowned the church bells. His forehead was knitted angrily under his fur cap.

The church-goers shuddered and felt they had seen the Evil One. Not even on that day, at their midsummer festival, might they forget malevolence and the bitter cold of winter! Theirs is a cruel lot who tread this earth.

The people seated in the shade of the church or on the walls of the churchyard waiting for the service to begin watched him wonderingly, as he strode up to the church door. The beautiful weather had been filling their hearts with delight at being able to tread the paths of earth and enjoy their existence, but when they saw Sintram, a presentiment of disaster came over them.

As he strode forward among the people, they marked with secret fear his manner of greeting. Happy was the man whom he passed pretending not to see, for he greeted only those who served his turn. His cap flew to the floor for the Broby parson, and he raised it to Marienne Sinclaire and the Ekeby cavaliers, but he took no notice of the Rector of Bro and the Judge from Munkerud.

Sintram entered the church and took his place in his pew, throwing his driving-gloves upon the seat with such force that the noisy rattle of the wolf claws sewn into the skin was heard all over the church, and some women who were already seated in the foremost benches, seeing the shaggy figure, fainted and had to be carried out.

But no one dared to turn him out. He disturbed the people's worship, but he was feared so much no one dared order him to leave the church.

It was in vain the old rector spoke of summer's high festival—no one listened to him. The people thought only of the cruelties of life and the winter's cold and the special disaster which Sintram's presence there foreboded them.

After the service they saw him climb the crest

of the hill on which the church stood. He gazed down at Broby Strait, and followed it with his eyes past the rectory and the three promontories on the eastern shore of the Löfven, and they saw him clench his fist and shake it over Broby and its green shores. Then his glance glided southward to the lower Löfven, to the blue headlands which seemed to shut in the lake, and northward for miles past Gurlita Cliff up to Björn Point, where the lake ended. He looked eastward and westward where the long hills edged the vale, and he shook his fist again; and every one felt that, if he had held a thunderbolt in his right hand, he would have flung it in wild delight over the quiet country and spread distress and death as far as he could reach, for he had so accustomed his heart to evil that he knew no pleasure except in misery. By degrees he had taught himself to love all things ugly and wicked. He was more crazy than the wildest madman, but no one realized it.

Wonderful stories went about the country after that. It was said that the key used by the sexton in closing the church broke off by the stem, for a tightly folded paper had been pushed into the key-hole. This paper had been given to the rector. It was a document intended, of course, for an inhabitant of another world.

Its contents were whispered abroad. The rector had burned it, but the sexton had watched the devilish thing as it lay in the fire. The letters shone red as on a black ground, and he had not been able to resist the temptation of reading it. He read, it was said, that the devil would lay waste all the country as far as the steeple of Bro church was visible. He desired to see the forest surrounding the church and bears and wolves dwelling in the abodes of men. The fields would lie waste, and the sound of dogs or cocks would be heard no more in the land. Sintram would serve his master by bringing ruin upon them all. This was what he promised to do.

And men looked into the future with silent dismay, for they knew the power of the Evil One was great—that he hated every living soul, that he desired to see the wilderness overspread the valleys, and that he would make plague or famine or war serve his turn in driving away every one who loved work—good heart-gladdening work.

The Lady Musica

WHEN nothing could make Gösta Berling his own glad self again after he had helped the young Countess in her flight, the cavaliers decided to seek the help of the Lady Musica, who, as you know, is a mighty fay, and comforts many sufferers.

And so, one evening in July, they opened the doors of the great salon at Ekeby, and took down the shutters. The sun — the late evening's big red sun — and the cool night were invited in.

The striped coverings were taken off the furniture, the piano was opened, and the muslin round the Venetian glass chandeliers was taken away. The gilded griffins supporting the marble tables shone again in the light, the white goddesses danced on the black panels over the long mirrors, and the multifarious flowers on the silken damask that covered the furniture gleamed in the evening light, and roses had been gathered and brought in — the whole room was filled with their scent. There were wonderful roses of unknown names which had been brought from foreign lands to Ekeby. There were the yellow roses, in which the veins showed red as in a mortal, and the creamy white with ragged edges, and the pink with their outer petals as colorless as water, and the dark red with their black shadows.

They brought in all Altringer's roses, which had been transplanted from foreign climes to gladden the eyes of lovely ladies.

Then the notes and music-stands were carried in, and the brass instruments and bows and violins of every size, for the Lady Musica was to begin in Ekeby halls to try to comfort Gösta.

They had chosen and practised Haydn's Oxford Symphony. Squire Julius wielded the conductor's baton, and each of the cavaliers played his own instrument. They could all play, or they would not have been cavaliers.

When all was ready, Gösta was sent for. He was still weak and spiritless, but he was pleased with the stately room and the beautiful music. For, as you well know, the Lady Musica is the very best company for those who are suffering. She is gay and playful as a child, she is fiery and engaging as a young woman, and good and wise as the old who have lived a righteous life.

And so the cavaliers began to play — so softly and tenderly. Little Ruster took it all very seriously. He pored over his music with his spectacles on his nose, kissed the sweetest notes out of his flute, and let his fingers play round the keys and holes. Uncle Eberhard sat twisted over his violoncello; his big wig had fallen over one ear, and he trembled with excitement. Bergh stood proudly with his long bassoon. He forgot himself occasionally, and discharged the whole strength of his lungs into his instrument, and then Julius thumped him promptly with the baton on his thick pate.

It was going very well — brilliantly. From the dead notes they charmed forth the Lady Musica herself. Spread forth thy mantle, dear lady, and carry Gösta Berling to the land of happiness where he was wont to dwell.

Oh, that it should be Gösta Berling sitting there so pale and spiritless, whom the old gentlemen are trying to amuse as if he were a child. Joy must be scarce now in Värmland. I know well why the old men loved him so much. I know how long the winter evenings can be, and how gloominess creeps over one's mind in those lonely homesteads. I know how they felt when he came there. Imagine a Sunday afternoon when all work was put aside, and your thoughts were dull! Imagine an obstinate north wind whipping the cold into the rooms, a cold which no fire on the hearth can mitigate! Imagine the one tallow candle, which must constantly be snuffed! Think of the monotonous tones of the psalm-singing coming from the kitchen!

And then comes the sound of sleigh-bells, strong feet stamp the snow off on the porch steps, and Gösta Berling comes into the room. He laughs and teases. He is life and sunshine. He throws the piano open, and he plays till you are surprised at the old keys. He can sing any song and play every melody. He makes every one in the house happy. He was never cold nor tired. The sorrowful forgot their grief when they saw him. Oh, what a kind heart he had! How sympathetic he was with the weak and poor! And what a genius he was! Yes, you should have heard the old people talk of him.

But now Gösta Berling sat silent and sorrowful, and in the midst of the music he burst into tears. He thought life—all life—was so wretched. He leaned his head on his hands and wept. The cavaliers were terrified. These were not the quiet, healing tears that music can call forth—he was sobbing like one in despair. They put aside their instruments, quite helpless. The Lady Musica was fain to lose courage, till she suddenly remembered that she had one more mighty champion.

It was the gentle Lövenborg, he who lost his bride in the cruel river, and who was Gösta's slave, even more so than the others. He now stole to the piano. He walked round it, touched it carefully, and caressed the keys with gentle hand.

In the cavaliers' wing Lövenborg had a wooden table, on which he had painted a keyboard and before which he had placed a music-stand. There he sat for hours, and let his fingers play over its black and white keys. There he practised both scales and études, and there he played his Beethoven. He never played anything but Beethoven.

But the old man never ventured upon anything

but the wooden keyboard. For the piano he had a respectful fear. It tempted him, but it frightened him also. The tinkling instrument on which so many polkas had thundered was his shrine. He had never dared to touch it. Think of the wonderful instrument with its many keys which could give life to the great master's works! He need only put his ear down to it, and he hears both Andante and Scherzo murmur inside. Yes, the piano is just the right altar at which the Lady Musica should be worshipped. But he has never played upon it. He will never be rich enough to buy one for himself, and he has never dared to touch this one. The Major's wife, too, has not shown any wish to open it for him. He has heard, of course, the polkas and waltzes and Bellman's melodies ring out upon it, but for such unholy music the old instrument could do nothing else than rattle and bewail itself. No, if Beethoven came, it would put forth its own true lovely tone. Now he thought the time had come for him and Beethoven. He would take courage and approach the shrine and gladden his young lord and master with the sound of its slumbering tones. He seated himself and began to play. He was very uncertain and very excited, but he scrambled through a few bars, tried to catch the right tone, wrinkled his forehead, tried again, and then covered his face with his hands and wept. Yes, dear Lady Musica, it was a bitter moment for him.

His shrine was no shrine. There were no pure, beautiful tones and dreams within it, no mighty, deafening thunder, no powerful rushing storm wind. Nothing of the unutterable euphony which sighed through Paradise had hidden itself there. It was but a tinkling old piano and nothing else.

But Lady Musica gave the crafty old Colonel a hint just then. He took Ruster with him; they went down to the cavaliers' wing and brought up Lövenborg's board with its painted keyboard.

"See here, Lövenborg," said Beerencreutz, when they returned; "here is your piano; play for Gösta!"

Then Lövenborg's tears ceased, and he sat down to play Beethoven to his suffering young friend. Now he would certainly be comforted.

In the old man's brain the lovely melodies rang. He could not but believe that Gösta heard how well they sounded. Gösta was sure to notice how easily he played that evening. There were no more difficulties for him to overcome. He made his runs and shakes with the greatest ease. He performed the most difficult feats; he could have wished the master himself had heard them.

The longer he played, the more enthusiastic he became. He heard every note with unnatural clearness.

"Sorrow, sorrow," he played, "why should I not love thee, because thy lips are cold, thy hands withered, and thy embrace can kill, and thine eyes paralyze?

"Sorrow, sorrow, thou art one of those beautiful proud women whose love is hard to win, but it burns stronger than that of others. Thou despised, I laid thee in my heart and loved thee! I kissed the cold from thy limbs, and thy love hath filled me with blessedness.

"Oh, how I suffered! Oh, how I longed for her after I lost her whom I held most dear. Dark night was within and without me. I lay low in prayer, in heavy unanswered prayer. Heaven was closed to my long waiting; from the star-besprinkled sky no sweet spirit came to comfort me.

"But my longing rent the darkening veil asunder, and thou camest down to me swaying on a bridge of moonbeams, thou camest in light, oh, my beloved! and with smiling lips. Happy angels surrounded thee. They carried garlands of roses, and played on cithers and flutes. It was happiness to see thee. But thou vanished—vanished again, and there was no bridge of moonbeams for me when I would follow thee! I lay on the earth wingless, tied to the dust; my wailing was like the roar of a wild beast, like the heavens' deafening thunder. I would have sent the lightning as a message to thee. I cursed the green earth—fire might blast the harvests and plagues kill the people. I called upon death and hell. I thought that the pain of everlasting fire was sweetness compared to my misery.

"Sorrow, sorrow, then wert thou my friend. Why

should I not love thee as men love those proud, beautiful women whose love is hard to win, but burns steadier than that of others?"

It was thus he played, the poor old mystic. He sat there, glowing with enthusiasm and emotion, hearing the most wonderful tones, certain that Gösta heard them too and was feeling comforted.

Gösta sat and looked at him. At first he was furious at the mockery, but by and by his anger vanished. The old man was irresistible as he sat there enjoying his Beethoven.

And Gösta remembered, too, that the man who now was so gentle and happy had been overwhelmed by sorrow—that he, too, had lost the woman he had loved. And there he sat now, beaming with happiness, over his wooden keyboard. It required, then, no more than that to make a man's happiness. He felt himself humbled.

"What, Gösta," he said to himself, "can you no longer endure? You have been hardened in poverty all your life; you have heard every tree in the forest, every tuft in the meadows preach to you of sacrifice and patience. You, brought up in a country where the winter is severe, and the summer joy is very short, have you forgotten the art of bearing your trials?

"Oh, Gösta, a man must bear all that life gives him with a courageous heart and a smile on his lips, else he is no man. Sorrow as much as you will. If

you love your beloved, let your conscience burn
and chafe within you, but show yourself a man and
a Värmlander. Let your glances beam with joy, and
meet your friends with a gay word on your lips!
Life and nature are hard. They bring forth courage and joy as a counterweight against their own
hardness, or no one could endure them.

"Courage and joy! It seems as if these were the
first two duties of life. You have never failed them
before, you will not fail them now.

"Are you worse than Lövenborg, who sits there
at his piano, or than any of the other cavaliers—
those courageous, happy, ever youthful men? You
know well that none of them has escaped suffering."

And then Gösta glanced round at them. Oh,
what a sight! They were all sitting seriously listening to the music which nobody heard.

Suddenly Lövenborg was startled from his
dreams by a gay laugh. He lifted his hands from
the keyboard and listened with rapture. It was Gösta's old laugh, his kindly infectious laugh. It was
the loveliest music he had heard in all his life.

"Did I not say that Beethoven would help you,
Gösta?" he cried. "You are all right again."

Thus did the Lady Musica cure Gösta Berling.

The Broby Parson

EROS, thou all-conquering god, thou knowest full well that it sometimes seems as though one of thy slaves had freed himself from thy power. Dead are all the kindly feelings which unite the children of men; madness would claim him, till thou comest in thy might, thou protector of life, and makest the wretched heart to blossom again like the rod of Aaron.

No one could be more miserly than the Broby parson; no one, by cruelty and wickedness, could have deviated further from the path of his fellowmen. His room was never heated in the winter; he sat on an unpainted bench; he dressed in rags, lived on dry bread, and raged if a beggar crossed his doorstep. He sold his hay and let his horse starve in the stable; his cows fed on the wayside grass and the moss growing on the walls of his house; the bleating of his hungry sheep was heard even on the highway. The peasants threw him bread that their dogs refused to eat and clothes that beggars scorned. His hand was outstretched to beg, his back bent in thanks. He asked alms from the rich; he loaned to the poor; if he saw a coin, his heart ached with anxiety till he had it in his pocket. Unhappy was he who was his debtor when the day of payment came.

He married late in life, but it would have been better if he had never done so, for his wretched, overworked wife soon died. His daughter earned her bread among strangers. He was growing an old man, but his years brought no alteration in his hunger for gain. The madness of the miser had him in its grasp.

But one fine day, in the beginning of August, a heavy calash drawn by four horses drove up the hill at Broby. A little old lady was coming in great haste, with coachman, footman, and lady's maid, to see the Broby parson — the man she had loved in her youth.

He had been tutor on her father's estate, and they had loved each other, but her family had parted them; now she was coming to Broby to see him again before she died. All that life could give her now was to see once more the lover of her youth.

She sat in the big carriage and dreamed. It was not over the Broby hills to the house of a poor vicar she was hurrying, but to the cool, thickly overgrown arbor down the path where her lover awaited her. She sees him: he is young, can kiss, can love her. Now that she was to see him again, his image stood unusually clear before her. He was so handsome, so very handsome. He burned with passion and filled all her being with rapture.

She was old now and sallow and wrinkled. Perhaps he would not recognize her with her burden of sixty years, but she had not come to be seen, but to see — to see the lover of her youth, whom Time had never changed, who was still young and handsome and warm-hearted.

She came from such a great distance that no tales of the Broby parson had reached her.

The calash rolled up the hill on the summit of which stood the parsonage.

"For mercy's sake," whined a beggar by the wayside, "give something to a poor man!"

The lady gave him a silver coin, and asked if that was Broby parsonage they saw before them.

The beggar turned a sharp, cunning glance upon her.

"That is the parsonage," he said, "but the vicar is not at home; there is no one in just now."

The fragile, little old lady looked as if she would quite fade away. The cool arbor disappeared; her lover was not there! How could she expect, after forty years, to find him there still!

"What may the gracious lady want at the parsonage?"

The gracious lady had come to see the vicar, whom she knew in former years.

Forty years and forty miles* have separated them, and for every mile she has left behind her she has lost a year, with its burden of sorrow and saddening memories — so that, as she stood at the parson-

*A Swedish mile is about 6¼ English miles.

age gate, she was but twenty again, without either sorrows or remembrances.

The beggar, standing gazing at her, saw her change under his eyes from twenty to sixty, from sixty to twenty again.

"The vicar will be at home in the afternoon," he said. "The gracious lady would do best to drive down to Broby inn, and come again later. I can answer for it that the vicar will be at home in the afternoon."

A moment later the calash rolled away, but the beggar, gazing after it, trembled, and felt inclined to fall on his knees and kiss the ruts the wheels had made.

At noon, well dressed, with silk stockings and brightly shining shoe buckles and ruffled shirt and wristbands, freshly shaved and powdered, he stood before the rector's wife at Bro.

"A grand lady," he was saying, "the daughter of an earl. How can I ask her to enter my miserable house? My floors are black, my rooms without furniture, my ceilings green with damp and mould. Help me, dear madam! Think of it! she is the daughter of a great earl!"

"Say that you are not at home!"

"Dear madam, she has come forty miles to see me. She knows nothing about me. Why, I haven't even a bed to offer her, not even a bed for her servants!"

"Well, let her go home again."

"Oh, don't you see what I mean? I would rather give all I possess, all that I have with so much care gathered together, than that she should leave without being my guest. She was twenty when I saw her last—that is forty years ago. Help me, so that I can receive her suitably. Here is money, if money is needed, but more than money is required just now."

Oh, Eros, women love thee; they would rather go a hundred steps for thee than one for any other god.

At Bro rectory the rooms and kitchen and pantry were turned out. Carts were filled with furniture and sent off to the vicar's house. The rector, returning from his confirmation class, came back to empty rooms, and, glancing in at the kitchen door to inquire about his dinner, found none.

No dinner, no wife, no servant girl! Well, it cannot be helped. Eros has willed it so, Eros the all-conquering!

And a little later in the afternoon the heavy calash came rolling up the hill again, and the little lady sitting in it wondered if another mishap would not occur, if it was really true that she was going to meet the one happiness of her life.

The calash swung against the parsonage gate, and there it stood. It was too wide—the gate too narrow. The coachman cracked his whip, the horses started forward, the footman came and swore, but the back wheels were firmly fixed and immovable.

The earl's daughter cannot enter the courtyard of her beloved!

But here comes some one—here he comes. He lifted her out of the carriage, and his arms had lost none of their old strength; she was held in an embrace as warm as in the olden days, as warm as forty years ago. She gazed into eyes as bright as if they had looked out upon twenty-five summers.

A storm of feeling overwhelmed her, greater than ever before. He had carried her once up the steps of the terrace, she remembered now, and although she had believed her love to be living all these years, she found she had forgotten what it was to be clasped in a pair of strong arms and to gaze into bright, young eyes.

She did not see that he was old: she only saw his eyes. She did not notice the black floor nor the green, damp rafters; she only saw his shining eyes. The Broby parson was a stately and beautiful man at that moment. He became beautiful whenever he looked at her.

She listened to his voice—his strong, clear voice —with its caressing tone, reserved for her alone. What did he want with furniture from the rectory, with food or servants? The little old lady would hardly have missed them; she was listening to his voice and looking at his glowing eyes.

Never, never in her life had she been so happy. How gallantly he bent before her—as gallantly and proudly as if she were a princess and he her chosen favorite.

He made use of many phrases in speaking to her, as the old do, but she only smiled and was happy.

Toward evening he offered her his arm, and they took a walk in the old, neglected garden. She did not see how ugly and ill-kept it was. The overgrown shrubs were clipped hedges to her, the ragged grass-plots spread into level lawns, long alleys of trees shaded her, and statues of Youth and Hope, of Truth and Love, gleamed white amid the deep green foliage.

She had heard he had been married, but she forgot it now. Who could remember such things? She was but twenty, and he was twenty-five—only twenty-five, and so strong in the pride of his youth! Was he to become the miserly Broby parson—he, that smiling youth?

Sometimes he seemed to hear a whisper of the ill fate in store for him—but the wail of the poor, the curse of the deceived, the looks of scorn, the lampoons and sneers, were not his yet. His heart held but a pure, unselfish love.

Could that proud youth so love gold that he would creep into the lowest mire after it, beg it from the wayfaring, suffer humiliation and insult, cold and hunger, for its sake? Would he let his child starve and torture his wife for this same miserable gold? Impossible! it could not be; he was a man as others were; he was no monster! Was it by the side of a shameless wretch, unworthy of his chosen profession, that his love walked that night? Oh, no, is not Eros all-conquering?

He was not the Broby parson that night, nor the next day, nor the next.

On the third day the gate had been lifted off its hinges and the calash rolled away as quickly as the horses, fresh after their three days' rest, could carry it.

What a dream it had been, what a beautiful dream! No, nothing could have spoiled the peace of those three days!

Smiling, she returned home to her castle and her memories. She never heard his name again, never asked any questions about him. She duly dreamed her dream as long as she lived.

The parson sat in his lonely house and wept like a man in despair. She had brought back his youth. Must he grow old again? Would the evil spirit return again, and would he become as despicable as he had been before?

Squire Julius

SQUIRE JULIUS carried his red chest down from the cavaliers' wing. He filled with fragrant Pomeranian brandy a green keg, which had accompanied him on many a journey, and into a large carved-wood lunch-box he put bread, butter, some fat ham, a ripe old cheese, and pancakes smothered in raspberry jam.

Then he went about bidding a tearful farewell to all the joys of Ekeby. He caressed, for the last time, the worn skittle-balls in the ninepin alley and the round-cheeked youngsters of the iron workers on the hill; he walked round the arbors in the garden and the grottoes in the park, wandered into stable and cow-shed, and patted the horses on the haunches, shook the vicious bull's horns, and let the calves lick his hands. His eyes brimming with tears, he at last went up to the great house, where a farewell breakfast awaited him.

Alas, this existence! Why must it hold so much bitterness? There was poison in the food, gall in the wine!

The cavaliers, as well as himself, were choked with emotion; a mist of tears dimmed their eyes, and their farewell speeches were broken by sobs. Alas, this existence! Henceforth his life would be one long sigh. Nevermore would his lips be parted in a smile. The songs would die in his heart as flowers die in the autumn soil. He must fade and wither like a frost-bitten rose, like a parched lily. Nevermore would the cavaliers see poor old Julius. Dark forebodings crossed his mind as shadows of windswept clouds pass over newly tilled fields. He was going home to die.

Blooming with health and well-being, he stood before them. Never again would they behold him thus; never again would they ask him when he had last seen his feet or wish they had his cheeks for skittles. Liver and lungs had already become affected by mortal ills that were gnawing and consuming him; he had long felt that his days were numbered.

If only the cavaliers would be faithful to the memory of the dead comrade! Oh, may they never forget him!

Duty called him. In the old home his mother sat waiting for her son. For seventeen long years she had awaited his return, and now she had sent him a summoning letter. Though knowing it would be the death of him, he would go home like a dutiful son.

Oh, beloved cavaliers' wing! Oh, heavenly feasts and glorious adventures! Oh, fair shore-meads and proud waterfalls! Oh, smooth white dance-floors! Oh, violins and horns!—life of happiness and pleasure!—to part with all that was to die!

Squire Julius stepped into the kitchen to bid

good-by to the servants. In an overflow of emotion, he kissed and embraced them all, from the housekeeper to scrub-women. The maids wept and bemoaned his fate: Alackaday, that so kind and merry a gentleman must die! that they would never see him again!

He ordered his chaise brought from the coach-house and his horse from the stable. His voice nearly failed him when he gave that order. So the chaise was not to be let mould in peace at Ekeby; so old Kaisa must be dragged from her accustomed manger! He did not wish to speak harshly of his mother, but she should have thought of Kaisa and the chaise, even though she failed to think of him. How would they stand the long journey!

Hardest of all was the parting with the cavaliers. Little rotund Squire Julius, built to roll rather than to walk, felt tragic to his finger-tips. He likened himself to the great Athenian, who amid the circle of weeping students calmly drained the poison-cup; to old King Gösta, who prophesied that there would come a day when the Swedish people would long to snatch him back from the mould.

He thought of the swan that dies singing, and sang for them his favorite ballad. Thus he wished to be remembered: a regal spirit that stoopeth not to lament, but departeth hence, borne on wings of melody.

When the last beaker had been emptied, the last

song sung, the last embrace bestowed, and he stood
with coat on, whip in hand, there was not a dry eye
about him, and his own eyes were so bedimmed by
the blinding mists of grief that he could not see.

It was then the cavaliers seized him and lifted
him high, while ringing cheers rose about him. They
put him down somewhere, he knew not where. A
whip cracked, and off he went. When he recovered
the use of his eyes he was out on the highway.

The cavaliers had certainly wept and seemed overcome by a feeling of loss; but their grief had not
stifled all the happy impulses of the heart. One of
them — was it the poet Gösta Berling, or Beerencreutz, the camphio-playing old warrior, or the life-
weary Cousin Kristoffer? — had managed matters
so that old Kaisa would not have to be taken from
her stall nor the mouldering chaise from the car-
riage-house. A big spotted ox had been harnessed
to a hay-cart, and after the red chest, the green keg,
and the carved lunch-box had been duly depos-
ited therein, Squire Julius himself was lifted, not on
to the chest, nor on to the lunch-box, but on to the
back of the spotted ox.

Such is man, too weak to meet sorrow in all its
bitterness! The cavaliers sincerely mourned with
the friend who was going away to die — that withered lily, that mortally wounded singing swan! Yet
their hearts grew lighter when they saw him depart
mounted on the ox's back, his fat body shaken by

sobs, his arms outspread for a last embrace, while his eyes sought pity from an unkind heaven.

Out in the road the mists began to clear for Squire Julius, and he presently discovered that he was seated on the jolting back of an animal. It is said that he fell to pondering what can happen in seventeen years. Old Kaisa was visibly changed. Could it be that the oats and clover at Ekeby had wrought this transformation? He cried—I do not know if the stones at the roadside or the birds in the bush heard him, but certain it is that he cried:

"May the devil martyr me, if you haven't grown horns, Kaisa!"

After some deliberation, he let himself slide very slowly off the back of the ox, climbed into the wagon, sank down on the lunch-box, and drove on, still in a brown study.

By and by, as he neared Broby, he heard timesure singing:

> "*One, two, three,*
> *Oh, hee, hee,*
> *Värmland's hunters are coming, see!*"

These sounds met his ears, but of huntsmen he saw none.

The merry young ladies from Berga and a couple of the Munkerud Judge's pretty daughters came swinging up the road, each with a little bundle of lunch dangling at the end of a long stick, carried

across her shoulder like a gun. They marched bravely
on, in the hot sun, singing all the while:

> " *One*, *two*, *three*,
>   *Oh*, *hee*, *hee*—"

"Whither away, Squire Julius?" they queried on
meeting him, without noticing the pall of grief that
shrouded his brow.

"I am departing from the house of sin and vanity," answered the Squire. "I can no longer dwell
amongst idlers and evil-doers, and am now going
home to my mother."

"Oh, it can't be true!" they cried. "You do not
want to leave Ekeby, Squire Julius?"

"Yes," said he, striking the red chest with his
fist by way of emphasis. "As Lot fled from Sodom
and Gomorrah, so do I flee from Ekeby. Now
there is not one righteous man to be found there.
When the earth under those sinners crumbles, and
the rain of sulphur comes pouring down from the
sky, I shall rejoice in God's just judgment. Good-
by, girls. Shun Ekeby!"

That said, he wanted to proceed on his way, which
was not at all what the merry young girls wished.
They were going up to Dunder Cliff to climb it;
but the road being a long one, they had taken a no-
tion to drive to the foot of the mountain in Squire
Julius's hay-cart. Happy those who can rejoice at
the sunshine of life and who need no gourd to pro-

tect their pates! In almost no time the girls had
it their way; Squire Julius obligingly turned in the
direction of Dunder Cliff. Smiling, he sat on his
lunch-box while the girls crowded into the cart.

All along the road grew buttercups and daisies.
Now and then, when the ox had to rest awhile, the
girls got out and picked flowers. Gorgeous wreaths
soon circled Julius's head and the ox's horns.

Further on they came upon a clump of bright-
leaved young birches and a tangle of dark-leaved
alder-bushes. Here they climbed out and broke off
branches to decorate the wagon, which soon looked
like a moving grove. All was fun and play.

As the day wore on, Squire Julius brightened
and mellowed. He divided the contents of his lunch-
box among the girls, and sang for them. And when
at last they all stood at the summit of Dunder Cliff
and viewed the wide landscape lying below, so lovely
and peaceful that tears came into their eyes on
beholding its beauty, the heart of Julius began to
beat fast, and words came pouring from his mouth
as he spoke of his beloved land.

"Ah, Värmland, my beautiful, my glorious Värmland! Often, when I have seen thee before me on
a map, I have wondered what thou didst represent;
but now I know what thou art. Thou art an old,
pious hermit that sits motionless and dreams, with
legs crossed and hands resting in his lap. Thou
hast a pointed cap drawn over thy half-closed eyes;

thou art a muser, a holy dreamer, and art very beautiful. Wide forests are thy dress. Long bands of blue waters and chains of blue hills border it. Thou art so simple that the stranger sees not how lovely thou art. Thou art poor, as the devout desire to be. Thou sittest still, while Vänern's waves wash thy feet and thy crossed legs. To the left thou hast thy mines and thy fields of ore; there is thy beating heart. To the north thou hast the dark, lonely regions of wilderness, of mystery, and there rests thy dreaming head.

"When I behold thee, majestic, serious, mine eyes fill. Thou art austere in thy beauty; thou art meditation, poverty, resignation. Yet back of thine austerity I see the gentle features of kindness. I see and adore! If I but glance into thy deep forests, if only the hem of thy garment touches me, my spirit is healed. Hour after hour, year after year, I have looked into thy holy countenance. What mysteries art thou hiding under lowered eyelids, thou spirit of resignation? Hast thou solved the enigma of life and death, or art thou still pondering it, holy giant? For me thou art the keeper of great serious thoughts. But I see beings creeping about upon thee, creatures who never seem to note the majesty of earnestness on thy brow. They see only the beauty of thy face and limbs, and are so charmed that they perceive naught else.

"Woe is me, woe to us all, children of Värmland! Beauty, beauty, and nothing more, we demand of life. We, the children of renunciation, of seriousness, of poverty, raise our hands in one long prayer and ask but for this one good, beauty. May life be like a rosebush, with flowers of love, wine, and pleasure, and may its roses hang within every man's reach; that is our heart's desire, and our land wears the features of sternness and renunciation. Our land is the symbol of perpetual meditation, but we have no thoughts!"

Thus he spoke as one inspired, his voice vibrant with feeling, tears glistening in his eyes. The girls listened in wonder and not without emotion. Little had they divined what depths of feeling lay hidden under that tinsel-surface of jests and shams!

When it drew toward evening, and they had again climbed into the hay-cart, the girls hardly knew whither Squire Julius was taking them, until he stopped at the door of Ekeby Hall.

"Now, girls, we'll go in and have a dance," said he.

And what think you the cavaliers said when they saw Squire Julius return with a withered wreath round his hat and the hay-cart full of girls?

"We might have known the girls had carried him off," they laughed; "otherwise we should have had him back hours ago." For the cavaliers remembered that this was by actual count the seventeenth time Squire Julius had tried to leave Ekeby. Once a year, with unfailing regularity, he set out never to return. He had already forgotten both this and every other attempt. His conscience was sunk once more in its twelve-month sleep.

A gifted man was Squire Julius, light-footed in the dance, the life of the card-table; pen, brush, and fiddle-bow he wielded with equal facility. He had a heart easily moved, fair words on his tongue, and a throat full of song. But what would all that have availed him, if he had not possessed a conscience, though it stirred but once a year, like the dragon-fly, which frees itself from the gloomy depths and takes wing only to live for a few hours in the light of day and effulgence of the sun.

Plaster Saints

SVARTSJÖ CHURCH is white both within and
without; the walls, the pulpit, the pews, the
reading-desk, the ceiling, the window-frames, the
altar-cloth, are all white. There are no ornaments,
no pictures nor coats-of-arms. Over the altar stands
a plain wooden cross with a white cloth draped upon
it. It was not always so; in the old days the ceiling was covered with paintings, and many, many
colored figures, both in stone and plaster, decorated that house of God.

Once, long, long ago, an artist in Svartsjö had
stood watching the summer sky and the clouds as
they travelled toward the sun. He saw the white,
shining masses lying on the horizon in the early
morning tower higher and higher, saw them expand
and rise to storm the heavens. They lifted sails
like ships and raised standards like warriors. They
were ready to usurp the whole sky. Before the sun,
the ruler of space, these growing monsters changed
their shapes and put on harmless forms. There lay
a devouring lion: he changed to a powdered lady.
There stood a giant with crushing arms: he laid
himself down like a dreaming sphinx. Some of them
covered their white nakedness with golden-edged
mantles; others drew rouge over their cheeks of
snow. There were plains, and there were forests.

There were walled castles with lofty towers. The
white clouds had conquered the sky; they filled the
whole blue arch of heaven and reached the sun
and shaded it.

"Oh, how beautiful," thought the pious artist,
"if longing souls could mount those towering hills
and be carried by them, as on a swaying ship, ever
higher and higher!"

And he suddenly comprehended that the white
summer clouds were the craft on which the souls
of the blessed departed travel.

He saw them there, as they stood on the shining masses with lilies in their hands and golden
crowns on their heads; the heavens echoed with
their song, and angels flew on broad strong wings
to meet them. Oh, what myriads of souls! As the
clouds spread out, more and more of them became
visible. They rested on the cloud-beds as water-
lilies float on the lake. They embellished them as
flowers adorn the meadow. What a jubilant ascent!
Cloud rolled up behind cloud, and all were filled
with heavenly hosts in armor of silver, with immor-
tal singers in mantles bordered with purple.

This artist had afterwards painted the ceiling
in Svartsjö church, and he had tried to reproduce
there the rising clouds of a summer sky carrying the
blessed saints to heaven.

The hand that wielded the brush had been strong
but somewhat stiff, so that the clouds resembled

the curly locks of a full-bottomed wig rather than expanding masses of soft vapor. And he had not been able to reproduce the godly travellers as they had appealed to his artistic fancy, but he had clothed them after the manner of men, in long red capes and bishop's mitres, or in black gowns and stiff ruffs. He had given them big heads and little bodies and supplied them with handkerchiefs and prayer-books. Latin sentences flew out of their mouths, and for those whom he considered holiest he had placed solid, wooden chairs on the clouds, so that they might be carried, sitting comfortably, into eternity.

Still, every one knew, of course, that saints and angels had never shown themselves to the poor artist, and so they were not greatly surprised that he had not made them celestially beautiful.

Nevertheless the good master's pious painting had appeared to many exceedingly beautiful and had roused much godly emotion. It might surely have been worthy to be seen by our eyes too.

But during the year when the cavaliers were masters of Ekeby, Count Dohna had had the whole church whitewashed. The painting on the ceiling was hidden, and all the plaster casts of the saints were taken away.

Oh, those plaster saints!

It were better for me if human ills would cause me as much sorrow as I have felt over their down-

fall, if man's cruelty to man could fill me with the
bitterness I have experienced for their sakes.

Think of it! There was St. Olaf, with a crown
on his helmet, an axe in his hand, and a fallen
giant beneath his feet; on the pulpit Judith stood
in a red skirt and blue tunic, with a sword in one
hand and an hour-glass in the other instead of
the head of the Assyrian conqueror. There was a
mysterious Queen of Sheba in a blue skirt and
red tunic, with one web-foot and her hands full of
sibylline books; there was a grey St. Göran, lying
alone on a bench in the choir, for the horse and
the dragon had long since been broken; there was
St. Christopher with the flowering staff, and St.
Erik with sceptre and mitre, wrapped to his feet in
a flowing, yellow mantle.

I have sat in Svartsjö church and grieved that
the figures were gone and longed for them. I should
not have cared so much if a nose or a foot had been
missing, if the gilding had faded, and the colors
had scaled away. I should have seen them through
the glamour of the old legends. It seems to have
been the case with those saints that they were always
losing their sceptres or ears or hands and had to be
mended and repaired. The congregation tired of it at
last, and would gladly have been quit of them, but the
peasantry would never have taken any steps toward
their demolishment if Count Dohna had not done
it. It was he that ordered them to be taken away.

I have hated him because of it as only a child can hate. I have hated him as a hungry beggar hates the stingy housewife who refuses him bread. I have hated him as the poor fisherman hates the stupid boy who disturbs his net or makes his boat spring a leak. Was I not hungry and thirsty during those long sermons? And he had taken away the bread that should have nourished my spirit. Did I not yearn for infinity, for heaven? And he had damaged my ship and torn the net in which I should have caught holy visions.

There is no room in the world of grown-up folk for a real hatred. How could I hate such a miserable little personage as that Count Dohna or such a madman as Sintram or an enervated woman of the world like Countess Märta? But when I was a child—it was fortunate for them that they had died so long ago.

The pastor was perhaps standing in the pulpit speaking of peace and forgiveness, but to our corner of the church his words never penetrated. Oh, if I had had the old plaster saints there, they would have preached to me so that I should have heard and understood.

But now I generally sat thinking of how it happened that they were destroyed.

When Count Dohna had declared his marriage dissolved instead of seeking out his wife and having it legalized, it aroused universal indignation, for

every one knew that his wife had left her home because she was being tormented to death. It seemed
almost as if he wished to regain the mercy of God
and the respect of men by some good work when
he undertook the repair of Svartsjö church. He
had the whole interior whitewashed and the paintings on the ceiling taken down, and he and his men
carried the plaster saints down to a boat and sunk
them in the depths of the Löfven.

How could he dare to lay hands on these mighty
ones of the Lord!

Oh, that the evil deed was permitted! The hand
that cut off the head of Holofernes—did it no longer
wield a sword? Had the Queen of Sheba forgotten the secret knowledge that wounds more fatally
than a poisoned arrow? St. Olof, St. Olof, you old
viking! St. Göran, St. Göran, you old dragon-killer!
Then the noise of your exploits has died, and the
nimbus of your miracles has faded! But perhaps
the saints did not want to use their power against
the destroyer; since the Svartsjö peasants were no
longer willing to pay for paint for their coats and
gilding for their crowns, they suffered Count Dohna
to carry them out and sink them in the bottomless
depths of the Löfven. They did not want to stand
any longer as unsightly blemishes in the house of
God. Oh, the helpless ones! Did they remember
when prayers and kneelings were offered them?

I thought of that boat with its burden of saints

gliding over the surface of the lake on a quiet evening
in August. The men who rowed took slow strokes
and cast frightened glances at the passengers lying
in the bow and stern; but Count Dohna, who was
also there, was not afraid. He took them one by
one in his own aristocratic hands and threw them
into the water. His brow was clear, and he breathed
deeply. He felt himself to be fighting for the pure
evangelical faith. And no miracle was performed
in honor of the old saints—they sank silently and
hopelessly to destruction.

Next Sunday morning Svartsjö church shone
white. No pictures disturbed the peace of inner
contemplation. With the soul's eye alone the pious
must see the glories of heaven and the faces of the
blessed. The prayers of men must rise on their
own strong wings to the Most High. They must
no longer clutch at the hem of the saints' mantles.

Oh, green is the earth, man's loved home, and
blue is heaven, the goal of his longing; all the world
shines in color; why, then, is the church white?
White as winter, naked as poverty, pale as fear!
It glitters not with frost as the winter forest. It
gleams not with pearls and lace as a white bride.
The church stands there covered with cold, dead
whitewash, without a statue, without a painting.

Count Dohna sat that day in a flower-decked
chair in the choir to be seen and praised by all
men. He would be honored now for mending the

old pews, destroying the ugly pictures and plaster saints, for setting new glass into the broken windows and having all the church whitewashed. There was no reason why he should not do this if he wished. If he wanted to appease the anger of the Almighty, it was right he should decorate His temple as well as he knew how. But why should he want to be praised for it?

Coming thither with unrepented harshness on his conscience, he ought to have knelt on the stool of repentance and prayed his sisters and brothers in the church to cry to God that He might endure him in His sanctuary. It would have been better for him if he had stood there as a poor sinner, instead of sitting honored and blessed in the choir, being praised because he wanted to be reconciled to God.

Oh, Count, He has certainly awaited you at the stool of repentance. He will not be deceived because men dare not censure you. He is still the jealous God, who makes the stones testify when men are silent.

When the service was over and the last hymn sung, no one left the church; the pastor mounted the pulpit to express the thanks of the people.

But he did not get so far as that. For the doors opened, and the old saints came back into the church again, dripping with water from the Löfven, covered with green mire and brown mud. They must

have felt that the man who threw them to destruction, who drove them from God's house and drowned
them in the cold, dissolving waves, was about to
be praised. The old saints wanted a word in the
matter. They did not love the monotonous wash of
the waves. They were accustomed to hymns and
prayers. They had been silent and let it pass, as
long as they believed it was for the glory of God.
But it was not the case now. There sat Count Dohna
in honor and glory in the choir, about to be extolled.
They could not bear that. So they rose from their
watery graves and marched into church and were
recognized by all the congregation. There went
St. Olaf with the crown on his helmet and St. Erik
with the yellow flowery cape and grey St. Göran
and St. Christopher; no more — the Queen of Sheba
and Judith had not come.

When the people recovered from their astonishment, a loud whisper went through the church,
"The cavaliers!"

Yes, it was the cavaliers' doing. They went up to
the Count, and, without saying a word, they lifted
his chair upon their shoulders, carried him out of
the church, and put him on the hill outside. They
said nothing and looked neither to right nor to left.
They simply carried Count Dohna out of the house
of God, and when that was done they took the
nearest path to the lake.

They challenged no one, and did not lose time

in explaining their thoughts about this matter. It was very simple. "We, the Ekeby cavaliers, have our own ideas about this affair. Count Dohna is not worthy to be extolled in church, so we carry him out. Any one who likes may convey him back again."

But he was not carried back. The pastor's gratitude was never expressed. The people poured out of church, for every one thought the cavaliers had done right.

They remembered the fair young Countess, who had been so cruelly used at Borg; they remembered how good she was to poor people, and how sweet she was, and what a comfort it had been to look at her. It was a pity to come with mad pranks to church; but both pastor and people felt that they had been on the point of making even worse sport of the All-knowing God, and they stood abashed before the barbarous old madmen.

"When men are silent, the stones bear witness," they said.

After this Count Dohna did not feel at ease at Borg. One dark night in the beginning of August, a covered calash drove up close to the old staircase. All the servants stood about it, and Countess Märta came out wrapped in shawls and with a close veil over her face. The Count supported her, but she trembled and shuddered. It was with the greatest difficulty they could persuade her to cross the hall and stairs. After her the Count sprang into the carriage, the doors closed with a bang, and the coachman sent the horses forward at a wild pace.

When the magpies awoke next morning she was gone.

The Count spent the rest of his life far in the south. Borg was sold, and has changed hands very often since then. All love it, but there are few who have owned it with any happiness.

The Pilgrim of God

CAPTAIN LENNERT, God's pilgrim, came one afternoon in August to the inn at Broby, and entered the kitchen there. He was on his way home to Helgesäter, which lay a few miles northwest of Broby, near the edge of the forest.

He did not know then that he was to be one of God's pilgrims on earth; his heart was filled with joy at the thought of seeing his home once more. His had been a cruel fate, but now he was home, and all would be well. He never thought of being one of those who may never rest under their own roof-tree nor warm themselves at their own fireside.

He was a jovial-tempered man, and as he found no one in the kitchen, he made as much stir there as an excited boy. He threw the wrong shuttle into the loom and entangled the cord of the spinning-wheel, and then, catching up the cat, he dropped it on the dog's head, laughing till the whole house rang to see the two comrades fly at each other with extended claws and blazing eyes and hair on end in momentary forgetfulness of their old friendship.

Attracted by the noise, the landlady came in, and paused on the threshold to gaze at the man who stood laughing at the quarrelsome animals. She knew him well, but when she last saw him, he was sitting in a prison cart with handcuffs on his wrists.

She remembered the affair rather more than five years ago. Thieves had stolen some jewelry belonging to the wife of the Lord Lieutenant during the winter fair at Karlstad. Rings, bracelets, and buckles, much prized by the great lady, being chiefly heirlooms and presents, had disappeared and were never found, but a report circulated through the country that Captain Lennert of Helgesäter was the thief.

The landlady could never understand how such a report could have arisen. Was n't Captain Lennert a good and honorable man? He lived happily with his wife, whom he had married only a few years ago, for he could not afford to marry earlier. Was he not in a good position, having his pay and the income from his farm? What could tempt a man like that to steal old rings and bracelets? And it seemed most astonishing to her that such a report should have gained credence and could be proved so conclusively that Captain Lennert was dismissed the service, was deprived of his Order of the Sword, and was sentenced to five years' hard labor.

On his part, he admitted having been at the fair, but said he had left Karlstad before he heard of the theft. He had found an ugly old buckle on the road, which he had picked up and given to the children. This buckle proved, however, to be of gold; it was one of the stolen articles, and became the cause of his misfortune. But the affair had really been arranged by Sintram. The wicked proprietor of

Fors had prosecuted and also witnessed against the
Captain. It seemed he wanted him out of the way,
for soon afterwards an action was brought against
Sintram himself, it having transpired that he had
sold powder to the Norwegians during the war of
1814. People imagined he had been afraid of what
Captain Lennert could say in the matter. As it was,
he was acquitted on the plea of insufficient proof.

The landlady found it hard to take her eyes from
the man in her kitchen. His hair was grey and his
back bent — he must have had a hard time of it;
but he retained his happy temper and his friendly
face. He was still the same Captain Lennert who
had escorted her to the altar when she was married and had danced at the wedding. He probably
still stopped on the road with every one and chatted
with every one he met as he used to do and threw
a copper to every child. He would still tell every
wrinkled hag that she grew younger and more beautiful day by day, and he was still capable of standing on a barrel and playing the fiddle for the dancers
round the Maypole. Ah, yes!

"Well, Mother Karin," he said at last, "are you
afraid of looking at me?"

He had really come there to find out how things
were going at home, and if they expected him there.
They would know that his sentence expired about
that time.

The landlady gave him only good news. His

wife had been as capable as a man. She had hired the farm from the new proprietor, and everything had prospered in her hands; the children were well, and it was a pleasure to see them. And, of course, they were expecting him. The Captain's wife was a severe woman, who never spoke all her thoughts, but the landlady knew very well that no one had eaten with the Captain's spoon nor sat in his chair since he had been away, and during the spring no day had passed without her going to the big stones on the top of Broby Hill to look down the road for his coming, and she had prepared new clothes for him, clothes which she had woven herself. You could know from these signs that he was expected, even if she spoke little about it.

"They don't believe I did it?" said Captain Lennert.

"No, Captain," replied the peasant woman, "no one believes it."

Then Captain Lennert had no wish to tarry longer, he wanted to go home at once.

It happened that outside the inn he met dear old friends. The Ekeby cavaliers had arrived—Sintram had invited them thither to celebrate his birthday—and the cavaliers lost no time in shaking hands with the released convict and welcoming him home again. Sintram did the same.

"Dear Lennert," he said, "you may be sure God had a meaning in doing it!"

"Faugh, you scoundrel!" cried the Captain, "don't you think I know it was n't God who rescued your head from the block?"

The others laughed, but Sintram was not at all angry. He had no dislike of people hinting about his dealings with the devil.

Well, and so they carried Captain Lennert indoors again to drink to his arrival; he might go home immediately after that. But things went wrong; he had not tasted any strong drink for five years; he had probably not eaten anything all day, and he was tired out with his long journey. The consequence was he became confused after the first few glasses.

When the cavaliers had got him so far that he no longer knew what he was doing, they insisted on his taking more, and they had no bad intention in doing this — it was due to a kindly impulse toward the man who had tasted nothing good for five years.

Otherwise he was one of the soberest of men, and, of course, he had had no intention of getting drunk just then — on his way home to wife and children. Instead of that, he lay on the bench in the tap-room and fell asleep.

And as he lay there, temptingly unconscious, Gösta took up a bit of charcoal and a little cranberry juice and painted his face. He made it a real malefactor's visage; he thought it just suited a man straight from prison. He gave him a black eye, drew a red scar across his nose, pushed his hair over his forehead in untidy locks, and darkened the whole face.

They laughed at his work. Then Gösta wanted to wash it away.

" Let it alone," said Sintram, "so that he can see it when he awakes; it will amuse him."

And it was left as it was, and the cavaliers thought no more of Captain Lennert. The revel lasted all night, and when they broke up at dawn, there was more wine in their heads than sense.

The question then arose, what was to be done with Captain Lennert?

"We will take him home," said Sintram. "Think how delighted his wife will be. It will be a pleasure to see her joy; I feel touched when I think of it. Let us take him home."

They were all touched at the thought. Good God! how glad she would be, the severe lady at Helgesäter.

They shook some life into the Captain, and lifted him into one of the vehicles which the sleepy ostlers had brought to the door long ago, and the whole crowd drove off to Helgesäter, some half asleep and almost falling out, others singing to keep themselves awake. They looked little better than a set of vagabonds, all of them with swollen, red, and imbecile faces.

They arrived at last, and leaving the horses in

the back yard, marched with a kind of dignity to the house-steps, Beerencreutz and Julius leading Captain Lennert between them.

"Gather yourself together, Lennert," they said to him; "you are at home now. Don't you see you are at home?"

He raised his eyes and became almost sober. He was touched that they had accompanied him home.

"Friends," he cried, and paused to make a speech. "I have asked God, my dear friends, why so much evil has come over me!"

"Shut up, Lennert, don't preach!" shouted Beerencreutz.

"Let him speak," said Sintram; "he talks very well."

"I have asked Him and have not understood — understand now. He wished to show me what good friends I had — friends who bring me home to see my children and my wife's joy. For my wife awaits me! What are five years of misery in comparison?"

Hard fists thumped on the door. The cavaliers had no time to listen to more.

There was a movement inside. The servant girls awoke and peeped out. They dressed hurriedly, but did not dare to open the door to the group of men. At last the bar was drawn aside. The Captain's wife herself stepped out.

"What do you want?" she asked.

Beerencreutz answered. "We came here with your husband."

They pushed Captain Lennert forward, and she saw him stand swaying toward her, drunk, with the face of a villain. And behind him stood that group of intoxicated reeling figures.

She stepped back, and he advanced with open arms.

"You went like a thief," she exclaimed, "and come home like a vagabond." And she turned to go in.

He did not understand, and tried to follow her, but then she gave him a backward thrust on the breast.

"Do you think I will take a man like you to be master over my house and my children?"

The door slammed, and the bar fell into its place.

Captain Lennert sprang at the door and began to shake it. Then the cavaliers could not restrain their mirth. He had been so sure of his wife, and now she would have nothing to do with him. They thought it was so ridiculous.

When Captain Lennert heard them laugh, he turned and wanted to fight them. They sprang aside and climbed into their cart. He rushed after them, but stumbled over a stone and fell headlong, and though he got up, he did not follow them any further. A thought struck his confused mind. Nothing happened in the world without it being the will of God.

"Whither wilt Thou lead me?" he said. "I am a feather, driven by the breath of Thy spirit. I am a ball in Thy hands. Whither wilt Thou lead me? Why dost Thou close the doors of my home against me!"

And he went away from his home, thinking it was God's will he should do so.

At sunrise he stood on the crest of Broby Hill and looked over the valley. The people did not think their friend had come. No poor and troubled soul had wreathed garlands of the evergreen cranberry leaves and hung them over the house doors. Over the thresholds he would tread no sweet-scented lavender or flowers from the hedges had been strewn. Mothers had not lifted their children high in their arms that they might see him as he came. The huts had not been tidied nor the dark hearths hidden by fragrant juniper. The men did not work with eager industry that he might be gladdened by the sight of well-tilled fields and straightly digged ditches.

Oh, as he stood there, his anxious eyes saw the ravages made by the drought, saw the scorched harvests, and that the people did n't seem to care to prepare the ground for the next year's crop. He looked up to the blue mountains, and the sharp morning sunshine showed him the tract of woods burned brown by the forest fires. He saw the way-

side birches nearly killed by the drought. There
were many small signs by which he could judge
— by the smell of mash which he perceived as he
passed the cottages, by the fallen fences, by the
small amount of stacked wood near the houses —
that the people were doing badly, that the famine
had come, and they were seeking comfort in indifference and in gin.

But perhaps it was well for him to see what he
did, for to him it was not given to see green harvests spring up on his own fields, nor to watch the
dying embers of his own fireside, nor to feel the
soft hands of his children laid in his, nor to know
the support of a good wife. Perhaps it was well for
him, whose heart was weighed down by great sorrow, that there were others whom he might comfort
in their poverty. Perhaps it was well for him that
it was such a bitter time of trouble, when the hardness of nature brought want to the poorer classes,
and those whose lot in life was more fortunate were
doing their best to ruin themselves. For not in vain
had the Broby parson sat among his parishioners
like a greedy miser instead of being a good shepherd to them, not in vain did the cavaliers reign in
waste and wantonness at Ekeby, not in vain had
Sintram instilled into them that wild belief that ruin
and death would overwhelm them all.

Captain Lennert stood on the hill at Broby,
and began to think that God perhaps had need of

him. And he was not recalled home by a penitent wife.

It must be remembered that the cavaliers never could understand the share they had in making the Captain's wife so stern. Sintram kept his own counsel. Much censure was bestowed by all the country side on the wife who was too proud to receive home such a good husband. People said that any one attempting to broach the subject to her was silenced instantly. She could not bear to hear his name mentioned. Captain Lennert made no attempt to change her mind.

It was the next day.

An old peasant was lying on his death-bed in Högberg village. He had received the sacrament; the strength of life in him was failing—he must die.

Restless as one about to set forth upon a long journey, he had his bed carried from the kitchen to the living-room and from the living-room to the kitchen, and by that they knew more than by the heavy rattle in his throat and the failing glance that his hour had come.

Round about him stood his wife and children and servants. He had been fortunate, rich, and respected, and his death-bed was not forsaken, nor did impatient strangers surround him in his last hour. The old man spoke of himself as if he stood before the face of God, and those around him witnessed with deep sighs and confirmative remarks to the truth of his words.

"I have been an industrious man and a good master," he said. "I have held my wife as dear as my right hand; I have not permitted my children to grow up without punishment and care; I have not drank. I have not moved my neighbor's landmark, I have not driven my horses violently uphill, I have never let the cattle stand starving in the winter, nor have I let the sheep swelter in their heavy fleeces in summer."

And round him the weeping servants repeated like an echo, "He has been a good master. Oh, Lord God! he has not driven the horses violently uphill, nor let the sheep swelter in their wool in the summer."

Unnoticed, a poor man had stepped into the house to ask for a meal. He also heard the dying man's words, where he stood silently on the threshold.

And the dying man continued, "I have reclaimed the forest and drained meadows; I have driven the plough in straight furrows; I have built barns three times as big to hold harvests three times as plentiful as in my father's time. I have three silver tankards made of bright dollar pieces, and my father had only one."

The dying man's words reached the listener at the door. He heard him bear witness of himself

as if he stood before the throne of God. He heard
the children and servants confirm his words.

"He drove the plough in straight furrows, indeed
he did."

"God will give me a good place in His heaven,"
said the old man.

"Our Lord will receive our master well," cried
the servants.

The man at the door heard the words, and fear
came over him who had been a shuttlecock in God's
hands for five long years—a feather driven by the
breath of His spirit.

He went up to the man and took his hand.

"Friend, friend," he cried, and his voice shook
with fear, "have you considered who the God is
before whose face you will stand soon? He is a
great and awful God! The earth is His field, and
He rides upon the storm. The wide heavens tremble under the weight of His foot. And you stand
before Him and say, 'I have ploughed straight
furrows, I have sowed rye and cleared the forest.'
Are you praising yourself before Him and measuring yourself against Him? You don't know how
mighty is the God to whose kingdom you are going."

The old man's eyes opened wide, his mouth
twitched with fear, and the rattle in his throat grew
deeper.

"Do not go to your God with proud words on
your lips," continued God's pilgrim. "The great

on earth are but winnowed chaff in His hand. His daily work is to create suns. He has digged the ocean and raised the hills; He has clothed the world with herbs. There is no worker like Him; you must not match yourself against Him. Bow down before Him, you passing soul! Lie deep in the dust before the Lord your God! God's storm is rushing over you! God's anger is upon you like fiery flame! Bow down, clutch at the hem of His mantle like a child, and pray for shelter! Lie deep in the dust and cry for mercy! Humble thyself, oh, soul, before thy Maker!"

The eyes of the dying man were wide open, his hands were folded, but his face had lighted up, and the noise in his throat had ceased.

"Oh, human soul, oh, passing human soul," cried the man again, "as surely as you humble yourself in your last hour before your God, so surely will He lift you like a child in His arms and carry you unto the bliss of His paradise!"

The old peasant gave a last sigh, and all was over. Captain Lennert bowed his head and prayed, and all those assembled prayed too with heavy sighs.

When they raised their eyes, the old peasant lay in quiet peace. His eyes still seemed to reflect the splendor of a glorious vision. His lips smiled, his face was beautiful. He had seen his God.

"Oh, thou great and beautiful human soul!" they thought, seeing him there, "thou hast now

burst thy bonds! Thou hast risen at the last moment to thy Maker! Thou hast humbled thyself
before Him, and He has raised thee like a child in
His arms."

"He has seen God," said the old man's son, and
closed his eyes.

"He saw the heavens open," sobbed the children and servants.

The old mistress of the house laid her trembling
hand in the Captain's.

"You have helped him over the worst, Captain."

He stood dumb before them. The gift of great
words and deeds had been granted him — he did
not know how. He trembled like a butterfly swaying on the case of its chrysalis, while its wings spread
themselves in the sunshine, glittering like the sunshine itself.

.   .   .   .

That was the hour which drove Captain Lennert
out among the people. Except for it, he probably
would have returned home and let his wife see his
real face, but from that moment he believed that
God had need of him. He became God's pilgrim
who carried help to the poor. The want among
them at that time was great, and there was much
misery which common-sense and tenderness could
alleviate better than gold or power could have done.

One day Captain Lennert travelled up to the

poor villagers who lived in the districts round Gurlita Cliff. The famine was very severe among them;
their supply of potatoes was used up, and they could
not sow the rye in the burned clearings, for they had
no seed.

Then Captain Lennert took a small boat and
rowed obliquely over the lake to Fors and asked
Sintram to give them some rye and potatoes. Sintram received him in a friendly manner; he showed
him over the big, well-provisioned granaries and
the full cellars, where the potatoes from last year's
harvest still lay, and let him fill all the bags and
sacks he had brought with him.

But when Sintram saw the little boat, he said
it was too small a craft for such a heavy load. The
wicked foundry proprietor had the sacks carried
into one of his big boats, and told his carter, strong
Måns, to row it across the lake. Captain Lennert
had only the little boat to look after.

Still he was left behind, because Måns was a
masterhand at rowing, and was immensely strong.
Captain Lennert sat, too, and dreamed while he
pulled his boat over the beautiful lake and thought
of the wonderful fate of the grain. Now it would
be cast into the black, ashy earth among the tree-
stumps and the stones, but it would germinate and
strike root in the wilderness. He thought of the soft,
clear, green shoots which would cover the ground,
and in thought he bent down and stroked their

soft tips. Then, too, he remembered how autumn and winter would go over the weak little shoots which had come up so late, and how sturdy and brave they would be when spring came, and they could begin growing in earnest. And his soldier heart was gladdened at the thought of the stiff stalks which would stand up so straight, yards high, with fine speary heads. The tiny pistol-like plume of the pistils would explode, and the powder of the stamens mount to the hill-tops, and then, in apparent strife and unrest, the ears would fill with the soft, sweet kernels. And afterwards, when the sickle cut them down, and the stalks fell, and the threshing flails thundered over them, when the mill ground the kernels to flour, and the flour was baked into bread—oh, how much hunger would have been stilled by the grain lying in the boat before him.

Sintram's carter pulled his boat to the landing-place at Gurlita Cliff, and many famished people came thronging to the shore. Then the boatman said, as he had been instructed by his master:

"The master at Fors sends you malt and rye, peasants. He has heard you are without gin."

Then the people went mad. They rushed down to the boat and even sprang into the water to snatch at the bags and sacks, but this had never been Captain Lennert's intention. He, too, had landed —and he grew angry when he saw this behavior.

He intended the potatoes for food and the rye for seed; he had never thought of asking for malt.

He shouted to the people to leave the sacks alone, but they would not listen to him.

"May the rye turn to sand in your mouths, and the potatoes to stones in your throats," he screamed at last, exasperated at the way they were tearing at the sacks of grain.

Then it seemed as if Captain Lennert had performed a miracle. Two women, pulling at a bag, tore a hole in it, and found it contained nothing but sand — the men who had lifted the potato-sacks felt how heavy they were, as if filled with stones.

It was sand and stones — all of it, nothing but sand and stones. The people stood in silent awe before the miracle-worker who had come to them. Captain Lennert was dumb for a moment with astonishment. Only strong Måns laughed.

"Row home, man," said Captain Lennert, "before the people find out that there never was anything but sand in the sacks, or I fear they may sink your boat for you."

"I am not afraid."

"Go, in any case," said the Captain in such an authoritative tone that Måns went. Then Captain Lennert told the people that Sintram had cheated them, but still they did not believe that a miracle had not been performed. The noise of it spread abroad, and, as the people's love for the extraordinary was great, it was generally believed that Captain Lennert could perform miracles. He won great influence over the people in that way, and they called him the Pilgrim of God.

The Churchyard

IT was a beautiful evening in August. The Löfven lay smooth as glass; a haze veiled the hills,
and there was a refreshing coolness in the air.

Colonel Beerencreutz of the bristling white
moustaches, short of stature and strong as an ath-
lete, came down to the shore of the lake, his camphio-
deck in his pocket, and stepped into a flat-bottomed
boat. With him were Major Anders Fuchs, his old
brother-at-arms, and little Ruster, who had been
drummer-boy with the Värmland Chasseurs and
for many years the Colonel's devoted friend and
orderly.

On the other shore of the lake lies the churchyard, the neglected churchyard of Svartsjö parish,
set here and there with slanting iron crosses that
rattle with every wind, and tufted as an unploughed
field with sedge and striped grasses, which seem to
have sprung up there to remind us that no two
men's lives are the same, but vary as do the blades
of grass. Here there are no gravelled walks, no shad-
ing trees save the great linden on the grave of some
old forgotten curate, but a stone wall, thick and
high, encloses the field.

A wretched, lonely place is this churchyard, ugly
as the pinched face of a miser withered by the curses
of those he has robbed of happiness. And yet those

who rest there are blessed, for they were lowered
into consecrated ground with hymns and prayers.

Aquilon, the gambler, who died by his own hand
at Ekeby, had to be buried outside the wall. He
who had once been so proud, so chivalrous—the
brave soldier, the fearless hunter, the gambler who
held fortune in his hand—had ended by dissipating
his children's inheritance, all that he himself had
acquired, and every penny his wife had saved. Wife
and children he had deserted many years before to
lead the life of a cavalier. One evening, the previous
summer, he had played away the farm that gave
his family the means of subsistence, and, rather than
pay that last gambling debt, he shot himself.

Since his death, the cavaliers had been only
twelve in number. No one had come to take the
place of the thirteenth; that is to say, no one but
the arch-fiend who on Christmas Eve had crept out
of the blasting-furnace.

The cavaliers thought the gambler's fate harder
than that of his predecessors. To be sure, they knew
that each year one of them must die. But what of it?
Cavaliers may not grow old. If their eyes are too
dim to distinguish the cards, their hands too shaky
to lift the glass, what is life to them and what are
they to life? But to lie like a dog outside the churchyard wall where the sod is trampled by grazing
sheep, wounded by spade and plough, where the way-
farer passes without slackening his pace, and chil-

dren romp and play without subduing their laughter
and merry chatter, where the stone wall will prevent
the sound of the trumpet from reaching him outside when the Angel comes to waken the dead who
rest within — that was indeed hard!

Beerencreutz rowed his boat across the Löfven,
gliding in the dusk of the evening over the lake
of my dreams, on whose shores I have seen gods
wander, and from whose depths rises my magic
palace. He rowed past the Lagö lagoons, where
spruces growing on the low sandy shoals shoot
straight up out of the water, and where the ruin
of the old pirate castle still crowns the steep rock-
island; he rowed on, past the pine grove at Borg
Point, where an old tree hangs over the cleft in
which a huge bear had once been caught, and where
old cairns and grave mounds bear witness to the
antiquity of the place.

He got out below the churchyard, and crossed
the mowed fields belonging to the Count of Borg
to the grave of Aquilon. He bent down and patted
the turf lightly, as one caresses the coverlet under
which a sick friend is lying. Then, taking out his
camphio-deck, he seated himself at the grave side.

"Our Johan Fredrik must be lonely out here,
and longs, no doubt, for a game."

"It's an outrage that a man like him has to
lie here!" protested the great bear-hunter Anders
Fuchs, sitting down beside the Colonel.

Little Ruster, the flute-player, with tears trickling from his small red-lidded eyes, said in a broken voice:

"Next to you, Colonel, next to you he was the best man I've ever known."

Those three worthy gentlemen sat round the grave and solemnly dealt the cards.

Looking out over the world, I see many graves —graves where once mighty men rest under a ponderous weight of marble. Funeral marches were played for them, and standards were dipped. I see the graves of those who have been much beloved. Flowers, caressed with kisses and watered with tears, rest lightly on their grassy mounds. I see forgotten graves and arrogant tombs, lying resting-places and others that say nothing. But never before have I seen the Right bower and the Joker with cap-and-bells tendered in tribute to the occupant of a grave.

"Johan Fredrik has won, as I expected," said the Colonel, proudly; "it was I that taught him to play. Now we are dead—we three—and he alone lives."

Then the Colonel gathered up the cards and, with his comrades, went back to Ekeby.

May the dead in his lonely grave have known and felt that he was remembered.

Primitive hearts bring strange homage to those they love. He who lies outside the wall of the churchyard, he whose body was not allowed to rest in holy ground, must be glad that there are those who still cherish his memory.

Friends, children of men, when I am dead I shall probably rest in the midst of the churchyard, in the tomb of my ancestors, for I have not robbed my nearest and dearest of their means of subsistence nor lifted my hand against my own life. But certainly none will come to me at eventide, when the sun is gone and the field of the dead lies desolate and lonely, to place in my bony hands the bright-colored cards.

Nor—which would delight me more, since cards tempt me little—will any one come with fiddle and bow, that my spirit, hovering round the mouldering earth, may be lulled in a flow of melody like the swan on the rippling wave.

Old Songs

MARIENNE SINCLAIRE sat in her room one quiet afternoon at the end of August arranging her letters and papers.

Disorder surrounded her. Large leather trunks and iron-tipped boxes had been dragged into the room, and her clothes covered chairs and sofas. Everything had been brought from wardrobes and garret and ebonized chests of drawers; silks and linen gleamed; her jewelry was laid out to be polished; shawls and furs were to be looked over and a choice made.

Marienne was preparing for a long journey. It was uncertain if she would ever return. She stood at a turning-point of her life, and she was burning a number of old letters and diaries. She did not wish to be burdened by remembrances of the past.

While sitting thus, she found a little bundle of old verses in her hands. They were copies of some old folk songs which her mother used to sing to her when she was a child. She untied the cord that held them together and began to read.

She smiled sadly after reading for a short time; the old songs held such wonderful wisdom.

Trust not in happiness, trust not in the expression of happiness, nor in roses and dewy leaves.

Trust not in a laugh, they said. See! Beautiful

Valborg drives in her shining coach, and her lips smile, but she is as sad as if the horses' hoofs and the wheels of her carriage had driven over her life's happiness.

Trust not in the dance, they said. Many feet swing lightly over polished floors, while the mind is as heavy as lead. Little Kerstin was gay and merry while she danced away her fair young life.

Trust not in the jest, they said, for many go to table with jesting lips while ready to die of sorrow. There sits the youthful Adeline and allows Duke Frojdenborg to offer his heart to her in jest, knowing it only requires that to give her strength to die.

Oh, you old songs, what are we to trust in—in tears and sorrows?

The sad heart is easily tempted to smiles, but he who is happy cannot weep.

The old songs believe only in tears, in sadness. Sorrow is the reality, the imperishable, it is the firm rock under the shifting sand. One can trust in sorrow and sorrow's symbols.

Joy is but sadness in disguise. There is, in fact, nothing on earth but sorrow.

"Oh, you comfortless songs," said Marienne, "your old wisdom runs short before the fulness of life!"

She went to the window and looked out into the garden, where her parents were walking. They

went up and down the broad paths, and spoke of all
that met their eyes, of the grass and the birds in
the sky.

"See! there goes a heart and sighs with sadness
because it has never been so happy before."

And it struck her suddenly that perhaps it all lay
with one's self, that joy and sorrow depended on
the different ways of looking at things. She asked
herself if it had been joy or sorrow that had overwhelmed her that year. She hardly knew herself.

She had lived through bitter trials, her very soul
had suffered. She had been crushed to the earth in
abasement, and when she came back to her home,
she had said to herself, "I will not remember anything ill of my father;" but her heart would not
consent. "He has drawn down such dreadful sorrow upon me," it said; "he has separated me from
the man I loved; he brought me to despair, when
he beat my mother. I bear no ill-will toward him,
but I fear him."

She noticed that she was obliged to force herself
to sit still, when her father came and sat down beside her. She longed to flee from him. She tried to
master herself, she talked to him as usual, and was
constantly with him. She could control herself, but
she suffered inexpressibly.

She finished by detesting everything about him
—his coarse, loud voice, his heavy tread, his large
hands, all the powerful, belligerent temperament.

She bore him no ill-will, but she could not approach him without experiencing a feeling of fear and dislike. Her subjugated heart revenged itself. "You would not allow me to love," it said; "but I am still your master. You will end by hating."

Accustomed as she was to keep a close watch upon all that passed within her, she knew but too well how that dislike deepened, how it grew day by day, and at the same time it seemed as if she were now bound forever to her home. She knew quite well it would be best for her to go out into the world again, but she could not bring herself to it after her illness. Still there was no relief to be found. She would be tortured thus, till one day she would lose her self-control and break out against her father; she would show him the bitterness of her heart, and after that there would be strife and sorrow between them.

Thus the spring and early summer had passed. In July she became engaged to Baron Adrian, to secure a home for herself.

One beautiful morning Baron Adrian had ridden up to the house, seated on a fine horse. His hussar jacket shone in the sunlight, his spurs and sword and belt glittered and beamed, not to speak of his own fresh face and smiling eyes. Melchior Sinclaire was standing on the hall steps and received him when he came.

Marienne had been sitting at the window sew-

ing. She saw him arrive, and heard every word he
said to her father.

"Good morning, Sir Sunshine," cried Sinclaire
to him. "You are devilishly fine. Are you not out
a-wooing?"

"Well, yes, uncle, that's just what I am," he answered, laughing.

"Is there no shame in you, boy? What have you
to keep a wife upon?"

"Nothing, uncle. If I had, never the devil would
I marry."

"That's what you think, that's what you think,
Sir Sunshine! But that grand jacket, you could
afford that, anyway?"

"On credit, uncle!"

"And the horse you are riding is worth much
money, I can tell you, boy. Where did you get it
from?"

"The horse is not mine."

That was more than the big foundry proprietor
could withstand. "God bless you, boy," he said;
"you truly need a wife who has some money. If
you can win Marienne, you can have her."

In this way they came to an understanding before
Baron Adrian had dismounted. But Melchior Sin-
claire knew very well what he was doing, for Baron
Adrian was a good fellow.

A little later the lover had gone to Marienne and
rushed at once into the subject.

"Oh, Marienne, dear Marienne, I have spoken to uncle already. I want you to be my wife; say you will, Marienne!"

She got the truth out of him. The old Baron, his father, had allowed himself to be cheated into buying some more empty mines. The old Baron had been buying mines all his life, and there was never anything to be got out of them. His mother was worried, and he was in debt, and he proposed to her now, so that he might save the house of his forefathers and his hussar jacket.

His house was the freehold property of Hedeby; it lay on the other side of the lake, almost opposite Björne. Marienne knew him very well; they were of the same age, and had been playmates. "You might just as well marry me, Marienne; my life is so wretched. I must ride on borrowed horses and cannot pay my tailor. It cannot go on much longer. I shall be forced to send in my papers, and then I shall shoot myself."

"But, Adrian, what kind of a marriage would it be? We are not in the very least in love with each other."

"Oh, as regards love, I do not care a scrap about that nonsense," he explained. "I like to ride a good horse and to hunt, but I am no cavalier, I am only a worker. If I could only get some money together, and could take the old estate in hand, and give my mother some peaceful days, I should be satisfied.

I should both plough and sow, I like the work so
well."

He looked at her with his honest eyes, and she
knew he spoke the truth, and was a man to depend
upon. She promised to marry him, chiefly to get
away from her home, but also because she had always
had a liking for him. But she would never forget
the month that followed the announcement of her
engagement—all that mad, miserable time.

Baron Adrian had become more sad and quiet
day by day. He called often enough at Björne, several times a day sometimes, but Marienne could
not help noticing how depressed he was.

He could still joke and laugh when with others,
but alone with her he was impossible—utterly silent,
dull. She felt she understood the reason; it was
not so easy as he had thought to marry an ugly
woman. Now he had taken a dislike to her. None
knew better than she how ugly she was now. She
had showed him plainly enough that she did not
expect caresses and protestations of love; but he
was miserable at the thought of her as his wife,
and it became worse and worse every day. Why
did he go about so miserable? Why did he not
break off the engagement? She had given him hints
enough. She could do nothing herself. Her father
had told her very plainly that her reputation would
not bear any more adventures in the way of engage-
ments. At that she scorned them both equally;

any way seemed good enough to escape from her captors. Then, only a few days after the betrothal feast, the change had come, suddenly and surprisingly.

. . . .

In the path just before the hall door at Björne there lay a big stone which had always been the cause of much trouble and provocation. Carriages were upset by it, horses and farm laborers stumbled over it, the dairy maids carrying their heavy milk-pails tripped over it and spilled the milk, and the stone was still allowed to remain there because it had lain there for so many years.

It had been there during the time of Melchior Sinclaire's parents, long before he thought of building Björne, and the great man could not understand why he should take it up now.

But it happened on one of the last days of August that two servant girls, carrying a heavy bucket, stumbled over the stone, fell, and hurt themselves seriously, and the angry feeling about the stone was again awakened.

It was only breakfast-time yet. The master was away taking his morning ride, but as the farm people were at home between eight and nine, Fru Gustafva ordered some of the men to come and dig up the big stone.

They came with spades and crowbars, and dug

and dragged, and finally got the old peace-breaker out of his hole, and they carried him away to the back yard. It took six men to lift him. Hardly had the stone been taken up when Melchior Sinclaire returned, and his eyes took instant notice of the fact. You can imagine he was furious. It was no longer the same place, he felt; who had dared to remove the stone?

Oh, Fru Gustafva had given the order! Of course, womankind had no heart in their bodies. Didn't his wife know he loved that stone? And he marched up to the stone, lifted it, and carried it from the back yard across the court and back to the place where it lay before, and there he flung it down again. Yet it was a stone which six men had lifted with difficulty. The exploit was greatly admired all over Värmland.

While he carried the stone across the courtyard, Marienne had been standing at the window in the dining-room watching him. She had never seen him so terrible. He was her master, that fearful man with the unconquerable strength; an unreasonable, capricious man, who never thought of anything but his own pleasure.

They were just eating their breakfast, and she had a bread-knife in her hand. Unconsciously she lifted it.

Fru Gustafva caught her wrist.

"Marienne!"

"What is it, mother?"

"Oh, Marienne, you looked so strange. I was afraid."

Marienne gazed at her mother for a long time. She was a little dried-up woman, grey-haired and wrinkled at fifty years. She loved like a dog, not counting the blows she received. She was usually cheerful, and yet she gave a sad impression, for she was like a storm-whipped tree on the sea-shore, she had never had peace for growth. She had learned to creep along by-paths if necessary; and she often dissembled, pretending to be more stupid than she was, to escape reproaches. She was in everything the work of a husband's hand.

"Would you grieve much, mother, if father died?" she asked.

"Marienne! You are angry with your father. You are always angry with him. Why cannot you make it right again, now you have a new lover?"

"Oh, mother, I cannot help it. Can I help shrinking from him? Do you not also see what kind of a man he is? He is hasty and uncouth; he has tried you till you are old before your time. Why should he be our master? He behaves like a madman. Why should I honor and obey him? He is not good—nor merciful. I know he is strong. He can kill us when he chooses. He can turn us out of the house when he will. Am I therefore to love him?"

But Fru Gustafva seemed another woman when

she answered. She had gained strength and courage, and spoke authoritatively.

"Be careful, Marienne. It seems to me that your father may have done right in barring you out last winter. You will see you will be punished for this. You must learn to bear things without hating, Marienne, to suffer without revenging it."

"Oh, mother, I am so miserable!"

Just after that it came. They heard the sound of a heavy fall in the hall.

They never knew if Melchior Sinclaire had stood on the hall steps and heard Marienne's words through the open door of the breakfast-room, or if it was only the physical exertion that occasioned the stroke. When they came out they found him lying unconscious, and afterwards they never dared to ask him about it. He too never allowed any sign to escape him that he had heard. Marienne never permitted herself to think that she had unconsciously revenged herself. But the sight of her father lying there on the same steps where she had learned to hate him took all the bitterness out of her heart.

He soon regained consciousness, and, after keeping quiet for a few days, was himself again — and yet not himself.

Marienne watched her parents walking together in the garden. It was always so now. He never went out alone, never left home, but grumbled over visitors and anything that separated him from his

wife. Age had come over him suddenly. He could
not undertake to write a letter; his wife must do
it. He would decide nothing alone, but asked her
advice about everything, and decided as she wished.
And he was always kind and mild. He felt the
change himself, and saw how happy his wife was.

"She is happy now," he said one day to Marienne, pointing to Fru Gustafva.

"Oh, dear Melchior," she cried, "you know very
well that I would rather have you well again."

And she really wished it. It was her greatest
delight to talk of the great man as he had been in
the days of his strength. She would tell you how
he could withstand a carouse as well as any of the
Ekeby cavaliers, and how he would make a splendid stroke of business and coin a pile of money
just when she thought he was bringing them to
beggary by his wildness. But Marienne knew she
was happy in spite of her mourning. To be all to
her husband was enough for her. They both looked
old and prematurely broken, and Marienne thought
she could see their future. He would by and by
become weaker, the strokes would come again and
again, and make him more and more helpless, and
she would guard and serve him till death divided
them. But the end might not be for many years yet.
Fru Gustafva would still keep her happiness for
some time. It must be so, thought Marienne. Life
was in debt to her.

For her, too, things were easier now. No anxious despair drove her to seek another master. Her bleeding heart had gained peace. Hate had torn it as well as love, but she thought no more of the suffering it had cost her. She was obliged to confess that she was a truer, richer, better woman than she had been before. What after all could she wish undone of all that had happened? Was it then true that all suffering was for the best? Could everything be turned to happiness? She had begun to look upon everything as good that developed her to a higher degree of humanity. Her old songs were wrong. Sorrow was not the only truth in life. She would travel now and seek for some place where she was needed. If her father had been in his old frame of mind, he would not have allowed her to break her engagement. Now Fru Gustafva had arranged it. Marienne had even received permission to give Baron Adrian the monetary help he needed.

She could also think of him with pleasure. He would be free. He had always reminded her in his manner and bright gaiety of Gösta, now she would see him gay again. He would again be the Sunshine Knight who had come in splendor to her father's court. She would give him an estate where he could plough and sow as much as his heart desired, and she would see him lead a lovely bride to the altar some day.

With such thoughts in her heart she sat down and wrote to him, giving him back his freedom. She wrote sweet persuading words — sense wound about with a jest, and yet she wrote so that he would understand how seriously she meant it. While she wrote, the footfalls of a horse were heard on the road.

"My dear Sir Sunshine," she thought; "this is the last time."

Directly afterwards Baron Adrian came straight up to her room.

"Why, Adrian, are you coming in here?" she exclaimed, looking round in horror at all the disorder.

He became shy and awkward at once and stammered forth an excuse.

"Oh, I have just been writing to you," she said; "see, you may as well read it at once."

He took the letter, and she sat and watched him while he read it. She was hoping to see his face light up with joy.

But he had not read far before his face grew fiery red; he threw the letter on the floor, stamped upon it, and swore, swore violently.

Then a gentle tremor went through Marienne. She was no novice in the lesson of love, yet she had not understood this inexperienced boy, this great baby.

"Adrian, dear Adrian!" she said. "What comedy have you been playing with me? Come and tell me the truth."

He came and nearly smothered her with caresses. Poor boy, how miserable he had been, and how he had longed for her!

After some time she looked out of the window. There walked Fru Gustafva and talked with the great land proprietor about flowers and birds, and here she sat and babbled of love.

"Life has made us two women feel its hardness," she thought, and smiled mournfully. "It would console us now, we have each got a big baby to play with."

Still, it was comforting that she could be loved so. It was sweet to hear him whisper of the charm she held, and how much ashamed he was of what he had said when he proposed to her. He had not known her power then. Oh, none could come near her without loving her; but she had frightened him so, he felt so subdued.

This was not happiness nor unhappiness, but she would try and live with this man.

She was only beginning to understand herself, and she thought of the words of the old song about the turtle-dove, that bird of longing. It said that the turtle-dove drank clear water, but always muddied it first with its foot so that it might better suit its pensive mind. She, too, could not go to the springs of life and drink of its clear waters—life pleased her better when touched with melancholy.

Death, the Deliverer

MY shadowy friend, Death, the deliverer, came in August, when the nights were pale with moonlight, to the house of Captain Uggla.

He dared not go directly to that hospitable home, for there are few who love him, and he who frees the soul from the burdensome flesh and opens to it the glorious life of the spheres does not want to be greeted with sobs and tears, but rather with mute joy. His delight is to ride through the air on fiery cannon-balls, he bears on his neck the hissing shell and laughs when it bursts, and the fragments fly. He whirls in the ghost-dance at the churchyard, stalks boldly into the pest wards of the hospital, but stands trembling at the threshold of the good man's home. Into the old birch grove behind the house he stole; in the grove, then full of protecting green, my shadowy friend concealed himself by day, but at night he could be seen standing near the edge of the wood, his scythe gleaming in the moonlight.

O Eros! Thou art the god that ever and anon hast guarded that grove. Old people tell how in times gone by lovers sought its seclusion, and now when I drive past Berga Manor, grumbling at the rocky road and the stifling dust, it gladdens my heart to see that grove with its silver-stemmed

bɪrches, associated in memory with beautiful love's
young dream.

But Death now lurked there, and the creatures
of the night saw him. Evening after evening, the
people at the manor heard the fox howl warnings
of his arrival. The black snake crawled along the
sand walk up to the very house; he could not voice
his warning, but they understood that he came as
a forerunner of the mighty deliverer. In the apple
tree outside the window of the Captain's wife'sroom
the owl hooted. For all Nature feels the presence
of Death, and trembles.

It happened that the Judge of Munkerud and
his family were returning late one night from a
party at the rectory in Bro, and when driving past
Berga they noticed a candle burning in the window
of the guest-chamber. They saw plainly the yellow
flame and the white candle and, wondering, they
afterwards told of seeing the burning candle in the
light summer night.

The jolly young girls at the manor laughed, and
said the Judge's people must have seen it in a trance,
for they had not a candle in the house, the last one
having been used up in March. The Captain swore
that no one had occupied the guest-room in weeks;
but his wife was silent and pale as a ghost, for she
knew that the white candle, which burned with so
bright a flame, was always seen when some mem-

ber of her family was about to be freed by Death, the deliverer.

Some days later, Ferdinand came home from a surveying trip in the northern forests, suffering from a fatal disease of the lungs. As soon as the mother saw him, she knew that he was doomed.

So he must go, that good son who had never caused his parents a moment's sorrow! He must leave the joys of earth, leave his beautiful betrothed, whom he adored, and the great estates which should have become his.

At last, when my shadowy friend had tarried a month, he took courage, and went one night to the house. He knew that hunger and want had been met there with smiling faces, so why should not he too be welcomed with joy?

That night the Captain's wife, who lay awake, heard rappings on the window-ledge and, sitting up in bed, she asked: "Who knocks?"

And it is said a voice answered, "It is Death."

Then she opened her window; she saw owls and bats fluttering in the moonlight, but Death she did not see.

"Come, friend and deliverer!" she said, in a half-whisper. "Why hast thou tarried so long? I have waited, I have called. Come and release my son!"

Then Death slipped into the house, pleased as a poor deposed monarch who in the decrepitude of old age receives again his crown; pleased as a child when called to play.

The next day the Captain's wife sat at the bed-side of her son and talked of the bliss of liberated spirits and their glorious life.

"They work," she said; "they create. Such art-ists, my son, such artists! When you come among them what shall you be? Ah! you will be one of the sculptors without mallet or chisel who form roses and lilies, one of the master-painters of the sunset glow. When the sunsets are most beautiful, I shall say to myself, 'This is Ferdinand's work.'

"My dear lad, only think of all there is to see and to do! Think of the seeds that must be wakened to life each spring, the storms that must be guided, the dreams that must be sent, and think too of the great journey through space from world to world!

"Remember me, my son, when you behold so much beauty. Your poor mother has never seen any place but Värmland.

"One day you will stand before our Lord and ask Him to let you have one of the little worlds that roll in space, and He will give it you. The one you receive will be dark and cold, full of cliffs and chasms, with no flowers nor animals. But you will labor on the star God gives you: you will bring thither light and warmth and air, you will bring herbs and nightingales and bright-eyed gazelles, you will have falls rushing down the ravines, you will build mountains and sow the plains with the reddest of roses; and when I am called, and my soul trembles at the long, long journey, loath to leave familiar scenes, then you, my Ferdinand, will be waiting outside my window in a shining golden chariot, drawn by birds of Paradise. My poor anxious soul will be taken up in your chariot, and I shall sit by your side, honored as a queen. Then we shall ride through space past twinkling stars, and as we come to these gardens of the heavens, each more beautiful than the other, I shall ask in my ignorance, 'Is it there or there we stop?'

"You will smile to yourself and urge on the bird-span. When we come to the smallest of worlds, but the loveliest of all, we shall stop before a golden palace, and you will usher me into my home of eternal joy.

"There the larders are filled and the bookcases too. The firwood there is not as here at Berga, for it does not obstruct the view of the beautiful world beyond. I can look out across sunny fields and boundless seas, and a thousand years are as one day."

So died Ferdinand, entranced by bright visions and smiling toward the glory of the future.

My shadowy friend, Death, the deliverer, had never known anything so blissful. True, there were those who wept by the deathbed of Ferdinand Uggla, but he himself smiled, when the man with

the scythe sat down on the edge of the bed, and
his mother listened for the death-rattle as for soft
music. When all was over, tears sprang to her eyes;
but they were tears of joy that fell upon the rigid
face of her son.

Never was my shadowy friend so honored as
at the funeral of Ferdinand Uggla! Had he dared
show himself, he would have come in gold-em-
broidered cloak and feathered biretta, and danced
at the head of the funeral procession. Instead, the
lonely, friendless old man, in his black mantle,
sat huddled on the cemetery wall and viewed the
pageant.

That was a wonderful funeral! Sunshine and
bright skies made the day glad; long rows of golden
rye-sheaves adorned the fields, the nasturtiums
in the rector's garden shimmered, light and transparent, and in the sexton's rose-garden shone
dahlias and carnations.

It was indeed a wonderful procession that passed
under the lindens that day! In front of the flower-
decked casket pretty children strewed blossoms.
There was not a mourning dress to be seen, not a
crêpe veil; for the Captain's wife had decreed that
he who died rejoicing should not be followed to his
quiet retreat by a gloomy funeral cortège, but by
a gay wedding train.

Close behind the casket walked Anna Stjärnhök,
the radiantly beautiful bride, in a wedding dress of

white, shimmering satin and wearing a bridal crown
and veil. Thus attired, she went to be married at
the grave of her bridegroom.

Following her came couple after couple, stately
matrons and dignified gentlemen. The ladies wore
dazzling jeweled buckles and brooches, strings of
milk-white pearls, and bracelets of gold. The ostrich
plumes on their lace-trimmed bonnets nodded
above their ringlets, and from their shoulders
floated shawls of fine-spun silk over dresses of bro-
caded satin. Their husbands were arrayed in their
best, with starched frills and gold buttons in their
high-collared dress-coats, and with waistcoats of stiff
brocade or richly embroidered velvet. Verily, it was
a wedding procession, as the Captain's wife had
wished it to be.

She herself walked next to Anna Stjärnhök on
the arm of her husband. Had she possessed a dress
of shining brocade, she would have worn it; had
she possessed jewels and a fine bonnet, she would
have worn those too in honor of her son's fête day.
But she had only the old black silk frock with the
yellowed laces, which had seen service at many a
festival—and she also wore it on this occasion.

Although the mourners were in gala attire, there
was not a dry eye among them, as they went toward
the grave to the faint tolling of the church bells.
They wept not so much for the dead as for themselves. There walked the bride; there the bride-

groom was carried; and here were they, arrayed as for a feast—yet, who that treads the green paths of earth does not know his fate is affliction, sorrow, unhappiness, and death! They wept at the thought that no earthly power could save them from the inevitable.

The Captain's wife did not weep; but she was the only one whose eyes were dry. When the burial service had been read, and the grave filled in, the mourners went back to their carriages. Only the mother and Anna Stjärnhök lingered at the grave to bid their dead a last farewell. The older woman seated herself on the mound, and Anna sat down beside her.

"Anna Stjärnhök," said the mother, "I have prayed God to let Death, the deliverer, come and take away my son. 'Let him come,' I said, 'and take him I love most to the quiet garden of peace, and I shall weep no tears save tears of joy; with nuptial splendor shall he be followed to his grave, and the red rose-bush growing outside my window I shall take to him in the churchyard. And now my son is dead. I welcomed Death as a friend, calling him by the sweetest of names. I shed tears of joy on the still, cold face of my son. In the autumn, when the leaves are fallen, I shall bring hither my red rose-bush. But do you who sit beside me know why I sent up such prayers to God?"

The Captain's wife looked hard at Anna Stjärnhök. The girl went pale, but said not a word. Mayhap she was struggling to silence inward voices, which there, on the grave of the dead, had already begun to whisper that now, at last, she was free.

"The fault is yours!" cried the mother.

The girl shrank as from a blow.

"Anna Stjärnhök, you were once proud and self-willed; then you played with my son, you won him, and cast him aside. He, like others, had to suffer it. Perhaps, too, he and we loved your money as much as we loved you. Then you came again, bringing blessings to our home; you were so strong and good, so gentle and patient! You cherished us with love, you made us so happy, Anna, that we poor beings lay at your feet. And yet I have wished that you had not come, for then there would have been no need of my asking God to shorten my son's life. Last winter he could have borne your loss, but after he had learned to know you as you are, it would have killed him.

"Know this, Anna Stjärnhök, who to-day have put on your bridal dress to follow my son to his grave, you would never have been allowed to accompany him to the church in that array, for you loved him not.

"I felt all the while that you had come to us out of pity, that you might relieve our misery. You did not love him! Think you that I do not know love when I see it, and perceive when it is lacking?

Therefore I prayed God to take my son before his eyes were opened.

"If only you had loved him! Oh, why did you come to sweeten our lives, when you did not love him? Had he not died, I should have been compelled to tell him that you were only taking him out of pity. I should have made him give you up and so wrecked his happiness. Rather than disturb the peace in his heart, I prayed that he might die."

She paused for a response; but Anna could not speak; she was still listening to the many voices in her soul.

Then the mother cried out in despair: "Happy they who can mourn their dead with tears! I must stand dry-eyed at the grave of my son, I must rejoice over his death. What unhappiness is mine!"

Anna Stjärnhök pressed her hand to her heart. She remembered the winter night when she had sworn by her love to be to these poor people a stay and a comfort, and she shuddered. Had all then been in vain? Was her sacrifice not one acceptable to God? Must it all be turned to a curse? But if she were to sacrifice everything, would not God then give His blessing to the work, and let her be a bringer of happiness, a help and comfort to others?

"What is required to make you mourn for your son?" she asked.

"That I shall no longer believe the evidence of

my old eyes. If I could feel that you loved my son, I should mourn his loss."

The girl arose, her eyes burning with rapture. Tearing off her bridal veil, she spread it over the grave; then taking off her wreath and crown, she laid them beside it.

"Now," she cried, "you see how I love him! I give him my crown and veil. I wed myself to him. Never shall I belong to another!"

The Captain's wife stood silent a moment, trembling all over, her face twitching; but at last the tears came — tears of grief.

My shadowy friend, Death, the deliverer, shuddered when he saw those tears. So he had not been greeted with joy even here, and this mother's heart had not really been gladdened by his coming.

He drew his cowl over his face and stole quietly away from the churchyard, disappearing among the rye-fields.

The Drought

IF the things of the world can love, if earth and
water can distinguish between friends and enemies, then I would gladly win their love. I would
wish that the earth did not feel my steps to be a
heavy burden, and that it forgave that for me it
was hurt by plough and harrow, and that it would
willingly open its arms to receive me when I die. I
would wish that the water, whose shining mirror
I break with my oar, had the same patience with me
as a mother with an eager child who clambers on
her knees without a thought to the silk dress donned
for the great occasion. I would be friends with the
clear air that trembles over the blue mountains and
with the shining, glittering sun and the beautiful
stars, for it often seems to me that dead things feel
and suffer with the living—the gulf between us
is not so wide as we imagine. What portion of the
world is there that has not taken part in life's circle?

The spirit of life still lives in dead things. What
does it feel while it lies in dreamless sleep? It hears
God's voice—does it hear the voice of men, too?

Oh, children of a later day! have you not noticed
this?—When hate and war fill the world, dead
things must also suffer. Then the ocean becomes
wild and rapacious as a robber, and the fields are
as hard and unyielding as a miser. But woe to him

for whose sake the forest sighs and the mountains weep!

It was a memorable year, the year that the cavaliers managed Ekeby. It seems to me as if the noise of men had disturbed the peace of the dead things of the world. How can I describe the infection that spread over the land? One might imagine that the cavaliers were the gods of the country side, and that everything was infected with their spirit —a spirit of wild thoughts and mad adventures.

If it were possible to write all that took place during that year among the people on the shores of the Löfven, it would amaze a world. For old love awoke, and new was kindled. Old hate blossomed again, and long-cherished revenge clutched its victim. One and all rose in the desire to grasp at the sweetness of life: dancing and playing, gambling and carousal, were what they longed for, and that which was hidden in the depths of men's souls became manifest.

This contagion of restlessness emanated from Ekeby; it spread first to the foundries and the gentry's mansions, and drove the people there to sin and ruin. We can follow it so far, because the old among us cherish the remembrance of what took place at some of the large estates, but we know very little of its effect among the people. Still none can doubt that the unrest of the times crept from village to village, from hut to hut.

Vice broke out where it had lain hidden before. If a rift existed between a man and a woman, it became a gulf; if a strong virtue or a firm will had been disguised, that also came forth, for all that happened was not evil; yet the times were such that the good often brought as much ruin as the evil.

It was like a tornado in the depths of a forest, where tree falls over tree, and one pine drags down another, and even the undergrowth is torn down by the falling giants.

But this unrest did not dwell with men alone; it spread abroad to every living thing. Never had the wolves and bears ravaged the country so; never had the foxes barked so fearlessly; never had the sheep gone astray so often in the forest, nor so much sickness destroyed the valuable herds of cattle.

If you would see the relation of things, you must go away from the towns and live in a lonely hut in a forest clearing, where you watch the charcoal-burning by night; or you must spend both days and nights upon the lake during the light summer months, when the timber-rafts journey slowly down to Vänern. Then you will learn to mark all the signs of nature and understand how the dead things of earth depend upon the living. You will see that unrest in the world disturbs their peace. The people know this. It is at times like these that the lady of the woods extinguishes the charcoal-stack, the sea-nymphs wreck the fishermen's boats, the nixies send sickness, and the gnomes starve the cattle. And it was so that year. Never had the spring flood carried so much destruction with it. Ekeby mill and foundry were not the only victims. Little streams that in the old days had possibly had strength enough to carry away an empty barn made a bold assault upon whole farmsteads and swept them away. Never had the thunder-squalls done so much damage before midsummer—after midsummer they came no more. Then came the drought.

During all the long days of summer there fell no rain. From the middle of June till the beginning of September, the parish of Löfsjö was bathed in unclouded sunshine.

The rain refused to fall, the wind to blow, the earth to nourish the harvest. Sunshine alone streamed over the earth. Oh, the beautiful sunshine, the life-giving sunshine! how can I tell of its evil work? Sunshine is like love. Who does not know the misdeeds it has done, and who can refuse to forgive it? The sunshine was like Gösta Berling; it gave joy to every man, therefore they were all silent about the ill it had caused.

A drought after midsummer such as this would hardly have been so ruinous in other districts. But the spring had come late in Värmland. The grass had not attained any height and would not grow taller; the rye received no nourishment just when it ought to bloom and broaden in the ear; the spring rye, of which all the bread was made at that time, bore thin little spears and stalks half a foot high; the turnips, planted late, would not germinate; not even the potatoes could suck any nourishment from the parched earth.

At such times fear awoke among the dwellers of the forest hills, and the fear descended from the hills to the calmer folk of the country side.

"God's hand is seeking some one," they say. And one and all smite themselves upon their breasts, and say, " Is it me? Oh, mother Nature, is it in horror of *me* that the rain keeps away? Is it in anger against *me* that the earth is scorched and hardened? And this everlasting sunshine, does it pour from a cloudless sky to heap burning coals upon *my* head? If it is not me, who is it that God's hand is in search of?"

And while the rye withered in the ear, and the potatoes drew no nourishment from the soil, and the cattle, with bloodshot eyes and panting from the heat, pushed one another about the drinking troughs, while fear of the future was crushing every heart, strange reports went circling about the country.

It was a Sunday in August. Service was over, and the people walked along the dusty roads in groups. Around them they saw charred forests and blasted harvests. The rye stood in stacks, but the sheaves were small. Those who had meadow clearing to do had easy work that year, but it happened sometimes that they set fire to the forest. And what the forest fires had left the caterpillars and locusts had taken. The pine wood had shed its needles and stood as naked as a birch wood in autumn, and the birch leaves hung ragged, showing only their veins in scraps of perforated leaf.

The sad congregation was in no want of a subject of conversation. There were many there who could tell you how hard they had fared during the famine years of 1808 and 1809, and in the cold winter of 1812, when the sparrows froze to death. Famine was no stranger to them; they had seen his grim hand before. They knew how bark was prepared for bread, and how the cows would learn to eat moss.

One of the women had made trial of a new kind of bread, consisting of whortleberries and barley flour. She had a piece of it with her and let people taste. She was proud of her invention.

But the same question hung over all, it stared out of all eyes, and was whispered by every lip: "Who is it, O Lord, thy hand seeks?"

A man in one of the gloomy groups that were going westward over the Sundsbridge and climbing the hill of Bro, paused for a moment before the road that led up to the house where the miserly vicar of Broby lived. He took up a dry twig from the ground, and threw it upon the parsonage road.

"Dry as that stick have his prayers to heaven been," he said.

Another man walking beside him also paused. He, too, picked up a twig and threw it where the first lay. "It is a suitable offering to that parson," he said. The third in the group followed the example of the others. "He has been like the drought; sticks and stones are all he has left us."

The fourth said, "We give him what he has given us."

And the fifth said, "I cast this to his everlasting shame. May he dry up and wither as this twig!"

"Dry fodder for the drought-bringing parson!" said the seventh.

People coming after them saw what they did and heard what they said. They had an answer now to their long questioning.

"Give him what he deserves! He has brought the drought upon us," was the opinion of the people.

And every one stopped and added his word and cast his twig, before he passed on.

In the corner between the roads there soon lay a heap of sticks and twigs—a monument of shame to the Broby parson.

This was all the revenge the people took. No one lifted a hand against the vicar or said a harsh word to him. Despairing hearts cast aside a little of their burden in throwing a dry twig upon that heap. They

did not revenge themselves; they only pointed out
the guilty one to the God of Retribution.

"If we have not worshipped Thee aright, it is
that man's fault. Be merciful, O Lord, and let him
suffer alone! We mark him with shame and dis-
honor, we are not one with him."

It soon became customary that every one passing
the parsonage road threw a dry branch upon the
heap. "May God and men see it," each wanderer
thought. "Even I despise him who has brought
upon us the wrath of God."

The old miser soon noticed the pile of branches
at the road corner. He ordered it to be taken away,
and some said he lighted his kitchen fire with it.
Next day there was another heap of dry branches
in the same place, and as soon as he had it cleared
away, a new one appeared. The dry twigs lay there
and whispered, "Shame, shame on the Broby parson!"

Those were the hot, dry dog-days. Heavy with
smoke and full of the smell of burning, the air lay
over the country as difficult to breathe as is crushing despair.

Thought grew giddy in the heated brains. The
Broby parson had become the demon of the drought.
It seemed to the people that the old miser sat and
kept watch over the windows of heaven.

The feeling that governed the people soon became known to the vicar. He understood that it

pointed him out as the cause of the misfortune. It was in anger over his sins that God let the earth suffer. The sailors who were in danger on the wild, wide sea had cast lots. He was the man who was to go overboard. He tried to laugh at them and their twigs, but when it continued for a week, he laughed no more. Oh, what childishness! How could those dry twigs harm him? He knew that years and years of hate took this occasion for expression. What of it? He was not used to being loved.

This kind of thing did not make him milder. Perhaps he had wished to reform after the sweet little old lady had left him. Now that was past; he would not be forced to amendment.

But by and by that heap overpowered him. He was obliged to think of it constantly, and the opinion that all cherished found an echo even in him. It was a most fearful testimony against him, that casting of dry twigs. He watched the pile, counting the branches that were added day by day. The thought of it grew and overwhelmed all other thoughts. The monument of shame undid him.

Day after day, he was forced to admit more and more that the people were right. He drooped and grew very, very old in a fortnight. His conscience was stricken, and he was ill, but it seemed as if it were all connected with that heap of dry twigs — as if his conscience could be silenced, and the burden of his years would depart from him, if only that heap of twigs did not grow larger.

At last he spent the whole day there guarding it, but the people were merciless — new twigs were always added at night.

. . . .

Ore day Gösta Berling drove down the road. The Broby parson sat by the wayside, old and stricken. He sat and plucked at the dry twigs, and laid them in rows and heaps, playing with them as if he had become a child again. Gösta was shocked to see his wretched state.

"What are you doing, pastor?" he said, and sprang quickly from the equipage.

"Oh, I am sitting here and doing nothing particular."

"You should go home and not sit here in the wayside dust."

"It is best, perhaps, that I stay here."

Then Gösta Berling sat down beside him.

"It is not such an easy matter to be a clergyman," he said, after a time.

"It is bearable down here where there are people," the Broby parson answered. "It is worse up north."

Gösta understood his meaning. He knew those big parishes in northern Värmland, where sometimes there was not even a house for their clergyman; the great forest parishes where the Finns lived in their smoky huts; the poor districts with two or three people to the mile, where the pastor was the only educated man in the place. The Broby parson had lived in such a parish for more than twenty years.

"They send us there when we are young," said Gösta. "It is impossible to bear the life there, and then one is ruined for all the future. There are many who have gone to destruction up there."

"That is it," said the parson; "loneliness destroys one."

"One comes there," said Gösta, "eager and fiery, and talks and persuades and thinks that all will soon be well, and that the people will soon take to better ways."

"Yes, yes, just so."

"But òne soon sees that words are of little use. Poverty stands in the way of any improvement."

"Poverty," repeated the Broby parson, "poverty has ruined my life!"

"The young clergyman goes up there," continued Gösta, "as poor as all the rest, and he says to the drunkard, 'Leave your drinking!'"

"And the drunkard answers," continued the Broby parson, "'Give me something better than brandy! The drink is a fur covering in winter and a cooling draught in summer. It means a warm hut and a soft bed. Give me this, and I will drink no more.'"

"And so," Gösta resumed, "the pastor says to the thief, 'Do not steal!' and to the evil man, 'You must not beat your wife;' and to the cripple, 'You must believe in God and not in the devil and in goblins!' But the thief answers, 'Give me bread!' and the evil man answers, 'Make us rich, and we will not quarrel;' and the cripple says, 'Teach me better.' But who can help them without money?"

"It is true, true every word," cried the old man. "They believed in God, but more in the devil, and most in the witches of the hills and the gnomes in the barns. All their rye was destroyed in the brandy-still. There seemed no end to the misery. Want reigned in most of the grey huts, and hidden sorrow made the tongues of the women very sharp. Discomfort drove the men to drunkenness. They cannot manage their fields and cattle properly. They distrust the squire and make game of the parson. What could you do with them? What I spoke to them from the pulpit they did not understand; what I tried to teach them they would not believe —and none to consult with, and none to help me keep my courage up."

"There are men who have borne it," said Gösta. "God's mercy has been so great to some that they have not returned from that life as broken men. Their strength has sufficed; they have survived the loneliness and poverty and hopelessness. They have done the little good they could and have not despaired. Such men have always existed and exist still. I would greet them as heroes and honor them as long as I live. *I* could not endure it."

"*I* could not," added the parson.

"The pastor up there," said Gösta, thoughtfully, "thinks he must become rich, an immensely rich man. No poor man can fight the evil there, and he begins to hoard."

"If he did not hoard, he would drink," answered the old man, "for he sees so much misery."

"Or become dull and lazy and lose all his strength. It is dangerous to live up there if you have not been born to it."

"He must harden his heart, if he is to hoard. He pretends at first — then it becomes a habit."

"He must be severe both with himself and with others," continued Gösta; "it is so difficult to amass anything. He must endure hatred and scorn; he must consent to freeze and starve and harden his heart. It seems, after a time, as if he forgot why he began to save."

The Broby parson glanced furtively at Gösta. He wondered if he sat and made fun of him, but Gösta was all seriousness and eagerness. He might have been speaking of his own case.

"So it has gone with me," the old man said gently.

"But God protects him," ejaculated Gösta. "He awakens within him a thought of his youth. When he has saved enough, he gives him a sign that his people need him."

"But if he refuses to see the sign, Gösta Berling?"

"He cannot withstand it," said Gösta, smiling happily; "he is so lured by the thought of the warm homes he will help the poor to build."

The parson looked down at the small erections he had made of twigs. The longer he talked with Gösta, the more he felt him to be right.

He has always had the idea of doing good when he has saved enough. He catches at this. Of course, he has always had that thought.

"Why does he not build the cottages then?" he asks, furtively.

"He is ashamed. People might believe that it is for fear of them that he does what he has always intended to do."

"He cannot endure being forced, that is the reason."

"He could do much in secret; much help is needed this year. He could find some one to distribute his gifts. I see it all," cried Gösta, his eyes beaming; "thousands shall receive their bread this year from one whom they have covered with curses."

"So shall it be, Gösta!"

A whirl of enthusiasm seemed to seize upon these two, who had filled their calling so badly.

Their youthful ardor to serve God and man was upon them. They revelled in all the good works they would perform. Gösta would be the vicar's assistant.

"We must get bread first," said the old man.

"We will arrange for school teachers and get some land-surveyors here who shall parcel out the ground; and the people must learn to till the ground and tend the cattle."

"We will make roads and take up unreclaimed ground."

"We will build locks at the Berg rapids, so that the way lies clear between the Löfven and the Vänern."

"All the riches of the forest will carry a double blessing when the way is open to the sea."

"Your head will be weighed down with blessings," cried Gösta.

The Broby parson looked up, and they read in each other's eyes the same fiery enthusiasm. But at the same moment their eyes were drawn to the heap of twigs.

"Gösta," said the old man, "this needs the power of a strong man, and I am dying. You see what is killing me."

"Get rid of it!"

"How, Gösta Berling?"

Gösta stepped close to him and looked him sharply in the eyes. "Pray God for rain," he said.

"You are to preach next Sunday; pray then for rain!"

The old man collapsed with fright.

"If you are in earnest, if you are not the man who has brought the drought upon us, if you have thought of serving God the Almighty with your savings, then pray for rain. That shall be the sign. We shall know by that if our will is His will."

When Gösta drove on down Broby hill he was astonished at himself and the enthusiasm that had seized upon him. After all, life could be glorious, but not for him. They would not take count of his services above.

. . . .

The sermon and the usual prayers were just finished at Broby church. The vicar was just on the point of descending the pulpit steps when he hesitated. Then he fell on his knees and prayed for rain.

He prayed as men pray in despair, with few words and without any real connection between them.

"If it is my sin that has called forth Thine anger, punish me alone! If there is any mercy in Thee, O Thou God of Grace, let it rain! Take the shame away from me! Let it rain at my prayer! Let rain fall on the fields of the poor! Give Thy people bread!"

The day was hot; it was almost unbearably suffocating in the church. The congregation had sat through the service as if unconscious — but at those broken words, that hoarse despair, every one awoke.

"If there is still a way of redress for me, give us rain!"

He was silent. The doors stood open. There came a sudden gust of wind. It sped along the ground, whirled up against the church, and sent a cloud of dust inside, full of sticks and bits of straw. The pastor could not continue; he stumbled down from the pulpit.

The people shuddered. Could this be an answer? But the gust of wind was only the forerunner of the thunderstorm. It came on with unparalleled rapidity. When the hymn had been sung, and the pastor stood at the altar, the lightning was already flashing, and the thunder drowned the sound of his words.

When the sexton played the voluntary, the first drops of rain pattered upon the green window-panes, and all the people rushed out to look at it. But they were not content only to look at it; some wept, some laughed, while they let the sharp thunder-shower stream over them. Oh, how great had been their need! How unhappy they had been! But God was good! God had sent rain. Oh, what joy, what joy!

The Broby parson was the only one who did not go out into the rain. He lay on his knees at the altar and did not rise. The joy had been too great for him. He was dead.

The Baby's Mother

THE baby was born in a peasant hut, east of the Klarälfven. Its mother had come there one day at the beginning of June seeking work. She had been unfortunate, she told the crofter's wife, and her mother had been so hard to her that she had been obliged to run away from home. She said her name was Elizabeth Karlsdotter, but she would not say where she came from, because, if any one told her parents, and they found her, she felt they would persecute her to death. She asked for no wage, only food and a roof over her head. She could work, weave or spin or look after the cows, —whatever they pleased. She might even pay for her keep, if they demanded it.

She had been cunning enough to come barefoot to the cottage, carrying her shoes under her arm; her hands showed traces of hard work; she spoke the language of the country, and was dressed as a peasant woman. They believed her.

The crofter thought she looked feeble, and did not count much upon her working capacity, but the poor thing must live somewhere, so she was allowed to stay.

There was something about her that made everybody on the farm friendly toward her. She had come to the right place, for they were serious and silent people, and the woman of the house took a fancy to her when she discovered the girl could weave huckaback. They borrowed a loom from the parsonage, and the baby's mother sat at the loom all summer.

It never struck any one that she required care; she was expected to work like a peasant woman all the time. And she herself liked best to work; she was no longer unhappy. The life with the peasants pleased her, though she was forced to dispense with all her accustomed comforts. Everything was taken so simply and calmly there. All their thoughts were centred in their work, and the days passed so evenly and monotonously that you lost count of them and thought you were still in the middle of the week when Sunday came round.

One day, at the end of August, there had been a scarcity of reapers in the harvest fields, and the baby's mother had gone out to help in binding the sheaves. She had over-exerted herself, and the child was born too early. She had expected it in October.

Now the woman of the house stood and held the child in her arms, warming it at the fire, for the poor little thing was cold, though it was a warm August day. Its mother lay in a little room opening out of the kitchen and listened to what they said about her baby. She could imagine the farm men and women stepping forward and looking at it.

"What a miserable little thing," they always

said, and afterwards the same phrase was always added, "You poor little thing—without a father!"

They did not mind his crying, they were convinced in a way that babies always cried, and when you considered everything, he was quite a big boy for his age. If he had only possessed a father, all would have been well, it seemed.

The mother lay and listened to them and wondered. This view of it suddenly grew to be of vast importance. How would the poor little thing get through life at all without a father?

She had made her plans before. She would remain at the farm for the first year; then she would hire a room somewhere and earn her living by weaving. She intended to make enough to feed and clothe the child herself. Her husband might continue to believe that she was unworthy to be his wife. She thought that perhaps the baby would grow up to be a better man if he was brought up by her than if a stupid, conceited father educated him.

But now the child was born, she could not see things in the same light. It seemed to her she had been selfish. "The child must have a father," she said to herself.

If it had not been so miserably weak, if it could have eaten and slept like other babies, if its head had not always hung so limply on its shoulder, and if it had not always been so near death every time it had a cramp, the question would not have been so urgent. But that helpless little baby must have a father.

It was not so easy for her to decide what to do, but she must do it at once. The baby was three days old, and in Värmland the peasants seldom waited longer before taking children to be christened.

What name should it bear in the church books, and what would the pastor wish to know about the mother? It was surely an injustice toward the child to write it in the church book as fatherless. It had come to this sad world, but seemed to long to go away again. Perhaps it would feel happier here if it had a father. If this child grew into a weak and sickly man, could she be responsible for depriving him of the advantages of high birth and riches? She had noticed there was usually great joy and excitement when a child was born. Now it seemed to her that life for the baby which everybody pitied must be a heavy burden. She wanted to see it sleep on silk and lace, as was befitting the son of a count. She wanted to see it surrounded by joy and pride. Yes, the baby must have a father.

She began to think she had committed too great an injustice toward its father. Had she a right to keep her baby to herself? She had no right. Such a precious little thing, whose worth it was impossible to measure, could she take it for herself alone? Surely that would not be right!

She had no desire to return to her husband. She

feared it would be her death, but her baby was in greater danger than she was; it might die any moment, and it had not been christened.

The great sin which had driven her from her home had passed away. She certainly had no love for any one but the baby which had no father. No duty could be too trying, if it put matters right again for the child.

She called the farmer and his wife and told them her story. The man set off at once to Borg to tell Count Dohna that his Countess was alive, and that a child was born and needed a father's care.

He came back late in the evening. He had not seen the Count, for he was abroad, but he had been to see the curate at Svartsjö and talked to him about it.

Then Countess Elizabeth learned that her marriage had been pronounced illegal, and that she no longer had a husband.

The curate had written a kind letter to her and invited her to make his house her home.

A letter from her own father to Count Henrik, which must have arrived at Borg a few days after her flight, was also forwarded to her. In that letter the old man begged the Count to hasten the legalization of the marriage, and that had probably shown the Count the easiest way of getting rid of his wife.

You can imagine Countess Elizabeth was more angry than grieved when she heard the farmer's tale.

All night sleep deserted her. The child must have a father, she repeated to herself over and over again.

Next day the farmer was sent to Ekeby to fetch Gösta Berling. Gösta put many questions to the silent messenger, but learned very little. Yes, the Countess had been in his house all summer. She had been strong and had worked. Now a child was born. It was weak, but the mother would be well again very soon.

Gösta asked if the Countess knew that her marriage had been dissolved.

Yes, she knew it now. She had heard it yesterday.

And as long as the journey lasted, Gösta was in a fever or shivering with cold by turns. What did she want with him? Why had she sent for him?

He thought of the summer they had spent on the Löfven shore. They had passed the days in jest and amusement, and she had been working and suffering.

He had never thought of the possibility of seeing her again. Oh, if he had dared hope for it, he might have gone to her a better man. What had he to look back upon but the usual mad exploits!

About eight o'clock in the evening, he arrived and was taken at once to her room. It was already twilight, and he could hardly see her where she lay. The farmer and his wife accompanied him into the room.

You must know that she, whose white face shone upon him through the half-darkness, was ever the highest and purest he knew in life, the loveliest soul that had put on earthly form; so, when he again experienced the blessing of her presence, he could have cast himself on his knees and thanked her for letting him see her again, but he was so overpowered with feeling that he could neither say nor do anything.

"Dear Countess Elizabeth," he only cried.

"Good evening, Gösta."

She gave him her hand, which had again grown soft and transparent. She lay silent, while he fought with his emotion.

She was not shaken by any stormy rush of feeling when she saw Gösta Berling. It only surprised her that he seemed to attach the greatest importance to her, when he ought to understand that it was all for the baby's sake, the baby who must have a father.

"Gösta," she said quietly, "you must help me now, as you promised once. You know my husband has deserted me, and my baby has no father."

"Yes, Countess, but there must be a way of changing all that. Now there is a child, it will be possible to compel the Count to legalize the marriage. You may be sure I shall do all I can to help you."

She smiled. "Do you think I will force myself upon Count Dohna?"

The blood surged in Gösta's head. What did she wish? What did she want of him?

"Come here, Gösta," she said, and stretched out her hand to him. "You are not to be angry with me about what I say, but I thought you, who are — who are —"

"A discharged clergyman, a drinking champion, a cavalier, Ebba Dohna's murderer, I know all my merit list —"

"Are you already angry, Gösta?"

"I would rather you did n't say anything more."

But the baby's mother continued: "There are many, Gösta, who would have wished to be your wife for love's sake, but it is not so with me. If I loved you, I should not dare to speak as I do now. For my own sake I should not ask for it, Gösta, but you see the child must have a father. You understand now what I am going to ask you to do. It is, I know, a great degradation for you, as I am an unmarried woman who has a child. I did not think you might do it because you were worse than others are, though, yes, I thought of that too. But I thought you might do it because you are so kind, Gösta; because you are a hero, and can sacrifice yourself. But perhaps it is too much to ask. It may be impossible for a man. If you despise me too much, if it is too distasteful to you to be spoken of as the father of another man's child, then tell me so! I shall not be angry. I understand I am asking too much of you, but the baby is so ill, Gösta. It is cruel that the name of the husband of its mother cannot be given at its christening."

He who listened to her experienced the same misgiving he had felt that spring morning when he rowed her ashore from the Ekeby barge and left her to her fate. Now he must help her to ruin her future, her whole future. He, loving her so, must do it.

"I will do all you wish," he said.

Next day he spoke to the rector of Bro, for Bro was the mother-parish of Svartsjö, and the banns would have to be called there.

The good old rector was touched at his story, and promised to take all the responsibility of guardianship and all such matters upon himself.

"Yes," he said, "you must help her, Gösta; she will go out of her mind, if you don't. She believes she has done an injury to the child in not being able to give it a father's care. She has an exceedingly sensitive conscience, that little woman."

"But I know I shall make her miserable," cried Gösta.

"That you must not do, Gösta. You must be a sensible man now, with a wife and child to look after."

In the meantime the rector would drive down to Svartsjö and arrange matters both with the curate and the judge, and the end of it all was that the banns were called on the following Sunday in

Svartsjö church between Gösta Berling and Elizabeth von Thurn.

Then the baby's mother was removed with all possible care to Ekeby, and the baby was christened there.

The rector talked to her on that occasion, saying she might still reconsider her determination to marry such a man as Gösta Berling. She ought to write to her father first.

"I cannot reconsider it," she said; "think if my child should die before it had a father."

When the third day of calling the banns came, Elizabeth had been up and well for several days. In the afternoon the rector came to Ekeby and married her to Gösta Berling. But none thought of it as a wedding. No guests were invited — they had procured a father for the child, that was all.

The mother beamed with quiet joy, as if she had gained a great aim in life. The bridegroom was wretched; he thought of her throwing away all the possibilities of her future life by this marriage with him. He noticed with dismay that he hardly existed for her. All her thoughts were given to the child. A few days later the trouble came; the child died in a fit of cramps.

It seemed to many people that the mother did not sorrow so deeply and so passionately as they had expected; there lay a glimmer of triumph over her.

It seemed as if she rejoiced that she had been

enabled to throw away all her future for the child's sake. When her baby went to the angels, he would still remember that on earth he had a mother who loved him.

.   .   .   .

All this passed very quietly and remained almost unnoticed. When the banns were called for Gösta Berling and Elizabeth von Thurn in Svartsjö, most people did not even know who the bride was. The clergy and gentry, who knew about the affair, were chary of talking about it. It almost seemed as if they feared that some, losing their belief in the power of conscience, might put an evil construction on what Countess Elizabeth had done. They were so frightened that any one might say, " See, after all, she could not conquer her love for Gösta Berling; she has married him now under false pretences." Oh, the old people were all so full of careful thought for her. They could not bear that any one should speak badly of her. They would hardly admit she had sinned. They did not wish that the soul which so feared evil should have a single stain.

Another event occurred at that time which was an additional reason why Gösta's marriage made so little stir. Major Samzelius met with a misfortune. He had become more odd and shy than ever, spent his time chiefly among animals, and kept quite a small zoölogical garden down at Sjö.

He was also a dangerous man, for he constantly carried a loaded gun with him, and sometimes discharged shot after shot, seldom paying any attention to what he was aiming at. One day he was bitten by a tame bear, which he had unintentionally wounded. The animal had flung itself upon him as he stood by the railing of its inclosure, and managed to bite him severely in the arm. Then it broke loose and made for the woods.

The Major was obliged to take to his bed, and died of the bite, though not till shortly before Christmas. If the Major's wife had known he was lying ill, she might have resumed the management of Ekeby, but the cavaliers felt certain she would not return before their year had elapsed.

Amor Vincit Omnia

UNDER the gallery stairs of Svartsjö church there is a lumber-room filled with grave-diggers' worn-out spades, with broken benches, with discarded tin numerals, and other rubbish.

In there, where the dust lies thick as if to hide it from human eyes, stands a casket inlaid with mother-of-pearl, in the most perfect mosaic. If one scrapes the dust away, it shines and glitters like a mountain wall in a fairy-tale. The casket is locked, and the key is in safe keeping. No mortal may peep into it, and no one knows what it holds. Not until the end of the century may the key be inserted, the cover lifted, and the treasures it contains be seen by man. So has he who owned the casket decreed.

On the brass plate on the cover is inscribed: *Labor vincit omnia;* but *Amor vincit omnia* would have been a more appropriate inscription, for the casket in the lumber-room is a testimony to the potency of love.

O Eros, all-conquering god!

Thou, O Love, art eternal! Old are the peoples of Earth, but thou hast followed them throughout the ages.

Where are the gods of the East, the mighty heroes whose weapons were thunderbolts — they who on the shores of sacred rivers took offerings of honey

and milk? They are dead. Dead is Bel, the powerful
warrior, and Thoth, the hawk-headed champion;
dead are the glorious ones that rested on the cloud-
beds of Olympus, so too the deedful ones who dwelt
within the walls of Valhalla. All the old gods are
dead save Eros alone, Eros, the all-conquering.

His work is in all that we see. He maintains the
race. Behold him everywhere! Where can you go and
not find the print of his foot? Has your ear distinguished aught in which the hum of his wings is
not the key-note? He lives in the heart of man and
in the slumbering seed-grain. Mark with awe his
presence in inanimate things!

What is there that does not throb with his life?
What that does not feel his power? All the gods
of vengeance will fall, all the powers of hate and
violence; but thou, O Love, art eternal.

Alone in the cavaliers' wing sat old Uncle Eberhard at his writing-desk—a fine piece of furniture
with a hundred drawers and a marble top, with
mountings of burnished brass—working with zeal
and diligence.

Oh, Eberhard, why have you not wandered in field
and wood these last days of the waning summer like
the other cavaliers? Those who worship the goddess
of wisdom pay the penalty. At sixty your back is
bent, the hair that covers your pate is not your own,
many and deep are the furrows on your brow, which
juts over hollow sockets, and the marks of age

are drawn in the thousand wrinkles round your toothless mouth. Death will take you the sooner from your desk for not letting Life tempt you away from it.

Uncle Eberhard had just finished his last line and had underscored it heavily. Taking from the various drawers the closely written pages of manuscript, different parts of his great work, the work that was to immortalize the name of Eberhard Berggren, he arranged them in a huge pile. He sat gazing at his labor of a lifetime in satisfied silence, when the door opened, and the young Countess came in.

There she stood, the idol of the old cavaliers, she whom they served and worshipped as grandparents serve and worship the first grandchild. Had they not found her in sickness and want and bestowed on her the good things of this world, as did the king in the fairy-tale with the beautiful beggar-maid he found in the forest? It was for her that the horns and the violins again sounded at Ekeby; for her that all on the great estate moved and breathed and labored.

She was lonely in the great house with her cavaliers gone, and wanted to see the cavaliers' wing — that much-talked-of room. She entered softly and looked around at the whitewashed walls and the yellow checkered bed-hangings, but on finding some one in the room she became embarrassed.

Uncle Eberhard rose to greet her and solemnly led her up to the big pile of manuscript.

" Look, Countess," he said, " my work is completed, and what I have written shall now be given to the world. A great thing is about to happen."

" What is going to happen, Uncle Eberhard?" asked she.

" Ah, Countess, it will come like a thunderbolt, a bolt that enlightens and kills! Ever since Moses drew him forth from the thunder-cloud of Sinai and enthroned him in the innermost sanctuary, he has sat secure, this old Jehovah. Now men shall learn what he is: illusion, emptiness, vapor — the stillborn child of our own brain. He shall sink into nothingness," declared the old philosopher, laying his wrinkled hand on the manuscript. "It is writ here, and when they read this the people must believe. They will see how stupid they have been, and will make fire-wood of their crosses, convert their churches into grain-lofts, and set their clergy to ploughing the earth."

" Oh, Uncle Eberhard!" exclaimed the Countess with a shudder, "are you such a terrible man as all that? Do such dreadful things stand there?"

"Dreadful?" repeated the old man. "Why, it is the truth. But we are like little boys, who hide their faces in a woman's skirt whenever they meet a stranger; we have accustomed ourselves to hide from Truth—the eternal stranger. But now he shall come and dwell among us and be known by all."

"By all?"

"Not only by philosophers, but by every one."

"And so Jehovah shall die?"

"He and all angels, all saints, all devils, all lies."

"Who will then rule the earth?"

"Do you think that any one has ever ruled it? Do you believe in the Providence that is said to care for sparrows and to number the hairs of your head? No one has ruled the world, nor ever will rule it."

"But we poor humans, what will become of us?"

"We shall be what we were before — dust and ashes. That which is burned out can burn no more; it is dead. We are only fuel enveloped by the fires of life, whose sparks fly from one to the other; we ignite, flame up, and die out. That is life."

"Oh, Uncle Eberhard, is there no life of the spirit?"

"None."

"No good, no evil, no hope, no goal?"

"None."

The young woman crossed over to the window. She looked out upon the yellowing autumn leaves, upon the dahlias and asters whose heads hung down on wind-broken stems; she beheld Löfven's troubled waves, the dark storm-clouds of the autumnal sky, and for a moment she became a prey to doubt.

"Uncle Eberhard," she sighed, "how drab and ugly the world is! How futile everything seems! I want to lie down and die."

Then she heard a murmur of protest in her soul, the strong currents of life, with its seething emotions, cried out for the happiness of living.

"But is there not something," she burst forth,—"something that can render life beautiful now that you have taken from me God and my hope of immortality?"

"Work," replied the old man.

A feeling of pity and contempt for that poor wisdom of his stole over her. Before her rose that unfathomable something; she felt the spirit that dwells in all things, and was sensible of the power that lies bound within seemingly dead matter, but which can develop into a thousand different forms of life. She gropingly sought for a name for the presence of the spirit of God in nature.

"Oh, Uncle Eberhard, what is work?" she asked. "Does it possess any virtue of its own? Name something else."

"I know of nothing else," he said.

At last the name she had been seeking for came to her—a name ofttimes sullied. "Uncle Eberhard, why did you not mention Love?"

A smile quivered on his toothless mouth, where the thousand wrinkles crossed.

"Here," said the philosopher, his clenched hand striking the bulky manuscript,—"here the gods are slain, Eros among them. What is love but a longing of the flesh? Why should it be regarded as something higher than other demands of the body? Make hunger a god, make fatigue a god, for they are equally worthy. Let there be an end to these superstitions. May the truth supplant them!"

"No, this is not truth," she thought, though unable to refute it.

"Your words have wounded my soul," she said, "but believe them I cannot. The gods of violence and vengeance you may be able to kill, but no others."

The old man took her hand and, placing it on the pile of manuscript, averred with the fanaticism of unbelief:

"When you shall have read this you must believe."

"Then may it never come before my eyes," she said; "for were I to believe that, I could not live."

Bowed with sadness, she left the philosopher. When she had gone, he sat a long while pondering.

That old manuscript, covered with blasphemous scribblings, has not as yet been tested before the world, and thus far Uncle Eberhard's name has not reached the heights of fame. His great work lies in a casket in the lumber-room of Svartsjö church. It is not to see the light of day until the close of the century.

But why did he lay it by? Think you he doubted that he had proved his point? that he feared persecution? Ah, you little know Uncle Eberhard!

KK

Understand, it was the quest for truth he loved, not his own glory. He sacrificed the latter, not the former, in order that a child whom he loved as a father might live and die in the faith she held most dear.

O Love, verily thou art eternal!

The Nygård Peasant Girl

NO one knows the place under the hill where the fir trees grow thickest, and deep layers of moss cover the ground! How should any one know it? It has never been trod by the foot of man, no tongue has given it a name, no pathway leads to the hidden place, great boulders tower around it, entangling junipers guard it, and the débris of the storm shuts it in; the cowherd has never discovered it, even the foxes despise it. It is the most lonely place in the forest, and thousands of people were seeking it.

What an endless stream of searchers! They would fill Bro church, and not only Bro, but Löfviks and Svartsjö church too.

The children of the gentry, who are not allowed to follow them, stand on the roadside or hang over the fence gates, as the great procession passes. The little ones have never dreamed that the world held so many people, such a countless multitude. When they grow up they will remember that long winding stream. Their eyes will fill with tears at the very thought of the overwhelming impression given by that endless procession passing along the road where only a lonely traveller, a few beggar waifs, or a peasant's cart were to be seen the long day through.

All who lived near the road started up and asked, "What has happened? Is the enemy upon us?

Where are you going, you people, where are you going?"

"We are searching," they answered; "we have searched for two days, we will search this day also, more than that we cannot do. We are going to search through Björne wood and the fir-covered hills west of Ekeby."

The procession first started from Nygård, a poor district among the eastern hills. The lovely girl with the thick black hair and red cheeks had not been seen for eight days. The broom girl whom Gösta Berling was to have made his bride was lost in the forests. No one had seen her for eight days.

Then the Nygård folk started to search for her; and every one they met joined them, out of every cottage some one came to help the searchers.

New arrivals often asked: "Nygård men, what is the cause of it all? Why did you let the girl go alone in such unknown paths? The forest is deep, and God had taken away her understanding."

"No one would harm her," they answered; "she, too, would harm no one. She went about as securely as a child. Who can be safer than she whom God must Himself guard? She has never lost her way before."

Thus the train of searchers had gone over the eastern forests that divide Nygård from the plain. On the third day it was passing Bro church, going to the woods west of Ekeby.

But wherever the stream of searchers passed, they awoke a storm of amazement, and some man from the crowd was obliged to pause and stand aside to answer questions.

"What do you want? What are you searching for?"

"We are seeking the blue-eyed, black-haired girl. She has lain down to die in the forest. She has been missing for eight days."

"Why has she lain down to die? Was she hungry? Was she unhappy?"

"She has never known want, but sorrow came to her this spring. She had seen the crazy parson, Gösta Berling, and had loved him for many years. She knew no better. God had taken her understanding."

"God had truly taken away her understanding, you Nygård men."

"In spring came the trouble; before that he had never looked at her. Then he told her she should be his bride. It was only a joke; he let her go again, but she would not be comforted. She went constantly to Ekeby. She followed in his footsteps wherever he went. He tired of her. When she was here last, they set their dogs at her. Since then no one has seen her."

Out of house, men, out of your houses! A human life is involved! A human being has lain down to die in the forest! Perhaps she is already dead! Perhaps she is still wandering aimlessly without finding the right way. The forest is wide, and her understanding is with God.

Follow the seekers, follow their train! Let the oats hang on the rafters till the thin kernels fall from the ears; let the potatoes rot in the ground; let the horses loose so that they may not die of thirst in the stables; leave the door of the cowshed open so that the cattle can go under cover for the night; let the children come also, for children belong to God, He is with them and leads their footsteps. They will help where man's wisdom fails.

Come all—men, women, and children! Who dares stay at home? Who knows but God intends to make use of him? Come all who hope for mercy, that your souls, too, may not wander aimlessly one day in a desert place, seeking rest and finding none! Come! God has taken her understanding, and the forest is wide.

Oh, who shall find the place where the fir trees stand thickest and the moss lies softest? Is not that something dark there near the hill slope? Oh, a brown ant-hill. Blessed be He who guides the steps of the foolish, it is nothing but a brown ant-hill!

Ah, what a long stream of people! It is no holiday procession on its way to greet a conqueror, to strew flowers in his path and fill his ears with shouts of joy; nor a pilgrim march with psalms and whizzing scourges on their way to the Holy Sepulchre;

nor an emigrant train on creaking wagons, seeking
a new home for the needy; nor an army with drums
and weapons. It is nothing but a crowd of poor
peasants in their working clothes of homespun and
ragged sheepskin, only their wives with their knitting in their hands and children on their backs or
dragging at their skirts. It is a wonderful sight to
see people united in a great aim, whether they go
to greet their conqueror, to praise their God, to seek
new dwellings for the needy, to defend their land —
but neither hunger nor the fear of God and not
war had called together these people. Their toil was
in vain, their labor without wage; they go but to
seek an idiot girl. So much exertion, so many steps
taken, so much anxiety, so many prayers, will they
not be repaid with more than the finding of a poor
crazy girl whose understanding is with God!

Oh, do you not love those people! When you
stand by the roadside and see them pass, do not
your eyes fill with tears as you see them march forward, deep in thought, men with harsh faces and
hard hands, women with brows wrinkled early, and
the tired children whom God will guide to the hidden place!

It filled the road—that stream of sorrowing
searchers. They probed the forest with earnest
looks and went forward gloomily, for they knew
they were probably seeking for a corpse and not
a living being.

Ah, that dark thing under the hillside, it is not an ant-hill, but an overturned tree! Praised be Heaven, only an overturned tree! But one cannot see very well where the fir trees stand so closely together.

The train of searchers was so long that the first of them, the strong men, were already at the woods west of Björne when the last stragglers, the cripples and work-worn old men and the women carrying their little ones, had hardly passed Bro church. They all disappeared into the dark forest. The morning sun lighted them in under the pines — the low evening sun would meet them when they came out again.

It is the third day of the search, and they are already accustomed to the work. They seek under the projecting hillside, where an unwary footstep could slip; under the fallen trees, where an arm or a leg could so easily be broken; under the close branches of the fir trees, which, sweeping down over the soft moss, invite one to rest.

The bears' and foxes' holes, the badgers' deep burrow, the black remains of the charcoal stack, the red cranberry bank, the fir tree with the white berries, the hillside laid waste by forest fires a month ago, the great boulder flung by the giant — they find all these, but not the place under the hillside where the dark thing lies. No one has been in there to see if it is an ant-hill or a fallen tree — or a human being. Oh, it is a human being, but no one has been in there to see her.

The evening sun saw them on the other side of the forest, but the girl whose understanding God had taken, had not been found. What would they do now? Would they go through the forest again? It is dangerous to do so in the dark, there are bottomless marshes there and precipitous cliffs. And how are they to find in the dark what they could not find in the daylight?

" Let us go to Ekeby!" cried one of the crowd.

" Let us go to Ekeby!" they all shouted together. "Let us go to Ekeby!"

" Let us ask those cavaliers why they set their dogs upon one whose understanding God had taken, why they drove an idiot to despair! Our tired children are crying, our clothes are torn, the oats hang in the rafters while the kernels fall from the ears, the potatoes are rotting in the ground, our horses are running wild, our cows are uncared for, we ourselves are tired to death—and it is all their fault. Let us go to Ekeby and call them to account! Let us go to Ekeby!

" During all the year every kind of evil has come upon us peasants. God's hand rests heavy upon us —and the winter will bring us the famine. Who is it that God's hand is seeking? It was not the Broby parson. His prayer did reach the ear of God. Who, if not these cavaliers! Let us go to Ekeby!

"They have destroyed the estate and driven the Major's wife to beg her bread on the wayside. It is their fault we are without work. It is their fault we are without bread. The famine is their work. Let us go to Ekeby!"

So the dark embittered men pushed down to Ekeby; hungry women with crying children in their arms followed them, and behind them came the cripples and old men. And anger followed like a gathering flood through the ranks, from the old men to the women, from the women to the strong men at the head of the procession.

It was the autumn flood coming. Cavaliers, do you remember the spring flood? New waves are coming down from the mountains, new ruin is threatening the honor and the glory of Ekeby.

A crofter, ploughing in a clearing of the forest, heard the angry shouts of the people. He unharnessed one of the horses, sprang on its back, and galloped home to Ekeby. "Ruin is upon us," he screamed. "The bears, the wolves, and the witches are coming to take Ekeby!"

He rode round the whole place, wild with fear. "All the forest witches are loose," he screamed. "They are coming to take Ekeby. Save yourself who can! The witches will come and set fire to Ekeby and kill the cavaliers."

And behind him could be heard the clamor and

yells of the oncoming crowd. The autumn flood was thundering down to Ekeby.

Did that approaching stream of fury know what it wanted? Was it fire, or murder, or plunder?

They were no longer human beings, they were the witches of the forests, the wild beasts of the wilderness. "We dark powers hidden in the earth are free for a single blessed moment. The lust of revenge has freed us!"

They were the spirits of the hills which dug for its ore, the spirits of the forests which felled the trees and fired the charcoal, the spirits of the fields which grew the corn; they were liberated now, and bent on destruction. Death to Ekeby, death to the cavaliers!

At Ekeby wine flows in streams, and gold lies in heaps in the cellars. The storehouses are filled with grain and meat. Why should the children of righteousness starve and the children of perdition have plenty?

But your time has now come, your measure is filled, cavaliers! You lilies who have never spun, you birds who have never garnered, the measure is filled! In the forest lies that which passes sentence upon you; these are her ambassadors. It is no lawyer or judge who sentences, but the dark thing that lies in the forest.

The cavaliers stood together in the main build-

ing and watched the people arrive. They knew what
they were charged with, and for once they were
innocent. If the poor girl had died in the forest,
it was not because they set their dogs at her—they
had never done that—but because Gösta Berling
had married Countess Elizabeth eight days ago.

But of what use to talk to those furies? They were
tired and hungry, revenge urged them on, and the
thought of plunder tempted them forward. They
came on with angry shouts, and before them rode
the crofter, driven crazy with fear.

The cavaliers had hidden Countess Elizabeth in
the innermost room. Lövenborg and Uncle Eberhard were to stay there and guard her, and the
others went out to meet the people. They stood on
the steps of the main building, unarmed and smiling,
when the first of the noisy crowd arrived there.

The people paused before that little group of
quiet men. There were those among them who were
ready to cast them on the ground and trample the
life out of them with their iron-shod boots, as the
workmen at Sund foundry had treated the manager
and inspector there fifty years before, but they had
expected barred doors and lifted weapons, resistance
and strife.

"Dear friends," said the cavaliers, "you are tired
and hungry; let us offer you some food, and you must
first taste a glass of our home-brewed Ekeby gin."

But the people would not listen to such talk,

they shouted and thundered; yet the cavaliers kept their tempers.

"Wait a bit," they said; "wait a minute. See, Ekeby is open to you. The cellars are open and the storehouses and the dairy. Your wives are fainting with fatigue, and your children are crying. Let us first give them something to eat. Afterwards you can kill us. We won't run away. But we have garrets full of apples; let us bring you some apples for the children!"

.   .   .   .

An hour later, the feast was in full swing at Ekeby. The biggest feast ever celebrated on the big estate took place that autumn night by the light of a shining full moon.

Armfuls of wood from the woodpile had been lighted, and the whole courtyard had been illuminated by bonfires. The people sat about in groups enjoying the warmth and the rest, while the good things of earth were spread before them.

Determined men had gone into the farmyard and taken what they desired. Calves and sheep had been killed and even some of the larger cattle, and they had been cut up and cooked in a handturn. Those hungry hundreds devoured the meat, and one beast after another was led out and slaughtered, till it seemed as though the whole cattle-shed would be emptied in one night.

The great autumn baking at Ekeby had just
taken place. Since the Countess Elizabeth's arrival,
the work of the house had again been resumed. It
seemed as if she never for a moment remembered
that she was Gösta Berling's wife; neither of them
referred to the fact, but instead of that, she made
herself mistress of Ekeby. As a good woman must
always do, she tried with burning zeal to overcome
the wastefulness and extravagance prevalent there.
And she was obeyed; the people experienced a kind
of pleasure in having a mistress over them again.

But of what use was it now that the kitchen rafters had been covered with bread, and that she had
taken charge of the cheese and butter-making and
the brewing, during the month of September, which
she had spent there?

For the people must have all there was in the
house that they might not burn Ekeby and murder
the cavaliers. Out with the bread and butter and
cheese! Out with the beer barrels and casks! Out
with the hams from the pantries! Out with the
brandy kegs and the apples!

How could all the riches of Ekeby hope to mitigate this people's wrath? If they go away without
any dark deed being done, we ought to be thankful.

But all that was done was chiefly for her sake, for
her who was mistress of Ekeby. The cavaliers were
courageous and practical men-at-arms; they would

have defended themselves if they had followed their own desires. They would have driven away that rapacious throng with a few sharp shots but for her, who was so gentle and sweet, and who begged that they might be spared.

As the night wore on, the feeling among the people grew milder. The warmth and rest, the food and drink, quieted their dreadful excitement. They began to laugh and joke—they were at the funeral feast of the Nygård girl. "Shame to him who fails in drinking and in jest at a funeral feast—there are they most needed!"

The children threw themselves upon the masses of fruit that were brought them. Poor cotter children, who considered cranberries and whortleberries delicious, threw themselves upon the clear Astrakan apples which melted in their mouths and the sweet oval-shaped Paradise apples, the yellow-white "lemon" apples, red-cheeked pears, and plums of all kinds, yellow, red, and purple. Oh, nothing is too good for the people when they deign to show their power!

As midnight approached, it seemed as if the crowd was preparing to break up, and the cavaliers ceased to bring forth fruit and wine, to draw the corks and tap the beer barrels. They drew a breath of relief, feeling that the danger was over.

But just then a light was seen in one of the windows of the main building.

All who saw it gave a shout. A young woman carried it.

It was seen but for a moment; she disappeared again, but the people thought they had recognized her.

"She had thick black hair and red cheeks," they cried. "She is here, they have hidden her here!"

"Cavaliers, is she here? Have you our child here? Her, whose understanding God has taken, here at Ekeby? You godless men, what have you done to her? You have let us be anxious about her for a whole week and seek for three days! Away with your wine and food! Woe to us, to have taken it from your hands! Out with her first, and then we shall know what to do with you!"

The newly tamed beast was again growling and threatening, and with wild leaps it rushed upon Ekeby.

The people were sharp, but the cavaliers were sharper. They sprang forward and barred the great doors. But what could they do against that crushing multitude! Door after door was burst open, the cavaliers were thrown aside, and they had no weapons. They were pushed among the crowd and could not extricate themselves. The people were determined to enter and find the Nygård girl.

They found her, they thought, in the innermost room. No one had time to see if she was fair or dark. They lifted her up and carried her out. She was not to be afraid, they said. It was only the cavaliers they were after. They had come to rescue her.

But the stream pouring from the building met another procession entering the yard. The corpse of a woman no longer lay in the most desolate place in the forest—a woman who had thrown herself over the high precipice, and died from the fall. A child had found her, and some of the seekers who still remained in the forest had lifted her upon their shoulders and brought her here.

More beautiful in death than in life was she. She lay looking very lovely with her long dark hair, and it was a splendid figure now that it rested in ever-lasting peace.

Lifted high on men's shoulders, she was carried through the crowd, and silence followed in her wake. Bowed heads greeted the majesty of death.

"She has died quite recently," the men whispered. "She had wandered about till to-day. We think she must have tried to escape the searchers and stumbled over the precipice."

But if that was the Nygård girl, who was the woman they had carried out of Ekeby?

The procession from the forest met the procession from the house; the bonfires lighted up all the courtyard; the people could see both the young women and recognized them. The other one was the young Countess from Borg.

Ah, what was the meaning of this? Was this a new

crime they had come upon? Why was the young
Countess here at Ekeby? Why had people said she
was far away or dead? In the name of justice, ought
they not to turn upon the cavaliers and trample
them to death under their iron-shod shoes?

A voice was heard far and wide. Gösta Berling
had mounted the balustrade of the stairs and was
speaking from there.

"Hear me, you beasts, you devils! Do you
think there are no guns and no powder in Ekeby,
you madmen! Don't you think I had the wish to
shoot you down like mad dogs, but she begged
us to spare you. Oh, if I had known you would
touch her, there is not one of you would be alive
now.

"What do you mean by this disturbance to-
night, and by coming upon us like thieves and robbers and threatening us with fire and murder? What
have I to do with your crazy lassies? How should
I know where they wander? I have been too kind
to her, that is all the trouble. I ought to have set
the dogs on her — it would have been best for us
both, but I did not do it. And I never promised to
marry her — I never did. Remember that!

"But now I say to you that you must release her
whom you dragged out of this house. Release her,
I say; and may the hands that have touched her
burn in everlasting fire! Don't you think that she
is as much above you as the heaven is above the

earth, that she is as tender as you are hard, and as good as you are evil?

"And I will tell you who she is. In the first place, she is an angel from heaven; and secondly, she has been the wife of the Count at Borg. But her mother-in-law was cruel to her, both by day and by night; she was forced to stand at the lake and wash clothes like a common servant; she was beaten and badly treated; none of your own women have been treated worse. Yes, she nearly threw herself into the river because she was so cruelly treated, and I wonder which of you, you rascals, were at hand to save her life. None of you were there, but we cavaliers, we did it. Yes, we did it.

"And afterwards, when her child was born in a peasant hut, the Count sent her a greeting, saying, 'We were married in a foreign land, we did not do it legally and as is ordained. You are not my wife, I am not your husband. I care not for your child.' And when she did not wish that the child should be inscribed as fatherless in the church books, you, of course, would have been too proud if she had said to one of you, 'Come, marry me; I must have a father for the child!' But she chose none of you. She chose Gösta Berling, the poor parson, who may never again expound God's word. I tell you, men, I have never done a harder thing, for I am so unworthy of her. I dared not look into her eyes, but I could not say 'No;' she was in such great despair.

"And now you may think what evil you will of us cavaliers, but to her we have done all the good we could. And it is for her sake we spared you. But now I say to you, release her and go your way, or I think the earth will open and devour you. And when you go, beg God to pardon you for frightening and troubling her who is so good and blameless. And now away with you! We have had enough of you!"

Long before he had finished speaking, the men who carried the Countess out had put her down on the stone steps, and now a big peasant came up to her, hesitatingly, and offered her his broad hand. "Thank you—and good-night," he said. "We intended no harm to the Countess."

After him came another and gave her a careful handshake. "Thank you—and good-night. The Countess must not be angry with us."

Gösta jumped down and stood beside her. Then they shook hands with him also.

So they came up, slowly and seriously, one after another, to say good-night before they went away. They were again tamed, they were again human beings, as they had been on the morning they had left their homes, before hunger and revenge had turned them into wild beasts.

They looked the young Countess in the face, and Gösta noticed how the expression of sweetness and innocence which they saw there brought tears to many eyes. They all showed a silent worship of the noblest they had seen; they were happy to see that one among them had such a great love for goodness. All could not shake hands with her. There were so many, and the Countess was tired and weak. But all could go up and look at her, and they could shake hands with Gösta; his arms could endure the shaking.

Gösta stood there as in a dream. That night had brought a new love into his heart.

"Oh, my people," he thought, "my people, how I love you!" He felt love for all the crowd who were marching away into the night, with the dead girl at their head; all those in coarse clothes and bad-smelling boots; all those who lived in the grey huts at the edge of the forest; all those who could not wield a pen, and often could not read; all those who had never known the richness and fulness of life, nothing but the strife for daily bread.

He loved them with a painful burning tenderness, which forced tears into his eyes. He knew not what it was he wanted to do for them, but he loved them each and all, with their faults and crimes and misfortunes. O God, if the day would ever come again that he should be loved by them!

He awoke from his dream. His wife had put her hand on his arm. The people had gone. They were alone on the steps.

" Oh, Gösta, Gösta, how could you!" She hid her face in her hands, crying.

"It is true what I said," he answered. "I never promised the Nygård girl to marry her. 'Come here next Friday, and you will see something amusing,' was all I said to her. I cannot help it if she cared for me."

"Oh, it was not that; but how could you tell the people I was good and pure? Gösta, Gösta, you know I loved you when I had no right to do it! I was ashamed, Gösta, I could have died of shame." And she shook with sobs.

He stood and looked at her. "Oh, my love, my darling," he said, softly. "How happy you are in being so good! How happy you are in having such a beautiful soul!"

Kevenhüller

THE gifted and versatile Kevenhüller was born
in the seventeen-seventies, in Germany. Being the son of a feudal count, he could have lived
in a great castle and ridden by the Emperor's side,
had he so wished. But that was not to his taste.

He would have liked to attach windmill-wings
to the highest tower of his father's castle, to convert
the Armorial Hall into a smithy and the Hall of
Dames into a watch-making establishment, and to
fill the castle with whirring wheels and working
levers. But as such things were not to be thought
of, he renounced all the grandeur and apprenticed
himself to a watch-maker. He learned all there was
to learn about cog-wheels, springs, and pendulums.
Moreover, he learned to make sun-dials, star-dials,
clocks with singing canaries and piping shepherds,
chimes whose marvellous mechanism would fill a
church tower, and watch-works so small they could
be set in a locket.

On receiving his certificate of mastership, he
shouldered his scrip and, with staff in hand, wandered from place to place to study everything that
went on wheels and rollers. Kevenhüller was no
ordinary watch craftsman; his desire was to be a
great inventor and world-benefactor.

When he had journeyed thus through many

countries, he came at last to Värmland, to study windmills and mining.

One fine summer's morning he happened to be crossing the market-place in Karlstad. In that same beautiful hour the Wood Nymph had seen fit to wander into the town; she was also crossing the square but from the opposite direction, and so met Kevenhüller.

Ah, that was an encounter for a watch-maker's apprentice! The lady had shining green eyes and a wealth of golden hair that nearly reached the ground, and she was garbed in shimmering green. Troll and pagan though she was, she appeared more beautiful to Kevenhüller than any Christian woman he had ever seen. He stood stock-still, and stared as if suddenly bereft of his wits.

The Nymph was fresh from the heart of the forest, where the ferns grow high as trees, and the giant firs shut out the sunlight, so that it falls on the creamy moss only in golden streaks, and where twin-flowers creep over lichen-clad rocks.

I should like to have been in Kevenhüller's place, to have seen her as she came with fern-fronds and pine-needles tangled in her flowing hair, a little adder round her neck, and bringing with her the fresh odors of resin and raspberry, of moss and twin-flower!

How the people must have stared! 'T is said that horses bolted, frightened by her long hair flying in the wind; that street urchins ran after her; that men dropped bridles and meat-axes to gape at her, while women ran shrieking for the bishop and the chapter to come and drive the witch from the town.

She herself walked on with majestic assurance, smiling at their consternation, and Kevenhüller noticed the small, sharp, feline teeth that glistened between her parted red lips.

To conceal her identity she wore a long cape, which hung from her shoulders down her back; but as ill-luck would have it, the cape did not cover the end of her tail, which trailed on the pavement.

Kevenhüller also noticed the tail, but it grieved him that a noble lady should be the laughing-stock of the town; so he bowed to her, and said, with delicate courtesy, "Does not your Grace wish to lift her train?"

The Wood Nymph was touched by the man's kindness as well as his politeness; and as she stood looking at Kevenhüller, it seemed to him that shining sparks flashed from her eyes into his brain.

"Kevenhüller," she said, "henceforth with your two hands you will be able to fashion any master work you wish, but only one of a kind."

So spoke she who can make good her word. For who does not know that the green-clad lady of the forest has the power to bestow the gift of genius upon those who win her favor.

Kevenhüller remained in Karlstad, where he

rented a workshop. He labored day and night, and in a week's time he had produced a marvel. It was an automatic carriage that could run up hill and down at a rapid or slow rate of speed, could be steered and turned, stopped and started, as one wished.

He became famous, and found friends everywhere. He was so proud of his carriage that he journeyed to Stockholm to show it to the King. And he did not have to be shaken in a jog-cart or lie on a hard wooden bench at way stations to wait for post-horses, but travelled now in his own conveyance, arriving at his destination in a few hours.

He went straight to the royal palace, and the King with the ladies and gentlemen of the Court came out to see him drive up. They could not say enough in praise of his invention. The King said:

"You might well give me that carriage, Kevenhüller."

Although the inventor demurred, the King would not be denied.

Kevenhüller then saw in the King's company a fair-haired court lady in a shimmering green gown and, recognizing her, he guessed that she had advised the King to ask him for the carriage. Filled with dismay at the thought of parting with his invention, and not daring to say "No" to the King, he ran the machine against the wall of the palace with such violence that it was smashed in a thousand pieces.

Upon his return to Karlstad, he tried to make a new carriage, but failed. Then the gift bestowed on him by the Wood Nymph struck terror to his heart. He had left the life of ease at his father's castle to become a benefactor to many, not to conjure witch-works of value only to one. Where was the good in being a master—ay, even the greatest of masters—if one could not duplicate one's inventions for the benefit of mankind?

The learned and versatile Kevenhüller, longing for some regular and sane occupation, became a mason and stone-cutter for a time. It was then he built the high tower down by the West End bridge, in the style of the seed-grain tower of his father's castle. He planned to erect a range of buildings with portals, ramparts, turrets, and courts, so that a veritable castle should stand on the shores of the Klarälfven. And there he hoped to make real the dreams of his boyhood. Every kind of industry and handicraft was to be carried on in the rooms of his castle. Millers, blacksmiths, watch-makers, dyers, weavers, turners, filers—all should have workshops there.

From stones of his own hewing he built his tower and fitted it with windmill wings, for the tower was to be a mill. That done, he was eager to begin work on the smithy. Then, one day, as he stood watching the strong, light wings turning in the wind, the old longing for creative work returned.

It was as if the green-clad nymph had again fixed him with her glowing eyes, and set his brain afire. He shut himself up in his workshop, tasted no food, took no rest, but labored assiduously for a whole week, at the end of which time he had produced a new marvel.

He appeared one day on the roof of his tower with a pair of wings. Some street urchins, seeing him, sent up a yell that could be heard all over the town. They ran up and down the streets knocking at every door, and shouting, "Kevenhüller is going to fly, Kevenhüller is going to fly!"

As he stood atop the tower calmly adjusting his wings, there was wild excitement in old Karlstad. Servants abandoned boiling pots and rising dough and ran into the streets; old women dropped their knitting and rushed out; the burgomaster and judiciary left their seats at the judge's table, the schoolmaster tossed the grammar in a corner, and the boys bolted from the class-rooms without asking leave. All Karlstad ran toward the West End bridge, which was soon black with humanity. The market-place was packed and the whole riverside swarmed with people.

Kevenhüller at last set out. One or two wing-strokes, and he was in space, hovering high above the earth. He drew in deep breaths of the strong, pure air, his chest expanded, and the old knight's blood began to surge in him. He dived like a pigeon

and circled like a hawk. His flight was as swift as the
swallow's, as certain as the falcon's. Looking down
upon the earth-bound crowds blinking up at him,
he wished he might make for them all a similar pair
of wings, so that they too could rise into the rare-
fied air. The thought that others might not share
his pleasure robbed him of all feeling of triumph.
Ah, that cruel Wood Nymph—if he could only
meet her!

Then with eyes almost blinded by the dazzling
glare of the sun, he saw some one flying toward him
on wings like his own, saw yellow hair floating in
the wind, billowing green silk, and a pair of shining
eyes. It was *she!*

Kevenhüller did not pause to reflect, but, with
furious speed, rushed upon the vixen to kiss or beat
her, he hardly knew which, but in any case to force
her to remove her curse from him. As he thrust out
his hands to seize her, his wings caught in hers and
he felt himself being whirled round and round, then
dashed down—he knew not where.

When he came to he was lying on the roof of his
tower, the demolished flying machine at his side. He
had flown against his own windmill, whose wings
had caught and hurled him down.

So ended his flying dream. He was again a de-
spondent man. Ordinary labor now irked him, and
he dare not make further use of his creative power.
Were he to fashion another marvel only to destroy

it, his heart must break; and did he not destroy it, the thought that his work was of no benefit to his fellows would drive him insane.

Once more he took up his scrip and staff, and set out in quest of the Wood Nymph. 'T is said that when he came to a forest he would enter and call:

"Wood Nymph, Wood Nymph, come, come! It is I, Kevenhüller, calling." But she came not.

He came to Ekeby in the course of his wanderings, and being well received, he decided to remain. So the company in the cavaliers' wing was augmented by a tall, strong, knightly figure, a man who could hold his own at the drinking-table and at the hunts. Memories of his boyhood returned, and he allowed his companions to call him Count. With his hawk nose, his bushy eyebrows, his pointed beard and uptwisted moustache, he grew to look more and more like an old German robber baron.

He became an Ekeby cavalier—no more, no less than others in that company of men whom people believed the Major's wife had sworn away to the Evil One. His hair turned grey, and his brain slept. He was now so old that he could no longer believe in the feats of his youth. Surely he was not the man who had made the automatic carriage and the flying machine! That was only a tale!

It was at that time the Major's wife was driven out from Ekeby and the cavaliers became the masters of her great estates. Then began a life that could hardly have been worse. A storm of recklessness swept over Värmland, and all kinds of madness broke out among the young. Evil was rampant, and good trembled. Men warred on earth and spirits in Heaven. The forces of nature had been let loose; wolves from Dovre came with witches on their backs, and the Wood Nymph appeared at Ekeby.

The cavaliers, thinking her some poor young lady in distress driven from home by a cruel stepmother, gave her shelter, honored her as a queen, and loved her as a child.

Kevenhüller alone knew her. At first he, like the others, was deluded; but one day, when she appeared in a dress of shimmering green, he recognized her.

There she sat amid silken cushions, while the old men made themselves ridiculous serving her. One was her highness's cook, another her chamberlain; one read to her, one was court musician, one court shoe-maker—all had been taken into her service.

The odious witch was supposed to be ill, but Kevenhüller knew she was only making fools of the cavaliers, and warned them against her. "Look at her small, sharp teeth," he said, "and her wild, shining eyes! She is the Wood Nymph. The powers of evil are at large in these awful times. I tell you she is the Wood Nymph come to destroy us. I know her of old."

But Kevenhüller had no sooner recognized her than the old eagerness for work came back to him. His brain began to seethe and burn; his fingers ached with longing for the touch of hammer and file. He put on his working-blouse and shut himself up in an old smithy.

A cry went out from Ekeby over all Värmland that Kevenhüller had begun work again, and people listened with bated breath to the sounds from the smithy—to the thud of the hammer, the rasping of the files, and the belching of the bellows.

A new marvel was forthcoming. What could it be?—they wondered. Would he teach them to walk on the water, or was he building a ladder to the Pleiades?

Nothing seemed impossible to a man of his sort. Had they not with their own eyes seen him hover in the air on wings? Had they not seen his horseless carriage running in the streets? He was a genius; therefore all things were possible to him.

One night he emerged from the smithy bearing in his hand a new invention. It was a wheel of perpetual motion. As it turned, the spokes glowed, radiating warmth and light. Kevenhüller had made a sun! The wheel gave forth so brilliant a light it set the sparrows twittering and turned the dark night-sky into a rosy dawn.

That was the wonder of wonders! Nevermore would the earth be cold or in darkness. His brain fairly reeled at the thought. The sun would continue to rise and set, but when it went down, thousands upon thousands of his fire-wheels would be shining in the land, and the air would tremble with warmth as on hot summer days. Then they would gather harvests in midwinter; raspberries and whortleberries would grow on the wooded hills the year round, and never again would the rivers be ice-bound.

Now that his invention was perfected, he was to revolutionize the world. His fire-wheel would be furs to the poor, sunlight to the miner. It would give motor power to machinery, added life to nature, and a bountiful and happy existence to mankind. Then came the thought that the Wood Nymph would never let him duplicate his wheel. Seized with rage and a desire for revenge, he wanted to kill her.

He tore over to the dwelling-house and placed his fiery wheel in the outer hall under the stairs, for he meant to set fire to the house and burn the witch. Returning to the smithy, he sat down and calmly awaited results.

Presently he heard shouts and cries. Evidently his design had worked.

"Yes—run, shriek, sound the alarm! She is burning, the witch you placed on silken cushions. Mayhap she is now writhing in torment or fleeing before the flames from room to room; for witches burn! How the green silk will blaze and the flames play in her yellow hair! Fear not her incantations, fire—let her burn! Here is one who because of her must suffer to the end of his days."

Bells rang, wagons rattled, hose lines were dragged out, water was carried up from the lake, and people came running from the neighboring villages. There were cries and wails and commands. A roof had just fallen in. Then came the awful crackle and roar of flames. But nothing disturbed Kevenhüller, who sat in the smithy rubbing his hands.

Suddenly he heard a crash, as if the heavens had fallen, and started with a jubilant cry. It was done! She had been crushed by the falling beams and destroyed by the flames.

He thought with regret of the glories and delights of Ekeby that must needs have been sacrificed to rid the world of her; the beautiful halls where happiness had dwelt, the tables which had groaned under the weight of delectable dishes, the priceless old furniture and the old silver and porcelain which could never be replaced. With a wild shriek he sprang to his feet. . . . His wheel, his sun, the model on which so much depended—that too was in the house!

"Am I going mad?" he gasped. "How could I have done such a thing?"

At that moment the door of the smithy opened, and there, on the threshold, stood the Wood

Nymph, smiling and lovely, her shimmering green dress undamaged, her hair unsinged!

She was as when he had first seen her that day in Karlstad; the tail showed between her dainty feet, and about her clung the spirit and odors of the wildwood.

"Ekeby is burning," she laughed.

Kevenhüller caught up a hammer to hurl at her, when he saw that she held his wheel in her hand.

"See what I have saved for you," she said.

The inventor fell on his knees before her.

"You have ruined my life," he cried. "It was you wrecked my carriage and destroyed my wings. Have pity on me now!"

"I see that you know who I am," said she.

"I have always known you," wailed the poor wretch; "you are Genius. Take back your gift and set me free! Why do you persecute me?"

"Fool!" answered the Wood Nymph, "I have never wished you harm. I gave you a great award, but if it does not please you, I can take it back. Only think well lest you should regret it later."

"No, no," he said; "take from me the magic power of working wonders!"

"First you must destroy this," she told him, throwing the wheel on the floor.

Instantly he swung his hammer and struck the glowing wheel, which to him was but a witch's tool and of no use to the world. Sparks flew, and flames danced round him, as the last of his wonders was demolished.

"I now take back my gift," said the Wood Nymph.

As she stood in the doorway, the glow from the fire outside streaming over her, she appeared more beautiful to him than ever — no longer sinister, but proud and austere.

" Madman," she said, "I never forbade your letting others copy your works; my sole desire was to spare the man of genius the artisan's labor."

Then she went her way, and for some days Kevenhüller was out of his mind. But in his madness he had burned down Ekeby, and though, luckily, no one had been injured, it was a great grief to the cavaliers that the hospitable home where they had enjoyed so many benefits should have been destroyed during their reign.

Ah! children of a later day, had it been you or I that met the Wood Nymph, would we, like Kevenhüller, have demanded that she take back her gift? Who in our time complains of having received too much from the Goddess of Genius?

Broby Fair

BROBY FAIR opened on the first Friday in October and lasted for eight days. It was the great autumnal holiday. It was preceded by a period of baking and slaughtering of cattle and fowl in every cottage; the new winter clothes were made ready to put on for the first time; holiday fare such as sandwiches and cheesecake stood all day on the table; the allowance of gin was doubled, and all work was laid aside. Every house made holiday. The servants and the work-people received their summer wages, and held long consultations about their intended purchases at the Fair. Folk from out of the way parts came marching in small groups, with their provisions on their backs, and long staffs in their hands. Many were also obliged to drive their cattle to the Fair for sale during this time of general poverty. Obstinate young bullocks and goats, which refused to move and braced their fore-feet stiffly against the hill slope, caused irritation to their owners and much amusement to the bystanders. The spare rooms in the large country mansions were filled with welcome guests; news was exchanged, and prices of cattle and furniture were discussed. The children dreamed of presents from the Fair and money given them to spend there.

And on the first market day, what a crowd of

people streamed up the Broby hills and over the wide market-place! Booths were raised, where the town shopmen spread out their goods, while the dale folk and the West Göthlanders piled up their wares upon endless rows of boards raised on trestles, over which white linen canopies hung. There were numberless rope dancers, hurdy-gurdies, and blind violin players; also fortune-tellers, sellers of sweet stuff, and gin shops. Beyond the booths stood rows and rows of copper and wooden utensils. Onions and carrots and apples and pears were offered for sale by the gardeners from the big estates, and wide patches of ground were covered by red-brown copper pans with shining tin linings.

Still it was noticeable at the Fair that there was want in Svartsjö, Bro, and Löfvik and the other Löfsjö parishes; trade went badly both in the booths and at the boards. There was more animation at the cattle market, for there were many who were obliged to sell both their horses and their cows to be able to survive the winter. There, also, the exciting barter and sale of horses took place.

Broby Fair goes gaily, for if you have money in your pocket for a couple of glasses of gin, you can keep your spirits up. And it was not alone the drinking that caused all the jollity; when the people from the lonely forest huts came down to the market-place in streams, they were frightened at first when they heard the roar of all that shrieking, laughing crowd, but when they came among them, they seemed to grow dizzy with pleasure and excited and maddened by the noisy life of the Fair.

Of course, there was a considerable amount of trade done among so many people, but still that, after all, was not the chief affair. The important thing was to get together a crowd of relatives and friends and carry them away to the cart and treat them to minced mutton and sandwiches and gin, or to persuade your sweetheart to accept a hymn-book and a silk dress, or to go and look for fairings for the little ones at home.

Every one who was not obliged to remain at home to look after the house and the cattle went to Broby Fair. The Ekeby cavaliers were there, and the forest dwellers from Nygård, horse-sellers from Norway, Finns from the northern forests, vaga-bonds from the roadway. Sometimes all the roaring mass would collect into a corner and wind about in circles round one central point. No one knew what was going on there before a couple of policemen fought a path through the crowd and put a stop to a fight or raised an overturned cart. The next mo-ment there was a new crowd around the shopman, who was wrangling with a quick-witted servant girl. Then about dinner-time began the great fight. The peasants had got it into their heads that the West Göthlanders used a short ell measure, and there was some quarrelling and disturbance round their boards, which later turned to violence. It seemed that to those who saw nothing but want and misery before them it was a pleasure to hit at something —it did not matter who it was or what they hit. As soon as the strong and pugnacious saw that a fight was going on, they rushed in from all' sides. The cavaliers intended to put a stop to it in their own way, and the dale folk hurried to the help of the West Göthlanders.

Strong Måns from Fors was the man who was in the very midst of it. He was drunk and angry. He had knocked a West Göthlander down and began to maul him, but at a cry for help the West Göthlanders rushed to the assistance of their countryman, and tried to compel Måns to release his victim. Then Måns turned over some piles of cloth from one of the boards, grasped the board itself, which was a yard broad and eight yards long and was composed of a number of thick planks, and began to swing it about as a weapon. Strong Måns was a fearful man. He had once kicked out the wall of the jail in Filipstad, and he could lift a boat out of the lake and carry it on his shoulders. And now you can imagine that, when he began to strike about him with the heavy board, the crowd retreated, as also did the West Göthlanders. But he came after them, swinging his mighty club about him. It was no longer a question for him of friends or enemies; he only wanted some one to fight with, now that he had a weapon.

The people fled in terror before him. Men and women shrieked and ran, but how was it possible for the women to get out of his way? Many of them had their children by the hand! The booths and carts, the oxen and cows alarmed by the noise, hindered their escape. In a corner between the booths a number of women had been cut off from retreat, and toward them the giant rushed. Did he imagine he saw a Göthlander among them? He raised the board and brought it down upon their heads. Pale and terrified, the women awaited the attack, huddling together to meet the fatal blow.

But when the board came whizzing down upon them, its force was broken upon the outstretched arms of a man. One man had not crouched under it, but raised himself above the others; one man had voluntarily taken the blow to save the many. The women and children were unharmed; the man had broken the violence of the blow, but he lay now senseless upon the ground.

Strong Måns did not lift his weapon again to rush on to further slaughter. He had met the glance of the man on whose head his weapon had fallen, and it rendered him powerless. He allowed himself to be bound and carried away without resistance.

But the rumor spread quickly over the marketplace that strong Måns had killed Captain Lennert.

They said that he who had been the people's friend had died to save the women and children.

Quiet stole over the wide plain, where life had lately roared in wildest excitement; trade slackened; the fighting ceased; the assemblies round the provision bags were scattered, and the rope dancers looked in vain for an audience.

The friend of the people was dead; they mourned him now. They all pressed silently toward the place where he had fallen. He lay stretched on the ground, quite unconscious; there was no wound to be seen, but the skull itself seemed to have been indented.

Some men lifted him carefully upon the board which the giant had dropped. They thought him still alive.

"Where shall we carry him?" they asked one another.

"Home," answered a harsh voice from the crowd.

Oh, yes, kind men, carry him home. Lift him on your shoulders and bear him home! He has been God's plaything. He has been driven like a feather before the breath of His spirit. Bear him home now. His wounded head has rested on a hard prison bench and on the straw in barns. Let it go home now and take its rest on a soft down pillow! He has borne unmerited shame and pain, and has been driven from his own door. Carry him home now! He has been a wandering fugitive trudging along God's ways where he found them, but the longing of his

heart was for the home whose doors God had closed
to him. Carry him home! Perhaps it stands open for
the man who died to save the women and children.

He comes now — not as a ruffian led forward by
his reeling boon companions. He is borne by sorrowing people, in whose homes he has dwelt, while
he alleviated their suffering. Carry him home now!

And they did so. Six men lifted the board upon
their shoulders, and bore him away from the market-place. As they passed, the peasants drew aside
and stood motionless, the men uncovering their
heads, the women bowing as they did in church
when the name of God was pronounced. Some were
crying and drying their eyes; some spoke of what
a man he had been, so good and so happy-tempered,
so useful and so God-fearing.

It was wonderful to see how, as soon as one of
the bearers grew tired, another stepped up gently
and slipped his shoulder under the burden.

So they carried Captain Lennert past the place
where the cavaliers stood. " I suppose we had better
go and see that he gets home safely," said Beerencreutz, leaving his place at the roadside to go up
to Helgesäter—and his example was followed by
many.

The market-place was almost deserted; the
people followed Captain Lennert up to Helgesäter.
One must see to it that he was taken home. All the
necessities which had to be bought must be left at

present; the fairings for the little ones at home were forgotten; the purchase of the hymn-book was not concluded; the silk handkerchief, which shone temptingly before the eyes of the young bride, was left on the counter. All followed to see Captain Lennert carried safely home to Helgesäter.

When the procession arrived at Captain Lennert's home, all was silent and quiet there. Again the Colonel knocked at the entrance door. All the servants were at the Fair. The Captain's wife alone was at home keeping guard over the house, and it was she who opened the door.

She asked, as she had asked once before, "What do you want?"

And the Colonel answered, as he had answered once before, "We are here with your husband."

She looked at him as he stood there, straight, and with his usual assurance. She looked at the bearers behind him, who wept, and at the great crowd of people beyond them. She stood there on the steps and gazed into hundreds of tearful eyes which anxiously watched her, and at last she looked at her husband lying unconscious upon the board, and then she pressed her hands against her heart.

"This is his real face," she muttered.

Without further questioning she bent down, drew back a bolt, and threw the doors wide open, and then walked before the others into the bed-chamber.

The Colonel helped her to open out the double bed and shake up the bolsters, and then Captain Lennert was again laid upon soft down and fine linen.

" Is he alive?" she asked.

"Yes," said the Colonel.

" Is there any hope?"

"No, there is nothing to be done."

There was silence for a moment, and then a sudden thought struck her.

" Are all those people crying for his sake?"

"Yes."

" What has he done for them?"

"The last he did was to allow himself to be killed to save their women and children."

Again she sat silent for a time.

" What kind of a face had he, Colonel, when he came home two months ago?"

The Colonel started. Now he understood—now for the first time.

" Why, Gösta had painted him!"

" So it was because of a cavalier's trick that I shut him out of his own home? How will you answer for that, Colonel?"

Beerencreutz shrugged his broad shoulders.

" I have much to answer for."

" But I think this must be the worst work you have yet done."

" And I have never trodden a more difficult path

than this to Helgesäter to-day. But there are two others that have a share in this."

"Who are they?"

"Sintram is one, and the other is yourself. You are a stern woman. I know that many have tried to speak to you about your husband."

"That is true," she answered.

Afterwards she asked him to tell her about the drinking revel at Broby.

He told her all he could remember, and she listened in silence. Still Captain Lennert lay unconscious. The room was filled with mourners, and no one thought of shutting out the troubled crowd. All the doors stood open. All the rooms, the staircases, and porches were filled with silent anxious men and women, and far out into the yard they stood in compact groups.

When the Colonel had finished his story, the Captain's wife raised her voice and said, "If there are any cavaliers here, I beg them to go away. It is hard for me to see them while I sit here by my husband's death-bed."

Without a word more, the Colonel rose and went out. Gösta did the same, and all the other cavaliers who had followed Captain Lennert home; the people made way awkwardly for the little group of humbled men.

When they had gone, the Captain's wife said, "Will some of you who saw my husband during these last weeks tell me where he lived and what he did?"

So those in the room began to bear witness about him to his wife, who had misunderstood and hardened her heart against him. They used the old language of the Bible—for the men who spoke had never read any other book—and in symbolic words taken from the good Book of Job and turns of phrases dating back from patriarchal days, they told her about God's pilgrim, about him who went about helping the people.

Time passed before they could tell her all they knew. While the twilight and evening fell, they stood there, and one after another, stepping forward, recounted his good works before his wife—his wife, who had not wished to hear his name mentioned. There were those who related how he had found them on beds of sickness and had nursed them. There were wild fighters there whom he had tamed. There were troubled souls whom he had helped, drunkards whom he had forced into sobriety. One and all who had been in unbearable trouble had sent for the pilgrim of God, and he had always helped them—at least, he had always awakened hope and trust.

All the evening the old Bible language echoed in the sick-room, and out in the yards the groups stood waiting for the end. They knew what was taking place indoors, and what was being spoken at the bedside was whispered from mouth to mouth outside. He that had something to say made his way forward gently. "It is one who can bear witness," they whispered, and made room for him. They came out of the darkness, told their story, and then sank back into the darkness again.

"What does she say now?" those outside asked when some one left the house. "What does the severe mistress of Helgesäter say?"

"She shines like a queen and smiles like a bride. She has moved his armchair to the bed and laid upon it the clothes that she herself had woven for him."

But a sudden silence fell upon the people. No one told them, all felt it at once — "He is dying."

Captain Lennert opened his eyes and looked about him, and saw all he had longed for. He saw his home, the people, his wife and children, and the clothes, and smiled. But he had only awakened to die. He drew a shuddering breath and gave up his spirit. Then all sound of speech died away, and a voice took up a funeral hymn. All joined in, and it was borne up by hundreds of voices; it was carried up on high.

It was Earth's farewell greeting to the passing soul.

The Forest Hut

MANY years before the cavaliers became the managers of Ekeby, a shepherd boy and girl used to play together in the forest, building houses of flat stones, picking berries, and setting traps. They had both been born in the forest. It was their home and mansion, and they lived peacefully with everything there, treating the forest beasts as you treat servants and domestic animals.

They looked upon the foxes and lynxes as their yard-dogs, and the weasels as their cats, and hares and squirrels were their playmates. Bears and elk were to them as cattle, and they caged owls and black-cocks; the pine trees were their servants, and the young birches were guests at their banquets. They knew the cave where the vipers lay twined together in their winter sleep, and bathing, they had seen the snakes swim toward them through the clear water, but they feared neither snakes nor gnome: they belonged to the forest, and the forest was their home. Nothing frightened them there.

Deep in the forest lay the hut where the boy lived. A steep forest path led thither; the hills stood round it and hid the sun, a bottomless marsh lay near and sent forth a frosty mist all the year round. It was hardly a tempting location for a home for dale folk.

One day they were to live together in the forest hut and earn their bread by the sweat of their brows. But before they could be married, the horror of war broke over the land, and the boy enlisted. He came home again without a wound or any damaged limb, but he had received a scar for life from that experience. He had seen too much of the wickedness of the world and man's cruelty to man; he no longer saw any kindness anywhere.

At first no one noticed any change in him. He went to the pastor with the girl he had loved since his childhood, and their banns were called. The forest hut above Ekeby became their home, as they had arranged years before, but there was no comfort in that house.

The wife went about her work, and looked upon her husband as upon a stranger. Since he had returned from the war, she felt she did not know him. He laughed harshly and spoke little. She was afraid of him.

He neither annoyed people nor did them any harm, and he was a good workman, yet he was not liked, for he believed evil of everybody. He, too, felt himself to be a hated stranger. The beasts of the forest were now his enemies; so were the hills which hid the sun and the marsh which sent forth the cold mist. The forest is a dreadful home for those who cherish evil thoughts.

He who would live in the wilderness must ac-

quire happy memories, or he sees nothing but murder and persecution among plants and animals, as
he saw before among men. He awaits evil from all
he meets with.

Jan Hök, the soldier, could not explain what
ailed him, but he saw that nothing ever prospered
with him. His home afforded little peace; the sons
grew up there strong but wild. They were courageous and hardy men, but they too lived in strife
with everybody.

His wife sought to while away her grief by prob-
ing the secrets of the wilderness, and sought for
healing balm in marsh and coppice. She mused upon
supernatural powers, and knew what sacrifices were
acceptable to them. She could heal sickness, and
gave advice to those in love-troubles. She gained
the reputation of being a witch and was shunned,
though she did much kindness to people.

Once she tried to speak to her husband of his
trouble.

"Ever since you went to the war," she said, "you
have been a changed man. What did they do to you
there?"

Then he had sprung up and been near striking
her, and it was the same whenever she mentioned
the war. He flew into a mad rage. He could not
bear any one to speak of it, and this soon became
known, and people were careful to avoid the subject.

But none of his comrades could say he had done anything worse than the rest of them. He had fought like a good soldier. It was the cruelty he had been a witness to which had so frightened him that afterwards he saw nothing else. All his troubles dated from the war. He felt all nature hated him, because he had taken part in such things. Those possessing wider knowledge could comfort themselves with the idea of having fought for their country and its honor. What did he know of such things? He only knew that everything hated him because he had spilled so much blood and caused so much harm.

At the time when the Major's wife had been driven from Ekeby, he lived alone in his hut. His wife was dead, and his sons were scattered. But at fairtime the forest hut filled with guests. Black-haired, dark-faced vagabonds turned in thither. They were most at home with those whom others avoided. Little shaggy-haired horses climbed up the steep forest roads, dragging carts loaded with iron implements, children, and rag-bags. Women, aged early, with features swollen from smoking and drinking, and men with pale, sharp faces followed the carts. And when they reached the forest hut, a merry life awoke there. They brought gin and cards, loud laughter and speech with them — they told of thieving and horse exchanges and bloody fighting.

On Friday Broby Fair had begun, and Captain

Lennert had been killed. Strong Måns, who had dealt him the death-blow, was a son of the old man in the forest hut. And when the vagabonds gathered together there, on Sunday afternoon, they passed the gin bottle to the old man oftener than usual, and talked to him of prison life and prison fare and trials, for they knew all about that.

The old man sat on the chopping-block in the chimney-corner, and said very little; his great dull eyes gazed upon the wild crowd filling the room. Twilight had come, but the firelight flooded the room. It shone upon rags, misery, and fierce want.

Then the door opened gently, and two women entered. It was the young Countess Elizabeth followed by the Broby parson's daughter. She looked strange to the old man, as sweetly, in her gentle beauty, she stepped into the circle of firelight. She told them that Gösta Berling had not been seen at Ekeby since Captain Lennert's death. She and her maid had been up in the forest seeking him all the afternoon. She noticed that there were men here who had journeyed much, and knew all the forest paths. Had they seen him? She had come in to rest and ask them if they had met him.

It was a useless question — no one had seen him. They placed a chair for her, and she sank down upon it and was silent for a time. All the noise in the hut had ceased. All looked at her and wondered at her, till she was frightened at the silence, started up, and sought for an indifferent subject to speak about.

She turned to the old man in the corner. "I think I have heard that you have been a soldier, father," she said. "Tell me something about the war."

The silence grew still more paralyzing. The old man sat as if he had not heard.

"It would please me very much to hear about the war from one who has been in it," continued the Countess, but paused suddenly, for the Broby parson's daughter was shaking her head at her. She must have said something unsuitable. All the people gathered there stared at her as if she had broken the simplest law of propriety. Suddenly one of the women raised her harsh voice and asked, "Isn't this the lady who was Countess at Borg?"

"Yes."

"That was different from running about the forest after a mad parson. A fig for such booty!"

The Countess rose and said farewell. She had rested sufficiently. The woman who had spoken followed them outside.

"The Countess will understand that I was obliged to say something, for it won't do to speak to the old man about the war. He can't bear the word. I meant no harm."

The Countess hurried away, but checked herself quickly. She saw the threatening forest, the overshadowing hills, and the misty marsh. It must be awful to live there for him whose mind was filled with evil memories.

She felt very sorry for the old man who sat there with the dark vagabonds as his only companions.

"Anna Lisa," she said, "let us return. They were kind to us in there, but I behaved badly. I will talk to the old man of happier things." And pleased at having found some one to comfort, she returned to the hut.

"I am afraid," she said. "I think that Gösta Berling is somewhere in the forest here, and he intends to take his own life. It is therefore important that he should be found and hindered from doing so. Anna Lisa and I think we have seen him sometimes, but he has disappeared again. He keeps in the neighborhood of the place where the Nygård girl perished. I have been thinking that I need not go all the way to Ekeby to find help. There are many strong men sitting here who could easily capture him."

"Go your way, men," cried the woman. "When the Countess does not think herself too great to beg us forest folk to do her a service, go at once."

The men rose and went to search.

Old Jan Hök sat motionless and gazed before him with dull eyes. Frightfully gloomy and hard he looked as he sat there. The young wife found no words to say to him. Then she noticed that a sick child lay on a sheaf of straw, and that one of

the women had a wound in her hand. She began
at once to nurse them. She was soon on good terms
with the chattering women, and let them show her
their babies. The men came back in an hour, and
brought Gösta Berling, bound, into the hut. They
laid him down on the floor before the fire. His
clothes were torn and dirty, his face looked thin
and his eyes wild. He had gone through much in
those days; he had slept on the damp earth, he
had buried his face and hands in the turf, dragged
himself over rocky ridges, and pushed through the
closest thickets. He had not followed the men voluntarily; they had overpowered and bound him.

When his wife saw him thus, she was very angry.
She did not unbind his hands, but let him lie on
the floor. She turned scornfully away from him.

"How dreadful you look!" she said.

"I had no intention of appearing before your
eyes again," he answered.

"Am I not your wife? Is it not my right to expect
you to come to me in your trouble? I have waited
for you with great anxiety these two days."

"I have been the cause of Captain Lennert's misfortune. How could I dare to show myself before
you? How could I?"

"You were seldom afraid, Gösta."

"The only service that I can do you, Elizabeth,
is to set you at liberty."

Unutterable scorn flashed from under her frowning eyebrows upon him.

"You would make me the wife of a suicide?"

His face grew angry.

" Elizabeth, let us go out into the silent forest and talk together."

"Why should not these people hear us?" she cried in a shrill tone. "Are we better than they? Have any of them caused more trouble and sorrow than we have? They are the children of the forest and wayside, and are hated by every man. Let them hear what sin and sorrow follow even the master of Ekeby, the beloved Gösta Berling. Do you think your wife considers herself better than they are— or do you consider yourself better?"

He raised himself painfully on his elbows, and looked at her with rising defiance. "I am not so worthless as you think!"

Then she heard the story of those two days. All the first day Gösta had wandered about the forest, deeply conscience-stricken. He could not bear to meet the eyes of a fellow-creature. But he did not think of dying. He meant to go into a distant country. On Sunday he came down from the hills and went to Broby church. Once again he wanted to see the people, the poor hungry Löfsjö people, whom he had dreamed to serve when he sat by the shame-stack of the Broby parson, and whom he had learned to love when they departed into the night with the dead peasant girl.

The service had begun when he came into the church. He crept up to a gallery and looked down upon the congregation. Cruel sorrow had then taken possession of him. He wanted to talk to them, to comfort them in their poverty and hopelessness. If he might have spoken in God's house, he would, hopeless as he was himself, have found hope and salvation for them. When he left the church, he went into the vestry and wrote the proclamation which his wife had already seen, promising that work should begin again at Ekeby, that food should be distributed there to the most needy. He had hoped his wife and the cavaliers would fulfil his promise when he was far away.

On leaving the vestry he saw a coffin standing outside the parish mortuary. It was roughly, evidently hastily made, but was covered with black crape and wreaths of whortleberry leaves. He knew it was Captain Lennert's coffin. The people had probably begged the Captain's wife to hasten the funeral so that the multitude who were present at the Fair might attend.

He stood and gazed at the coffin, when a heavy hand was laid on his shoulder. Sintram had come up to him.

"Gösta," said he, "if you wish to play any one a real trick, lie down and die. There is nothing so

wily as to die; nothing that so cheats an honest
man, suspecting nothing. Lie down and die, I say!"

Gösta listened with dismay to what Sintram said.
He bewailed the miscarriage of well-laid plans. He
had wished to destroy all the Löfsjö country and
see desolation round the Löfven shores. That was
why he had made the cavaliers lords of the country
side, that was the reason he had allowed the Broby
parson to impoverish the people, that was why
he had called down the drought and the famine. At
Broby Fair the decisive blow was to have been
struck. Wearied by misfortune, the people would
give themselves to murder and theft. Afterwards
the law would prosecute and impoverish them still
farther. The famine riots and all kinds of adversity
would lay waste the country, till at last it would
grow so bad and hateful that no one could live
there, and it would all be Sintram's work. It would
be his joy and pride, because he was wicked. He
loved desolate waste and unbroken ground—but
that man, who had been clever enough to die at the
right moment, had spoiled it all.

Then Gösta asked him what purpose it would
all have served.

"It would have pleased me, Gösta, for I am
wicked. I am the bear from the hills, I am the snow-
storm over the plain; I love to kill and persecute.
Away, say I, away with men and their work. I hate
them! I let them run through my claws, and allow

them to gambol,—that is also amusing for a time,
—but now I am tired of that game, Gösta; I want
to strike, I want to spread death and ruin."

He was mad, quite mad. He began those devilish tricks many years before in fun, but now wickedness had taken the upper hand, now he thought
himself a spirit from hell. He had cherished and
fostered the evil within him, till it had taken mastery over his soul. Thus, like love and trouble,
pride too can make people mad. He was furious,
was the wicked foundry proprietor, and in his anger
he began to pluck at the crape bands and wreaths
on the coffin; but Gösta cried, "Don't touch the
coffin."

"See, see, am I not to touch it? Yes, I shall cast
my friend Lennert out upon the ground and trample on his wreaths. Don't you see all the harm he
has done me? Don't you see in what a splendid grey
calash I have come here?"

Gösta Berling saw that a pair of prison wagons
with the county police and court servants stood
and waited outside the churchyard wall.

"See, see, am I not to send the Captain's wife at
Helgesäter some thanks for her having sat down
yesterday to hunt among old papers for proofs
against me in that gunpowder affair you know of?
Am I not to teach her that she would have done
better attending to her brewing and baking than in
sending the police after me? Am I not to be repaid

for the tears I shed in entreating Schärling to allow
me to come here and offer a prayer by my good
friend's coffin?"

And he began to pull at the crape again.

Gösta Berling stepped up to him and caught at
his arm.

"I will give anything if you won't touch the
coffin."

"Do what you like," said the madman. "Call for
help if you wish, I can still manage to do something
before the police come. Fight me if you like. It will
be a fine sight here in the churchyard. Let us fight
among the wreaths and the pall and the crape!"

"I will purchase peace for the dead at any price.
Take my life—take all!"

"You promise great things, my boy."

"You can prove me!"

"Well, then, kill yourself!"

"I can do that, but the coffin must first be safely
under ground."

So it was arranged. Sintram made Gösta swear
that he would not be alive twelve hours after Captain Lennert's funeral. "Then, I know, you will
never have time to be a good man," he said.

This was easy for Gösta Berling to promise. He
was glad to be able to give his wife her freedom.
His stricken conscience had driven him on and
on till he was now wearied to death. The only thing
that distressed him was that he had promised the

Major's wife not to die as long as the Broby parson's daughter remained in service at Ekeby. But Sintram declared that she could no longer be considered a servant after inheriting all her father's money. Gösta objected that the Broby parson had hidden his riches so well that no one could find them. Then Sintram smiled and said the money was hidden among the pigeons' nests in the steeple of Broby church; and with that he departed. Afterwards Gösta went up to the forest again. It seemed to him it would be best for him to die on the spot where the Nygård peasant girl had killed herself. He had wandered about there all day; he had seen his wife, and had not been able to kill himself at once.

All this he told his wife while lying bound on the floor of the forest hut.

"Oh," she said sorrowfully, "how well I recognize all that! All heroics and bravado! Always ready to thrust your hands into the flames, Gösta, always ready to throw yourself away! How great it once seemed to me! And how much I prize calmness and sense now! What good could you do to the dead by making such a promise? The coffin could have been raised again, and new crape and new wreaths could have been made! If you had laid your hand on the good man's coffin, there before Sintram's eyes, and sworn to help the people whom he had tried to ruin, how I should have prized your

oath! If you had thought,when you saw the people
in church, 'I will help them; I will devote all my
strength to assisting them,' and had not laid the burden upon your weak wife and old men with failing
strength, I should have prized that too."

Gösta Berling lay silent a moment.

"We cavaliers are not free men," he said at
length. "We have promised one another to live for
pleasure and for pleasure alone. Woe to us all if
one fails!"

"Woe to you," said the Countess angrily, "that
you are the most cowardly of the cavaliers and the
last in amendment. Yesterday afternoon all eleven
sat at home in the cavaliers' wing, and they were
very gloomy. You were absent, Captain Lennert
was dead, and the honor and glory of Ekeby was
destroyed. They left the toddy glasses untouched,
and would not show themselves before me. Then
Anna Lisa, who stands there, went to them. You
know she is a sharp little woman, who, for many
years, fought on despairingly amid neglect and
waste.

"'To-day I have been home again seeking for my
father's money,' she said to the old cavaliers, 'but
found nothing. All the notes on hand are cancelled,
and all the drawers and cupboards stand empty.'

"'It was a great pity,' replied Beerencreutz.

"'When the Major's wife left Ekeby, she bade
me look after it. If I had found my father's money,

I would have rebuilt Ekeby. But when I found nothing at home that I could carry away with me, I took a few twigs from the shame-stack, for I shall be overwhelmed with shame when my lady returns and asks me what I have done with Ekeby.'

"'Don't take the blame of what you could not help,' answered Beerencreutz again.

"'But I did not bring them for myself alone,' continued the Broby parson's daughter. 'I took some for the good gentlemen. If you please, gentlemen, my father, after all, is not the only man who has caused shame and sorrow in the world!'

"And she went from one to another and laid a few twigs on the table before each. Some of them swore, but most of them admitted she was right. At last Beerencreutz said, with the calm of the thorough gentleman, 'That is well. We thank you, Anna Lisa. You may go now.'

"When she had left the room he struck his fist on the table so that the glasses jumped.

"'From this moment,' he said, 'I am a total abstainer. Never shall drink bring anything of the kind upon me again!' And with that he rose and went out. They followed him by and by, all of them. Do you know where they went, Gösta? To the river, to the promontory where the mill and forge stood, and they began working there. They began to drag out the beams and stones and clear the place. The old men have had hard times lately, trouble has gone over many of them, and now they could not endure the disgrace any longer of having ruined Ekeby. I know well that you cavaliers have always been ashamed to work, but the others have taken the disgrace upon themselves. And more than that, Gösta, they intend sending Anna Lisa to the Major's wife to bring her home again. But you—what are *you* doing, Gösta?"

He still found wherewith to answer her. "What do you expect of me, of a discharged clergyman—an outcast from men and despised of God?"

"I went to Bro church to-day, Gösta, and I have a greeting for you from two women. 'Tell Gösta,' said Marienne Sinclaire, 'that a woman does not wish to feel ashamed of the man she has loved.' 'Tell Gösta,' said Anna Stjärnhök, 'that all is well with me now; I manage my estates myself, and people say of me that I shall be a second Lady of Ekeby. I think no more of love, only of work. But we all grieve over Gösta. We believe in him and pray to God for him; but when—when will he be a man?'

"See, then, are you an outcast from men?" continued the Countess. "You have won too much love, Gösta; that has been your misfortune. Both men and women have loved you. If you laughed and jested, if you but sang and played for them, they forgave you everything. What it has pleased you to do has satisfied them. And you dare call

yourself an outcast! You think you are despised of
God! Why did you not stay and see Captain Lennert's funeral?

"As he died during the Fair, his fame had spread
far and wide, and after morning service thousands
of people gathered at the church. All the churchyard and the wall and the field outside were covered with people. The funeral procession formed
before the vestry hall. They only waited for the
old Rector. He was ill and had not preached, but
had promised to officiate at Captain Lennert's funeral. At last he came, walking with bowed head,
absorbed in his own dreams, as he is often nowa-
days, and placed himself at the head of the procession. He noticed nothing unusual. The old man
had headed many a funeral procession, and he went
along the well-known path and did not look up. He
read the prayers and cast the earth on the coffin
and still noticed nothing unusual. But then the sexton raised the hymn. I never thought the sexton's
voice, which at other times sang alone, could have
the power of waking the Rector from his dreams.

"But the sexton was not to sing alone. Hundreds and hundreds of voices joined his: men,
women, and children sang. Then the old man
seemed to awaken. He passed his hand over his
eyes, and stepped up on a heap of mould to gain
a better view. Never had he seen such a crowd of
mourners. The men wore their old battered funeral

hats, and the women their white aprons with the
wide tucks. They all sang; all their eyes were filled
with tears—they all mourned.

"Then the old Rector trembled and grew frightened. What could he say to all those people in
trouble? He must say something to comfort them.

"When the hymn was finished, he stretched out
his arms toward the people.

"'I see,' he said, 'that you are in trouble, and
trouble is more difficult to bear for those who are
to tread the paths of life for many years than for
me, for I shall soon be called away.'

He paused dismayed. His voice was too feeble,
and he hesitated in his choice of words.

"But soon he began again. His voice had regained the vigor of his youth, and his eyes shone.

"He made us a splendid speech, Gösta. First he
told us all he knew about God's pilgrim; afterwards
he reminded us that no outer brilliance nor great
talent made this man so highly honored—it was
because he always kept in God's paths. And he
prayed us for God's sake—for Christ's sake—to
do the same. Every one should love his neighbor
and help him. Every one should do as Captain
Lennert did, for no great talent was required for
that—only a devout mind. And he explained the
meaning to us of all that had happened during
the year. He said it had been the preparation for
a period of love and happiness which was certainly

to be expected now. He had seen the goodness of men break forth during the year in scattered rays; now it would shine like bright sunlight.

"And it seemed to all of us that we heard a prophet's voice. We were all ready to love one another; all desired to be good.

"He raised his eyes and hands and prayed for peace upon the country. 'In the name of God, let all strife cease! Let peace dwell in your hearts and in all nature! May the dead things of the world and the beasts of the field and the plants in the earth feel peace and cease from strife!'

"And it seemed as though a holy quiet sank over the world. It seemed as though the hills and the valleys smiled, and the autumn mists clothed themselves in rose color.

"Then he called for a helper for the people. 'Some one will come,' he said; 'it is not God's will that you should perish. God will call some one who will feed the hungry and lead them into His way.'

"Then we all thought of you, Gösta. We knew the Rector was speaking of you. The people who had heard your proclamation went home talking of you, and you were wandering in the forest seeking your death! The people need you, Gösta. Far and wide in the cottages they are talking of you, and saying that if the crazy parson from Ekeby will help them, all will be well. You are their hero, Gösta. They all look upon you as a hero!

"Yes, Gösta, the old man meant you, and that ought to make you desire to live. But I, Gösta, your wife—I say to you that you should simply go and do your duty. You must not dream of having been sent by God—everybody is that, you know. You must do the work without heroics. You are not to dazzle and astonish people; you must do it so that your name is not too often on the people's lips.

" But consider well before you break your word to Sintram. You have won a certain right to death, and life hereafter may not offer you much pleasure. It was once my wish to return to my father's home in the south, Gösta. For me, so laden with sin, it seemed too much happiness to be your wife and to follow you through life. But I shall remain here now. If you dare to take up your life again, I will remain with you. But do not expect any joy from it, Gösta. It is the heavy path of duty I must force you into. You must not expect words of gladness and hope from me. I will place all the sorrow and misery we two have caused as a guard about our hearth. Can a heart that has suffered as bitterly as mine love any more? Tearless and joyless I shall walk by your side. Consider well, Gösta, before you make your choice. It is the pilgrim's path of penance we must tread."

She did not wait for an answer. She motioned to Anna Lisa and left the cottage. When she entered the forest, she began to cry bitterly and wept till she reached Ekeby. When she arrived there, she remembered that she had forgotten to talk of happier things than the war to Jan Hök, the old soldier.

There was silence in the hut after she left.

"To the Lord be all praise and honor!" cried the old soldier, suddenly. They all gazed at him. He had risen to his feet and was looking about him eagerly.

"Evil, evil, has everything been," he said. "All I have seen since my eyes have opened has been evil—evil men and evil women; hate and anger in forest and field. But she is good. A good woman has stood in my house. When I sit here alone, I shall remember her. She will be with me in the forest paths."

He bowed over Gösta, untied his hands, and raised him. Then he took his hand solemnly.

"Despised of God," he said, nodding his head, "that is just it! But you are not that now, nor am I since she has stood in my house. She is good."

Next day old Jan Hök went to the high sheriff, Schärling. "I will take my cross," he said. "I have been an evil man, therefore my sons are wicked too." And he begged to be sent to prison instead of his son. But that was, of course, impossible.

One of the most beautiful of old stories is the one which describes how he followed his son, walking beside the prison cart; how he slept outside his prison; how he never deserted him till he had served his sentence. That, too, will find its narrator some day.

Margarita Celsing

THE Major's wife returned to the Löfsjö district a few days before Christmas, but it was not till Christmas Eve she came to Ekeby. She had been ill during all the journey. She had inflammation of the lungs and high fever, still no one had ever seen her happier or heard more kindly words from her lips.

The daughter of the Broby parson, who had been staying with her since October at the foundry at Älfdal, sat by her side in the sledge and would willingly have hastened the journey, but she could not prevent the old lady from stopping the horses and calling up each passer-by to ask for news.

"How is it with you here in Löfsjö?" she asked.

"All goes well with us," was the answer. "Better times are coming. The crazy parson at Ekeby and his wife are helping us."

"A good time has come," said another. "Sintram is gone. The Ekeby cavaliers work; the Broby parson's money was found in the steeple of Bro church. There was enough to raise again the glory and honor of Ekeby and to supply bread to the hungry."

"Our old Rector has awakened to new life and strength," said a third. "Every Sunday he tells us about the coming of God's kingdom. Who would sin any more? The millennium approaches."

The Major's wife drove on, asking all she met: "How is it with you? Are you in any want?"

And the fever and the sharp pain in her breast were lulled when they answered, "There are two good and rich women here: Marienne Sinclaire and Anna Stjärnhök. They help Gösta Berling to go from house to house and see that no one starves. And no more grain is wasted in the gin-stills now."

It seemed almost as if the Major's wife sat in her sledge and held a long thanksgiving service. She had come to a holy land. She saw old, wrinkled faces light up when they spoke of the days that had come, and the sick forgot their pains in praises of the days of joy.

"We would all be like the good Captain Lennert," they said, "we would all be good. We would believe good of others. We would not harm any one. The Kingdom of God would then be hastened."

She found them all moved by the same spirit. At the big estates, food was being given to the most needy. If there was work to be done, it was done at once, and all the foundries were in full swing.

She had never felt herself stronger than now as she sat and let the cold air stream in on her aching breast. There was no house she could pass without stopping and asking questions.

"All is well now," the cottagers answered. "We were in great want, but the good Ekeby gentlemen

are helping us. The lady will be amazed to see all
that has been done there; the mill is nearly finished,
the forge is at work again, and the burned house is
rebuilt to the eaves."

It was the famine and the late heart-shaking
events that had transformed them all. Oh, it would
last but a short time! Yet it was happiness to return
to a land where every one tried to serve his neighbor, and where they all tried to do good. The
Major's wife felt she could forgive the cavaliers,
and she thanked God for it.

"Anna Lisa," she said, "I, old woman as I am,
sit here and feel that I am already in the paradise
of the saints."

When she reached Ekeby at last, and the cavaliers hurried forward to help her out of the sledge,
they hardly recognized her, she was as kind and
gentle as their own young Countess. The old men
who had seen her in her youth whispered to each
other, "It is not the Major's wife of Ekeby — it is
Margarita Celsing who has come back."

Great was their joy to see her return so kind and
so free from all revengeful thoughts, but it was soon
changed to sorrow when they found how ill she
was. She had to be taken at once to one of the guest-
chambers and put to bed. But she turned on the
threshold of the room and spoke to them.

"It has been God's storm," she said, "God's
storm. I know now that all has been for the best."

Then the door of the sick-room closed, and they saw her no more.

There is always so much to say to those who are about to die. Words crowd to your lips when you know that in the next room lies one whose ears will soon be closed forever. "Oh, my friend, my friend," you would say, "can you forgive me? Can you believe I have loved you in spite of all? Oh, my friend, I thank you for all the happiness you have given me!"

You would say this and much, much more.

But the Lady of Ekeby lay in burning fever, and the voices of the cavaliers could not reach her. Would she ever know how they had labored, how they had taken up her work, how they had saved the honor and glory of Ekeby? Would she ever know?

Soon afterwards the cavaliers went down to the forge. All work was at a standstill, but they threw more coal and new pig-iron into the furnaces and prepared for smelting. They did not call the black-smiths, who had gone home to enjoy their Christmas, but worked themselves at the furnaces. If the Major's wife would only live till the hammers were started, they would tell her their story.

Evening came on and night. While they worked, several of them thought how strange it was that they should again be spending Christmas Eve in the forge.

Kevenhüller, man of many acquirements, who had been the master builder of Ekeby mill and forge during this stirring time, and Kristian Bergh, the strong captain, stood at the open furnaces and took charge of the smelting. Gösta and Julius drew coal. Some sat on the anvil under the heavy hanging hammer, others on the coal trucks and piles of pig-iron. Lövenborg, the old mystic, was talking to old Eberhard, the philosopher, who sat beside him on the anvil.

"Sintram dies to-night," he said.

"Why to-night?" asked Eberhard.

"You remember we made a contract last Christmas. Now we have not done anything uncavalier-like, and he loses."

"If you believe that, my dear fellow, you must also admit that we have done much that has not been cavalier-like. Firstly, we did not help the Major's wife; secondly, we began to work; thirdly, it was not quite correct that Gösta Berling did not kill himself when he promised to do so."

"I have thought of that too," said Lövenborg, "but I think you don't quite grasp the subject rightly. To work for our own narrow interests was forbidden us, but not to do that which love or honor or our own everlasting salvation required. I think Sintram has lost."

"You may be right."

"I will tell you why I am sure of it. I have heard

his sleigh-bells all the evening, but they are not real sleigh-bells. We shall soon have him here."

The little man sat and stared toward the forge door, which stood open, and at the big bit of blue sky, dotted by a few stars, that was visible beyond.

After a few minutes he sprang up.

"Do you see him?" he whispered. "There he comes creeping in. Don't you see him in the door-way?"

"I don't see anything," replied Eberhard. "You are sleepy, my dear fellow, that is all."

"I saw him quite distinctly against the light sky. He wore his long wolfskin coat and fur cap. Now he is in the shadow there, and I cannot see him. See, there he is near the fire. He stands close to Kristian Bergh, but Kristian certainly does not see him. Now he leans forward and throws something into the fire. Oh, how wicked he looks — take care, friends, take care!"

As he spoke, a sheet of flame shot out of the fur-nace and covered the two smiths and their assist-ants with a shower of cinders and sparks. But no harm was done.

"He would be revenged," whispered Löven-borg.

"You are too crazy," cried Eberhard. "You ought to have had enough of such things."

"You may think that and wish it, but it doesn't do much good. Don't you see, my dear fellow, how he stands there by that beam and grins at us? But really—why, I believe he is loosening the hammer!"

He sprang up, dragging Eberhard with him, and a moment later the hammer fell with a thundering crash upon the anvil. A screw had given way, but Lövenborg and Eberhard had barely escaped death.

"See, brother, he has no power over us," said Lövenborg triumphantly. "But it is evident he wanted to be revenged."

He called to Gösta Berling.

"Go up to the womenkind, Gösta; he may show himself there, and they are not so accustomed as I am to such sights. They might be frightened. And be careful of yourself, Gösta, for he is very furious with you, and he may have power over you because of that promise."

Later every one knew that Lövenborg had been right, and that Sintram had died on Christmas Eve. Some people said he hanged himself in prison. Others thought that the officers of the law had quietly made away with him, for it seemed possible he might win the lawsuit, and it would never do to let him go abroad among the Löfsjö people again. Others there were who believed a dark gentleman came in a black carriage drawn by black horses and carried him away from prison. Lövenborg was not the only one who saw him on Christmas Eve. He had also been seen at Fors and in Ulrika Dillner's dreams. Many people would tell you how often he was seen till Ulrika Dillner moved his body to Bro churchyard. She turned away all the wicked servants and engaged new ones at Fors, and since then no more ghosts have been seen there.

.   .   .   .

It is said that before Gösta Berling reached the house, a stranger had called and left a letter for the Major's wife. No one recognized the bearer, but the letter was carried in and laid on the table beside the sick woman's bed. Directly afterwards she became unexpectedly better, the fever abated, the pain diminished, and she was able to read the letter.

Our elders willingly believed that the improvement in her condition had been caused by the influence of the dark powers. It was to the advantage of Sintram and his friends that the Major's wife should read the letter.

It contained a document, written with blood on black paper. The cavaliers would certainly have recognized it. It had been written last Christmas Eve in the forge at Ekeby.

The Major's wife lay and read it. It said that, inasmuch as she was a witch and sent the souls of cavaliers to hell, she was doomed to lose Ekeby. This and more of the same kind of nonsense she read. She examined the date and the signatures, and

saw this note appended to Gösta Berling's name:
"Because the Major's wife took advantage of my
weakness to lure me away from honest labor and
has kept me a cavalier at Ekeby, because she made
me the murderer of Ebba Dohna by informing her
that I was a discharged clergyman, I sign this paper."

The Major's wife folded it slowly and replaced
it in the envelope. Afterwards she lay and thought
over what she had just learned. She understood
with bitter grief that such had been the people's
thought about her. She was a witch and a sorceress
to all those whom she had served, to whom she had
given work and bread. That was her wage, such
would be her reputation. They could think no better
of a woman who had been faithless to her husband.

But what cared she for the outside world! They
stood afar off, but those poor cavaliers who had
lived by her grace and knew her well, even they
believed it or pretended to believe it to gain an excuse for appropriating Ekeby. Her thoughts moved
rapidly. Anger and revenge burned in her feverish
brain. She ordered the Broby parson's daughter,
who, together with the Countess Elizabeth, was
watching beside her, to send to Högfors for the
manager and inspector. She wanted to make her
will.

Again she lay thinking. Her eyebrows were
drawn together; her features were convulsed by
awful pain.

"You are feeling very ill," said the Countess softly.

"Yes, worse than ever before."

There was silence again, then the Major's wife spoke in a hard, harsh tone. "It is wonderful to remember that you, even you, Countess, whom all love, have also been a faithless wife."

The young woman started.

"Yes, if not in deed, still in thought, and there is no difference. I, lying here, feel that it makes no difference."

"I know it does n't."

"And yet, Countess, you are happy now. You may own the man you love without sin. No dark shadow stands between you when you meet. You can belong to each other before the world, love each other by broad daylight, and go side by side through life."

"Oh, dear lady!"

"How have you the courage to remain with him, Countess?" cried the old woman with rising excitement. "Do penance, do penance, while there is time! Go home to your father and mother before they come and curse you. Dare you count Gösta Berling your husband? Leave him. I will give him Ekeby. I will give him power and might. Dare you share that with him? Dare you accept honor and happiness? I dared to do it, and do you remember how it went with me? Do you remember the Christmas

dinner last year here at Ekeby? Do you remember
the jail in Schärling's house?"

"Oh, but we sin-laden creatures walk together
without happiness. I am here to watch that no joy
shall abide at our hearth. Do you not think I long
to go home? Oh, bitterly do I long for the protection and support of my home, but I shall never feel
them. I shall live here in fear and trembling, knowing that all I do leads to sorrow and sin, knowing that in helping one I am harming another. Too
weak and foolish for life here, yet forced to live it,
bound by an everlasting penance."

"With such thoughts we deceive our hearts,"
cried the Major's wife, "but that is weakness. You
will not give him up, that is the whole reason."

Before the Countess could answer, Gösta entered
the room.

"Come here, Gösta," said the Major's wife at
once, and her voice grew even sharper and louder
than it was before. "Come here, you whom everybody in Löfsjö is praising—you who will win the
reputation of being the deliverer of the people! You
shall hear how things went with your old friend,
when you allowed her to tramp through the country
scorned and deserted by all.

"I will tell you first what happened in the spring,
when I went home to my mother, for you ought to
know the end of that story.

"In March I made my way on foot up to the

Älfdal forests, Gösta. I looked little better than a
beggar-woman by that time. They told me when
I arrived there that my mother was in the dairy. I
made my way there and stood a long time silently
at the door. All round the room there were long
shelves on which stood shining copper pans filled
with milk, and my mother, who was over ninety
years old, lifted down pan after pan and skimmed
it. She was strong enough, yet I noticed that it told
upon her to straighten herself sufficiently to reach
the pans. I did not know if she had noticed me, till
after a time she spoke in an extraordinary shrill
voice.

"'What I desired has then happened,' she said.
I wanted to speak and ask her forgiveness, but it
was quite useless. She did not hear a word, she was
stone deaf. After a time she spoke again.

"'You can come and help me,' she said.

"Then I went forward and helped her to skim the
milk. I took down the pans in their right order and
put them into their places and took off the right
depth of cream, and she was pleased. She had never
trusted any of the servants to skim the milk, but
I knew of old how she liked to have it done.

"'Now you can take this work upon yourself,'
she said. And by that I knew she had forgiven me.

"After that it seemed as if she lost the power of
working any longer. She sat quietly in her armchair
and slept nearly all the day, and she died a fortnight

before Christmas. I would willingly have come here sooner, but I could not leave my old mother."

She paused; it was beginning to be difficult for her to get her breath, but she mastered herself and continued.

"It is true, Gösta, that I was glad to keep you here at Ekeby. You make every one wish to be near you. If you had shown any desire to settle down, I should have given much power into your hands. I always hoped you would find a good wife: first I thought it would be Marienne Sinclaire, for I saw she loved you even when you lived as a wood-cutter in the forest. Later I thought it would be Ebba Dohna, and I went over to Borg one day and told her that I would leave Ekeby to you if she married you. If I did wrong in that, you must forgive me."

Gösta knelt by the bedside with his forehead against the edge of the bed. He groaned heavily.

"Tell me, Gösta, how you mean to live! How are you going to keep your wife? Tell me; you know I have always wished you well!"

Gösta answered her smilingly, though his heart was breaking with remorse. "In the old days, when I tried being a workman here at Ekeby, you gave me a crofter's hut to live in, and that is still mine. This autumn I have put it in order. Lövenborg has helped me, and we have whitewashed the ceiling and papered the walls and painted them. The little inner room Lövenborg calls the Countess's boudoir,

and he has hunted in all the peasant huts for pieces
of furniture that have found their way there from
auctions at the old estates. He has bought them,
and there are high-backed armchairs and chests with
bright mountings there now. But in the bigger room
stands the young mistress's loom and my turning-
lathe. Household furniture and all kinds of things
are there already, and Lövenborg and I have sat
there many evenings and talked of the time my
young Countess and I shall live in the crofter's hut.
But my wife hears of this for the first time. We intended telling her about it when we should leave
Ekeby."

"Continue, Gösta!"

"Lövenborg always said it was necessary to have
a servant girl in the house. 'In summer it is bless-
edly beautiful here on the birch promontory,' he
said; 'but it will be too dull in the winter for the
young wife. You must get a servant girl, Gösta.'
And I was quite of his opinion, but I could not see
how I was to afford to keep a servant girl. Then
one day he came there with his music notes and his
table with the painted keyboard and placed it in
the cottage. 'You, Lövenborg, are to be the servant girl, then?' I said to him. He answered that
probably he would be needed. Was it my intention
that the Countess should cook the dinner and carry
wood and water herself? No, I did not mean she
should do anything at all as long as I had a pair of

hands to work with. But he still seemed to think it best there should be two of us, so that she might sit all day in the sofa corner with her embroidery. He said I had no idea how much attention a little woman like that required."

"Go on, Gösta," said the Major's wife; "this eases my suffering. Did you think your young Countess would consent to live in a cottage?"

He wondered at her scornful tone, but continued: "Oh, I dared not hope it, but it would be so beautiful if she would. It is thirty miles or more to any doctor here, and she, with her light hand and tender heart, would have work enough in binding wounds and stilling fevers. And I thought how all the troubled would find their way to the beautiful lady in the crofter's hut. There is so much trouble among the poor which a kind hand and a warm heart can lighten."

"And about yourself, Gösta Berling?"

"My work will lie at the carpenter's bench and the turning-lathe. I want to live my own life now. If my wife will not follow me, I must live it alone. If all the world's riches were offered me, they would not tempt me now; I want to live my own life. I shall be a poor man among the peasants, and shall live to help them in any way I can. They need some one who will play polkas for them at their weddings and Christmas feasts; they need some one to

write their letters to their absent sons—and that
will be my work. But I must be poor."

"It will be a gloomy life for you, Gösta!"

"Oh, no, my lady, it won't, if there are two of
us who uphold each other. The rich and gay will
probably come to us as well as the poor. We shall
have sufficient happiness in our crofter's hut. The
guests will not mind very much if the food is prepared before their eyes, nor feel shocked if two must
eat at every plate."

"And what good will it all do, Gösta? What
praise will you gain?"

"Great will be my fame if the poor care to remember me a few years after my death. I shall have
done sufficient good if I have planted a couple of
apple trees at the house-corners, if I have taught
the village fiddlers a few of the old master's melodies, and if the shepherd boy learns a few new songs
to sing in the forest paths. You must believe me,
dear lady, I am the same crazy Gösta Berling I have
always been. A village fiddler is all I can be, but
that is enough. I have many sins to make good, but
tears and grieving are not for me. I will give joy to
the poor—that shall be my penance."

"Gösta," said the Major's wife, "that would be
too humble a life for a man of your capacities. I
will leave Ekeby to you."

"Oh," he exclaimed in fear, "do not make me

rich! Do not lay such duties upon me! Don't separate me from the people!"

"I will give Ekeby to you and the other cavaliers," repeated the Major's wife. "You are a trustworthy man, Gösta, whom the people bless. I say
as my mother said, 'You can take this work upon
you.'"

"No, my lady, we cannot accept it—we who
have suspected you and caused you such sorrow."

"I will give you Ekeby, do you hear?"

She spoke severely, harshly, without a trace of
kindness. He was seized with dismay.

"Do not put such temptation in the way of the
old men! It will make them sluggards and drunkards again! God of Heaven!—rich cavaliers! What
would become of us?"

"I will give you Ekeby, Gösta, but you must
promise then to give your wife her liberty again.
You know such a refined little creature is not fit
for such as you. She has already suffered too much
in the bear-country. She longs for her own bright
fatherland. You must let her go. That is the reason
I give you Ekeby."

But at this Countess Elizabeth came forward and
knelt beside the bed. "I don't long any more for
my own country. The man who is my husband has
solved the problem and found for me the life which
I can live. No longer need I go cold and hard beside him to remind him of repentance and penance.

Poverty and want and hard work will perform that mission. The paths that lead to the poor and the sick I may tread without sin; I fear no longer the life here in the north. But don't make him rich, my Lady, or I dare not remain!"

The Major's wife raised herself in bed. "All happiness you require for yourselves!" she cried, and shook her clenched fist at them; "all happiness and blessing! No, Ekeby shall belong to the cavaliers so that it may be their ruin! Man and wife shall be separated so that they may be ruined! A witch am I—a sorceress am I—and I will drive you to ruin! Such as my reputation is, so shall I be."

She clutched the letter and flung it in Gösta's face. The black paper fluttered out of the envelope and fell on the floor. Gösta recognized it only too well.

"You have sinned against me, Gösta. You have misunderstood the woman who has been a second mother to you. Dare you refuse to take the punishment? You shall receive Ekeby, and that will ruin you, for you are weak. You shall send away your wife to her old home so that no one will have the power to save you. You shall die with a name as hated as my own. Margarita Celsing is believed to be a witch. Your fame shall be that of a spendthrift and a grinder of the poor."

She sank back upon her cushions, and all was quiet in the room. In the silence there fell the dull thud of a heavy stroke; then another and another.

The steel hammer had begun its wide-sounding work.

"Hear it," said Gösta; "there resounds Margarita Celsing's fame. It is not the mad prank of drunken cavaliers. It is the conquest hymn of labor raised in honor of a good old worker. Listen to what the hammer says—'Thanks for good work and for the bread you have given to the poor! Thanks for the roads you have made and the ground you have cleared! Thanks,' it says, 'and sleep in peace; your work will live and prosper! Your house will ever be a haven for heaven-blessed labor! Thanks,' it says, 'and do not judge us harshly who have gone astray. You who are starting upon the journey to the plains of peace, think kindly of us who are still in life.'"

Gösta was silent, but the steel hammer continued to speak, and all the voices that had ever spoken in kindness to the Major's wife blended in its strokes; and gradually the strained look left her face, her features relaxed, and it seemed as if the shadow of death had already fallen upon her.

The Broby parson's daughter came in and announced that the gentleman from Högfors had arrived. The Major's wife sent him away; she would not make the will.

"Oh, Gösta Berling, man of many conquests," she said, "you have conquered once again. Bow down and let me bless you."

The fever redoubled its fury, the death agony began. The body was tortured by great pain, but the soul knew little of it. It was looking in at the gate of heaven which was opened for the dying.

So an hour passed, and the short death-struggle was over. Then she lay so peaceful and beautiful that those standing round her were deeply touched.

"My dear old friend," said Gösta, "once before I saw you like this. Now is Margarita Celsing come to life again! Now she will never give place again to the Major's wife of Ekeby."

.   .   .   .

When the cavaliers came in from the forge, they were met by the news of her death.

"Did she hear the hammer?" they asked.

She had heard it, and with that they were obliged to be content. They learned afterwards that she had intended leaving Ekeby to them, but that the will had never been written. They always considered this a great honor, and prided themselves upon it as long as they lived. But no one ever heard them bewail the riches they had lost.

It is said, too, that on that Christmas Eve, Gösta Berling, standing by the side of his young wife, made his last speech to the cavaliers. He was troubled over their fate, now they were all to leave Ekeby. The trials of old age awaited them. A cold welcome meets the old and dull even from the hospitable. The impoverished cavalier who is obliged to seek board in a peasant's hut has no joyous days. Separated from his old friends and the old adventurous life, alone and solitary, he fades away. And so he talked to them, to those light-hearted men hardened against all chances of fate. Once again he called them gods and knights who had arisen to bring back joy to the ironland in iron times. Still he bewailed that the garden where butterfly-winged joy had abounded should have been filled with destructive caterpillars, and that its fruit was shrivelled. He knew well that joy was a blessing to the children of men, and that it must exist; but like a great mystery the question still hung over the world how a man was both to be joyous and to be good. He said it was both the easiest and the most difficult of things. They had not been able to solve the riddle before, but now he believed they had all learned the lesson. They had all learned it during that year of joy and of want, of happiness and of trouble.

Oh, good Sir Cavaliers, for me, too, the bitterness of parting hangs over this hour! This is the last night we shall spend together. I shall not hear again your merry laughter or your gay songs. I must part from you and all the happy people of the Löfven shores.

You dear old men, you gave me good gifts in the old days. You brought the first knowledge of life's many vicissitudes to one living in great loneliness. I saw you take part in mighty battles round the lake of my childhood's dreams. But what have I given you?

Still it may please you that your name will be mentioned in connection with the dear old places. May all the splendor which belonged to your lives descend upon the country where you lived! Borg still stands and Björne, and Ekeby still lies beside the Löfven, beautifully surrounded by the rapids and the lake and park and smiling forest meadows, and when you stand on its broad balconies the old legends swarm round you like summer bees.

But speaking of bees, let me tell you one more old story. Little Ruster, who, as drummer-boy, marched at the head of the Swedish army when it entered Germany in 1813, was never tired of describing the wonderful country in the south. The people there were as tall as steeples, the swallows as big as eagles, the bees as large as geese.

"Well, and the beehives?"

"Oh, the beehives were just like our own beehives."

"How did the bees get into them?"

"Well, that was their own affair," said little Ruster.

Dear reader, may I not say the same? The giant bees of Fancy have thronged about us for a year and a day, but how they are to enter the beehives of Reality is surely their own affair!

THE END

www.ingramcontent.com/pod-product-compliance
Lightning Source LLC
Chambersburg PA
CBHW020454020726
47493CB00001B/27